Until Then

The Blue Collar Boys Series

SARA MILLER

Copyright © 2025 by Sara Miller All rights reserved.

No part of this publication may be reproduced, distributed, or transmitted in any form or by any means, including photocopying, recording, or other electronic or mechanical methods, without the prior written permission of the publisher, except as permitted by U.S. copyright law. For permission requests, contact Sara Miller.

This book is a work of fiction. The characters and events in this book are fictitious. Any similarity to real places or persons, living or dead, is purely coincidental and not intended by the author or is used fictitiously.

The author acknowledged the trademark status and trademark owners of various products, brands, and/or establishments references in this work of fiction. The publication/use of these trademarks is not associated with or sponsored by the trademark owners.

Without in any way limiting the author's (and publisher's) exclusive rights under copyright, any use of this publication to "train" generative artificial intelligence (AI) technologies to generate text is expressly prohibited. The author reserves the rights to license uses of this work for generative AI training and development of machine learning language models.

Paperback ISBN: 979-8-9919263-0-0

E-book ISBN: 979-8-9919263-1-7

Cover Design by Melissa Doughty—Mel D. Designs

Interior Illustrations by Alica Clarie

Playlist

1. After You (feat. Calle Lehmann) by Gryffin

2. These Tears by Andy Grammer

3. Irony of Loneliness by Jason Mraz

4. I Know She Ain't Ready by Luke Combs

5. Start Nowhere by Sam Hunt

6. Be Yourself by Wilder Woods

7. Bits and Pieces by JP Cooper

8. Part Of It by Jordan Davis

9. I Like Me Better by Lauv

10. Amen To That by Dylan Scott

11. Automatic (feat. Jake Miller) by Fly by Midnight

12. Feel Good (feat. Daya) by Gryffin

13. Slow Down by Alana Springsteen

14. Gravity by John Mayer

Dear Reader,

WRITING IS ALWAYS DEEPLY personal and, often times, extremely emotional. Greer's story was no different. In fact, it lived in my mind for years, but I was always hesitant to write it, as it reflects very personal fears. It explores the complicated emotions involved in loss, grief, and healing.

At some point in life, we will all be affected by loss. It enters unannounced, leaving us broken and questioning everything we thought we knew about ourselves and the world. But with loss comes healing—a journey that differs for everyone. I wanted to reflect that reality in this story.

For Greer, life as she knew it vanished in a heartbeat. But I always knew her story would be one of hope and healing, of finding the light even when it feels like you are lost in the dark, and realizing that you don't have to journey through grief alone. Throughout the book, Greer learns that you can't put a timeline on healing and that it is not a linear path, but with love, resilience, and the support of others, it is possible to move forward.

I believe I've written Greer's story to be raw and realistic. This book includes content that may not be suitable for some readers, such as death of a spouse, flashbacks, discussions of physical injuries, the death of a parent (off page), anxiety, and post-traumatic stress. While I hope I have handled these topics with care and honesty, your well-being matters deeply to me. Please protect your heart and mental health, and take care while reading Greer's story if these themes feel difficult for you.

My hope is that as you read, you'll connect with these characters and find comfort in your own experiences. If you are navigating loss—now or in the past—I hope you'll be reminded that healing is possible, even when it feels out of reach, and that you don't have to face it alone.

I am honored to share *Until Then* with you.

With love,
Sara

For anyone lost in the dark . . .
keep moving forward.
Your light is out there.

For Blake . . .
it's your love;
it just does something to me.
You believed in me even
when I had my doubts.

For Noodle Bear . . .
you're beautiful,
you're amazing,
and I love you.

"If there ever comes a day when we can't be together, keep me in your heart, I'll stay there forever."

—Winnie The Pooh

Prologue

DEATH COMES FOR US all. You can't control it. You can't change it. You can't stop it.

For some, they sense Death approaching. They can prepare to lessen its sting. For most, it happens unexpectedly, leaving them no way to brace for impact.

Death came for us like that. One minute, I was on a trip with the man who was my whole world, and in the next, a semitruck running a red light changed everything. When I came to, there was no pleading or bargaining or fighting. In fact, I wasn't even aware Death waited patiently nearby.

All I saw was my husband—crumpled over, bleeding and gasping for air.

All I smelled was gasoline and burning rubber and blood.

All I felt were razor-sharp pains in my abdomen and a sharp stabbing sensation in my leg—unable to move, to help.

All I heard was someone yelling help was on the way.

All I asked was for him to hold on until then.

All I tasted was my own sorrow when he took his final breath.

I begged and pleaded then, but Death wasn't listening. It was focused only on turning the tragic page of the final chapter of one man's beautiful story.

In the end, Death walked away with the man I loved, leaving me behind. And me?

I was desperate to rewrite the ending of our story. But how could I when I was fighting like hell just to breathe?

1

Greer

L IFE SUCKS AND THEN you die. Or, if you're like me, you're the one left behind to start over.

"Mama, that one needs a blue Post-it. Blue is for books." I gingerly lift a few weighty novels and nestle them within a medium moving box. The afternoon sun filters through the shutters, casting a warm glow on the wooden floors of my childhood bedroom. It's moving day, and these books and I are making the journey to a new home.

It's only a small part of my collection though. The rest remains locked away in a storage unit, a crime against books everywhere. But they're not alone—everything from my old life is shelved right alongside them.

"Greer, honey, all the boxes are going into your new house, so what does it matter?" As my mom loads various books into the box, humming to herself, I'm brought back to another moment, to another person who didn't always understand my particular nature.

"You got so mad at me, but you know my method was top-notch."

"What did you say?" Mom looks at me, her eyes narrow in curiosity as she wrangles the top of the box closed, fighting with the tape dispenser.

"Oh, uh, nothing." It's easy to forget not everyone talks to the dead. I steal a glance at the only framed photograph on my bedside table—me with a huge smile and the man who left me too soon with his arm slung around my waist. I hardly recognize myself in the picture. It's been a long time since I've felt genuinely happy and not just faking it for the benefit of those around me.

"You know my love for organization, Mama, so I'm not sure what you expected when you agreed to help me pack." My words are gruff as I attempt to ground myself in the present even though my mind dances between the boxes and shadows of memories.

I've always lived on the life principle that everything has its place, organization is key, and lists are lovely. Even if, on occasion, I procrastinate until the last moment, I've worried about whatever it is enough and have ninety million possible plans of attack to accomplish it.

"Boy, do I know it." Mom smiles. "I still remember when you and Brian started dating, and he asked Daddy and me what to get you for Valentine's Day. The look on his face when we said office supplies." She bursts into a fit of giggles at the memory. Tears well in my eyes as I try to picture it: his face, his smile, his laughter.

Mom notes the faraway look on my face. She grazes her fingers along my arm, pulling me from my reverie. Not one to push or prod, she begins folding my shirts and dresses from the closet. My mom is the kindest soul you'll ever meet. She's funny, adventurous, and definitely a little messy. The opposite of everything I am or, at least, everything I am now. Death has a way of altering a person, in ways not everyone can see, in ways not even we can see ourselves.

Continuing to pack in companionable silence, I can't help but notice how much larger the room feels. Moving back in with my parents as an adult was never part of my life plans, but sometimes, Life throws you a curveball and your plan changes. I know how blessed I am to have the two people who love me most in the world, aside from Brian, welcome me home with open arms. These four walls have been a solid base, offering me a sense of safety and comfort amid confusion and pain.

A low hum of indie guitar wafts from the radio, filling the room with heavy lyrics I could get lost in. Mom continues her rhythmic packing, humming along to songs she's heard repeatedly over the last few months. Making eye contact, she offers a gentle smile.

"Big week, huh?" she says. "Moving into your new house and the last week of school."

Big is an understatement. Everyone talks about moving as some kind of exciting adventure. I suppose maybe it is, a fresh start, new beginning. For some, at least.

I'd rather have my old beginning.

My old adventure.

My old life.

"Yeah, I guess," I murmur, my voice trailing off. My gaze drifts around the room as the soothing notes of the guitar wash over me, calming my rising anxiety that tightens my chest.

"You guess? Shouldn't all *this* be right up your alley?"

I grab several notebooks containing hundreds of worn pages from hours of therapy. I run my hand over the leather covers as the weight of both past and present presses against me. These notebooks have been silent witnesses to my journey through grief. I load them along with a small hoard of office supplies into another small box. Little pinpricks of anticipation, of change and uncertainty, build under my skin.

Inhale. Exhale. I remind myself over and over until my heart rate settles.

The room, now filled with the scent of cardboard, seems to expand, releasing echoes of laughter and tears. I glance at the framed photograph again. The weight of its memories seem to press down on me, and with effort, I force my attention back to the task at hand.

"Yeah, under any normal circumstance it should be, but these aren't normal circumstances." My words linger, spoken to my mom but also to the ghost of the life I once knew.

"No, they're not, but you'll get through this too. I promise." My mother, ever the optimist.

"You're right. Gah, I don't know, Mama. All of this"—I gesture wildly around the mess of my room—"is just pissing me off today. I don't want to *have* to move, and with my new job I get two rounds of torture. Speaking of, you're going to help me pack my classroom, right?"

"Greer, you're not even having to pack that much." Her voice is serious, having lost her earlier pep.

And I know she's right. I'm not packing a whole house, just my childhood bedroom. A mere sampling of a life fully lived for thirty-two years.

"Plus," she adds, "it could also be a good thing. If you want it to be."

A box tucked under the bed catches my toe. I carefully take it from its hiding space, knowing exactly what's inside. After wiping off the layer of dust, I caress the cover of the old photo album. With a heavy heart, I flip through its pages, photo after photo showcasing memories of the joy my life once contained. There Brian is, his face, his smile. My fingers trace the lines of our smiles frozen in time when life was simpler, more certain.

The slow melody from the radio fills the room as memories of Brian flicker through my mind. Each note wraps around me like a comforting embrace, a lifeline that has seen me through both joy and sorrow. It's more than just music to me; each melody or note is like stitches binding the fabric of my memories. They've danced within me in moments of celebration; but in times of sorrow, they've supported me and made me feel not so alone in my grief.

"I know, Mama." My fingers tremble as I carefully place the photo album in the box, close it, and drag tape along the top of it. "It's just hard."

"We know, sweetie. Losing Brian was hard on all of us. You know . . ." she says. "You can stay here with Daddy and me for a bit longer. Give yourself time to settle in at your new school. You've been through more than enough this year." Looking at me from the corner of her eye, she loads up another box.

People always say to expect the unexpected from Life. But I never considered that in a few seconds, Death might alter my entire course and take me right back to square one—or square zero for that matter.

Sterile hospital walls became my world. Even now, I can recall the constant beeping machines, the smell of antiseptic, the murmur of medical staff discussing my prognosis, and the whispers about Brian's death.

Shaking my head, I stack another box near the door. "Thanks, Mama, but I've lived here since the accident. You and Daddy have done enough."

And they have. My parents hovered in those bleak hallways, concern etched on their faces. But even then, Mom's smile remained. Mom always finds the joy in the face of uncertainty. I think she knew I would need that smile because it wasn't just the loss of Brian or my injuries—ruptured spleen and broken leg—that she worried about. It was the internal wounds she knew would haunt me for weeks and months to come.

Their unwavering support was a lifeline among the shattered remains of my old life. People *we* once considered friends weren't able to handle the depths of my grief and drifted away one by one, leaving me to tackle my recovery alone. Ten days I spent in that hospital; days filled with surgeries, a haze of medications, restless nights, and flashbacks.

As I reach for another box, my scalp prickles, and I recall the endless minutes I spent locked away in my own mind, reliving my nightmare over and over. As the weeks and months passed, I wondered if I'd ever close my eyes and not see the accident.

"You say that as if you've been some kind of burden on us," Mom says. "Greer, sweetheart, your daddy and I would do anything for you." Mom looks at me over her shoulder, sipping water out of a water bottle.

"I know you would." Warmth seeps through the window and permeates my skin as thoughts tumble through my mind at a rapid pace. I never contemplated returning to the familiarity of *our* home after being released from the hospital. The mere thought of returning alone to the home we shared together was overwhelming. My parent's house became my refuge—a warm and safe place to land.

My eyes well with tears as my heart beats against my ribs. Reaching down, I rub the long scar on my right calf. Numerous pale-white scars riddle my body, reminding me that I survived.

My physical wounds healed, and through intensive therapy, the mental scars have started to as well. Every day, every step, every breath, feels both intimidating and oddly familiar. I know my parents know how much this move scares me, but I don't want to burden them any longer.

"Time heals," the doctors always told me.

But I'm not so sure.

I've learned there is no script for grief or loss. For me, I know it's time to start over, to move on, to face the unknown on my own two feet even if it feels overwhelming and unnerving. I'm moving onto the next chapter of my life even though I wish I didn't have to write it without my husband.

"So . . ." Mom says, knowing my mind is spinning. "When should we pack up your classroom? Will the school help transport everything to your new one?"

"Um, yeah." I startle back to the present, my voice fading as I escape down the hallway to grab a few garbage bags. I take a few moments to myself before returning to my room. "They've actually been really great. All I have to do is pack and label the boxes, and the school will move them over."

Mom smiles. "Well, that's just wonderful. Are you nervous for the move?"

"Which one?"

"Both, my love."

"The new school will be fine. I'm good at my job and will be at any location. I'm not even worried about moving down to second grade. If anything, it'll give me something new and challenging to focus on."

She nods her head. "And the other one?"

"I—" I take a settling breath as my fingers toy with the hem of my pale-teal shirt.

"You what?" She rests her hands on the box in front of her.

"I don't know, Mama. I don't know how I'm supposed to feel. I'd rather not have had to move in with you and Daddy in the first place. I'd rather be living in my old house with Brian. But that's not possible anymore. I can't live in that house, not without him." Tears cloud my vision. "I've imposed on you and Daddy for too long. Whether I'm ready or not, it's time for me to move on."

Mom ties her golden blonde hair in a twist. "You know, Greer, if I'm being honest, I'm excited for you but also a little nervous too."

"Why are you nervous?" I force a laugh. "I'll be across town, not in Australia. Plus, you'll get to decorate my new house."

The words *new house* tumble around my mind. The house Brian and I filled with memories for eight years now stands empty. Shortly after I moved in with my parents, they and Brian's parents moved our items to a storage unit. My parents used to ask me what I wanted to do with the house, and I know someday soon I'll have to figure that out.

It's hard to live a new (and unwanted) life when you're surrounded by what was and the possibilities of what could have been. Constantly reminded that you lived and he died.

I'm sure if I went back to our house, I could still smell his fancy coffee in the kitchen, hear his laugh bouncing off the walls, and see the worn spot on the carpet from his desk chair. Every room, every surface, holds a memory. But the thought of stepping into that house feels like I'll drown in a tidal wave of memories. It's time I swim.

"I know. I know." Mom takes a settling breath, emotion clogging her throat. "I've—well, we—have loved having you back home. With everything that happened . . ."

You mean nearly dying in a car crash or watching my husband die or the surgeries or the recovery or the fact that my body or mind won't let me forget what happened? You have to be specific, Mom.

"Mama, I'll be fine. I am fine. Everyone can stop worrying. Plus, I can't live with you and Daddy forever."

"Well." She pauses her packing, looking at me with a grin.

Sighing, I stretch a piece of tape across the top of a box. The scratching of the dispenser fills the silence in the room. Walking down the short photo-lined hallway, I find my gaze catching on our wedding photo. Averting my eyes, I quicken my steps, placing the box into the stack in the living room.

"Mother," I holler, "I refuse to be a thirty-two-year-old woman still living at home. I get that a lot of bad shit has happened to me this year, but I have to do this." I snag another small moving box, then take my time folding and taping it into form. I grab another and another.

I finally closed on my new house a little over two weeks ago. A brand new, 2,000-square-foot house with three spacious bedrooms and a three-car garage. Why I need a house this big for one person, I'll never know. I blame the master bathroom and view. It's in a new community with only a few other houses on the block, and the house sits on a large corner lot that backs up to a wooded preserve.

The empty spaces wait for me to fill them with life, like blank pages eager for a story. Silent hallways and empty bedrooms in my new home whisper secrets of a fresh start. It's pristine, untouched, and isolated. The irony of the situation isn't lost on me: Seeking solace in a home devoid of memories will only serve to amplify the void left by those that never will be.

Mom places her hand on my shoulder, pulling me from yet another thought spiral. Shivers wrack my body. Her touch threatens to unravel me, but I can't do that anymore; I can't fall apart. It's been months. It's time to move on. *Right?*

I turn toward her, and she tugs me into her arms. I know it'll be hard for them when I move out. It's easy for me to forget sometimes that not only did they almost lose me, but they lost Brian too.

"People would understand, Greer. You know they would."

Laying my head on her shoulder, I wrap my arms around her waist, the soft fabric of her dress tight in my grip. "I don't need them to understand. I'm fine."

"Are you though?" Her words are barely audible.

"Yeah. I'm okay." The quiver in my voice betrays the knot of regret tightening in my chest.

The truth is, I'm trying, but I'm not sure when I'll actually feel *good* or *fine* or *okay*. Because no one ever tells you the truth about life—it's beautiful and unpredictable and occasionally really fucking sucks.

2

Greer

The furniture store looms ahead of me as I turn into the nearly empty parking lot. Dread fills my stomach as I catch sight of the extensive list sitting on the passenger seat. After dinner last night, Mom helped me determine what pieces of furniture I needed to "make this new house a home." Her words, not mine.

I'd made a plan to get here early because if I'm forced to furnish a new home, I at least want to do so in a crowd-less store. Armed with a fresh coffee and list, I ditch my truck and set off toward the entrance. I'm halfway across the parking lot when I notice a sandy-colored dog, all alone, furry body tucked back into the corner of a playpen outside the neighboring pet store, hoping no one notices him. But I do.

Looking both ways, I limp across the crosswalk, my leg a bit stiffer this morning. His deep brown eyes meet mine. And I'm done. Finished.

He stands, his tentative gaze never leaving mine. As I get closer, his tail wags side to side. When I stop near his playpen, he wiggles erratically.

"You're a good boy, aren't ya?" My cheeks, a bit out of practice, ache from the giant smile I know I'm sporting.

"Oh, that's Duke." Startled by the sudden voice, I wheel about as a young man comes to stand beside me. "He's one of our old-timers." A vibrant smile extends across the man's entire face. For a moment, that's all I can focus on. For me, seeing a genuine smile is a rare sight. Even after eight months, most smiles I'm gifted are still born out of pity for the widow.

"What do you mean?" I glance around the makeshift pet adoption area, noting a few other dogs roughhousing.

I place my hand a foot or so in front of Duke. He takes a few cautious steps forward, nose bobbing up and down as he smells me. He nuzzles his cold nose into my outstretched hand, pushing into it like he wants more attention than what I'm doling out. Soft tan fur slips between my fingers as I smooth my hand over the top of his head and scratch behind his ears.

His eyes close, surrendering to my affection. When I stop scratching, he pushes my hand again. I can't help but wonder how long it's been since he's felt the loving touch of someone. For me, I can calculate it down to the second.

"Oh, Duke, here has been with us a long time." The man slides his hands in his pockets. "Most of our elderly dogs never get adopted out. Kind of sad actually."

Stepping into the playpen, I squat down, and Duke pushes his way between my legs. With both hands, I hold the sides of his face, my thumbs caressing his soft fur. Our eyes never lose contact. When he lays his head to the side and puts its weight fully into my left palm, my heart flutters. Instinctively, I sweep my hands down his face before patting his sides.

"Well, I'll be. I've never seen him do that before." Confusion drips from the man's voice.

"Yeah?"

"Normally, he's not one to approach people, let alone share affection. Tends to keep to himself. We bring him to every adoption event, and it's like he doesn't even try."

Tends to keep to himself. The words reverberate within my mind, slicing at my fragile heart. It's something I'm quite familiar with. I've been doing the same thing for the last eight months. The man's words and close proximity create a nervous energy that swirls through my body. I've never been one to talk to someone I don't know, let alone a man I don't know.

"I'm Matt by the way." Holding out his hand, he waits for me to shake it. I go for the awkward small wave instead. Unfazed by my lack of social graces, he asks, "And what's your name?"

"Greer!"

Duke jerks his head out of my hand at my loud tone. His eyes seem to say, "What was that?"

"God, I'm sorry. I'm Greer. What kind of dog is he?"

"A golden-lab mix as far as we can tell. Owners surrendered him one day. No explanation. He's been with us ever since. I think he likes you." Matt smiles again, and his eyes twinkle. I recognize that twinkle—he thinks I'm available. If only he knew what he'd be signing up for.

I can already hear my sister telling me to "get back out there" and "Brian wouldn't want you to live your life alone and unhappy." Gemma will never understand what it's been like for me. Not only did I lose my husband, I lost my best friend. I lost everything I knew, including the Greer I used to be. Even though I'm done with physical therapy and only see my therapist occasionally now, it's a daily battle to keep my thoughts from clawing at me and dragging me back to that night.

Gemma makes it sound so simple, so easy to meet someone new. And, okay, objectively Matt is handsome in a country-surfer boy kind of way. Losing my husband didn't rob me of my ability to appreciate a handsome man. Sure, we could date, fall in love, do all the things happy couples do—and then he could die. I don't know if I can risk the potential of losing someone so important to me again.

It's not that I haven't thought about opening my heart again. I'm young and, according to Gemma, the probability of me finding someone is relatively high. She means well with her nudging, but I can't help but wonder if I'm ready for that next chapter.

Shaking myself out of my swirling thoughts, I turn my focus back to Duke. He saunters around me sniffing at my legs and low back. Standing back up, I notice he doesn't put much weight on his back leg and has a bit of a limp, just like me. With a final lap around my legs, he sits at my feet and leans his whole body into me.

"Whoa there, big guy," I say. "You're a lot too big to be using me for a leaning post." With a gentle pat to his head, I step back. He doesn't like the space and scoots close to me once again. I'm better prepared this time and brace my previously injured leg as he leans all of his weight into me. My hand smooths over his ears, noting the sprinkles of gray hair.

"Well, I think that's that then." Matt tuns to gather some papers from his table.

"That's what then?"

"He's adopted you." He holds outs a small stack of papers for me to take.

"What? No, he has not. Dogs can't adopt people." A nervous laugh erupts out of me. I cannot be adopted by a dog right now. It's only been a week since I moved into my new house. Just one week of living on my own, trying to function on my own, and being alone.

Duke looks longingly at me. Nudging my hand in search of more affection, he stirs something inside me. A swirl of warmth and fear. I'm sure it wouldn't take much to care for him, but I'm also uncertain if my heart can handle the attachment I already feel forming with him. Glancing at Matt, I offer him another awkward smile.

He nudges my arm, offering me the paperwork. "It's not every day a dog finds their human."

My gaze moves from the paperwork down to Duke's piercing brown eyes. My heart wars with my mind, the fear of losing something, again, firing off warning bells.

Duke sighs deeply, pawing at my foot. When I glance down, the tether between us pulls taut. In this moment, we share a longing for a connection neither of us realized we needed. A twinge stirs beneath my ribs, making me wonder if I'm betraying Brian's memory by bonding with someone new—even if it's only a dog.

As if sensing my internal battle, Duke jumps up and places his paws on my stomach. Grasping his face, I lean in close and nuzzle him. He gives me a big ole lick, and while I expect the slobber to gross me out, it doesn't.

"Yeah, okay, buddy, you can have me."

Mom is already here when Duke and I pull into the driveway. She had texted me earlier saying she'd done some *light* shopping for dishes. There is nothing light when it comes to her, and my guess is I'll have dishes coming out of my ears.

This house is an open concept with the kitchen, dining, and living rooms blending into one cozy room. Crisp white walls are met with neutral wood flooring. White cabinets are accompanied by a wood island and pantry door, quartz countertops, and even a barnwood-covered fireplace. The real reason I bought this house though is that it overlooks a wooded preserve.

"Greer, honey, what in the world took you so long?" Mom shouts from the kitchen as I slam the garage door shut.

"What're you doing, Mama?" Sure enough, boxes full of white ceramic plates, bowls, and coffee cups cover the island.

"Oh, just unpacking. No more paper plates for you." Her back is turned to me as she places more salad plates onto the second shelf in the cabinet.

"Did you buy everything they had? You know it's just me living here, right? Not like I'm going to need a place setting for twelve anytime soon."

I struggle with the many bags of dog supplies I purchased and set them on the kitchen island. Cool air from the ceiling fan brushes over my heated skin. Then I tug Duke's leash.

"It's okay. She won't bite." It's hard not to feel bad for the ole guy. I'm sure people will someday have to tug me by the leash too to get me to willingly meet someone.

"Who won't bite, dear?" Mom pushes an unruly swath of hair out of her face. She freezes when her eyes catch sight of me and Duke. "Um, Greer, I thought you were going to look at furniture?"

"I did." Patting Duke's head again, I unhook his leash and set it on the counter.

"That, dear daughter, is not furniture."

"Nope." I smile. "It's a dog."

"I can see it's a dog. I'm more curious whose dog it is?"

"Mine." Gesturing to Duke, I say, "Duke, meet Mama. Mama, meet Duke." I skirt around her to search for a pair of scissors in the junk drawer I've already created while they continue to study one another. After locating a pair, I cut the tags off the supplies I bought: silver dog bowls, a cozy tan dog bed, dog shampoo, bags of treats, and a few dozen toys. The giant squeaky hot dog was an absolute necessity.

Duke pads softly into the room, seemingly hesitant to freely move around. I don't blame him; I'd be just as nervous going from isolation in a dog shelter to a strange new home with a strange new woman.

New home.

Every time I think those words, it feels like a sucker punch to the gut.

Duke stares out the large black-framed windows (the best part of the house) to the backyard. I set the scissors down, then step around the island and open the back door. He trots confidently over the threshold onto the back porch.

"Greer?" Mom leans over my shoulder, watching the dog. "How did you end up with a dog instead of furniture? You've never owned a pet in your whole life. Remember that time you wanted a betta fish?"

Who doesn't remember my betta fish? I can still see lonely, fifth-grade me, desperate for a friend, thinking a blue-and-yellow-colored fish was the right choice. By the time I realized my mistake, I was on Dory number four.

Shaking away the memory, I state, "He adopted me." Warm afternoon heat greets us as I guide Duke to the lawn, preparing to set some ground rules. "This is where you'll go potty, okay? Not in the house. Out here, okay?" He tilts his head back and forth in understanding.

"Adopted you? How does a dog adopt you?"

"I don't know. That's just what Matt said. I was in the parking lot and saw him across the way at the pet adoption event outside the pet store, and he took one look at me and decided I was the one, I guess." Not wanting to drag out this conversation, I turn quickly and head into the house, leaving my very confused mother in my wake.

"Matt? Who's Matt?" She sputters, sliding the door shut behind her.

I don't respond.

Mom breaks down empty boxes. Duke bumps into her legs sniffing his way around the house.

Desperate to drop this part of the conversation, I all but whisper, "Matt? Oh, he's just the dog adoption guy."

"Oh really?" She drags out the *oh*, and my eyes roll.

"Don't 'oh really' me. It wasn't like that."

"If you wanted it to be, it could be." She grabs her handbag and keys.

"Mama," I groan, her words feeling like they're pressing into my spine, nudging me forward. "It won't be, okay. It's just . . . too soon."

She smiles, reading my unspoken thoughts. "It's not too soon, my love. I didn't mean anything by my comments. There isn't a timeline attached to starting your life anew after tragedy. And if there were, the only one who could decide that timeline would be you." She swings open the front door, and before I can stop him, Duke darts into the front yard.

"Duke!" I yell. Practically running over my mom, I dash into the yard, trying to catch up to him. "Elderly dog, my ass." Duke runs down the side yard between my house and the neighbor's. "Duke, come back here!"

That's when I see him. All six feet, scruffy face, suspender-wearing, lumberjack of him. The man holds an axe held high above his head preparing to take a swing.

Duke bounds toward the looming figure, and my heart lurches into my throat, panic surging through my veins. "Oh my god—stop! Please stop!"

The man freezes, lowering his weapon. It rests in the crook of his shoulder, further solidifying him as the perfect candidate for a calendar model—rugged lumberjack edition.

"Jesus!" He fully turns toward me, brow creased. "What is wrong with you?"

Breaths escape me in short, rapid bursts now that Duke is no longer in danger. "Duke, come here, boy."

"Lady, my name isn't Duke, and if you want me to come over there, you'll have to buy me coffee first." He sports a stupid smirk, and I roll my eyes, glad to have been spared ridiculous pickup lines when Brian and I met in college.

"C'mon, boy. Let's go inside." Gesturing toward Duke, I ignore lumberjack man's attempt at flirting. All I care about is getting my dog safely inside and away from him and away from the tumult of emotions surging through my body. I've only had Duke for a few hours, and I've already almost lost him.

Lumberjack man lowers his axe and sets it against a hunk of tree. In slow motion, he slides his thumbs beneath black suspenders and pulls them away from his body. Embarrassment leeches from my pores because it's at this exact moment my brain notices the way his gray shirt, dampened with sweat at the neckline, is completely plastered to his chest, leaving very little to the imagination.

As if they have a mind of their own, my feet fumble closer to Duke, who's equally hypnotized and sitting patiently in front of him.

"Like I said before," lumberjack man says, "my name isn't Duke. Although, you are pretty close." His intense gaze never wavers from mine. A new emotion trickles through my body, one I feel down to the very tips of my toes. *Get it together, Greer.*

Sighing out my embarrassment, I inhale annoyance. "My dog's name is Duke. I really am sorry he bothered you, but you didn't have to be so aggressive with him."

Looking from me to my dog and back to his axe, he bursts into a loud, boisterous laugh. "Oh man, did you think I was trying to kill your dog? Lady, I was chopping wood." With weathered hands, he points behind him, where I spy a large log and a pile of cut firewood. "I didn't even see your dog. All I heard was you screaming."

Gnawing on my lower lip, I dig the toes of my shoe into the grass. "Okay, well, I'm sorry for assuming you were an axe-wielding dog murderer. I suppose that was a randomly bizarre assumption to make."

"Thank you for the apology. It's not every day you get accosted for chopping wood." Squatting down, he places his hand out for Duke to smell. Within seconds, Duke sits between his large muscular thighs, a feature I'm trying my best to ignore, and stares into his face. Lumberjack man rubs Duke's ears and runs his hands down Duke's body.

"Okay, that's a bit dramatic, don't ya think?" I say. "I did not accost you. He just adopted me, and I've never had a dog before, and when he ran away, all I could think was that he would get lost or hurt, and I'd really not like to lose anything else I love because I've had quite enough of that this year, so when I saw you about to swing that axe, I might have jumped to the worst-case scenario." Every word rushes out in a single breath. Gathering what little morsels of confidence I can muster, I bring my gaze back to his face.

His smile blinds me. "He adopted you?"

"Well, yeah, I guess." I fidget with the hem of my shirt. "I mean, that's what Matt told me, but I also think maybe Matt was just looking for an 'in' to ask me out. So, yeah, that's my dog, Duke."

"Well, aren't you just the sweetest." He's petting Duke but studying me. "He's an old-timer. Not too many people adopt old-timers." Standing again, he holds his hand out toward me. "Name's Luke."

Without hesitation, I place my hand in his. "Greer."

"Nice to meet you, Greer." He gently squeezes my hand, then lowers our hands between us. "You just moved in, right?"

"Last weekend."

"I saw your car a few times coming home from shift. Sorry I haven't made the time to come say hi and welcome you to the neighborhood."

"From shift?" He doesn't release my hand, nor do I try to pull away. It's slightly sticky with sweat, but I don't mind, even though it feels strange holding his hand. Not bad strange, just *strange* strange. Brian was the last man I held hands with.

Duke sidles up next to me, once again pressing his body into mine. With my free hand, I sink my fingers into his fur.

"Yeah, I work with the fire department." Only now does he release my hand, and my audible inhale causes the corner of his mouth to turn up.

"I thought firemen weren't allowed to have facial hair?" My eyes widen at my outburst.

He grins, rubbing his hand along the brown stubble. "Yeah, we aren't, but I've had the last few days off."

"That's cool." *That's cool? Good lord, Greer.*

His gaze flicks down to my left hand. "I like to camp and hunt when the weather is nice. Do some scouting and whatnot. Your husband like the outdoors?" Luke clears his throat, motioning toward my house.

"Oh, no. He's dead." *Okay, well, that's one way to explain it.*

His smile falls. "I'm sorry. I just—I saw your wedding ring and assumed."

I rub my thumb over the bottom of the band, grounding me into the present and hoping my senses return. "Yeah, sorry, I just blurted that out. I promise, I know how to be around people. Or, at least, I did before everything happened. But it's clear I've forgotten how to people because you're the second person today who's gotten to witness my awkward attempts at socialization. And my parents wonder why I never go out. *This* is why I never . . ." I trail off, hoping he'll save me from my misery.

"Just breathe. It's okay." His voice is soothing, sincere.

Inhale. Exhale.

It's been so long since I've been around other people aside from my parents, doctors, or coworkers that I'm out of sorts, like I don't quite know where I fit in anymore. It's not as if I set out to isolate myself away from the world.

It still stings remembering how Brian's and my friends couldn't handle the depths of my grief and how easily they disappeared after the funeral. When they stopped coming around, I told myself they were more of his friends anyway. But I know I used it as an excuse to slide further away from social gatherings or any sort of relationship. I knew my social skills were lacking, but I didn't realize I was that far removed from the semi-social Greer I used to be.

After a few calming breaths, my embarrassment and nerves exit my body. "You must be really good at your job, huh?" I say. "Dealing with people who word vomit all over you?" Duke's velvety ear slides from my fingers.

Another laugh bubbles from Luke as he drags a hand through his long brown hair, wavy from sweat. "Word vomit? I've never heard that term before, but it works. And yes, I'm pretty good with people's word vomit. Part of the job."

"Greer, honey?" My mom calls from the driveway. "Is everything okay? I really need to be getting going."

I glance over my shoulder. She's looking down the side yard right at us. "Yeah, Mama. I'm good. Be right there." I turn my attention back to Luke. He's peering over my shoulder at my mom. Even from here, I see the sparkle in her eyes.

"I better get going," I say. "Sorry again for the whole murdering my dog thing and the word vomit thing. Just, well,"—*breathe*—"okay, I'm going to go now." Shuffling backward, Duke follows at my side. "I'll see you around, Luke-not-Duke."

Before I round the front of my house, I can't seem to help it as I glance back where my new neighbor is still standing, looking my way. With a smile and another awkward wave, I duck out of sight and walk down my driveway.

"You good?" Mom's eyebrows rise as she unlocks her car.

"Yeah." I roll my eyes, frustrated by my lack of social skills. "Just embarrassing myself in front of my new neighbor."

"Oh, I'm sure . . ." Her voice fades as she slips into her car. I kneel down to hear her better. ". . . it's not that bad. He looked very nice."

Leaning in, I place a kiss on her cheek. "Yep, real nice."

"Okay, well, let me know what day the furniture will get delivered, and I'll come over to help you arrange it."

I shake my head at her overzealous joy of decorating. "Of course, I'll let you know, but I am capable of doing things on my own, you know?"

"Of course you are. You can do anything on your own, but you're in luck because you don't have to." She winks, closes the door, and puts the car in reverse. As her car fades into the distance, I wonder if maybe she's right.

From the corner of my eye, I spy Luke with an armful of wood. His back muscles stretch and strain under the fabric of his shirt as he adds each log to the growing pile. I'm still staring when he pivots, catches my gaze, and gives me that dazzling smile that tries to reawaken some dormant part of me. Maybe Mom is right. Maybe it's time I let some people back in?

3

WATER DRIPS OFF THE freshly washed fire truck, a low hum of idle chatter filling the cavernous space as my crew gathers their belongings to head home after a long shift.

"Well, hi there, Luke." The familiar voice brings a smile to my face. Ms. Carol has been coming around the station for as long as I can remember, always flirting with the guys and stirring up trouble. I spy her leaning against her car door, gray hair up in her signature clip with her equally signature shit-eating grin spread across her face. I stifle a laugh. I swear she's got an uncanny ability of being around the station at the perfect moment. Peeling my sweaty shirt over my head, I throw it into the pile of clothes to be washed later.

"Will I see ya later today?" Ms. Carol says. Her keys dangle from her hand and jingle loudly.

"C'mon, Ms. Carol, as if you need to ask. You know I'll be there."

"You're a good man." Her eyes are bright as she gives me a thumbs-up.

Not ten seconds later, Hunter is at my side, elbowing me in the ribs with an expression I really don't have the time or energy for right now. "Um, should I be concerned about that?"

"What the hell are you talking about?" I bend down to grab a new shirt. Ms. Carol's eyes remain fixed on us, and a nervous laugh tumbles out of me. "C'mon, Hunter. You know how Ms. Carol can be."

"That is very true, sir. She might be pushing seventy-eight, but that hasn't stopped her from looking." He shoves me again, and I stumble into my gear bag.

Sliding a soft green shirt over my head, I distract myself by shoving a few other items into my bag. Sweat drips into my eye as I peek over at Ms. Carol. With another devilish smile, she slams her car door and skitters down the block to the coffee shop that's already got a line out the door.

"You know I help her around the house," I say. "And it's time to clean her gutters. There's definitely nothing to worry about." After gathering my empty coffee tumbler, I sidle up to where Hunter is leaning against his police cruiser, fidgeting with his laptop. He typically stops by the station to say hi before he starts his last shift of the week.

At six years old, Hunter and I joined the same T-ball team and have been best friends ever since. We decided early on to attend the same college, but when his father got sick sophomore year, he returned home, leaving me behind to finish my business management degree. We always knew we'd end up in careers helping others, but he ended up wearing a badge, and I ended up on a fire truck. Last year, I was promoted to captain.

Looking over the rim of his coffee cup, a smirk appears on his lips. "Cleaning out her gutters, are ya?" It's a good thing I'm his best friend because not everyone can handle his goofy, sarcastic attitude.

I ignore him and head inside to refill my cup. Firehouse coffee notoriously tastes like shit, so on my way home, I'd normally stop by Ground Up, the local coffee shop, a few blocks down from the fire department. But today is one of those rare days when the idea of forced socialization makes my skin crawl. My shift felt like an eternity, and I'm more than ready to be home.

And I'd be lying if I said I wasn't curious about what my new neighbor is up to. I'd been so annoyed the other day when she came screaming and hollering at me, but the moment those blue eyes met mine, I was speechless. I smile, recalling her rambling mess of thoughts—or "word vomit" as she called it. As far as neighbors go, she won't be half bad.

A few guys coming on shift tilt their heads toward me in greeting as I snag my wallet and keys from the kitchen counter. The urge to play the part of energetic-and-personable Luke tugs at my gut, but exhaustion claws through the feeling.

Heat blasts my face when I open the bay door and head out to my truck. Hunter is still leaning against his car, sunglasses and cowboy hat doing little to hide his true intentions—to give me shit.

Growing up, our moms would tease that it was our life's mission to cause trouble and break hearts. They were partially correct. I mostly tried keeping people happy so they wouldn't call the cops on us. And where breaking hearts was concerned, that was Hunter's expertise. I fell firmly into the category of getting mine broken, over and over.

"I like how you ignored my question." He nudges my foot with his boot.

"Hunter, stop being ridiculous. I'm just helping her clean her gutters. You know she lives alone, and the last thing we need is that woman getting on a ladder."

"Facts." He snorts. "Although, I kind of wish it was more salacious than that. Ain't it about time you got yourself back out there?"

"Just because I don't jump from woman to woman like you doesn't mean I'm not out there." I huff a frustrated breath.

"I'm just fucking with you. What's wrong?"

"Nothing. I'm fine."

"Mm-hmm, because *fine* definitely means you're not fine. C'mon, man, what's got you all mopey this early in the morning?" He crosses his feet at the ankles, tucks his black sunglasses into his shirt pocket, and turns his all-knowing gaze on me.

Nervous agitation prickles just beneath my skin. I grip my coffee, then run my other hand absentmindedly down my face. "I am not mopey. And it's nothing, just saw Sadie last night on a call." I grit my teeth at her name.

He chokes on his coffee. "Sadie?"

"Yeah." I'm hoping he drops it because Sadie is the last person I want to think or talk about.

"Sadie? As in the woman who left you high and dry for some fuckboy in Montana? That Sadie?" Hatred emanates from him as he freezes in place.

One great thing about best friends: They've always got your back. Especially when you get your heart broken after catching your girlfriend having a secret relationship with some random cowboy in Montana.

"What other Sadie is there?"

"Shit, what is she doing back in town? Thought she was too good for Suncrest Valley."

"Me too. Maybe she was just too good for me." Because apparently that's my thing—I'm the guy all the girls love for a time but never the long haul.

Sometimes I wonder if my radar is set to finding women in need. Even as a teenager, it was the same old story. I'd meet a girl, help her, fall for her, and then she'd be gone. Maybe someday, I'll find the right woman, one who wants to be with me forever.

"Shut the fuck up, you know that's not true. Sadie was not too good for you. You just fell for a girl you thought you knew. Hell, we were all shocked by what went down."

I take an aggressive sip of scalding coffee. I suck in a breath, trying to play it off like it wasn't that hot. "Maybe I missed the signs that she really wasn't into me."

"Yeah?" His fingers hover over the screen of his phone as he peers up at me. "What signs?"

"For starters, I always called her."

"Okay, but we all know you're a needy bastard." Tossing his cowboy hat onto the passenger seat, he slides into his cruiser.

"What's so wrong with wanting to keep up with another person? Hear about their day? Hear their voice?" I unlock my truck, and then I toss my gear into the back seat. My tackle box and fishing poles catch my eye. The urge to find a creek and get lost for a few hours tempts me.

Firemen catch so much shit about sitting in recliners all day, but people have no clue about the severe lack of sleep and rest that plague us. Yesterday alone we had fifteen calls in our twenty-four-hour shift. As captain, that also means fifteen calls of increased anxiety not knowing what we're heading into and fifteen call's worth of paperwork to double-check and submit. My brain rarely gets a moment of reprieve. Now, I'll go home to rest and recover for the next two days before coming back to do it all again.

"Nothing is wrong with that." Hunter buckles his seat belt. "You know that's not my thing. Guess some women don't work that way either. Okay, what else?" Hunter never seems willing to put in the work for a relationship, giving just enough before he's off to the next thing.

"Okay, here's one for you: The only time she invited me over was when she needed something done." I push the ignition button on my key fob, and the engine rumbles to life.

"Ah, golden-boy Luke." Sarcasm drips from each word. "You know that's your biggest problem."

"What are you even talking about?" I walk over and stand beside his door.

"You can't say no to people."

"Is it so wrong to be a nice guy?" I inhale deeply, removing my ball cap, smoothing my hair down, and brushing my fingers along my stubble.

"No, there's nothing wrong with being a nice guy. But there's everything wrong with letting people take advantage of your kindness."

"I don't." I slam my ball cap onto my head, then raise my hands in the air. He's got me there.

"Yes, you do. Look me in the face right fucking now and tell me you don't let people take advantage of that heart of gold in your chest?" His eyebrow slants in a "you know I'm right."

"I—shit." Any explanation I have catches in my throat. I officially want to be anywhere but here.

"Exactly. You're a good man, but that doesn't mean you have to bend over backward for everyone all the time."

"Okay." I swing my arms out and let a loud exhale whoosh from my lungs. "And what does that have to do with Sadie?"

"It's not just Sadie, man. It's all your past girlfriends." He looks over to check the time on his dash. "You want to fix 'em, do everything for 'em, make 'em happy. Which is all good and grand to some extent, except I don't think you worry about yourself being fucking happy. It's like you forget you're a worthwhile person who doesn't have to be everyone's *go-to guy* to have them like you."

Built-up tension trickles down to my hands. "I don't do it so people will like me."

"Oh, you don't? What do you get out of it then?"

Backing up toward my truck, I play it off with a smirk. "The simple joy of helping someone else."

"I call bullshit." Hunter turns the ignition to his cruiser, then the engine hums to life.

"I don't know, man. It's just who I am, I guess."

"Whatever you say, Luke. Maybe someday you'll meet a great woman and realize it's you they want, not shit you do for them."

"I can only hope."

"So, what's on tap before your date with Ms. Carol?"

"It's not a date, asshole. I'm just cleaning out her gutters." I throw him the middle finger.

"Yeah, yeah, I'll bet you are." He smirks, grabbing the handle.

"Is your mind ever not filthy?" I holler over the noise of the engine. "You know what? Don't answer that. If you must know, *Dad,* I'm going home to shower, sleep for a few hours because we were up most of the night, and then, who knows, maybe I'll see what my new neighbor is up to."

"Say what now? New neighbor?" He clutches his chest. "I'm hurt, Luke; you're holding out on me. How gorgeous is she?"

"She's beautiful." Greer's face flashes in my mind—hair piled in a messy bun, nervous sweat glistening on her forehead.

"You ask her out yet?"

"What? Of course not. She seems like a very nice woman, but it's complicated." *That's one word for it.*

"How long's it been again?"

"Long enough." It's not like I haven't been tempted, but I've not met a woman I truly connected with to want to take things to that level.

"You have to get laid. Maybe it'll make you less mopey."

"Fuck off. I'm not mopey. I just—"

"Whatever man," he says, shaking his head, then starts to close his door. "I gotta go. Catch you at the lake Sunday, right?"

"Wouldn't miss it," I reply, my words fading as he drives away toward the police station.

Jumping into my truck, I sigh in relief as I finally drive across town toward home. Suncrest Valley isn't a big town by any means. It gives one the ability to choose a more urban or rural lifestyle. Before being promoted, I lived in an apartment near the library, but now I prefer living on the outskirts of town.

Working in real estate is in my family's blood. Growing up, it was clear Dad wanted my sister, Sutton, to join the family business. Sutton being Sutton, she quickly transformed it into the town's number-one real estate company only a few months after he passed away. About two years ago, she helped me land my current house. It's not the ten acres of land near the Onyx Mountains I hope to someday call my own, but it's a happy medium.

Wind rushes inside the cab of my truck as I roll down the window. I make the turn on my street, and my eye catches on an old Ford truck parked on the street in front of Greer's house. Curiosity begs at me to go next door and say hello, but I head inside my home instead. Hunter's probably right, and I doubt Greer wants to deal with my piss-poor attitude. Nothing a little sleep won't fix.

Today is our friend group's summer kickoff party, and one of my favorite days of the year. Being on the department makes it hard to get the group together more than once a month, but once our summer kickoff happens, most of us focus less on working overtime and more on making up for lost time with our family.

As kids, our core group usually consisted of me, Sutton, and Hunter. After joining the fire department, I met Vinnie and Adam. We're an eclectic group, but we share a deep love for nature. When Hunter bought his boat, we began frequenting the lake regularly. Years back, Sutton and Grace initiated a grand summer kickoff party, which has become one of my favorite traditions.

I open the door to my navy-blue truck, and then I toss in a handful of beach towels and slide a small cooler across the seat. My phone buzzes in my pocket, and I pull it out quickly thinking it's one of my friends needing some last-minute item from the house.

"Shit." I groan seeing Sadie's name stretch across the screen. I contemplate not answering, but I'm sure she wouldn't be calling if it weren't an emergency. I press accept and hold the phone to my ear. "Hey, Sadie."

"Luke, I'm so glad you answered." There's some sort of clanking noise in the background.

"You just caught me. I'm headed to the lake. What's up?" I slide into the driver's seat and buckle up.

"Oh man, I could really use your help."

I lift my hat and wipe sweat from my forehead. "Like I said, I was just headed to the lake. Can it wait?"

"Not really. My car broke down, and I didn't know who else to call."

Dammit. "Where are you at?" I swear, someday she'll get a vehicle that isn't a total junker.

"I'm outside the grocery store."

I know it's going to make me late. I know my friends will give me endless amounts of shit, but . . . "I'm on my way. It's too warm to wait outside, so go inside the store." I end the call and head in the direction of the market.

The parking lot is swarming with people, but I see Sadie's rusty green car in a spot at the back of a row. I text her I'm there, and soon, she's strutting across the lot. And I do mean strutting. She is clad in tiny pink shorts and a tight white tank top; it's as if she's trying to put on a show for me. There's too much baggage between us, and I'm pleasantly surprised at the lack of reaction she causes.

I tap on the hood of the car. "Pop it open."

"I can't thank you enough for coming. I know how much today means to you." She would; she's attended the summer kickoff party a few times.

"Yeah, it does, so the faster I can figure out what's wrong with your car, the faster I get there." I'm annoyed, but I'm not sure if it's at my uncharacteristically gruff tone or the fact that I answered the call in the first place. It doesn't take long to find the bad connection between the spark plugs and battery. I use a socket to tighten them down and give her car a jump-start. After sputtering several times, it finally revs to life.

"You're a lifesaver, Luke!" Sadie jumps out of her car and rushes to give me a hug. Peeling myself out of her arms, I twirl up the jumper cables and hand them back to her.

"Okay, well, I'm going to head out now." I slam the hood of her car closed.

"Oh, okay. I just thought . . ." Her voice fades off.

I shake my head. "I gotta go. Bye, Sadie." I wave as I pull out of the parking lot.

It's late by the time I arrive at the lake, and, of course, the entire parking lot is full. After several laps, I find a spot big enough to squeeze my truck into. Jumping from the cab, the scent of summer wildflowers assaults me. I grab a small ice chest and duffle bag, and then I beeline it to the marina.

"Well, well, well," Adam says, "look who finally decided to grace us with his presence." He maneuvers the boat up to the dock.

"Hey, Luke." Grace, Adam's wife, reaches for the cooler of beer I'm holding, and I step onto the deck. "Glad you could make it out."

"Kickstarting summer wouldn't be the same without you!" Hunter grabs a beer from the ice chest.

"Only because of my grilling expertise." I take a beer from his outstretched hand.

"That too." Vinnie leans against the front rails. "What took ya so long?"

"Got caught up." I deflect. We've all been friends for so damn long that I know exactly how they'll react.

"Wouldn't have anything to do with Sadie being back in town, would it?" Sutton takes the beer offered to her from Hunter, her eyebrows raised in a judgmental question toward me.

"What the fuck, man?" Hunter jerks back in disgust, his voice bordering on a yell. "Tell me you did not."

"No, nothing like that."

Our conversation halts as Adam guides the boat across the lake toward a hidden cove we found a while back. Ignoring his insinuation, I settle back, allowing my body to unwind as we coast over the waves, the summer sun warming my shoulders. This is exactly where I need to be today. As a boy my dad taught me to fish and hunt, even took me camping any chance he got. It's because of him I'm usually outdoors.

Hunter, unrelenting in his teasing, fixates on me with a smirk. "I mean, I know it's been a long-ass time."

"Hunter," I say, "I told you it's not like that. I'm over her." And I am over her. Sure, I used to fall into the trap of getting physical with Sadie, even after we broke up. But having sex with someone you know doesn't actually love you anymore and who only asks to see you for sex made me get tired of that quickly.

"Why were you late then?" Hunter asks. "You're never late." He sits down across from me, close enough to Sutton that she glares at him and scoots down.

Shaking my head, I inwardly groan, frustrated that he can never just let things go. "Her car wouldn't start."

"Jesus, Luke." Sutton takes a long pull from her beer.

"Bro, why?" Adam says. "She's not your girlfriend anymore."

"I know." I slip my shirt off and smear sunscreen over my chest and shoulders. "It wasn't like that at all. I was packing my truck when she called. Her car is a piece of shit, and the stop was on the way to the lake."

"Yeah, okay," Hunter says. "But what're you gonna do when she calls again?" He rests his arm across the seat behind Sutton, his perceptive gaze drills through me, challenging me.

"Listen," Sutton says. "What Hunter is doing a terrible job of saying is"—she glares at him, but he just blows her a kiss—"we worry about you. You can't drop everything every time someone calls or texts or stops you at the corner to ask you to build them a barn."

"You guys will never let me live that down, will you?"

"Nope," they all say in unison.

I am so sick of this conversation. As if any of them would decline their boss's request to help build a barn when actively trying to get promoted. It's not as if this is a new habit I've developed. Growing up, I was always at Mom's and Dad's heels. When I got older, I enjoyed lending a hand to our neighbors, especially when they started paying me a few bucks. It didn't take long for me to become the guy who could do anything, fix anything, build anything. I liked it, feeling needed, which is part of the reason why I chose the career I did.

"*No* is a full sentence." Grace elbows me.

I roll my eyes. "Are we riding or beaching first?"

A chorus of grunts and headshakes follow, clearly annoyed by my quick subject change.

"Let's ride first." Sutton grabs the wakeboard and slips her feet into the boots. She winks, and I know I'm being let off the hook.

"Oh hell yeah, babe!" Hunter yells. With a few quick steps, he lets down the dive platform.

"When will you realize I am not your babe?" Sutton slides into the water. Adam carefully pulls the boat forward, giving her enough slack to get situated.

"When will you realize you are?" Hunter smiles brightly. He might act like a playboy, but I know his heart has always belonged to Sutton.

"Let's go, Adam!" Sutton slaps the rope on the water.

"She hates you." Vinnie laughs.

"Nah." Hunter stares longingly at her as she stands up. "She loves me."

"If y'all could figure it out, that'd be great." I smile, lay my head back, and close my eyes. "Hey, did I tell you guys I have a new neighbor?"

"New neighbor?" Grace leans in close. "What are they like? How old are they? Please tell me it's a woman. We need more estrogen in this group."

Water splashes along the side of the boat as we speed up. Sutton treads from side to side. It didn't take her long to become an excellent wakeboarder after Hunter taught her last summer. It's natural for her to excel at anything she sets her mind to.

"Not sure, Grace. I only met her briefly the other day." I don't bother mentioning I haven't stopped thinking about her. She was so nervous and agitated, but it all made perfect sense when she blurted out her husband was dead. I'm no stranger to death, and I've seen firsthand how much it can change someone.

"Just don't become the friendly neighborhood handyman." Adam ribs me.

"Shut the fuck up. I am not *that* bad."

"Yeah, you are!" They all scream at the same time my phone buzzes in my pocket. Sadie, again. Shaking my head, I silence my phone and zip it into my duffle bag.

With no threat of further interruptions, I settle onto the bench seat, allowing the sun to sink into my skin. They might constantly bust my ass, but they're family, and I know they're just looking out for me. Who knows, maybe they're right. Maybe I don't have to do things for people to get them to like me. Maybe I'll meet someone who will like me for me.

4

Greer

The clock ticks loudly, the sound sharp in the room, as excited tension permeates the air.

"Okay, everyone," I say loudly, "the bell is about to ring. Make sure you have your belongings. And don't forget—"

"You love us!" My students rush in for a last-minute hug. They'll never truly understand how much they anchored me and gave me a reason to wake up every morning after all that happened. Their constant talking, silly questions, and squabbles kept my mind blissfully occupied. But as I watch them prepare for summer, my heart clenches with the reminder that time is fleeting. In just minutes, they'll leave my classroom and we'll be but mere memories to each other.

"Okay, okay, be careful you don't knock me over! Yes, I love you, and I hope you have a great summer!" The final bell echoes through the hallways, and my fifth graders disperse with squeals of laughter. Each goodbye is an ending of one chapter and the beginning of another. Summer has officially begun.

I turn from the door, and empty desks stare back at me. Silence, something every teacher craves, engulfs me. Sighing, I gather up a few belongings before heading to pack the rest of my desk. Mom came a few times after school this week, so most of my things are ready for the transfer to the new school.

"Hey, Greer!" My co-teacher, Lucy, sweeps into my room. "You going out to lunch with us? I can't believe it's your last day." She plops into my chair and spins in a circle.

"Oh, lunch? Where are you guys going?" My stomach drops as I once again ponder whether to join or not.

"Just over to the taco shop. You should come."

"I really wish I could, Lucy, but my parents are coming over today." The excuse comes naturally. We both know I have time for lunch. Problem is, I'm not even sure I know how to say yes to anything anymore.

"Okay." Her smile flatlines. From my history, she'd probably already guessed I would say no. She stands from the chair and removes posters from the wall. We lapse into silence working side by side.

My coworkers, students, and parents all knew what had happened to me, something that comes with living in a small town like Suncrest Valley. After missing the first three months of the year, I returned with the goal of distract, distract, distract. I tried joining various committees, but my self-imposed isolation took control, and every attempt felt like a battle between what I wanted and what I was capable of.

It was hard, facing death, living, and then having to pick up the pieces. It shouldn't have shocked me when people took my behavior as a signal that I'd rather not be bothered. Even if, looking back on it, I wanted to be bothered, I just didn't know how to let other people in, to let them see my pain. I wanted to explain it, to show them the weight I carried, but I couldn't find the words, and silence seemed safer than trying to break through the walls I'd built around myself.

Lucy radiates energy, and sometimes I wonder if maybe I should have given our friendship more of a chance. We'll be at different campuses next year, so I know it's probably too late now and probably not worth the effort.

"Congrats on the new place by the way." Lucy smiles, rolling the posters and handing them to me. "It's exciting."

"Exciting isn't the word I would use."

"I get it." She steps closer. "This whole situation is really shitty. I'm sure you'd rather be living your old life, in your old house. But, well, things are different now."

"I know." My heart lodges in my throat, and my lungs constrict, as if a heavy weight is pressing down on my chest.

"I know it hurts. It probably always will, but—and I mean this in the nicest way possible—it's okay to allow yourself to move forward with your life." Her soft hands grasp the outsides of my arms as tears track down my cheeks. Her words nestle between my ribs.

"Keep in touch." She pulls me into a hug. "I mean it."

"Thanks, Lucy. I will."

We both know I won't.

With a parting wave she exits. I'm frozen, watching the doorway she just vanished through. Between Mom and Lucy, it's like the universe is shouting at me to be brave and move forward, to let people in. Message received.

Sunlight beams into my eyes, blinding me for a moment as I turn onto my street. Distant trees from the preserve are dark shadows against a backdrop of the pinks, blues, and yellows that paint the sky.

As my new home comes into view, my heart tumbles through a mix of memories and uncertainties. Dad and his Ford truck are already in the driveway with a small, rented trailer holding pieces of furniture I purchased.

It's hard to admit that I could have easily filled this house with a lifetime's worth of belongings. Lord knows Brian and I had just about everything under the sun with memories built into every item. Our dining table that was always covered in puzzle pieces; a worn-in couch from movie nights; the rug that hosted an endless number of dance parties; our bed, where we made love and talked of everything we wanted out of life.

I could fill every inch of this new house with the memories of us. Guilt gnaws at me every day because, the truth is, I don't want them here. I can't have them here. Not yet. Maybe not ever. But I'm also not sure it feels right to leave them in a lifeless storage container either.

This unfamiliar life of mine is hard enough. Each day is a minefield of memories brought on by the smallest of things—the slightest scent of a cologne he wore or even the melody of a song we loved. Thoughts of *what should have been* consume me. Someday, I'll be ready to face the past, but, until then, that life, *our life*, can remain safely tucked away in that unit across town.

Flipping open the visor mirror, I tuck a few loose golden strands behind my ears, forcing a practiced smile before taking a steadying breath and tiptoeing into my new life.

"Hiya, sweet pea!" Dad shouts as he unlatches the tie downs. "How was your last day?" Although he's never been much of an outdoorsman, he sure does like to dress the part in his signature overalls and boots.

"It was great, Daddy."

He wraps me in a quick hug.

"Where's Mama?" I ask.

"Oh, she and that realtor lady, Sutton, are inside. House is most likely decorated by now."

"You're probably not wrong." With a quick smile, I make my way across the yard and up the front walkway. Light coming from the open door marks my path as excited chatter fills the air. I spot the two women at my large kitchen island, and Duke greets me at the threshold.

"Oh, Greer!" Sutton squeals when she notices me. "Your house is looking amazing."

"Thanks." I give Mom a side hug. The house is bare and hardly finished, but I appreciate the comment all the same. When I decided to move out of my parent's house, I'd enlisted Sutton Bradley to be my realtor. She was always part of the *in crowd* in high school, always put together and confident. Two things I'm not very good at. Although we came in and out of each other's orbits, we were never really friends. I feel her now, tugging at that familiar bond between us, and each time I'm near her, I'm tempted to tug back.

"Sutton has some wonderful decorating ideas!" Mom says. "Maybe she could help you."

"Oh, um." Butterflies whoosh through my belly at Mom's suggestion. I know what she's trying to do. "Yeah, that could be fun."

Sutton must sense my hesitation because she quickly replies, "My services are offered, if you ever want them. Hey, my brother, a few friends, and I are going to the lake again tomorrow. You should join us."

I stare at her, unsure when I started giving off the signal that I want to *people.*

"It could be fun, Greer." Mom fusses with a display of fake plants and candles.

Sutton's invitation hangs in the air, waiting for me to reach out and grab it. My heart hesitates, caught between longing to say yes to the lifeline of potential friendship she's thrown in my direction and the fear of starting something that might not last. I know everyone wants me to say yes. Hell, I'd love to say yes, but every time something stops me.

"My brother lives next door." Sutton says. "Maybe you've met him?" For now, it seems she's given me a free pass on her invitation.

Tingles spread along my palms. "I didn't know Luke was your brother." It's like I can see my hopes of avoiding my new, very handsome and alluring neighbor fly out the open front door, as if Life has other plans for me.

Inhale. Exhale. In my head, I repeat the words Brian would always say when he could sense my anxiety growing.

"You'll love him." Her smile is radiant. "Anyway, I forgot to give you your mailbox key. Make sure you drop this form at the post office for your change of address. And"—she looks around—"I think that's it. I'm really happy for you, Greer. This is going to be so good for you."

"Thanks, Sutton." I'm almost positive my bucket of what everyone thinks is good for me is officially overflowing. I love how much they care for me, but it's overwhelming sometimes because I wish I knew what was good for me. Most of the time, I feel like I'm blindly moving in the direction I hope I'm supposed to be going.

"Okay, well, I'll leave you to it," Sutton says.

Coming around the island, I'm wrapped in a tight hug. At first, I stand there, awkward and wide-eyed before settling my arms around her waist.

"There you go," Sutton whispers in my ear. Her warmth seeps into my heart, tugging at that little crack longing for friendship. She releases me and wraps my mom in a similarly tight hug before exiting on a cloud of energy.

Mom laughs. "Well, I quite like her. She's going to be good for you."

My eyebrows perk in confusion, but I'm too tired to overthink her statement now.

"C'mon, Mama, let's go help Daddy." My hand envelops hers as I drag her back out the door.

We unload the trailer rather quickly, and they offer to help me build some of my new furniture, but I tell them I want to do it on my own. After waving goodbye, I walk back inside. My ever-present nerves settle beneath my pale skin. Little by little, this house is beginning to feel different—less overwhelming, less empty.

I gather my tools and the instructions, then attempt to assemble some of the items I purchased while Duke sits nearby. I only make it halfway through the ridiculous instructions for a side table when I realize I should have taken my parents up on their offer to help. Giving up for the night, I toss down my Allen wrench and head to get ready for bed.

It's quiet here at night, something I noticed when I first moved in. Silence bears down on me, a stark contrast to the usual noisy background that once accompanied my life. With Brian, our days were always filled with music or his idle chatter. With my parents, they were always talking or, you know, doing whatever else parents do when they don't remember the walls are thin.

I pour a few fingers of whiskey, then slip out onto my back patio. The night is cool; a slight breeze rustles my hair, and my pink nightgown swishes around my legs. Grass tickles my feet as I gingerly step into the yard. Wind whispers through the trees, an owl hoots from somewhere nearby, and a soft glow of light comes from the window next door, pulling my attention.

"Hey, neighbor."

Not expecting a deep voice to sneak up on me, I startle and almost spill my drink. A shriek works its way up my throat, but I cut it off before it has the chance to run free. I press my free hand to my heaving chest and look at the man who almost chopped my dog in two the other day.

"Sorry, didn't mean to sneak up on you."

He's standing in the middle of his yard, moonlight casting him in shadows. I don't need a watch to know it's nearing midnight.

"Hey," I say lamely. I know what keeps me from sleep at night, but I wonder what's kept him awake tonight.

"Couldn't sleep," he answers, as if reading my thoughts. The atmosphere warms as he approaches wearing nothing but a gray T-shirt and a soft pair of navy shorts that I definitely don't notice riding dangerously low on his hips.

"Whiskey girl?" He asks, tipping his own tumbler in my direction.

"Of course." I bite my lip, trying to control my grin.

"What brings you out so late?"

"Um . . ." I take a sip of the amber liquid.

"Shit, I'm sorry. You don't have to answer that."

I gift him a smile. "It's okay. Just trying to find a way to answer that's not depressing."

"Who cares as long as it's honest?" He steps closer, his bare feet inches from my own.

"It's harder at night," I whisper, tilting my face back to his. "There's nothing to distract my thoughts from straying to places I'd rather not revisit."

He nods his head before taking the last sip of his drink. "How did it happen?"

Strangely, I know exactly what he's asking. *How did your husband die?*

"Car accident." My answer is quick, automatic. I'm surprised I even have to tell him because most people always seem to know my story already.

"That's fucking brutal." I appreciate his lack of condolences. Those don't bring people back.

"It was," I respond, my voice firmer.

"How long?"

"It's been eight months."

"Greer . . ." he says.

"I know," I reassure him. "Death is an asshole."

He clears his throat and nods his head. "I'll cheers to that." He must note my confused look because he quickly follows with, "My dad. Six years ago. Cancer."

"Shit." I release a breath.

"Yup. And"—he reaches toward me but drops his hand to his side—"I know it's not the same as what you're going through, but I'm here if you ever want to talk."

"Thanks." My muscles calm at his offer.

"You settling in okay?" He shifts side to side, lowering his empty glass.

"That's the million-dollar question these days." I laugh. "You want more?" I nod to his empty glass. He hands it over, and I slip inside to the safety of my kitchen. Looking over my shoulder, I see he's moved closer to my patio with his back turned toward the preserve. This might be the first time the butterflies in my stomach don't feel like an angry hurricane. Shaking away the start of a thought spiral, I pour a splash of dark amber liquid into each glass and head back outside.

"Thanks," he says when I hand him his glass. "You were saying?"

"To be honest,"—I take a sip, curious as to why I feel the need to be honest with this man in the first place—"this isn't the plan I had for my life, but I'm doing okay. I think." Why is it so easy to confide in a stranger I don't know a thing about?

"Life does tend to have a plan of its own even if we disagree with it. Those your parents over here earlier?"

I nod, and he continues. "Do you have any siblings?"

"Yeah," I smile at his rapid-fire questions. "Gemma is younger than me, but she lives in California, so I hardly see her. Speaking of siblings, a certain realtor of mine failed to mention my neighbor was her brother."

He laughs then, and I'm mesmerized by the crinkles beside his eyes. "That sounds like my little sister. She loves holding onto information and then dropping it like a bomb into the middle of a conversation."

"Little sister? So, you're what—thirty-four?" I'm not entirely sure why I care.

"Just turned thirty-five in February."

"Let me guess, Pisces?"

His eyes catch mine and refuse to let them go. "Yep. You?"

"Scorpio. Not that I know much about zodiacs and stuff. Lucy, she's this woman I work with, well, used to work with before they transferred me; she loves astrology."

"Transfer?" This man doesn't miss anything.

After a deep breath, I explain that my school is transferring me to second grade at another elementary school because they need someone with more teaching experience to be the lead teacher. He nods along and interjects with other questions as they pop up. I surprise myself by answering each one.

"I'm not sure how you do it," he says.

My forehead scrunches, not sure of his meaning.

"You've had a lot of huge life changes," he says. "More than most people can handle."

"I don't really have a choice but to handle it, you know? Tell me more about you." I hope he'll let that particular strand of conversation go. We talk for a while longer, and he tells me more about his family and job. As the temperature drops a few degrees, our conversation fades off.

We stand together under a sky full of stars, both of us lost in thought but content to be with one another. It feels nice, being near Luke, someone who has an intimate experience with loss, someone who seems to know when to dig deeper but also doesn't feel the need to fill every moment with constant chatter.

Luke clears his throat again. "Well, I'm going to head to bed. G'night, Greer."

"Good night, Luke." I watch him as he takes long, steady strides across the grass before disappearing into his house.

I toss back the rest of my drink, then take another deep breath of fresh air and go inside. Clicking the lights off one by one, the house takes on an eerie ambiance. I flip off my bedroom light and dash toward the bed, my feet slapping against the hardwood floors. I hop onto the mattress, banging my knee in the process.

"Ah, fuck." I roll over, trying to rub away the pain.

Cool sheets press against my legs as I slip beneath the covers. I squish various pillows on either side of me, and then I pull the covers up to my chin. After a few readjustments, I am perfectly cocooned in the middle.

Unable to stop the sudden memory, I allow it to play through: Brian sleeping on the left and I'm on the right, always ending up plastered together, butt to butt, right in the middle of the bed. I hate that something as simple as a mattress is now a daily reminder of what I've lost. I hate that it's no longer *our* bed. It's just mine. I hate sleeping in the middle, but it's less lonely here.

Darkness fills my vision as I watch the ceiling fan spin round and round, silence roaring in my ears. One by one, I attempt to quiet my thousands of thoughts. Ones of Luke and Brian, but mostly thoughts of me and my life, everything that was and everything that will be.

Eventually, I give up and close my eyes, knowing soon enough my mind will be anything but silent.

5

Greer

Unknown: Hey girl, want to meet for coffee?
Me: Who is this?
Unknown: Woman, it's Sutton.
Me: Oh hey, how are you? Sorry, didn't have your number saved in my phone.
Unknown: Best be changing that quick.
Unknown: So . . . coffee?
Me: What about it?

I pour steaming coffee into my favorite mug, the rich aroma mixing with the crisp summer air. I quickly add her to my contacts.

Sutton: Do you drink it? Want to meet up at Ground Up?
Sutton: 10:00?
Sutton: You're on summer break, right?
Sutton: They've got those really good cinnamon rolls.
Sutton: I love those things. I think they must put some kind of drug in them.

I can't help the giggle that escapes me as my phone pings incessantly, her messages flooding in back to back.

I am convinced there are only three types of texters in this world: those who write organized and thoughtful paragraphs; those who type in a series of never-ending texts, their thoughts flitting from one thing to the next; and then there are those who don't text. I'm unsurprised to learn Sutton falls firmly into category two.

Sutton: Please say yes.

It's hard to remember the last time, if there ever was one, where someone was this exuberant and desperate to hang out with me. Shuffling into the living room, I picture her already dressed to perfection, phone in hand, ready to tackle the day into submission. The perks of being a teacher are that I have zero to-do lists. I'm content to stay in my flamingo nightgown and cozy socks for as long as I want. Which, I suppose, won't be for very long today.

Sutton: Please :)
Me: Are you done yet?
Me: Wait, don't answer that or I might never get a word in. Why do you want to go to coffee with me?

Sutton: Because I want to.

Sutton: Does there have to be a reason?

I sigh and say aloud, "Message received, Brian." *I can do this. I don't have to be so alone anymore.*

Me: Fair point. 10:00 works.

Sutton: OMG! I'm so excited!

Sutton: It'll be so fun to catch up and not be focused on finding you a house.

Sutton: Speaking of, I gotta run to a few showings.

Despite the early hour, Sutton's excitement is infectious, and a reluctant smile tugs at my lips at the same time a flutter of anticipation settles in my chest.

"Oh man, Duke." I reach down to scratch his head. "Am I really going to do this?" He barks. Even my dog thinks I need more friends.

Slipping on my house shoes, Duke and I venture into our shared sanctuary. The concrete pad under my awning, though modest, opens to a large grassy yard. A line of pine trees stands guard, creating a natural barrier between the preserve and neighborhood. If I listen hard enough, I can just make out the trickling of water from a nearby stream.

I take a deep breath, then exhale slowly, letting the subtle scent of pine trees and wet foliage wrap around me. The dew-covered grass tickles my ankles as we walk farther into the yard. Duke playfully darts off to the side and circles around me.

I'm surprised at how *not* terrifying it's been living on my own. Aside from my college dorm room, I've never truly lived alone. When I'd decided to move out of my parents' house, I'd built it up in my mind that I was moving to some far-off land that'd be filled with monsters and orcs, pain and loneliness. But it's not been like that at all. In fact, I almost feel more settled, more at peace now that I'm here. A bittersweet smile tugs at my mouth. Brian would be proud of me. *Would be.*

"You like it here, don't ya, buddy?" I giggle, something I don't do much, but it's a welcome distraction from the sudden gravity of my thoughts. He continues his morning zoomy ritual around the yard, the wet grass causing occasional slips. Yet, he remains unfazed. The leg I thought might have been permanently injured appears to have mysteriously healed.

Turning toward the tree grove, I notice the trees aren't as densely packed together as I originally thought. There even looks to be a small path that leads into the area. Peering between them, I spot a larger, more open grassy area where morning sunlight filters through. Careful not to trip, I step over rocks and walk the last few steps until I'm standing on the edge of the tree line.

"Good morning, Brian." The words sail away on a whisper, and I hope they reach him.

A slight breeze moves through the yard, as if the trees are whispering good morning back. Distantly, I imagine Brian, wherever he is, saying hello to me. Placing the coffee mug on the ground beside me, I stretch my arms from side to side, reaching them high toward the sky before letting them fall with a loud exhale.

"Beautiful." A deep voice pierces the silence, jolting me from my thoughts.

"Jesus, Luke, you keep doing that!" I yell and step forward as I look over my shoulder. He's a vision in his fireman's uniform, matching blue pants, and a collared shirt.

"Yeah, sorry 'bout that." He doesn't look sorry.

"It really is beautiful here and *normally* so quiet." I tease, turning my gaze back to the view ahead. "Headed to work?"

"Yeah, I am. Chief asked me at the last minute to help teach a class." He pauses, furrowing his brows and shaking his head before continuing. "But I've got some time off soon." He takes a few long steps, then he stops to my left. At first, he caught me off guard, but now his close proximity feels safe, inviting even. Feelings I'll overthink and obsess over later.

A light silence settles between us for several minutes as we enjoy the tranquility of our little slice of nature.

"You ever been out there?" He gestures to the makeshift dirt path leading into the preserve.

"Not yet. All I've managed to do is make my house livable. Correction: I've helped my mom make my house livable. In fact, it's more than livable. It's—shit!" I pause my sudden stream of consciousness. "There I go again." Closing my mouth, I give him a sheepish grin.

"It's okay." He takes another step closer. Warmth settles over my skin. "I like listening to you ramble."

"Rambling is one word for it. There's something about you, Luke Bradley." My voice fades off as I turn my gaze to Duke who's rooting around various bushes.

"Yeah . . ." he says as a sudden smile lights up his whole face. "Okay, well, I guess I better head out. Have a good day, Greer." His retreating footsteps sound behind me as Duke settles to my right, watching him leave.

"You too." I peek over my shoulder to see if Luke's heard me.

He's standing there at the corner of his house, one hand holding on to it, watching me. He grins, nods his head, and disappears from sight.

"Alright, doggo. Let's go figure out what I'm going to wear." I slide the back door open, and Duke runs in and heads straight for my bedroom, making himself completely at home in the bed.

"Or maybe we can find a good reason for me not to go. We could do that, right?"

Just then my phone rings, *Mama* flashing across the screen. I press the speaker button as I step into my large walk-in closet.

"Hi, Mama."

"Good morning, my Greer. How did you sleep?" The soft, rhythmic sound of whisking filters through beyond her voice.

"I slept okay."

"Just okay?"

Her question prods at me. She knows I rarely sleep well since the accident. Some nights, I'll pass out readily into bed and sleep soundlessly the whole night through. On rare occasions, I sleep and dream of Brian. Others, I'm unable to fall asleep, my mind a never-ending hurricane. Worse yet are the nights I'm ripped from sleep by a version of the same nightmare of the accident.

"I'm not really in the mood to discuss it. I need to figure out what to wear."

Thumbing through my meager collection of clothes, I'm suddenly very aware of my lack of clothing. I've never been much for fashion. Give me jeans and T-shirt or a sundress, and I'm good to go. During recovery, I needed clothing that made maneuvering my hardwired leg and crutches easier, so my wardrobe became a collection of athleisure wear and teaching clothes.

"God, B, even my clothes are depressed." I muse.

"It's Mama, baby. Not Brian." Her voice clogs with brief emotion, and she sniffles.

Only she, Dad, and my therapist know I occasionally talk to Brian. It brought me comfort when I was in the early days of my war with grief. At first, I was embarrassed. Ashamed, even. Always worrying that people would think I wasn't quite right in the head. But my parents never judged me or made me feel silly. Talking to Brian is easy and, like now, if I slip into conversation with him, they gently nudge me back to the present, where he doesn't exist.

"Sorry."

"No need to be sorry." She takes a loud sip. "Now, tell me why you're fussing over what to wear? Where are you off to today?"

"Coffee."

"Coffee? You're going out for coffee and need to figure out what to wear?" Confusion pours through the line as she tries to piece together my dilemma. "Don't you go to Ground Up at least once a week? Pretty sure no one will care or even notice what you're wearing."

I hear the telltale sound of a bowl and spoon clattering to the ground. "Shit," my mom says.

I love her to bits, but unlike me, she's a disaster in the kitchen. "Technically," I say, "I'm meeting someone there. And before you jump to conclusions—"

"You're meeting someone? Oh, Greer, I'm so happy—"

"And there are those conclusions I told you not to jump to. It's not a big deal. Just meeting Sutton for coffee." I toss a light purple sundress and white slip-on sneakers on my pale-pink bed before popping into my bathroom and turning on the shower.

"Well..." A sharp intake of breath is the only indication my mom gives of her excitement. If I had her on FaceTime, I know she'd likely be sporting a huge grin. "That's just wonderful. Sutton seems like such a nice girl. I'm sure you'll have a great time."

"Thanks, Mama. I gotta get ready though, so I'll call you tonight. Love you."

"Love you!" She yelps as more clattering sounds in the background. I end the call, then toss my phone on the counter.

If there were any part of my house that I loved more than my backyard and view, it'd be my bathroom. Bigger and more luxurious than any I've ever had, it boasts a large walk-in shower with a freestanding tub inside. The back wall is covered in black hexagon tiles while the adjacent walls are adorned with white subway tiles. Before this house, I was never a take-a-bath type, but I've been converted with this shower-tub combo.

After I slap on a minimal amount of makeup—a sweep of rose blush and mascara—I slip my dress over my head. The fabric caresses my body, and goosebumps erupt across my skin. Nervous excitement flutters in my stomach as I step into my sneakers, catching sight of but ignoring the scars on my legs.

"There's nothing I can do about them," I say. "I've accepted them. I bet no one really notices them anyway, right, B?"

"Right," I answer for him.

I head out of my room, grabbing my keys and crossbody bag. All the while, Duke matches me step for step.

"Okay, Duke, you'll be a good boy while I'm gone, right?" He sits dutifully by the garage door. At the last minute, I grab my book (because who goes anywhere without a book?) and crouch down to his level.

"Yeah, you'll be a good boy. I'll be gone a little bit." I stand and give him a little twirl. "Do I look okay?"

He cocks his head and wags his tail.

"Great, I'm gonna take that as a yes. Okay, I'm off."

I slide into my SUV and close the door behind me. It takes a few tries before I can get the key into the ignition. People always thought I'd have trouble driving after the accident, but driving is one thing I don't have trouble with at all. It's the thought of socializing that's got my nerves on overdrive today.

I reverse out of my driveway, releasing a calming breath, and head toward the coffee shop. I open the window hoping the butterflies assaulting my stomach will fly away.

"Why am I nervous? It's just coffee." I picture Brian sitting next to me. He always helped me make sense of things. I still remember our late-night study sessions and him unwinding the worries of my brain about some paper I had due, something a professor said, or some random thing I said when I was thirteen.

"I know, I know. But it's *just* coffee with a potential new friend. Yes, I know it could be really good. Okay, fine, I'll admit it. I might feel like I need to throw up, but I am excited. That's good, right?" It's starting not to hurt as much now when he doesn't answer.

It's a quick drive to the coffee shop and after checking the clock I nod, happy to realize I'm a full twenty minutes early. Plenty of time to make sure the coffee shop hasn't decided to spontaneously pick up and move somewhere else. Plenty of time to internally freak out as if I've never had coffee with someone before.

I groan and bang my forehead against the steering wheel, cursing how much social anxiety plays a role in my life. I've had friends and have attempted to make new ones before. All throughout elementary and high school, I'd find myself on the periphery of various groups of people, but, no matter what I did, I never found myself in the center of one. Eventually, I'd just fade into the background and the relationship would fizzle.

When I met Brian in college, my life took a social one-eighty. I was quiet and reserved; Brian was loud and friendly. I was more of a homebody; Brian was the outgoing, adventurous type. With his help, I broke out of my little introverted bubble. When we moved back to Suncrest Valley, we stayed in contact with most of them and tried to hang out as often as we could. Although I didn't like all his friends, it was easy and fun. For once, it felt like maybe I'd finally found genuine, long-lasting friendships.

But then Brian died and those friendships faded away, just like all the others. Maybe it was me. Maybe it was them.

"God, Greer, it'll be fine. You know Sutton."

I tuck my hair behind my ears, and then I flip down the visor mirror to smooth down any flyaways. Why is it that someone hasn't created a handbook for making adult friends? It'd be like Tinder but for people who want to hang out, drink coffee, read, hike, go to shows, or sit silently in each other's company. Until now, I probably wouldn't have used it, but even I can admit my mom's probably right—I need to find my people.

"You've got this, babe." With confidence, I speak the words Brian would have said. After a final deep breath, I swing the truck door open and head inside.

The moment I step into Ground Up, the rich aroma of freshly ground coffee beans envelops me like a warm hug. The walls, adorned in a deep navy hue, are accentuated by rustic wooden accents, which lend an earthy warmth to the space. The usual hustle and bustle is hushed today, and I'm able to secure a table near the window with a perfect view of the street.

"Hey, can I get ya anything?" A voice behind the register greets me as I sit down.

Glancing over, recognition sparks in my mind. She isn't the familiar barista from the morning rush. Instead, I recognize her as a former schoolmate. Her auburn hair is elegantly secured in a claw clip with tendrils framing her face. Draped in a deep-teal apron that contrasts the delicate lace of her dress, she exudes an effortlessly romantic vibe.

"Yeah," I smile. "But I'm going to wait for my friend—I mean, my person I'm meeting to arrive." Only I could make talking a task worthy of needing a doctoral degree.

"Oh, that's cool. I'm normally on the afternoon and night shift, but you look so familiar. What's your name?" She comes around the bar, wiping tabletops and throwing trash away.

"Um, Greer." My voice catches. After clearing my throat and with more confidence and semblance of normalcy, I repeat, "Greer Ashbury. I'm pretty sure we went to the same high school, right?"

"Yes!" Her eyes light up in recognition. "Okay, now I know who you are. You were a year ahead, but I never forget a face." She walks behind the bar, abruptly ending the conversation. If you can even call it that.

Bells tingle as Sutton energetically bursts through the door. She spots me immediately and beelines to our table. I note the black pencil skirt and white collared shirt she's wearing, the classic pumps and smooth hairdo. Sutton's knack for style and sophistication is unforgettable.

"You came!" she shouts.

"I came." I know my cheeks must be bright red.

She approaches the table and sets her handbag in the chair before rounding the table. I'm already opening my arms, preparing to give her another awkward hug.

"I'm a hugger," she states plainly.

Grinning, the butterflies in my stomach land and settle. "That's okay. I don't mind." *Why don't I mind?* Slipping out of my chair, wallet in hand, I ignore the thought and head to the counter. "Should we order?" When I don't hear a response, I glance back at Sutton. She's just standing there, staring at me with a serene smile on her face. "You okay?"

"Yep, perfect now."

Her statement makes no sense, so I ignore it and place my order for a dirty double chai. As I finish, I motion for Sutton to place her order.

"Same as Greer. Oh! And one of your cinnamon rolls." She elbows my arm, giving me a side-eye.

"Okay." The barista looks from Sutton to me. "Are you two on a date?"

If we'd had anything in our mouths, it surely would have ended up on her face. Instead, our loud laughs fill the coffee shop, causing some annoyed glares from patrons.

"Well, no, not in the sense that I want to fall madly in love with her, get married, and have babies. But . . . yes? We're on a friendship date." Sutton's confidence pours from her and a warm, welcoming smile lights up her whole face. She wraps her hand around my waist, laying her head on my shoulder.

"A friendship date?" The barista looks utterly confused.

"Well, you see,"—Sutton raises her head, then looks at the barista's name tag—"Navy? Gosh, that's a great name. Wait, you went to school with us, right?" She pauses briefly, nodding yes to her own question. "Well, Greer and I have always known *of* each other, but we were never friends. She called me when she was ready to buy a house, and I loved her vibe. Made me wonder why we never became friends in high school. But then I realized we weren't meant to be friends then. We're meant to be friends now." She grins at me like that's the most normal explanation in the world. My body settles further, and I return her smile, loving that she rambles like me.

Navy eyes us curiously. "Well, *that* was a very thorough explanation. Good luck with your . . . friendship date. Hopefully it all works out. I'll bring your drinks and pastry out shortly." She abruptly turns her attention to the espresso machine and begins prepping our drinks.

"So . . ." I hate the awkwardness of beginning a conversation, my fingers twisting in my dress as I search for the right words.

"Can I tell you something, Greer?"

"Of course." We take our seats at the table.

"I hate small talk."

I release a deep breath. "Oh, thank god."

"Right! There is nothing worse than small talk. I try it all the time, but it doesn't take me long to deep dive—"

"Exactly," I interrupt, but immediately pull back. Embarrassment crawls over my skin at my outburst. I haven't been around people my own age socially much this last year, so it's hard not to talk a million miles a minute. I know I'm more of an introvert, but with the right people, my extroverted tendencies seem to emerge.

Sutton places her hands over mine, providing a sense of strength to my suddenly frazzled nerves. "If you can't talk about the deep stuff, what's the point? Am I right?"

"Okay, on that note . . ." I pause, toying with my wedding ring. "Why did you suddenly decide, after all these years, to invite me to hang out? Like you said, we weren't friends in high school, and we don't really run in the same circles. I mean, technically, I don't run in any circles these days."

"Yeah." She looks longingly out the window, then turns her attention back to me. "Your question is valid. But I don't know if I have an answer for you. At first, it was all about business, right? But after working with you and getting to know you a bit, you seemed kind of—"

"Sad? Depressed? Broken? All of the above?" I supply with an expectant look.

"Actually, no," she replies firmly. "You didn't seem like any of those things. At least not all the time. Yes, I could see glimpses of them, but mostly I just felt a connection to you. Like maybe we might have a lot in common?"

"So, this isn't a pity thing for the grieving, lonely widow?" I'm not afraid to admit I'm lonely because I know I am. Muriel, my therapist, is the one who helped me see just how much my self-isolation had exacerbated the emotion. We've been talking recently about me getting out of my bubble sooner rather than later. I know my awkwardness may contradict that desire, but it doesn't make it any less true; I would love a few friends, just not the kind that show up because they feel sorry for me.

"Greer, come on. Give me more credit than that. This is not a pity thing."

Navy brings our order to the table, assessing the suddenly serious nature of our conversation. "Everything, okay?"

The coffee cup's warmth centers me. I look from Sutton to Navy before saying, "Yep, everything is okay. Just getting to the nitty-gritty of things right quick."

"Yeah, small talk sucks." Navy says, setting the pastry down as Sutton and I share a smile.

A few quiet moments pass as we sip our drinks, being careful not to burn our mouths. Settling back in my chair, I absorb the energy from Sutton's presence

"The thing is"—Sutton twirls her finger over the edge of her coffee—"I don't have very many close friends."

I cut her an incredulous look.

"Okay, yes, I have friends. I know. It's kind of hard not to when my brother is the town golden boy, and he's never shooed me away like an annoying little sister. What I mean is, I've recently realized that I don't have any super-duper close girlfriends and, while working with you, I wondered if maybe you didn't either."

"I don't. I mean, we used to have friends, but after"—my scalp prickles—"the accident, they just kind of disappeared. If it's not Mom or Dad, I don't really have anyone anymore." *I don't have anyone anymore. God, that's depressing.* Distracting myself, I take a sip of coffee, my tongue stinging from the heat.

My confession doesn't faze Sutton. She passes me a fork and digs into our cinnamon roll.

"Was it hard?"

"Yes."

"I didn't know . . . Brian." She looks at me, seeming to ask permission to say his name. I give her a nod, and she continues, "But I remember hearing about it."

Settling my breathing, I pick up the fork and bring a piece of warm, gooey cinnamon roll to my mouth. Spices explode on my tongue while the dough melts in my mouth. I can't help the moan that escapes.

"Right? I told you they were good." Sutton shoves a bite in her mouth, getting icing on her chin. She may dress like a debutante, but this tiny view of her unrefined eating habits makes me curious what she's like when the world isn't watching.

"So good." A genuine smile peeks through as I settle into myself. Into my body. Into this moment. In the back of my mind, I just barely see Brian's face and his encouraging smile.

"So, how are you, Greer?"

"I'm not too sure." I place my fork on the side of the plate.

She takes a sip of her coffee. "Okay. Want to talk about it?"

"Not really." Little ants of nervousness suddenly emerge under the surface of my skin, and I reach for my handbag. I'm actually not shocked Sutton jumped right to the hard stuff, she did warn me, but for the first time in a long time, I don't want to talk about the past.

As if she senses my hesitation, Sutton's hand clasps mine across the table. "Don't go. It's okay if you don't want to talk. Stay, spend time with me."

I shake out the trepidation in my body, hating how hard this is. "I'm sorry. It's just hard to talk about it with people sometimes." *Most people.* Luke's face appears in my mind. "And I'd rather talk about other things right now?

"I get it." Sutton smiles, and those little ants retreat. "I promise, it'll be okay."

"Okay." I nod and slip my handbag back onto my chair.

And with Sutton, it really is okay that I wasn't ready to spill my guts to her. I know if this friendship continues with her, she won't always let me off the hook so easily, but I'm thankful that she does today. Baby steps.

We spend the next hour lost in conversation. Sutton rambles away with any thought that pops into her head, happy to lead the conversation. As the minutes tick by, it surprises me how good it feels to be here, fully present.

For the better part of a year, I've avoided interactions with most people. Each day started with facing my grief and tucking it away so I could function somewhat normally. One seemingly innocent question though could send me right back into the pits of despair, and then I'd have to start back over, tucking away the pieces of my broken heart, bit by bit. Isolating became my defense mechanism, but even I know it's not something I can, nor want, to maintain forever.

"You know what, Greer?" We gather our belongings and throw away our trash.

"What's that?"

"I think this is the beginning of a very beautiful friendship."

After another hug, Sutton hustles out the door to her car. I couldn't wipe the smile from my face even if I tried.

"Well, that seemed to go well?" Navy stands behind the bar, arms crossed over her chest.

"You know,"—I look back at her over my shoulder—"I think you're right."

"Must be nice, having a friend." She tosses the words out before disappearing into the kitchen. I watch the door swing on its hinges and an idea forms in my mind. *Yeah, it is.*

6

*T*HWACK.

Pulling the axe from the center of the wood, I feel reverberations vibrate through my hands. The air around me carries the scent of freshly cut wood as I wheel the axe behind my shoulder, taking aim once more. Another precise *thwack* echoes around me, splitting the log in half.

Beads of moisture drip from my brow, soaking my shirt. With a quick swipe, I clear the sweat before grabbing another piece.

It's June and the warmth of summer is setting in, the air damp with humidity warning of a coming storm.

Splitting the log easily in two, I set my axe against the sturdy base. Rough bark scratches my arms as I load up several pieces and carry them to the stack on the side of my house.

Being a lumberjack isn't a hobby I intentionally set out to do. When I was little, I'd find Dad in the backyard almost daily, swinging this same axe, adding wood to a pile. He'd get caught up talking to neighbors who'd stop by. That's one thing he was good at—attracting people to him, like moths to a flame. The sheer amount of wood we had stored at the house always confused me. But when he was asked about it, he'd just say, "We take care of family, and that means keeping 'em warm."

As a young boy, I strived to make my parents happy. Where they went, I'd be right behind. When I turned thirteen, Dad finally taught me how to use an axe. At first, my weak arms couldn't match his skills, but over time, I became stronger and stronger. Sometimes, while chopping wood together, we'd talk about life, but mostly we just worked in companionable silence.

After I learned of his cancer diagnosis, I became even more focused trying to do everything he did. I didn't think my mom or Sutton should be doing backbreaking work, so I stepped up, taking over majority of his tasks.

After he passed, my body and mind craved physical release. Chopping wood became a form of therapy for me. I wonder now if maybe he felt that way too. Most days I'm out here, swinging this damn axe, and when I do, the weight of the world fades. Even if only for a little while.

From the corner of my eye, a sandy-brown dog runs past and into my yard. He turns sharply before zipping back to his side. I shake my head, and my eyes wander over to his owner, my breath catching in my chest.

Greer.

She stands there, arms braced across her middle, watching her dog run circles around our joined yards like a racetrack. I'm dumbstruck watching her, much like I am every time I lay eyes on her. Even when I'm not around her, the image of her standing in her nightgown, illuminated by the early morning sunlight fills my thoughts.

Today, she's wearing a light pink sundress, her feet bare. Golden waves of hair hang well past the middle of her back. When she turns to grab a toy, a rather large scar on the lower half of her leg catches my eye. You'd have to suffer a serious injury to get a scar like that. I wonder if it has something to do with her husband's death.

It's hard to remember when Greer moved next door. House went from empty to full of her overnight. One night I ended up meeting her parents as they left her house. They seem like good people. A bit too enthusiastic and definitely protective.

"You'll keep an eye out for our girl?" Her father asked me.

"Yes, sir," I assured him. It's already proven to be an easy task.

Seems I can't keep my eyes from finding her any chance I get. I'll catch a glimpse of her in the yard with her dog or reading on her back porch. I've been tempted to approach her many times, but she always has this faraway look on her face, lost in her own thoughts. So I let her be.

"He's dead." I hadn't expected her to blurt those two words out in such a matter-of-fact way. They hung heavily in the air between us. In my line of work, I know horrible things can happen at any moment, but she seems so young to be a widow.

The other night under the stars, I had to deny the urge to pepper her with questions. I'm surprised how long we talked and how honest and open she was. A few times, I thought she was going to disappear inside, but she stayed. I was already curious about Greer, but now that curiosity rages like an inferno in my chest.

Grief is a motherfucker. I know that firsthand. For some, they retreat internally, wanting to be left alone to process. If you nudge them too much, they might not ever find their way back to the light. Mom was like that. I, on the other hand, was the opposite. I wanted to fix everything, wanted to lessen the burden I know losing our dad caused for Mom and Sutton.

A chuckle escapes Greer as her old fool of a dog runs between her legs about knocking her on her ass in his attempt to get his energy out. You'd never know he was such an old guy based on his speed and agility. The only proof he's not as young as he acts is his gray-tipped ears and matching luster in his coat.

"Hey now, dog!" She wags her finger at him. "You gotta be careful with me, remember?"

The dog, Duke-not-Luke, sits on his haunches, head canting side to side in understanding. She runs her hand over the top of his head, rubbing his ears. Her wide smile never leaves her face. I've never been drawn toward a woman like I am to Greer, nor have I met a woman as naturally beautiful as her.

Hooking my fingers in my suspenders, I watch them. Greer tosses a brown and yellow toy. Duke immediately rushes after it, catching it mid-air. Once it's in his mouth, he trots back to her, squeaking the toy as loudly as possible. She tosses it again, but this time, it lands near me.

As I reach to retrieve the squeaky hot dog, I hear another laugh escape from Greer. Duke bounds toward me, his ears flopping up and down, and sits at my feet. When my gaze turns toward Greer, she's looking at me with rosy-colored cheeks.

"Hey, boy, is this your hot dog?" I ask Duke, squeaking and shaking his toy back and forth. I rear back and toss it for him.

"Hey, you," I say. Greer's frozen as I take a few tentative steps in her direction.

She looks side to side as if someone else magically appeared in her yard. "Hi." Her mouth quirks up on the side.

"How've you been?"

"I've been g-good." She looks back at her porch. It doesn't take a genius to sense her desire to run and hide in the safety of her home. "I love this neighborhood."

"Same. I really love that," I say, pointing to the wooded preserve behind our houses.

"You go in there?"

"Yeah, I hike back there a lot." Duke drops the toy at my feet, so I toss it farther this time. "If you follow that little path, it leads to a small lake. It's a nice place to drop a line every now and then."

"Drop a line?" She purses her lips.

"Fishing." I smile, noticing her shoulders lower. "You ever been fishing?"

"Um, no. I can't say that I have. I know, how can you grow up in a state like this and never go fishing? Dad isn't really the outdoorsy type, so we never went." She shrugs, a smile so close to appearing.

"We should go sometime." Without thought, I step close, crowding her. Freckles dust over her nose and cheekbones. She's so beautiful. The pink fabric of her dress rustles in the breeze, and my fingers reach out, unable to resist touching the corner.

"Really?" Her eyes zero in on where my fingers toy with her dress. My heart rate speeds up as her breathing evens out. I've never felt like *this* around another woman before. I barely know her, and yet, she pulls me to her.

"Yes, really." My immediate response brings her eyes back to mine. I could get lost in them. "Would you like to go fishing with me?"

At first, I'm not sure she's going to answer because she stands completely still, eyes staring intently into mine. I see her mulling it over, as if she's going through all the possible reasons why she shouldn't say yes.

"I barely know you," she says, "and you want to take me fishing at a lake somewhere out there?" She gestures broadly toward the trees.

I laugh. "I see your point, but we're neighbors now, and it's not like I'm asking you to go right this second. We've got plenty of time to get to know each other. And, if needed, I can provide excellent references before I take you *there*." I make a similar gesture as hers. "Plus, it'll be fun." I'm hoping like hell my desperation isn't that obvious and that she says yes. Her eyes narrow. My fingers twitch in apprehension.

"Yes," she finally whispers. "I think maybe I would like to go fishing with you *someday*."

"Great, I'm looking forward to *someday*." Letting the fabric of her dress fall from my fingers, I step back, trying to convince my heart to slow.

"Awesome."

I love her sweet smile. Duke bumps into her leg, and she hisses out in pain.

"Duke, you gotta be careful."

Squatting down, she tosses his toy again before rubbing the bottom of her leg, the one with the large scar. I'm desperate to ask her about it, but I tuck that question away for later.

"Sorry, he gets so rambunctious," she says. "I'm not quite back to normal yet."

"That's okay. Normal is overrated anyway." She tilts her head up to study me. Not a stitch of makeup covers her pale complexion. I wonder how soft her skin is. "Hey, a few friends are coming over tonight for a bonfire and card games. You should stop by."

"I—um, no." Her reply is automatic. "I wouldn't want to impose."

"Greer, you wouldn't be an imposition." Needing to get back to work, I head to my yard. "Tell you what,"—I turn back to her, holding my hands out to each side. Her shoulders raise minutely—"if you feel up to it, stop by. If not, no hard feelings."

"I—it's hard for me. You know what? Never mind." She worries her lip between her teeth and fidgets with her hands. "I'm not making any promises, but we'll see." She stares at her feet before looking me square in the eyes.

There ya go, Greer. It's just me.

With a nod, I walk back to my side and place a new log on the stump. She's still standing there, dog at her feet, watching me as I reach for my axe. It slices through the air before cleaving the wood, the sharp sound cutting through the silence. I replace it with another piece and swing again, the rhythm of the blows steady and familiar. I don't have to look to know she's still watching me—her gaze one I can feel without seeing.

The best thing about Suncrest Valley is its cool summer nights. About once a month, our group likes to get together and blow off steam. The guys and I are all first responders, which makes it all too easy to exhaust yourself physically and mentally and become jaded. It can be easy to forget about the simple joys of real life—hanging out with friends, drinking beer, eating good food, and playing games. The group voted without me, and my house became ground zero for our get-togethers because according to them, I have the best yard.

Arguably, it is. It's the perfect backdrop, but I'm positive they chose my house because I'll do the cooking. I've got my mom to thank for my skills in the kitchen. "Full belly, full heart," she always says.

After adding a few more spices to the meat mixture, I form the burgers while Sutton finishes the veggies for the salad.

"Did I tell you I went for coffee with Greer?" she says.

"Oh yeah?"

"She's a quiet one, isn't she?"

"I guess so."

"Have you talked with her much since she moved in?"

"Few times, yeah. You know a lot about her?" I place the last burger patty on the tray before turning to wash my hands. I'm hoping Sutton will have some insider information.

"She was in my grade in high school. Always seemed good at school but was kind of a loner." After tossing the ingredients together, Sutton turns to get the dressings from the fridge as well as the potato salad I made earlier.

"I didn't know she went to school with us."

"Didn't know who went to school with us?" Hunter steps into the kitchen to grab another beer.

"Greer Ashbury." Sutton's tone is sharper than normal.

"You know what happened to her, right?" Hunter leans back on the counter, crossing his feet at the ankles.

"No," I lie. I know Greer said her husband died in a car accident, but I don't know any details. When it comes to her, I know I have to tread lightly. Any information I can learn now will save me from putting my foot in my mouth later.

"Her husband died," Sutton murmurs.

"She did tell me that."

"Did she tell you she was in the car with him?" Hunter's voice rises as he takes a swig of his beer. My hands pause.

That explains so damn much.

"I can't believe you don't remember this, man?" Hunter says.

"Remember what?" I question, focusing on the burgers. How can he think I'd willingly remember every detail of every call? Why wouldn't I block out really bad shit when I've got patients to attend to? Hell, my own mind would be a minefield if I allowed every detail to take root.

"I swear," he shakes his head. "It was last year. We went on that call, the one where the car got sideswiped by the semi. Took you guys forever to get them both out. Husband was dead, and she was wrecked. Never saw so much blood before. You could barely see what she looked like."

It clicks then, and my stomach plummets. I do remember this call. It was my first major incident acting as the on-scene commander after being promoted. It was something we'd never seen before. I remember jumping into the incident command role and pushing the horror of it all to the back of my mind.

I faintly recall her refusing to let go of her husband's arm even as we tried to remove her from the car. She kept saying, "Get him first. Please, get him first." But we'd already called his time of death, and she was our priority. We'd eventually gotten her out of the car, broken and bloodied, and into the back of the ambulance. By then, she'd gone silent.

I see it perfectly in my mind now: the medic closing the doors, her lying there, staring at everything and nothing.

"That was her?" I exhale. Sutton takes a sharp breath, eyes fixed on me as she nods her head. I knew Greer was grieving the loss of her husband, but this is more complicated than I ever thought possible.

"Why were you two talking about Greer Ashbury when I came in?" Hunter inquires.

"She's Luke's new neighbor," Sutton answers. "We went to high school together, and I helped her buy the house next door. Even met for coffee."

"No shit?" He swigs his beer and clears his throat. "Well, this is a heavy conversation for a cookout. She's not one of your new projects, is she?"

"No, asshole, she's not." I grab the tray of patties and hold the back door open. "Burgers will be up soon."

"Jesus," Sutton says to Hunter, "are you not capable of reading a room?"

He shrugs. "Sorry, babe, my bad."

"Don't *babe* me." She snatches the side dishes. "Get the rest of the stuff, will you? Least you can do is help set up the food." Sutton disappears out the door ahead of me.

"Guess you two are back to frenemy territory?" I ask.

"Nah." He smiles. "She loves me. So, did you invite Greer over tonight?"

"Yeah, but I don't know if she'll come over. She's a little reserved and very hesitant."

"I'm sure watching your husband die in front of you would fuck you up. Just promise me—"

"Hunter," I say sternly, signaling the end of the conversation. I love the guy, but he really could use a lesson or two in emotional tact. I'm not looking at Greer like someone to fix or some kind of project. Hopefully soon he'll see that too.

Voices fill the yard an hour later as everyone pulls up a chair around the fire. Crackles and pops fill the dips in conversation as night darkens around us. Our group varies in size from month to month due to other obligations, but I'm happy to see everyone here tonight.

Vinnie shuffles several decks of cards, and excitement builds as he passes them out one by one. Most of us grew up playing games. Bullshit is one of our favorites. I, of course, am the reigning champ, which pisses Hunter off. That man cannot lie to save his own life.

A glow from Greer's house catches my eye. I can't explain why, but she's burrowed herself into my mind, and each minute I spend with her makes me want more. A shadow passes in front of a window, and I contemplate going over to invite her over to join us. Figuring there's no time like the present, I set my cards down and push out of my chair.

"Be right back," I say to no one in particular.

"Hey man, where the fuck you going?" Hunter calls after me. "You afraid I'm gonna whoop your ass tonight?"

"Hunter," Vinnie says, then laughs, "you know you're never going to win. You are the worst liar. Remember that time in high school when we TP'd our math teacher's house? If memory serves, it took you less than five minutes to spill the beans to your mother."

"My mom is scary though!" Hunter shouts.

Their voices fade as I walk across our yards to Greer's back door. Tapping on the sliding glass door, I step back, placing my hands in my pockets. Her shadow approaches the door, but she doesn't open it.

"Greer?" I ask. "It's Luke."

The door whispers open as she pulls back the white curtains. "Luke?" She's barely visible through the opening.

"Hey, uh, I know I mentioned it earlier, but we're hanging out playing bullshit if you want to join us."

A soft rustle echoes as she places the curtains behind a small hook, revealing herself completely. An oversized sweater drapes over her shoulders, its fabric inviting to the touch. In cutoff shorts, her bare legs and feet capture my attention. A subtle, alluring scent lingers, and a few damp tendrils of hair escaping her top knot hint at a recent shower. Desire floods through me. She consistently takes my breath away, her presence constantly pulling at me, as if the very sight of her makes everything else fade into the background.

"Bullshit?" Her forehead wrinkles.

I laugh. "Yeah, it's a card game we play."

"Never heard of it." She leans against the wall's edge. "So, maybe I'll pass."

"It's okay, we'll teach you. Plus, you can't miss out on Hunter getting his ass kicked again."

"Who's Hunter?"

"My best friend. Sutton's there too." I hope knowing Sutton is there will make her feel more comfortable joining us for a bit of fun.

"Greer!" A yell fractures the cocoon around us. "Come over and play with us!" Hunter's boisterous laugh follows.

Greer chuckles and steps onto her patio. "Hunter?"

"The one and only."

"Greer," Sutton shouts. "Ignore Tweedle Dipshit, but for reals, come hang out!"

Greer takes a few steps more, and I can't help but smile as I spy her purple toenails. As if drawn by an invisible force, my body leans toward her, catching the thick scent of vanilla and sugar in the air.

"Did you just . . . sniff me?" She stifles a giggle.

"Sure did," I admit. "Are you baking?"

Glancing over her shoulder, unaffected by my nearness, she grins. "Yes. How did you know?"

"You smell delicious. Shit,"—I shake my head—"I mean something smells delicious." I don't know what it is about this woman, but now I'm losing my ability to speak.

"I baked some cookies. My mom's recipe." She turns fully to me now, stepping close. I could easily wrap my arms around her waist.

"Should I . . ." She gestures toward her kitchen.

"Yes!" I blurt out. "Bring you." *Fuck me.* "I mean, bring them. The gang will love you forever."

Greer looks toward the fire, back to me, and then glances inside her house. She's contemplating, and I pray like hell she says yes.

"Okay, let me grab them. Want to come in?" Her hand closes around my wrist. I'm not sure she's aware she's done it.

I nod and she releases me. I follow closely behind her. Her house is warm and inviting, a large open room adorned with a simple modern decor that complements the cozy space.

"Wow, this place is gorgeous."

"Oh, that's my mom," she says while plating the cookies on a tray. "She loves to decorate, so she's using this as a perfect opportunity to *Better Homes & Gardens'* the shit out of it."

She moves around the kitchen, plating cookies, cleaning pans, not saying much more. Greer moves around the kitchen with an unhurried grace, every movement reminiscent of a dancer. The oversized sweater she wears hints at the contours of her body underneath. Wide hips and generous thighs.

"You done?" she asks with raised eyebrows.

Startled, I shake my head trying to clear visions of her legs wrapped around my waist as her ass sits on the counter. "Done?" I croak.

"Checking me out." She juts out her hip, a smile playing across her face.

"I was not—Okay, that's a lie. I was totally checking you out." I shrug my shoulders. "Can you blame me? Not when you answer the door looking like that." I gesture up and down, indicating her sexy-as-fuck, girl-next-door self.

At that, she releases a belly laugh. Her face instantly transforming. "We better go before I change my mind, Casanova."

I revel in her laugh and the genuine smiles she's freely sharing with me tonight, as if she feels safe enough to venture out of her cocoon. While she finishes arranging the cookies, I take in the details of her home. The colors, cozy furniture, everything reflects a sense of warmth that matches Greer herself. It's the empty picture frames scattered throughout that break my heart. I remember my mom doing the same thing after we lost Dad.

With cookies in hand, she steps next to me and whispers, "I may not be very good at this."

Placing my hand on the small of her back, I lead her out the door. "That's okay, Greer. No one asked you to be." Her shoulders relax as we walk across the yard. From the corner of my eye, I spy yet another shy smile tugging at her lips. There's a soft breeze in the air, carrying the scent of cookies and quiet sounds of the night. A perfect backdrop for whatever seems to be unfolding between us.

"Yes!" Hunter yells. "Greer, come help me bullshit my way to the podium." He jogs over to us, then takes the tray from her. "You brought cookies?"

"Homemade too." She crosses her arms.

Hunter elbows me in the ribs. "We're keeping her." He's already devouring the cookies as he heads back to where our friends wait.

I glance at Greer and notice her smile fall and eyes gloss over. "You okay?" I ask.

She nods, closing her eyes and taking a calming breath. It's a familiar sight, and I recognize it as a method to help curb anxiety. I know I shouldn't, but the need to touch her is overwhelming. She doesn't open her eyes as I slip my hand into hers. The smoothness of her palm a direct contrast to mine.

When her eyes finally open, I'm lost in a cerulean sea. Her piercing gaze makes my heart pound against my ribcage.

"Yeah, I'm okay," she says. "I mean, I'm not, but I will be. My mind likes to . . ." She squeezes my hand, not finishing the thought. I can only imagine the minefield her mind has become.

The crackling flames cast a warm glow over us, laughter and conversation filling the air. As we join the circle, I can't shake the feeling that tonight marks a turning point, not just for Greer, but maybe for us.

Gesturing for Greer to take my seat, I sit on the ground at her feet. For a few moments, she thumbs through her cards, listening to Hunter explain the rules of our game, which haven't changed since my dad taught us to play when we were kids.

"I just try to get rid of all my cards without being caught lying?" she asks.

"Yes, ma'am," Vinnie answers from across the fire. "Are you a good liar, Greer?"

"I'm not much for lying." She lifts her shoulders, and her leg brushes my arm when she crosses her ankles. A jolt of electricity bolts through me. With a slight adjustment, I lean farther into her. I don't know what's happening, but my body craves to be close, to touch.

"You're in good company then, Greer," Sutton reassures her. "The only one good at lying in this game is Luke." Sutton points at me as she stuffs a cookie in her mouth.

"Oh really?" Greer looks down at me, nudging me with her bare foot.

"Really. It's all about the poker face, G."

Hunter hands me some cards, and we begin our game. Playing with three decks of cards makes the first few rounds lame because no one is sure who has what. I still can't believe they haven't caught on that I've learned to keep count of the cards. Definitely makes winning easy.

The fire casts shadows over our faces, and laughter mingles with the night air. As the game progresses, I find myself more focused on Greer's every move, every breath, every small laugh than on the cards in my hand. The unspoken connection between us tugs at my heart as the minutes tick by. I almost don't care about winning. Almost.

"Bullshit," Vinnie tells Adam.

"Damn it, Vinnie." Adam picks up the cards from the pile in the middle.

"That's another rule," I say quietly to Greer. She leans down to hear me better; her thigh pushes harder into my shoulder as pieces of hair fall around her face. "If your bullshit gets called, you have to take all the cards in the middle."

"Got it," she says.

The longer we play, the more relaxed she becomes. Her shoulders remain low, and she effortlessly adds to the flow of conversation and shit-talking. No one pushes her to talk, yet she surprises me again by divulging information about her parents, sister, job, and new house. As I peer around the fire, everyone seems as captivated by Greer as I am.

Warmth and friendship envelop us as our game continues. It doesn't take long for Hunter, Greer, and me to be the ones with the fewest cards. I'm so close to victory, and the caveman inside me hopes I get to show off a win to the beauty sitting next to me. Tension builds as each card is played. And with every round, I inch closer to victory, a silent challenge between me and Greer, hidden beneath laughter.

"Two aces," Hunter says.

I know he's lying. Greer knows he's lying too.

"Bullshit." Her eyes narrow on him.

"You sure about that, Greer?" He smirks.

"Yep. Bullshit."

"You know, Greer . . ."

"Flip the cards, Hunter," she says as a devious smile forms on her lips.

"Shit. You're good, girl." He flips his cards and reveals two 3s, then he grabs the massive stack in the middle. "You better be ready, Luke. She's coming for ya."

Without thinking, I slide my hand around her ankle and squeeze gently. An audible inhale from her causes me to drop it quickly, and I wonder if maybe I overstepped her physical boundaries.

"Oh, I hope so." I wink up at her. "Four 5s."

"Bullshit." She says the word before I can even place my cards in the middle.

My brow crinkles as I look up at her. We're both down to our last cards, and I know if she bullshits me now, she wins. "You sure?"

"Not about most things these days, but this?" She raises an eyebrow. "Yes. Bullshit."

I reach for the discarded cards and flip them over. The collective gasp from the group can be heard for miles. A giant smile breaks across my face as I look at her. Our shared laughter and surprise break the tension.

And then, she winks at me. She fucking winks at me. If seeing Greer like this means I have to lose every game for the rest of forever, sign me up.

"No way!" Vinnie throws his hands up in the air.

"That's unbelievable." Grace applauds Greer.

"Damn, man," Adam says. "You got your ass kicked by a newbie!" He leans over to give his wife an affectionate kiss. Envy threads through my heart.

"You're my hero, Greer." Hunter knocks his chair down as he rushes over to pick her up, wrapping his arms around her in a giant hug. She wraps her arms around his shoulders, easily accepting his show of affection.

Sutton snorts. "Oh man, Luke, if you could see the look on your face right now. Classic. Someone take a picture for the wall of fame. We'll name it *the day a king was dethroned*." Sutton swats Hunter on the shoulder. "C'mon, Hunter, put Greer down and help me clean up." Hunter sets Greer on her feet, then he and Sutton head into my house together.

As the laughter and congratulatory remarks surround us, I can't help but be entranced by the way Greer's confidence and playfulness have stolen the spotlight. She added a whole new layer to the evening, and I find myself wondering what comes next.

"Greer, it was so nice to meet you." Grace stands and gives her a quick hug. It's obvious Greer has caught on to what an affectionate group we are.

"Sorry, man," Adam says. "We'd stay and help clean up, but I'm working overtime in the morning." We high-five, and he wraps his arm around me. "We like her."

My eyes dart to Greer. Her smile is wide and bright as Vinnie says goodbye to her. "Yeah, but—"

Adam holds me out away from him. "No buts man. Just roll with it and let it be what it's gonna be." He grabs Grace's hand, and they walk to their car.

Vinnie is next to leave, followed closely by Hunter and Sutton who live fairly close to one another.

"Be gentle with her," Sutton says as she hugs me goodbye.

"I will be."

Now, it's just Greer and me standing alone next to the fire.

"Tonight was fun," Greer says, her face stoic. My desire to know what she's thinking runs deep.

"Yeah. Fun for you. I didn't know you were a card shark."

"You're not the only one who can count cards, big guy." I've lost count of how many times she's giggled or laughed tonight. With deft fingers, she unclips her hair, and it tumbles in waves down her back. Staring into the flames, she runs her fingers through her hair, scratching at her scalp. The movement causes her sweatshirt to rise, exposing a bit of her toned stomach.

"I—" she starts to say when she notices me staring at her. "Look, Luke, we should . . ."

I know I shouldn't, but I can't seem to look away. My eyes finally track back to hers.

"It's only been eight months," she says, "so this is all new to me." She hesitates before continuing in a clearer voice. "I think you're very handsome and extremely nice."

"You think I'm handsome, do ya?" I smirk, trying to lessen the tension that has sprung up. Her eyes lose focus and I wonder where she went.

"Of course I think you're handsome. I'm not blind."

"You're gor—"

"But," she interrupts, "I'm not sure if I'm ready for anything more than friends right now."

Taking a deep breath, I stand and grab my chair. "Okay."

"Okay?"

"Yep." I give her a reassuring smile. "Whatever way you're willing to let me get to know you, makes me a lucky man."

It's only a few strides to my back porch, where I place the worn camping chair with the others. I'll return them to the garage another day. Her soft shuffling footsteps mingle with the evening breeze behind me. She gathers her own chair, the fabric rustling lightly, and adds it to the pile. Neither of us moves as unspoken words swirl between us.

Unable to control it, I slip my hand into hers. "Let me walk you home."

She looks down at our hands but doesn't let go. Her eyebrow slants slightly. "I'd like that."

The grass is cool under our bare feet, moisture clinging to our ankles. Her hand is small in mine, her grip firm. As we near her back porch, I spot Duke through the patio door.

"Hiya, boy," she says when we near the door. She turns to face me fully, but doesn't drop my hand. "Thanks for walking me home." Her eyes meet mine, her tongue sneaking out to wet her lower lip.

If this were any other woman, I'd be tempted to lean in to savor those sweet lips of hers, but Greer isn't any other woman. I'm lost here—in her eyes, her scent, the knowledge of her loss.

"Thanks for kicking my ass tonight, G." I know I shouldn't, but I pull her hand to me anyway and give it a gentle kiss. "And about what you said—about not being ready for anything more right now—that's okay." I drop her hand and step away. "There's no timeline."

The night wraps around us, holding the unspoken promise of *more*.

7

*T*HE MOMENT OF IMPACT *happens so quickly. One minute we're talking about our trip and the next...*
Lights.
Noise.
Glass.
Silence.
His eyes look directly into mine.
"Hi, babe," he says.
"Brian?"
"What are you doing back here?"

"Brian, we have to get out. Can you move? We have to get out. You have to get out."

"No, Greer, you do."

Jolting awake, I attempt to sit up in bed, but the dampness of my skin causes the fabric of my sheets and nightgown to cling uncomfortably. The struggle to untwist my gown does nothing to ease my chest's panicked rising and falling. Finally free from the confines of fabric, I flop back onto my pillow, each breath shallow and jagged.

Focusing, I inhale deeply, hold it for a count of four, and release it for another count of four. I've never been so thankful for a breathing technique in my life; it's saved me countless times over the last year. My therapist taught it to me as a way of dealing with my anxiety. Minutes pass as my heart rate slows and my breathing evens out. After a few more rounds, I feel rooted in the present.

Typically, by the end of the day, my body is ready for rest, but it's like the instant my head hits the pillow, it stubbornly refuses to close its tabs, forcing me to lie there as the heavy, roaring silence fills my ears, suffocating me until I eventually drift off into a nightmare-induced sleep.

"I just want to sleep like a normal person," I say, even though Brian won't answer. "I haven't had a nightmare since I moved into this house. I thought I was getting better."

There's no timeline.

Luke's words from the other night echo in my mind. It'd be a lot less confusing and overwhelming if there were a timeline. I'd know exactly when I could stop being angry or sad. I'd know when the nightmares would end. I'd know if it was okay to be attracted to my neighbor.

Shaking off thoughts of Luke, I pull my legs out from my tangled sheets, the carpet soft beneath my feet. With a final calming breath, I glance over where the clock reads 7:00 a.m. A brief shock tumbles through me because I can't remember the last time I've slept this late.

A rustling and groaning fills the air as Duke wakes. Rolling over in his bed, he meets my gaze with his sleepy eyes. With a few deliberate stretches, he rises slowly, then after taking a few steps, he settles at my feet. He's grown accustomed to my early mornings and poor sleeping patterns. If I'm awake, he's awake, faithfully following wherever I go.

I stretch my arms above my head, my nightgown rides up allowing the cool air to kiss my thighs. Summer is in full swing, but without keys to my classroom, I've got a whole lot of nothing on my to-do list. My phone vibrates from where it's charging on my bedside table.

Sutton: Morning, sunshine.
Sutton: I feel like you're awake.
Sutton: You're awake and just reading these, aren't you?
Me: I'm awake.
Sutton: Good. Now, get out of bed. The world is waiting.
Me: Do you ever run out of energy?

"C'mon, old man bones," I tell Duke, "let's go make coffee." He's slow to rise, stretching his body before exiting our room. Growing up, our house was always filled with photos of our family adventures, a tradition I carried on when I got married. My empty walls glare back at me now, begging me to do something with them—anything—that might make this place feel like it's mine.

I reach for the can of coffee, taking comfort in the familiar, simple task of placing the coffee liner, measuring out an even scoop, pouring in fresh water, and feeling Luke's hand in mine—*wait, what?* A sudden roaring sound startles me and my cup slips from my fingers, shattering on the floor.

"What the hell?" I try to clear my brain as I grab a broom from the pantry. The roaring continues, fading in and out. I scoop up the broken bits of glass, taking care not to slice my feet open, and toss them in the nearby trash can. Meanwhile, the noise has gotten louder as if it's right on my back porch.

"Alright, what the—" I'm dumbstruck when I fling open my white curtains and spot Luke mowing my lawn. His broad shoulders strain through his shirt as he maneuvers the riding lawn mower back toward his house. Sweat dampens the fabric in the dip between his pecs.

I'm frozen, entranced watching him drive the mower, knees splayed out due to his thick jean-clad thighs. Luke Bradley is built like a brick house with a wide chest, broad shoulders, and a trim torso. Today, he's wearing his baseball cap backward.

I swallow past the lump in my throat. My fingers twitch and my body tingles as I'm pulled back to memories of the other night—his rough hand caressing my leg, my body coming alive when I caught him staring at me, and his grip when he held my hand. It felt like emerging from the dark and experiencing the world for the first time. But no one, aside from Brian, has ever made me feel like that.

It's too early, I'm not supposed to feel those feelings or let someone touch me like that, except that's all I seem to think about when I look at Luke. Mom's advice comes back to me, and I realize suddenly they're the same Luke voiced the other night. *There's no timeline.*

"It would be a helluva lot easier if there were a timeline!" I shout at Luke through the glass. Shaking my head, I stomp onto my patio until I'm in his line of sight.

"Hey!" I yell, suddenly angry and prepared to unleash hell on him. "Luke!" I holler again, louder this time, even waving my arms above my head so he sees me. Duke thinks I'm playing and takes it as an opportunity to run circles around me, squeaking that damn hot dog toy.

"Not now, Duke. Luke!"

Suddenly, Luke's eyes meet mine, and the engine cuts off.

"Greer?" His brow furrows. I'm sure he's wondering why I'm out here in my nightgown hollering at him while Duke runs laps around me like a maniac.

"What are you doing?" I realize too late that I'm still yelling and drop my arms.

Time slows as he stands up on the mower, swings his leg back over the machine, and steps away from it. With the bottom hem of his shirt, he wipes at the sweat on his upper lip. A small sliver of his toned stomach catches my eye.

Huffing a breath, I bring my eyes back to his, and a damn smirk crosses his face. Because, of course, he catches me ogling him. He knows I like what I see.

"What's up, G?" He stops short of my patio and tucks his thumbs into the pockets of his jeans.

"What are you doing?"

"Mowing the lawn."

"I can see that. But why? It's also really early. Are you trying to torture me?"

His chest rumbles with a laugh. "Definitely not trying to do that. But if I don't get this done soon, it'll be a jungle out here."

"I know why people mow lawns. I'm not an idiot. I mean, why are you mowing *my* lawn?" I place my hands on my hips.

Luke drops his gaze to the ground in front of him, bringing a hand to grasp the back of his neck. "Because . . ."

"Because what, Luke?"

"I just thought maybe it would make things easier for you." His gaze slowly makes its way back to my face.

I shake my head. "What do you mean?"

"I just," he places his hands back in the pockets of his jeans. "I just thought with your leg and all that, mowing the lawn might be difficult for you. Plus, I was going to be mowing mine and a few other people's today, so I figured why not." With a shrug, he meets my eyes once more.

Every time we've talked before, he's been nothing but calm and confident, but today he seems nervous or maybe that's guilt I'm picking up on? But wait, why would he feel guilty? Besides mowing my lawn, he hasn't overstepped—And then it hits me. Someone told him more about the accident.

My stomach drops because this right here is exactly why I don't like people knowing the details of what happened. They always look at me differently and treat me like I'm not capable or about to shatter into a million pieces. I want people to see me for who I am and not what happened to me.

"My leg?"

"Well, yeah," he gestures to my left leg, the various scars visible beneath my short nightgown. "I'm not blind, G. I see your scars, and I notice you limp sometimes when you play with Duke."

"It's getting better," I say, crossing my arms.

"What happened to it?"

"Why bother asking when it's clear someone already told you all about it."

"Actually, I was there," he blurts.

The words hang in the air between us.

"You...were...*there*?" My breath catches as I drop my hands to my sides and fidget with the fabric of my nightgown.

Luke takes a deep breath, muttering to himself, "Fuck. This is not how I wanted to tell you." He gestures to the gray wicker chairs on my back patio, and we sit. The air around us is still, as if nature itself is waiting on bated breath for what Luke will say.

At first, he says nothing. Just sits silently with his hands steepled between his thighs, gaze fixed on the ground in front of him. Suddenly chilled, I tuck my legs beneath me, pulling my nightgown down to cover them.

"The night of the accident," he finally says. "I was the captain on duty and the incident commander."

My shoulders slump with an invisible weight. It's one thing for people to know about the accident and have an unclear understanding of what really happened; it's a whole other thing knowing Luke witnessed to the worst moment of my life.

"I didn't realize it at first. Before you came over, Sutton and I were talking—"

"You were talking about me?" Agitation floods my system. I know people talk about me and what happened all the time, but I was kind of hoping things might be different with Sutton and even with Luke.

"Yes, we were, but—shit—this sounds worse than it actually is." His hands slide over his face and around his neck before taking his ball cap off. There's a slight curl to his hair that's damp with sweat. He twists his hat in his hands. "I swear it's not how it sounds. Sutton just mentioned that you and she went for coffee."

I nod my head. "Yeah, we did."

With a calm inhale, his eyes meet mine. "Anyway, Hunter came in and wanted to know what we were talking about. When Sutton told him your name, he was surprised I didn't remember that we'd responded to the accident."

"Hunter was there too?" I interrupt.

"Yes, he was one of the officers on scene."

"So the other night at the bonfire, you all—what? Rehashed the whole scene?" I clench my fists, amazed at how a moment that irrevocably changed my life is now fodder for conversation.

"No, Greer. *No.*" He hangs his head, shaking it back and forth. "He mentioned it, and it all came back to me."

My spine straightens, and my shoulders tense. "Well, since you were there, you know what happened."

"Actually, I don't—" he pauses, rubbing his hands together before saying, "You know what? This is not how I expected to have this conversation."

"I'm sure," I quip, my voice sharper than intended. My heart and mind shut down, a cold wave of uneasiness settles around me.

"Listen, Greer," he leans forward, arms stretching the sleeves of his shirt, and places his hand on my knee.

My cheeks flush from his invasion of my space. I'm not sure if I want to cry or throw up.

"When you're ready to talk about that night, we can," Luke says, his voice low and impatient. "If you never want to talk about that night, that's fine too."

"Okay, but . . ." His words echo in my head, distorting and merging with the sound of my racing heartbeat. It's like the ground beneath me has crumbled, leaving me teetering on the edge of an abyss. "I wasn't prepared for this."

"Me either, but we're neighbors. Friends even?" Another boyish shrug. "I see your leg bothers you."

"You're very observant." Feigned sarcasm drips from each word. The grin on his stupid, handsome face pulls me back from the edge. This isn't Luke's fault, and, if anything, I'm glad this confession of sorts came out today and that he didn't try to hide it from me for fear of hurting me.

"I'm already out here, and I'd like to do this for you. Please let me."

"Who says I need your help?" My eyebrows rise in question.

"Well," he clears his throat, taking his hand from my knee. *I wish he'd put it back.* "No one actually."

"Look, Luke," I untuck my feet and cross them at the ankles. His attention catches on the newly exposed skin. My stomach whooshes because I really like the way he looks at me, and I probably shouldn't. "I appreciate it, but I'm not asking for you to be there for me in that way. I want—need—to learn how to help myself and do things on my own now."

"Okay." His voice is steady as he stands from the chair and puts his hat back on.

"Okay?" I mimic.

"Yep. I'm sorry for overstepping."

"Apology accepted." I nod and force a smile.

Taking a few backward steps, he reaches down to scratch Duke's head, "I can't promise it won't happen again. It's something I'm working on. But we're friends and neighbors, so if you need me,"—he gestures to his house—"don't hesitate to ask. I'm right next door."

Standing from my chair, I watch him return to his side of the yard. He glances back at me and rubs his hand over his mouth and down his neck. Without losing eye contact, he throws his legs over the mower and starts the engine. It's not until he turns it back toward his side of the yard that he looks away.

"C'mon, Duke," I mumble. "I need coffee."

The mower's ruckus continues as I putter around my house. I don't know what it is about Luke. He just appeared in my life and has somehow nestled himself under my skin.

Maybe I was too harsh on him?

I gravitate toward my back windows. My eyes track him as he goes back and forth across his lawn. Even from this distance, I zero in on his forearms and biceps straining as he maneuvers the machine. He pauses to wipe sweat from his brow and looks right at me.

"Shit!" Before I can look away, he juts his chin toward me and grins. Duke nudges my leg. "Yeah, I know."

For the second time this morning, I fling open the sliding door, and make my way across the yard. He never breaks eye contact, and with each step, tingles trickle down my spine. I stop directly in front of him.

"Hi," I say.

"Good morning."

"I'm sorry."

"No need to apologize." He reaches for my hand, and I reach back, the touch tentative at first, as if testing the waters.

"It's weird knowing that you know and that you were there."

"I know." *Inhale. Exhale.*

"I broke my leg in several places and ruptured my spleen during the accident. I had a few surgeries to repair the injuries." He pulls me closer until my knee bumps his. I don't exactly understand this urge to tell him these things, but I continue anyway. "I graduated from rehab with flying colors, but the doctor says I will most likely always have occasional problems with my leg. I'm able to work out, and it's stronger now. Yes, it causes me issues from time to time and probably always will."

His rough thumb brushes back and forth over the back of my hand. Heat crawls up my arm, hairs standing on end.

"It's not that I don't appreciate your *sort of* offer to help." I side-eye him, trying to ignore the buzzing in my ears. "I'd just like to do things for myself too. It's always been"—my heart jumps to my throat—"Brian or Mom and Dad doing everything for me. I just . . ." My breathing accelerates.

"It's okay, sweetheart. Just slow down."

"I know everyone wants to help, but I don't need their pity. And I'd just like to learn how to do some of this on my own. Even with my messed-up leg." I suck in a deep breath. Duke brushes his head against the bare skin of my thigh. Luke has yet to take his eyes from mine.

I like the grin that appears on his face. "Would you like me to teach you?"

"Say what now?"

"You heard me. Would you like me to show you how to use the riding mower, and then you can mow the grass?"

His hand is warm against mine. Inching closer, I place my other hand on his knee. He closes his eyes as his lower lip disappears between his teeth. The action pulls me in and suddenly I don't want to be angry or guilty or any other emotion.

I just want to *feel.*

I reach forward, sliding my hand along the rough stubble on his jaw and cup his cheek. His jaw clenches as my thumb pulls his lip from between his teeth with an audible pop.

"Greer?" His voice is low and husky. My eyes follow my own movements. My thumb gently traces the skin below his eye. Goosebumps slither up my neck. His skin is sun-kissed, and he has grooves around his eyes. From anger? Laughter? I'm overcome with a need to know this man who draws me to him.

"Greer?" he repeats with a rough whisper, opening his eyes. They pull me into their depths, and I'm lost in swirls of autumn. I know the desire in his eyes matches mine.

"Yes?" I whisper, lowering my hand from his face, tucking it into my side.

"What do you want?" He casually releases my other hand with a gentle squeeze.

"Everything," I tell him. *Wait, what?* "I mean, y-yes, I would love it if you showed me how to use this thing."

"Okay, sweetheart."

My cheeks burn, a flush moving down my neck to my chest.

"But," he says, "even though you look beautiful, you might want to change out of your nightgown."

I jolt, shaking my head to clear the fog. Looking down, I groan realizing I've come out here in my pajamas. Again. Will this man ever see me in anything else? Guilt lodges in my throat at the thought of wanting him to see more of me more often.

"Oh god, I'm—I don't know what that was. I am so sorry."

"Stop apologizing. Now, go get changed."

Duke's bark startles me. With a weak smile, I dash inside.

Inhale. Exhale. I remind myself again, thinking back to all the times Brian said the same words when I was speaking too fast or he could sense my rising anxieties.

As I'm throwing on my cutoff jeans, T-shirt, and sneakers, my phone buzzes from the nightstand.

Sutton: I have no showings today. Want to get brunch?

Sutton: Please. Don't make me be a lonely goose today.

Me: Whatever energy drink that runs through your veins, give me some, will ya?

Her messages ping in one after the other, making me laugh. Ever since we had coffee together, my days have been filled with strings of texts from Sutton. She'll send a text or meme or GIF about literally anything. I've begun to anticipate the alert from my phone signaling a new message. I'm not sure if it's her incessant texting or some other wizardry, but it's been easy opening up to her, telling her pieces of *our* life and even hinting at the details of the accident.

Sutton has yet to shy away from anything I've told her, and she's never left me hanging. I knew I was lonely, but I hadn't realized how desperate I was for a friend until Sutton found me. And I think maybe she was too.

Sutton: No magical energy potion here. Just me.

Sutton: So, brunch?

Me: I can't.

A smile breaks across my face as I think of Luke outside, waiting for me. A lightness fills my chest. Usually, when I talk about my past, it's hard and overwhelming, but somehow, with Luke, it feels good. It feels right. The conversation we just had was probably the most honest I've been with anyone aside from my therapist lately. Sure, Mom and Dad are incredibly supportive, but I sometimes feel bad burdening them with my grief while they have their own to deal with. It's not every day Death almost claims your daughter and rips her life to shreds.

Gemma tries to connect with me, but she lives thousands of miles away. As much as I'd love for us to have a close sisterly bond, it's just not in our cards. Even with Sutton, I know I'm holding back. I'm afraid if anyone sees all of my scars, they'll leave me too.

Sutton: Why? :(

Me: Luke is teaching me to use the riding lawn mower.

Sutton: Why would you want him to do that?

Me: Because using a regular mower would take forever. Plus, he offered, and I embarrassed myself so . . .

Sutton: What? How did you embarrass yourself?

Me: I temporarily lost my ability to think, and my hands might have done a little walkin'.

Sutton: G, this isn't a Shania Twain song. I need details!

My face flushes, remembering the way his skin felt under my palm. "God, Brian, what's going on with me."

I've only known the touch of one man. Memories of Brian's skin on mine, his hands on my body have played in my daydreams often since I lost him. My own hands have mapped and brought pleasure to my body with the memories. Missing his touch, his kiss, his weight.

Now there's Luke.

He reaches for me without thought, holding my hand, caressing my arm. I shiver at the memory of his hand grasping my ankle. Every time our skin meets, electricity zips from the contact and shoots out the top of my head. But that electricity also feels tainted with guilt because I like the way Luke's hands feel on me, and I like the way it feels to reach for him.

"How dare I feel tempted to do new things? How can I live a life when you can't?"

Sutton: Girl, I don't know what's going on, but you better be prepared to spill all details.

Me: Of course. Later though?

Sutton: Ground Up at 11:00. Tell my bro I say hi.

Sutton: Gah, I'm dying in anticipation. Can't you give me one teeny-tiny detail?

Me: I gotta go now. Pray for my grass.

Sutton: Ah, the queen of avoidance.

The queen of avoidance? I grab a ball cap and throw my hair up into it. I don't avoid things, do I? Hell, I'm pretty sure I've done my due diligence starting therapy a few weeks after the funeral.

I know at first I was an iron vault, struggling to tell myself the story, let alone say it aloud to others. Every time Muriel and I had a session, I'd try to talk, but the words would become trapped. Unwilling to be said. Over time, it became less difficult. I ripped open every scar, laying my bits and pieces out for a complete stranger to figure out.

I thought my scars had healed and faded, but maybe not?

"G!" Luke shouts from the yard. "Get a move on, girl!"

When I reemerge from the house, he's waiting for me with a bright smile. Inhaling deeply, I bury my racing thoughts away. I'll deal with them eventually, but today is not that day.

8

Greer

Cool air greets me as I swing open the door to Ground Up. I had rushed through a shower after my impromptu mowing adventure; my damp hair cascades loosely down my back. I hastily picked an outfit this time, figuring if Sutton judged me based on appearance, she wasn't the friend I needed.

I'm still flying high after Luke's lesson on the riding mower. It's like he knew what I needed. I'm so used to getting myself worked up when I can't *get* something, but Luke was calm and patient with me as I figured out how to drive and maneuver the mower. He was confident I could do it, and for some reason, I trusted him implicitly. I was actually surprised he left me to traverse our yards, creating satisfying lines. Although, I did see him several times in the periphery tending to various tasks in his yard.

Every now and then, I'd catch him watching me. Like the awkward dumbass I am, I smiled and waved like I was on a ride at Disneyland. And he would wink. I swear, that wink does something to me.

As I approach the door, I note how unusually calm Ground Up is this morning. Normally, there's not an open seat, and you end up having to take your items to go. The scent of freshly made coffee hangs in the air, assaulting my senses. There's something inexplicably comforting about the aroma.

Sutton and Navy are busy chatting at a table near the register. As I enter, Sutton spots me and springs up from her chair for a hug. For someone who's been averse to any sort of physical touch for the last year, I find it interesting that I don't seem to mind it from any member of the Bradley family. There's just something about them that draws me in and makes me *want* to soak up their warmth.

"Hey, girls," I say. "Sorry I'm late." I give Navy a slight wave, and she returns it with a smile.

"Hey, Greer. What'll you two have? Same as last time?" Navy asks while tying her teal apron around her waist.

"Actually," I say, "I'll have triple espresso over ice with almond milk and whip cream." I quickly scan the pastry case. "Oh, and another cinnamon roll. Do you want to share this time, Sutton, or should we get our own? Maybe we should each get one because I could eat a dozen right now."

Navy's mouth hangs open and her brows knit together. "Who are you, and what have you done with the Greer I met last time?"

Sutton snorts. "Separate cinnamon rolls today, Navy. And I'll have whatever the hell she just ordered to drink."

"Okay. I'll have those out soon." Navy turns, grabbing shot glasses to begin our drinks.

"Sooo," Sutton says, "how was your morning?" She draws out each word.

I shake my head.

"Well, first of all, why the hell does your brother insist on getting up at the asscrack of dawn all the time? I swear, it's like the sun comes up, and Luke is up."

"Sounds about right. He's always been that way. Our dad was an early riser, and Luke takes after him in a lot of ways."

"But it's not even the fact that he's up that early because I'm always up early. It's the fact that he's up and loud. I swear he was rearranging his garage yesterday. And the wood chopping? I think he's preparing for the apocalypse or something."

"He does chop a lot of wood." Sutton doesn't even try to hide her grin.

"Funny." I roll my eyes. "And then today, he's out there before the sun's even up mowing the goddamn lawn. Who mows the lawn that early in the morning on a freaking Wednesday?"

Navy appears at our table and sets our drinks in front of us. She turns to the counter and grabs our cinnamon rolls. "Here ya go. Anything else I can get for you?"

"Why don't you join us?" Sutton asks.

Navy's eyes widen in surprise at the invitation. "Why?"

"Well…" Sutton takes a sip of her iced coffee. "It should be illegal how good this is."

"I know, right," I say. "Coffee is the nectar of the gods. But especially when Navy makes it." She beams at my comment, her cheeks taking on a slight flush.

"Anyway," Sutton continues, turning toward Navy. "We're friends now. It's clearly dead in here today, which is really bizarre. Plus, Greer is about to spill the beans about feeling my brother up."

I sputter my coffee, coughing as it goes down the wrong pipe. "That is not what I said."

"Are you sure?" Navy asks. I suspect she's a lot like Sutton and me and struggles to make new friends. I sensed it the first time we were in here, like she was jealous of the friendship date Sutton and I had.

"Of course we are sure," I say. "Now, get a drink because I refuse to relive this mortification more than once." I raise my eyebrows at Sutton. The Cheshire Cat grin spreading across her face tells me she's enjoying this more than any normal person should.

Within minutes, Navy pulls up a chair, cup of coffee and cinnamon roll in hand. "Okay, so what's this about you and Luke? Which, by the way, bravo. He's so handsome."

"Yeah, Greer," Sutton says, "tell us. How does one end up groping my brother? At seven a.m? On a Wednesday?" She emphasizes each phrase.

"First of all," I say, "it wasn't anywhere close to groping."

"Stop delaying," Navy butts in.

"Like I was saying, he was out there being so damn loud mowing the lawn, and then he decided to mow *my* lawn, so of course I went out there to give him a piece of my mind."

"Of course." Navy snickers.

"Anyway." I roll my eyes. "He said he wanted to help me because he notices my leg bothers me sometimes."

"Sounds like my brother."

"Well, that made me even more pissed."

"Because it's totally normal to be pissed when someone offers to do something nice for you," Navy deadpans.

"No, I was pissed because I realized someone told him about the accident."

"Oh." Sutton crouches down in her seat. "That might have been mine and Hunter's fault."

"Yes, I know." Pausing, I gather my emotions and tuck them away. "And it's fine, really. I was just really shocked to learn that Luke and Hunter were there at the scene. People don't normally have a firsthand account of my nightmare. So then I shut down."

"Why?" Navy and Sutton prompt.

"Because I knew he pitied me, and I despise pity." I stab at the cinnamon roll with my fork, desperate to divert my attention from the wave of emotions tumbling through me. Heat creeps up my neck, and my scalp prickles.

"Pity?" Sutton inquires.

"Yes, pity," I grumble. I'm not sure I want to talk about this, but the words pour out anyway. "Everyone knows about the accident, and suddenly, people feel sorry for me, wanting to do things for me. I don't need help because they pity my situation.

Sure, my leg is wonky sometimes, but I'm not helpless. I can do things on my own."

"Of course you can," Navy reassures softly. "No one is saying you can't."

"I . . . well,"—my mind falters—"I guess that could be true."

"Okay," says Sutton, "so you got pissed at my brother because you assumed he's helping you out of pity? Please continue . . ."

"Here I was trying to holler at him, but instead, he apologized for overstepping. So, then I went inside to be more mad at him, only to end up feeling guilty instead."

"And the reason for that is?" Navy's tone is soothing, but her questions are direct.

"Are you a therapist or something?" A smile plays on my lips as I take another sip of my coffee.

A grin lights up her whole face. "My mother is, and I'm a barista, so technically no but maybe in a roundabout way?"

"Greer, why were you really upset with Luke?" Sutton's gaze is steady but gentle.

A hush falls over the table. Typically, this is the moment when I'd evade and escape any probing questions. I haven't discussed what happened with anyone except in therapy. Yet, with these women, I couldn't stop the words from spilling out if I tried.

"I know people want to help me and feel sorry for me, but I have to learn to navigate life on my own. I don't have Brian anymore, and he was always the one to do everything. And I don't want to keep relying on my parents. They've done so much for me already. I don't want to burden them any longer."

"Greer." Sutton reaches forward, folding my hand in hers. Navy's hand settles on my forearm, applying gentle pressure. "You are not a burden."

"It feels like that sometimes."

"Does it really?" Navy questions, her brow arching as she leans back in her chair. "Or is that how you think others see you?" Her words linger in the air, and my pulse quickens, like she's peeled back a layer I wasn't ready to confront.

I hesitate, unsure how much truth I'm willing to admit, and we all dig into our food. With each bite, Navy's words begin to resonate. Mom and Dad have never expressed any negativity toward me after the accident. In fact, they leaped immediately into action to assist me. No hesitation, no questions asked. That's what parents do, right? Even Gemma did her best in the days following the funeral, but eventually she had to go home.

Thinking back on it, no one at work treated me differently when I returned. Sure, Bill, the maintenance supervisor at my school would assist me throughout the week, carrying heavy things to the classroom or even helping me bring items from my car inside, but that was just the kind of man he was. My students also pitched in, running errands or carrying things when I needed help. But I never sensed pity from them; they were just sweet kiddos eager to lend a hand. Half the time, I don't think they even noticed my scars or limp because they were always asking me to play with them during recess.

"Maybe you're right," I concede.

"Meaning?" Sutton takes a sip of her coffee.

"Meaning"—I hold the cold glass between my hands—"maybe I portrayed myself as a burden in my mind. Maybe I feel like a burden to myself. Maybe I pity myself." The last part sneaks out before I can stop it.

"Oh, Greer," Navy says, and both women once again cradle my hands in theirs. "You've been through hell."

"I know," I say, my voice barely above a whisper. Sutton squeezes my hand, urging me to continue. "It's exhausting living in my mind, and I'm just really sad. Really fucking sad."

"You have every right to be sad," Navy states.

"It's hard to imagine what it's like for you, Greer."

"I'm fucking exhausted living like this," I blurt. "Every day, I fight the memories of the accident. Physically, I'm healed, but I'll never be like I was. And then there are my scars. It's so damn hard to try to move on when my body constantly reminds me that I lived and he died. Sometimes, it feels like the guilt will bury me alive. And"—I wipe the tears dripping down my cheeks, then push my plate aside—"I don't know how to move on. And I know it's time. I know I need to."

Sutton sighs. "Who says you have to move on, G?"

"No one. Me. I don't know." I cover my face.

"Do you want to know what we think?" Navy asks. "Or would you rather we just listen?"

My hands lower to cover my heart, soothing my surprise shining through. Most people insert themselves into your emotional turmoil and immediately attempt to give advice or try to commiserate, but now I've met two women who are willing to sit here and merely listen to me ramble if that's what I need from them.

"Honestly," I begin, tears lining my eyes. "It's been me alone with these thoughts for so long, I'd really like to hear what my friends think."

"Greer, life is hard." Navy's voice is resolute and filled with empathy. "Really fucking hard. More so for some than others. But you couldn't have controlled what happened. The accident wasn't your fault. It's not fair to yourself to take responsibility for your husband's death. Plus, what does guilt accomplish? Does it change what is? No, it doesn't. It's a dumb fucking emotion that keeps you stagnant, preventing you from moving forward, leaving you trapped in the dark."

"You'll never forget Brian or what happened," Sutton adds. "But the fact remains, it happened, and now here you are. Maybe Navy is right—don't focus on trying to move on, focus on moving forward."

I ponder their words for a moment. I've had countless therapy sessions, but this, with Navy and Sutton, feels more freeing and more comfortable than most of those sessions.

"Sooo . . ." Sutton smiles. "Back to Luke and the whole grass situation."

I chuckle. "Well, then I realized I was too harsh on him, went out to apologize, spilled my guts about the real reason I was upset, and then he offered to teach me how to use the lawn mower so I could do it myself."

"And you said what?" Sutton asks.

"Well . . ." I hesitate.

"Is this when the touching starts?" Excitement fills Navy's voice, and her eyes brighten.

"Mm-hmm."

"Uh-uh, girl," says Sutton, crossing her arms over her chest. "Spill. What happened between you and my brother?"

"Isn't this awkward? Me talking about this stuff when it involves your brother?"

"I mean," says Sutton, "if you start telling me you gave him a handy or something, yeah. But if you keep it PG, it's all good."

Shame slithers up my spine, searing into my cheeks. It hadn't been anything sexual, but in that moment, I'd felt things I hadn't felt in a very long time.

"Oh god, what did I say?" Sutton's eyes widen.

"N-nothing," I stammer. I can still feel his skin beneath mine and hear the huskiness of his voice. He'd asked what I wanted, but I couldn't be sure if he meant physically or something else.

"Greer," Navy begins, "have you been with anyone since?"

"Of course not," I say. *Why would she think that was a possibility?* It hasn't been that long since I lost Brian. Yes, I'm a woman. Yes, I have needs. But it's nothing a good memory or two and battery-operated friend can't help. Wouldn't moving on so quickly be disrespectful to his memory and our life together?

"Explain," Sutton insists.

"You guys don't really want to talk about this, do you?"

"Yes, we do," they say in unison, making us all smile.

"Brian is—*was*—the only man I've ever been with. Sure, in high school, I had a boyfriend or two, but it was never like *that*."

"And . . ." Navy keeps her eyes locked on me.

"And nothing. It's probably too soon."

"You're the only person who can determine how you move through your grief." Navy takes the last sip of her coffee.

"I like you," Sutton tells her with a giant grin on her face.

"Yeah, well,"—Navy's cheeks take on a rosy hue—"I like you girls too. Greer, I'm curious if you've ever asked yourself when will it have been long enough?"

"I—well, I don't know." I admit, befuddled.

"Do you do other stuff . . . like by yourself?" Sutton asks.

"Well, yeah, of course," I say. "I'm human." I'm not shocked or even the slightest bit embarrassed about this line of questioning. I'm not shy about my own sexuality.

"And is it Brian you still see when you close your eyes?" My heart skips a beat at Navy's words because I can't recall the last time a memory of Brian helped bring me to climax.

"In the beginning, that's where I found Brian. It felt safe there, with him. I could pretend my hands were his, my words were his. I could pretend."

"And now?" Sutton's eyes implore me to be honest.

"Now,"—I inhale, steeling myself before confessing—"I'm not sure I want to pretend anymore, and that makes me feel guilty as hell."

"Remember what we said about guilt?" Navy reminds me. "Guilt is a dumb emotion that keeps you where you were, not where you are."

"I'm sure Brian wouldn't want you to live the rest of your life alone," Sutton says quietly.

"He wouldn't," I say, "but I'm also . . ." I'm embarrassed to admit the next part.

"Also . . ." Navy encourages.

"Afraid."

"Afraid of?" they ask together. I love how easily the three of us have clicked.

"I don't know how to be with anyone but Brian. What if I do something wrong? What if they do something I don't like? What if, while I'm with someone else, I think of Brian? That seems fucked up to me."

"First of all," Navy says, sitting straighter in her chair, "you won't do anything wrong, and neither will he. You're clearly not the type to jump into anything physical with just anyone, so I can only assume that *when* it happens, you'll communicate with each other."

"Thoughts of Brian may come to mind," Sutton adds. "That seems natural, and maybe it'll be a sign that what you're doing or about to do is too much for you at the moment. Who knows? But you'll communicate that with him."

"You can't live your life worrying about what *could* happen, G," Navy says. "You just have to live it fully and out loud for whatever time you have left." Navy pops up when the coffee shop door opens, revealing a man in bike wear. She returns behind the counter to take his order.

"She's right, Greer."

"Of course I am," Navy hollers over the noise of the espresso machine as she quickly makes the man's drink.

"So, what really happened?" Sutton nudges my foot.

"I don't know, actually. He asked me if I wanted him to teach me how to use the lawn mower, and it's like I was suddenly floating. I didn't want to be angry or guilty anymore. I just wanted to touch him. To feel him."

"Oooh, tell us more," Navy butts in, returning to her chair.

"It's like I was lost to the feeling of him, the sound of him, the smell of him."

"And? What else?" Sutton's unable to control her grin.

"And he . . . let me. He closed his eyes and let me lose myself to the sensation. Then, he asked me what I wanted, and I said everything."

Both girls sigh, reaching forward to grab one of my hands.

"Girl," Navy says, "this is a good thing."

"Is it?" I ask.

"It could be," Sutton replies. "If you want it to be."

"But what if Luke isn't into me like that?"

"Ask him." Navy quirks her brow.

"Oh yes, that sounds exactly like something I would do, 'Excuse me, Luke, I recently lost my husband, but I'm really attracted to you, and I also feel guilty and scared to be with another man. Want to help me out?'"

"Exactly like that." Navy nods.

"I think you might be surprised what you find out, G," Sutton says. "Just talk to him." Sutton lets go of my hand and fidgets with her purse. "Communication is key."

"You're both right. God." I laugh. "I act like it's so hard, and yet here I am spilling my guts to the two of you, who I'm just getting to know."

"Yeah." Sutton smiles. "But sometimes your heart knows it's safe to open up before your head catches up."

"I do feel safe," I say, "with you girls, I mean. Is that a totally weird thing to say?"

"Not at all," Navy says, "because my heart's telling me the same thing. Which is insane because I keep that sucker locked down." Navy pushes away from the table and looks at her watch.

"I don't mean to dash out of here," Sutton says, "but I need to get home. I need to help Mom prepare lasagna."

"Yeah," Navy says, "I need to get going too. My shift is almost over, and I've got to get my son." Navy returns behind the coffee bar and removes her apron. She's gathering up her bag when she notices our wide-mouth stares.

"You guys okay?"

"You have a son?" We ask in unison, as seems to be the new norm for our trio.

"Yeah, I do. He's almost two." A wistful look moves across her face. "He's at his dad's house right now, but I get to have him for the next three days."

"Navy, this is . . ." Sutton begins.

"Amazing," I finish.

"Yeah, well,"—Navy pauses, coming close and grabbing my hand again—"I know a thing or two about moving forward, Greer. I understand *some* of what you're going through. Just trust yourself to know that you'll know what your next right step is. That you'll know when you're ready and who you're ready for and what you're ready for."

"But what if I never find someone?" I ask.

"Seems like you already did." At Navy's words, Luke's face comes to mind.

"Luke is a great man." Sutton looks right at me. "Just think about it."

On the drive home, our conversation plays over and over in my mind. It's just past one p.m., and I'm surprised how long the three of us talked. It's amazing how much lighter I feel, how safe and seen I felt.

Just think about it.

My decision is made by the time I arrive home, and as I step out of my car, I allow the guilt resting on my shoulders to fall away. I take my first steps *forward*.

9

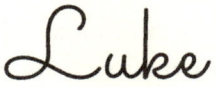

"Hey, big bro," Sutton says, settling down next to me on a patio chair.

"Hey, sis. How goes it?"

We're on the back porch at Mom's house, preparing for our weekly family dinner. I suppose biweekly is more accurate. Shift work is a real pain in the ass sometimes.

"It's been a crazy few weeks, actually," Sutton says. I hand her a cold beer, and she takes a small pull. "I've closed on three houses this month."

"Wow, congrats. Town sure is growing fast." My sister is three years younger than me, but impresses me daily—she's driven, successful, yet grounded and focused on our family.

"It really is. So, what's new? I feel like I haven't seen you since the bonfire."

The setting sun casts a golden light across the backyard. Mom's garden of summer flowers seems to glow like Christmas lights. Besides early morning, this is my favorite time of day. Everything begins to settle in for the night, and a quiet calm takes over my body. Tonight, however, Greer takes center stage in my mind.

"Nothing much. Just working and hanging out at home."

Her face instantly lights up. "Yeah? And how's Greer?"

A laugh rumbles from my chest. "Well, she 'bout busted my ass the other day."

"Oh yeah? For what?" she asks coyly. It's clear as day that she knows all about what happened between Greer and me.

"Trying to mow her lawn."

"I heard." She tries to stifle her giggle, but it tumbles out anyways, soft and brief, before she quickly takes a sip of her drink in an attempt to hide it.

I haven't been able to get the situation with Greer out of my mind. Her spark of stubborn independence splayed me open. I didn't mean to overstep. I thought for sure I fucked up when she vanished inside, but I felt her watching me. When she came back out, she was a woman on a mission—shoulders back, eyes focused. And then, as she often does around me, words spilled out of her.

The more I remember from the accident, the more I know there's no way Greer walked away unscathed. For Christ's sake, her husband had been killed. But hearing about her injuries? That gutted me. When she'd confessed wanting to learn things on her own? That sobered me. When she touched me? That scorched me.

"Did she tell you everything?" I bring the beer to my mouth.

Sutton side-eyes me. "You mean the groping?"

"Is that what she called it?"

"Well, yes, kinda."

I can still feel Greer's hand on my hand, my face. Her thumb brushing along my mouth, her eyes caressing my skin. I'd never in my life been touched or looked at like that by a woman. Every swipe of her thumb across my skin stole my breath. I've replayed the moment many times since then.

"Rest assured,"—I attempt to calm the heat rising on the back of my neck and will my body not to react—"it was not groping. I don't know what it was, but it was something."

"You know," Sutton says, then hesitates. "She felt guilty."

"Shit." My stomach bottoms out. After game night, she told me she wasn't ready for more, which is fine. I meant it when I said there was no timeline. But then, she was the one to initiate physical contact. So, yes, it took me by surprise, but she did nothing wrong. It's not every day you find yourself lost in the eyes and hands of someone as captivating as her. I guess I have a lot more to learn about grief than I previously thought.

"I think it's something you should talk to her about."

Looking over at Sutton, I know she's right. Greer and I might have just met, but there's something between us. I *felt* it that first day she accused me of trying to murder her dog and that night drinking whiskey under the stars. Even the morning when I saw her standing in her yard in nothing but her nightgown, *something* stirred within me. But the night we played cards? And when she laid her hands on my face? Those moments ignited it.

"There's something between us, Sutton. I don't know what it is, and it feels sudden, but I also know I can't ignore it. Every time I'm with her, it's like I'm just. . . pulled toward her."

"I know." She sets her beer down and stands from her chair. "You do?"

"Mm-hmm." She squeezes my shoulder before walking on bare feet toward the table. "It's not going to be easy, Luke."

"What won't be easy?" Mom chimes in from the back door.

"Luke's met a woman." Sutton pulls out a chair and sits.

"Keeping secrets from your mom now, Luke Bradley?" Mom winks at me as she begins serving dinner. She's always been our rock, and I'm thankful we've kept a close relationship even after losing Dad.

I shake my head. "Not keeping secrets, I promise."

"Well, then," Mom says, "why are you stalling? Tell me all about her."

We dig in and Mom listens closely as I tell her about Greer. Mom only adds her two cents occasionally. Every now and then, her eyes cloud over, and I know she's thinking about Dad, know she's wishing she could take Greer's pain away even though she's never met her. That's just how Mom is.

"Sutton's right," Mom says as she begins clearing dishes, but I stay her hands. She shakes her head and smiles but lets me take over cleaning up. "Losing someone you love is incredibly difficult. There are so many emotions attached to everything you do or think or say *after* you say goodbye. It won't be easy, for either of you."

"I know it won't," I say. "But I also can't ignore whatever this is. Does that even make sense?"

"Makes complete sense, Son. And you shouldn't ignore it. Life is short. Just be easy on yourselves as you begin this journey and communicate."

"Just don't give up on her," Sutton says as she disappears into the house.

That's not even a thought in my mind.

Rain pounds down on my metal roof, creating a rhythmic melody that pulls me from sleep. Glancing at the clock, it's around three a.m. I've been working a lot this week and planned to sleep in today, but clearly nature has other plans.

I sit up, scratching my chest and attempting to wipe the fog from my brain. As if she isn't on my mind most of the day anyway, my new neighbor has now infiltrated my dreams.

Not that I'm complaining.

As my eyes adjust to the soft yellow glow from the kitchen light, I realize I forgot to close my shutters the night before. From my bed, I notice Greer's window is illuminated next door.

I approach the window, telling myself I just want to make sure she's okay, and open the shutters fully. Greer's main light is on. A shadow moves behind her sheer curtains. *What is she doing awake this early?* Suddenly, her curtains part, revealing Greer. One of her sheer nightgowns covers her body, her figure illuminated by the light behind her. This woman has curves for days. Her mouth moves as if she's talking to someone else, but

I suspect she's talking to herself, a habit I've noticed before, or to Duke, who's bound to be nearby.

I should close the shutters, but I can't look away. Greer's hands sweep up her body as she gathers her hair, twisting it into a knot at the top of her head. My gaze wanders and I try hard not to notice the shadow between her thighs or the fact that I'm getting hard just looking at her.

As if she senses being watched, she looks up directly at me and jumps back, her hands grasping the center of her chest. I'm certain if I were closer, her face and chest would be flushed that beautiful rosy color. Her hands drop to her sides, and she gives me her standard awkward wave. I wave back as her eyes rake over my body. I'm standing here in nothing but a pair of old station shorts. I lean in, placing both hands on the windowpane, content to let her take her fill.

She fidgets with the fabric of her nightgown, and when her gaze returns to mine, I can't help it; I wink. A stunning expression graces her face as she lets out a full belly laugh—a sound I wish I was close enough to hear.

That tempting lip of hers slips between her teeth as she slides her curtains closed. Surprisingly, she doesn't walk away. Instead, the shadow of her slips her nightgown up and over her head. She turns to the side, giving me a perfect view of her silhouette. It's only a few seconds before she disappears out of sight.

"Fuck me," I mutter, shaking my head. "Two can play that game, sweetheart." Without bothering to close the shutters, I drop my shorts, possibly count to thirty, and head to take a shower. A very cold shower.

On any given day you'd find me outside, but a rainy day like this is a perfect opportunity to stay inside all day and do nothing. Something I don't do very often. After throwing together some breakfast, I try to make some headway in my newest book. I'm only five chapters in when a sudden burst of hollering from next door shatters the silence.

"What the hell?" Tossing the book on the coffee table, I follow the noise. As I open the sliding door, Duke darts across my yard and disappears from view. More hollering ensues, but I can't quite make out what Greer's saying. I open my door just enough to step onto the patio.

"Duke! You come back here right now!"

Wet sloshing alerts me to Duke running at full speed back across my yard. I step to the edge in time to see her reprimand him with a pointed finger. He sits immediately.

"What the hell?" she says. "You goofy dog, you can't come inside like that!"

I chuckle, thoroughly amused watching her give this fool dog the what-for. He looks like he's been through a mud wrestling match, covered in mud from paws to ears.

"You okay over there?" I call out.

"Do I look okay to you?"

"You look more than okay, but your dog, on the other hand, looks like he's rolled in the creek."

Without bothering to put on shoes, I stroll over to her patio. Rain pelts down, spattering my shirt and jeans.

"You're not wearing shoes," she says as I duck under the safety of her awning.

"No, I'm not." She can't seem to look away from my bare feet. "Uh, G, my eyes are up here."

She quickly shakes her head and huffs a breath. "I know where your eyes are."

"Mm-hmm." I grin, enjoying watching her squirm.

"Oh, please! As if *you* weren't looking at me," she says, a playful glint in her eyes. Greer crosses her arms which pushes her breasts closer together in the low-cut tank she's wearing.

"I was definitely looking, and I'm pretty sure you liked it."

She opens her mouth to reply, narrowing her eyes on me. "You sure are something, Luke Bradley."

"So are you, Greer Ashbury."

Duke's tail swishes back and forth over the concrete as he looks from her to me. I file away her sweet smile for later.

"I really wasn't planning on trying to wash a dog today," she says, "but I guess I have no choice."

"Let me go get the hose, and I'll help."

Before I can take a single step, Greer stops me.

"I can do it, Luke."

"Shit . . . I did it again, didn't I?" She nods. "Okay then, what should I do?"

"Want to keep me company?"

"Absolutely."

She raises her shoulders slightly and wiggles her hips. "Great! Um, I'll be right back."

Greer disappears inside, leaving Duke and me on the patio. Glancing around, I notice she's added a new rug and table. My curiosity is piqued by the book discarded on the table, but before I can investigate further, she's back with a bottle of shampoo, a brush, and several towels. Duke, looking chastened, hasn't moved an inch.

"You like to read?" I gesture to the book as I sit down.

I'm not sure she's heard me because she looks around like she's lost something.

"Um," she says, "do you think I could borrow your hose?"

Without answering, I duck back into the rain and jog to my house. My clothes are completely soaked when I return with a garden hose and nozzle. She takes them from my hands and steps under the stream of rain dripping off her roof to hook it into the spigot.

After successfully getting the hose working, she smiles her cute little smile. Leading Duke over to the edge of the concrete, she hoses him down. I try not to notice the splashes of water covering her toned legs or how her rosy nipples are clearly visible under the thin fabric of her tank top.

"I do like to read," she finally answers, her hands busy massaging shampoo into Duke's coat. Poor dog looks like he's been caught in a bubble factory.

"That's a lot of soap."

She braces her soapy hands on her hips. "Yeah, I think *maybe* I used too much."

"Fuck." I groan. It's torture sitting here doing nothing, trying to be a gentleman as her clothes get wetter by the minute. "You sure you don't want some help?"

"Nope. So, what were you doing up so early today?"

"Rain woke me up." *Great, now all I can picture is her in a wet nightgown.* "You?"

"Bad dream."

"Want to talk about it?"

With the nozzle in one hand, she uses the other to scoop off some bubbles covering Duke's fur, flinging them onto the grass.

"I dream about the accident sometimes." She looks at me then, gauging my reaction.

"Is that what you dreamed about last night?" She flushes, but nods. "If you ever want to talk, you can always come over."

"You know," she says, "I was wondering something."

"What's that?"

"Why do you always leave your light on?" The water finally runs clear, so she turns the hose off and grabs a nearby towel. Duke isn't as patient and starts wiggling when she covers him. Her shorts slide high on her thigh, revealing a cluster of freckles I'd like to explore. My fist flexes, fingers itching to touch the patches of newly exposed skin when her tank rides up her back.

"My eyes are up here, Luke."

"I know," I say, dragging my eyes over her glistening skin.

"Luke."

The breathy way she says my name snaps me out of it. "What were you asking?"

"Your lights,"—she laughs—"why do you keep them on?"

At first, I'm not sure what she's referring to, but then it dawns on me that she's talking about the kitchen light.

"Oh, it's something my mom and dad always did."

I step forward, unable to resist, and squat down next to her, needing to do something, anything, to keep from dragging her to me. With the other dry towel, I dry Duke's ears. She huffs.

I smile. "I want to help."

"I don't need you to help." She plops down on the ground, shoulders slumped.

"I know you don't, but I *want* to. It has nothing to do with me pitying you and everything to do with the fact that I just enjoy helping those around me in whatever way I can. Let me help you, Greer, okay?"

Her skin is warm beneath my palm as I slide my hand over her bare shoulder. She gives me a quick nod.

"Thank you." I squeeze her shoulder before continuing to dry Duke. "Growing up, my parents always wanted me and Sutton to know they were there for us, so they left the kitchen light on to remind us that we always have someone to talk to if we need them."

"Oh, I really like that."

I really like how soft her eyes become.

"You sound close to your parents."

"Yeah, I'm a mama's boy through and through, and Dad was my best friend."

"It sucks losing someone you love."

"It does, but it gets better."

With a brief nod, she grabs the wet towel from my hand and drops it by her back door with a thud. Our hands collide as we both reach for the dog brush. Her sharp intake of breath tempts me. Neither of us pulls away. Despite the chill in the air, my blood heats. I want nothing more than to pull her to me.

"Luke . . ." *Damn, a man could get used to hearing his name said like that.*

Not allowing her to stew in whatever emotions are rolling through that mind of hers, I wrap my hand around her wrist, feeling her pulse thrum beneath my thumb. Then, I grab the brush with the other. She allows me to hold her wrist for a few moments more before she pulls away and tucks it against her stomach. I kneel down to brush Duke at the same time Greer sits cross-legged nearby.

We talk for a while longer as rain continues to fall around us. Greer goes on and on about the romance book she's reading. I smile, loving how animated she gets, but even more so because she's actually letting me brush Duke's fur. Tufts of loose hair drift around the patio, and she collects what she can as they float by her. The whole time we talk, our eyes keep finding their way back to each other.

Suddenly, Greer stops talking and stands abruptly. "I have to go," she says. I grasp her calf, the bumps of her scars rough beneath my hand, and smooth my palm down to her ankle.

"Stay," I say. "It's okay."

She twists her fingers together. "I'm nervous."

"Don't be nervous. It's just me."

It takes great effort to pull my hand away, but I do, and she sits back down. Duke stops his wiggling when she rubs behind his ears.

"What else are you doing today?" she finally asks.

"Until I heard you hollering in the yard, I was planning on relaxing at home."

"And now?"

My eyes cut to hers. "I was wondering if you like lunch."

She knits her eyebrows. "Um, yes, I like lunch. Why? You got something in mind?"

"Yep, let's get this cleaned up, and I'll make us some turkey sandwiches and lemonade." The sweet smile she gives me in return is all the confirmation I need.

10

With flour-covered hands, I grab my phone as it buzzes on the counter, alerting me to a multitude of messages. Most are from the group chat with Sutton and Navy, but there's one from an unfamiliar number.

Unknown: Hey, you.

My cheeks flame recognizing the greeting.

Me: Hi, Luke.

Biting my lower lip, I quickly add his name to my contact list.

Luke: Hope you don't mind, but I stole your number from Sutton.

Me: You could have just asked for it, silly.

Luke: You're not the only one who's nervous. So, what are you up to tonight?
Me: Nothing much. The girls are coming over.
Luke: Oh yeah? I'm jealous.
Just then a few messages from the girls ping through.
Navy: Almost to your place.
Sutton: Me too!

I step away from the kitchen and turn the lock on the front door open, nerves dancing along my skin. I am filled with equal parts excitements and nerves that I have actual friends coming over. Storms continued to roll through town over the last few days, but they were a welcome distraction to the summer heat. There's nothing better than a few rainy days snuggled up with a good book and trying new recipes.

I turn my attention back to the kitchen counter and dust the biscuit dough with a fine layer of flour. A cloud of white hangs in the air, catching the glow of the kitchen lights. My hands move with a practiced rhythm, kneading the dough with firm, steady movements. I am most definitely not making homemade biscuits because a certain neighbor of mine mentioned his love for them.

The front door slams against the wall with the force of Navy's arrival. She stumbles inside, juggling pizza boxes and several grocery bags.

"A little help!" she calls out, her arms straining under the weight of her groceries.

Abandoning the dough, I hustle over and relieve her of the pizza boxes. "What's all this?"

"Pizza. What's it look like?" Navy rolls her eyes, heaving the grocery bags onto the counter.

"I see that. I meant, *this*," I gesture broadly over the pile of grocery bags.

"Oh, you're already baking." Navy pokes at my clump of dough, raising an eyebrow.

I place the pizza on the counter and playfully bump her with my hip. "Yes, I am."

"Biscuits?"

"Yep. And what all did you bring?"

Navy drifts over to the living room and drops her bag next to the sofa. Without saying anything, she perches on the arm of the couch, kicks off her sandals, and covers her bare feet with fuzzy pink socks she pulls from her bag like she's been here a million times. Once upon a time, I'd have been running around cleaning and preparing for guests, but not with Navy and Sutton. There's an unspoken ease between us I've always craved in friendship.

"I'm glad to see you're in troll attire as well." She gestures to my faded purple sweats.

"Are you really even friends if you can't be around them looking like a bridge troll?" I say, smiling playfully as she jumps up to join me at the kitchen island and sets about unpacking items from the grocery bags.

"Exactly."

"So, what all did you—" The front door slams against the wall again, interrupting my question. I should probably look at the damn thing before it punches a hole through the wall.

"Hey, girls!" Sutton calls from the entryway. When she rounds the corner, her mouth drops, seeing Navy and me. "Oh, thank god. Let me change." Sutton's dressed in denim jeans, a peach-colored blouse, and white sneakers, so I'm not entirely sure why she feels the need to change.

"Navy," I say, "are you avoiding my question?"

"What?" she says. "No, I'm not avoiding anything. What is she doing?" Navy stares in the direction Sutton disappeared.

"Changing, apparently." I turn back to my biscuit dough, rolling it out flat. The dough's smooth texture settles the jitters beneath my skin. The scent of butter and flour fills the kitchen.

"Why is she changing?" Navy asks, her hands frozen on the grocery bag's handles, a quizzical expression etched across her face.

"Because"—Sutton says, popping back in the room—"I wanted to wear my comfy clothes, but I didn't know what you girls would be wearing, so I brought options." She's changed into a matching set of mint-colored loungewear, her movements suddenly light and carefree, as if the very act of shedding her previous outfit lifted a weight off her shoulders.

"But you still look cute and shit," Navy deadpans.

Sutton strikes a pose. "Do I ever not look cute and shit?"

"You look great, Sut," I say. "I think Navy's questioning her own clothing choice." I flick my head toward her stained shirt that proudly reads *I bake and I know things*.

"Meh," Sutton says, "it's just us girls. Who cares? So, what are we doing?" Sutton joins us at the island and washes her hands. The kitchen, now warm from the oven, buzzes with her infectious energy.

"I'm making biscuits," I say. "Not sure about Navy because she refuses to answer my question." I grab a glass jar, then cut out perfect spheres of dough and place them on the pan.

"Well," Navy says, "I thought maybe we could make a batch or two of cinnamon rolls."

"Like Ground Up cinnamon rolls?" Sutton and I ask.

"Is there any other kind?" Navy takes out the rest of the ingredients. "These biscuits look great, G." Navy washes her hands, eyeing my kitchen. I have a sneaking suspicion that she's mentally ranking the status of my kitchen.

"They do," Sutton says, "but there has to be like two dozen here. Why do you need this many biscuits?"

"Uh, no reason," I say.

"Bullshit." My eyes meet Sutton's, and my cheeks flush when Sutton winks at me. The Bradleys sure have a thing for winking.

Navy begins washing dishes but turns at Sutton's giggle. "What did I miss?"

"Oh, you know," says Sutton, "just that a certain man next door, whom I love and adore, just so happens to love homemade biscuits."

"You're so lucky," Navy says drying her hands. "My neighbor is eighty-four and wears nothing but flannel pajamas."

"That's hot," Sutton says as her eyes rove over every inch of my home. "I love what you've done with your house."

With the last of the biscuits prepped for the oven, I turn my attention to getting Duke's dinner ready. Sutton takes it upon herself to give herself a tour, running her hand over different pieces of furniture, pausing every so often to briefly inspect a frame or trinket before moving on.

After Duke's eaten, Navy and I get to work on the cinnamon rolls. Without a recipe in sight, Navy spouts each measurement, and I add them to the bowl. We quickly mix and measure the ingredients. Sutton is still perusing my home, stopping again at various picture frames placed around the room and on the walls. I know my hope that she *won't* notice the contents, or lack thereof, in each frame is a long shot—not with her keen eye.

"What's up with you, Sut?" Navy abandons the kitchen to join her.

"Oh!" Sutton startles when Navy shoulder-bumps her. "It's nothing," she adds quickly, brushing it off with a small laugh, though her eyes flicker with curiosity.

It's not nothing. It's obvious to anyone paying attention that every single frame in my house is empty or still contains stock photos of happy people I don't even know.

"Care to explain?" Navy points to an empty frame.

"Explain what?" I set the cinnamon roll dough to the side to rise before gathering plates and drinks for dinner. I avoid eye contact but catch a glimpse of sympathy in Navy's expression. They exchange a quick look before Sutton breaks the silence.

"Greer, why are all these frames empty?"

"Oh, *that*." I choke out a laugh. "I just haven't gotten around to filling them yet." The lie tastes bitter on my tongue. I know they'd think I was strange if I told them the truth. The image of my locked storage room swirls in my mind.

From the corner of my eye, Navy's toe catches on a box tucked under the table. She carefully takes it from its hiding space. Wiping off the layer of dust, she turns her gaze to me. She caresses the cover of the old photo album, then begins to flip through photo after photo showcasing memories of the joy from my life with Brian.

"You two look so happy together." Sutton's words float in the air between us as she gently turns each page.

"Wow, was that your house?" Navy inquires.

I stand on my tiptoes, peeking over the island and couch to see she's landed on a picture of Brian and me holding the keys to our first home. We were so happy that day. We didn't have a single thing to put in the damn house, but we'd bought it together. Our first *adult* adventure.

"Yeah, it is," I say. "Who's ready to eat?" My stomach twinges with guilt at my quick subject change.

They close the photo album. But instead of tucking it away, Sutton carefully displays it on a nearby shelf. We gather our food, then cozy up with blankets and settle in on my couch.

"How are you girls?" I ask.

"Ugh," says Navy, "Ground Up has been way too busy lately, and having to work the opening shift is driving me insane. I need sleep and a vacation."

"I feel you," Sutton adds. "It's like everyone and their dog needs a house. Too bad I can't go on a trip right now."

"Yeah, me either." I take a huge bite of pizza.

"G, aren't you literally on vacation right now?" Navy says. "You can do whatever you want."

"You are not wrong," I say, "but what would I do? Where would I go?"

"Anywhere," they quip.

"You gotta get out more." Sutton shoves a piece of pizza in her mouth, and Navy looks on in shock. "What?" Sutton mumbles around a mouthful of pizza.

"You eat like a pig," Navy says. "That is . . . unexpected."

Sutton shrugs and continues to shovel pizza in. Suddenly, she exclaims, "We should go out!"

"Why would we do that?" Navy asks.

"Because, Navy," Sutton says, "we are hot, available women in need of social lives."

"Who says we need a social life?" Navy asks. Sutton cuts a glare at Navy, who then says, "Um, okay, yes, we definitely need a social life."

"Do I have to?" I moan.

"Yes, you do," Sutton says. "We talked about this already, remember? Moving forward." Sutton's smile chips away at the shell around my heart.

"What did you have in mind?" I ask.

"Dancing!" Sutton blurts.

Sighing, I place my plate on the coffee table. I knew she was going to suggest dancing.

"I do not dance." Navy tosses her plate on top of mine and snuggles deeper into the couch. Her foot hangs off and strokes Duke's side. He's content, enjoying the extra attention.

"C'mon, Navy," Sutton says, "it'll be fun."

Navy groans and pulls the blanket over her head. I gather our plates, then meander into the kitchen. It's on the tip of my tongue to tell Sutton I can't go, but instead I am totally honest.

"I haven't danced since the day Brian died. It was kind of our thing. We used to go all the time."

Like prairie dogs, their heads pop up over the back of the couch. Those pesky butterflies flutter in my stomach because I know Sutton and Navy are preparing to get me to share more.

"All the more reason that you should come out with us." Sutton's eyes are glassy as she places her hand over Navy's. "Right, Navy?"

Navy glances at her. "Oh, yeah, absolutely. Dancing will be great," she says, her tone light.

"I bet Luke and everyone will go too," Sutton says. It's not hard to hear an uptick in her voice when she mentions his name.

"I'm sure he has other things to do than go dancing with me," I say, then quickly add, "I mean, us."

Navy waggles her eyebrows, not letting my slip of tongue go unnoticed. "Oh really?" she grins.

"It'll be fun," Sutton says, her voice calm and reassuring. "Plus, if it isn't, at least we'll be together."

"Ugh, fine," Navy says. "Rowan goes back to his dad's next weekend, so let's go Friday?"

Wide, expectant eyes turn to me. I ignore the *no* on the tip of my tongue and instead say, "Sure."

"Yeah?" They grin ear to ear. Those butterflies officially take flight at the surprise in their voices.

Nodding my head, I sink back onto the couch. "Forward, right?" Sutton crawls over the couch and lays across my body.

"You got it, babe. Forward."

"Now that that's decided," Navy says, "can we talk more about your sexy-as-fuck neighbor?"

My phone buzzes as a text from Luke pings through.

Luke: Hope you're having fun. Good night.

Me: Good night.

Sutton groans reading the messages over my shoulder and falls to the floor.

"Well, well, well," Navy teases, taking my phone. "Spill, G. How are things?"

The oven timer pings, giving me a momentary reprieve from her prodding. Truth is, things have been good. Better than good even. I'm surprised how okay I've been living on my own, having my own space, even if my house remains devoid of any personal touches. And I'd be lying if I said I haven't enjoyed getting to know Luke and that I can't stop thinking about him or looking for him or hoping he stops by.

"Things are good. Luke has been great."

"I bet he has," Navy mumbles.

Rolling my eyes, I switch out the pans of biscuits. "It's not like that."

"Do you like him?" Navy asks.

Sutton elbows her in the arm.

"What?" Navy says. "It's an honest question."

"I know," Sutton says through clenched teeth, her eyes bright in anticipation.

"Luke is . . . unexpected," I say. And that's the truth. I'd envisioned moving into my house, starting my new job, and getting through to the next day. Nowhere in this vision did I ever imagine meeting someone like him. Every time he's near, he reminds me what it feels like to want and be wanted in return. "He's really sweet and patient."

"And handsome?" Navy adds. Sutton gestures impatiently for me to continue.

"It's unfair, really," I giggle. "But he makes me nervous. I don't know how to do this."

"*This?*" Sutton asks. "As in crushing on someone new?"

I nod.

"Well," Sutton says, "if it makes you feel any better, he's crushing on you too."

"And how would you know that?" Navy asks.

Sutton lifts a shoulder with a sly smile as heat tickles up my neck and my cheeks flush.

"Has he said anything to you?" I ask.

"Uh-uh," Sutton says. "That's for you two to figure out, and dancing is a perfect opportunity."

Outside, the sun sets and stars wink into being. Our conversation never stalls, moving from one subject to the next as we finish our baking. A lot of things about this new chapter of my life have been unexpected, especially finding Sutton and Navy. I've never felt so at ease and accepted by two people before. It makes it easy to lay bare something that's been weighing on my heart.

"Sutton," I say. "I have a favor to ask." She's scanning through Netflix titles as Navy and I finish cleaning the kitchen. After wrapping a plate of goodies that I'll bring to Luke later, I return to my spot on the couch.

"What kind of favor?"

Just rip the Band-Aid off. "I need a realtor."

She springs up from the couch, turning to face me. "But you just moved in?"

Shaking my head side to side, I reassure her. "No, I'm not moving, but I do have a house to sell." Sutton's eyes gloss over already guessing which house.

"You have another house?" Navy asks.

"I still own mine and Brian's house."

"Are you sure?" Sutton's voice clogs with emotion.

"Yeah, I am. It's just sitting empty, and I don't plan on moving back into it, so I think it's time." They share a look, silently communicating their shared understanding of this complicated life of mine

"Gosh," Sutton sniffles, wiping snot running from her nose. "I'm sorry, this is just . . . this is just . . ."

"A good thing?" I smile brightly, trying on her sunny-side-up attitude, hoping maybe it'll rub off on me permanently.

"Yeah, babe," Sutton says. "It can definitely be a good thing if you want it to be." Wiping her eyes and nose, she pulls the blanket up under her chin. "I'm really glad I met you girls."

Navy places her hand on Sutton's leg. "Me too."

"Me three," I add. And I am. If there's anything I'm certain of, it's that meeting Navy and Sutton has been a wonderfully good thing.

We spend the majority of the night ignoring the movie, choosing instead to talk about anything and everything. It's late by the time they leave, and I should be exhausted, but my body is wired.

Growing up, I was always envious of all the girls who had tight-knit groups. How could these girls find so many close friends to spend time with on girl's night or trips, celebrating their lives together, while I could barely keep one or two friends in my life? I could never seem to find people I fit with. It's exciting that maybe it's my turn to experience what I've always coveted from afar.

The TV's glow fills my great room, the room warm from the oven and endless conversation. Duke jumps into the pile of blankets on the floor and buries his nose. One by one, I take blankets from his makeshift bed, folding and placing them in a wicker basket. The tray of goodies I'd prepared for Luke catches my eye.

"It's not that late. I'll just pop over and see if he's awake." Duke doesn't bother moving.

After slipping on my sandals, I dip into the yard. The air is cool and moist after days of rain. Goosebumps pebble over my bare legs. The glowing light behind his shutters illuminates the ground at my feet. I take a few calming breaths, then step onto his patio and rap lightly on the glass.

The night stills around me, waiting alongside me on bated breath for him to answer. He doesn't, so I knock a little louder this time. Still, he doesn't come to the door, and I can't see any movement behind the curtains.

"Maybe he's already asleep," I say aloud. I'm halfway back to my house when I hear him.

"Greer?" His voice is heavy with sleep.

"Hi." I wheel around to face him. Holding the tray of goodies in one hand, I give him yet another awkward wave with the other.

"Everything okay?"

Stepping back onto his patio, my eyes immediately zero in on his very shirtless chest. He runs his hands through his sleep-tousled hair. His stomach muscles move and flex as he stretches his hands above his head. I can't help but stare at his broad upper body with hair sprinkling his chest and stomach before it disappears beneath the waistband of those damn blue shorts. Shorts that hide nothing. I'd only caught a glimpse of him that morning when he thought I wasn't looking, but I saw enough that even icy water on my face couldn't cool me down.

My eyes are locked on his body when he clears his throat, dragging his hands down his chest and over his stomach before resting them on his hips.

"Eyes are up here, sweetheart."

"Yeah, I know." Seconds tick by as I take my time cataloging every visible speck of skin. By the time I make it to his eyes, I've forgotten what I came over here for. He adjusts himself, but I've already seen the heavy length of him straining against the fabric.

"G, baby, you're killing me here."

"Oh, uh, sorry about that." Tilting my smile to one side, I don't bother hiding my peaked nipples or the chill bumps or the fact that it's suddenly very, very warm out here.

"No need to be sorry. Everything okay?" This time it's him who bites his lower lip. *Pay attention, Greer.*

I shake my head in a weak attempt to clear the haze of lust. "Everything is great."

"Okay. Not that I mind you being here, but do you need something?"

"Um . . ." My eyes drop to his chest and stomach. I flex my hand to keep from reaching for him. "Yes, I mean, no, I don't need anything. I came to bring you these." I shove the plate of goodies at him. He steps close, crowding me. Close enough that I'm overwhelmed by the masculine scent of his body wash. So close I could reach out and touch him if I wanted to.

"Did you make me biscuits?" His voice is low and measured.

"I did. Oh, and cinnamon rolls, too. Not the cheap tube kind either. They're actually the Ground Up recipe. I was just going to make you biscuits, but then Navy and Sutton came over and Navy brought the ingredients, so we ate pizza, baked, and hung out. Do you know—"

"Slow down, sweetheart. Just breathe." I blush but do as he commands.

Inhale. Exhale.

He takes my free hand and leads me toward the sliding door. The broad muscles of his back are now on full display. The light above the sink casts a soft glow over the cozy space. Normally,

I'm one who loves to admire the inside of someone's house, but right now I couldn't care less. I only have eyes for him.

He takes the plate from my hand and sets it on the counter. "You didn't have to make me anything."

"I know, but I did anyway."

"Thank you." He smiles. I love watching his mouth when he speaks. His hand is gentle under my chin as he brings my gaze to meet his. I most definitely wasn't staring at his lips.

"You're welcome. I'm sorry I woke you up." Without thought, I rest my palm on his bare stomach, and he covers my hand with his.

"I like being woken up by you." Silence and anticipation fill the empty spaces in the room.

"I should, uh, let you get back to bed." It takes great effort to pull my hand from under his warm one.

Neither of us moves away.

"I'm glad you had a fun time with the girls."

"Me too. It's been a while. Actually, it's been forever because I've never had that. A girl's night, I mean. I'm kind of a loner if you haven't gathered. It's not like I want to be a—"

"Woman," he interrupts. "Do you ever breathe when you talk? Because I'm starting to think I need to be prepared to catch you when you pass out." He invades my space to brace his hands on each side of my face, and I cover them with mine. I know I've got a goofy smile, but I can't help it; he makes smiling easy.

"Sorry," I mumble. "I told you that you make me nervous."

"And I told you the other day,"—he steps closer, and his thighs brush mine—"it's just me. No need to be nervous. Would you like to eat some of these with me?"

Luke tugs my lower lip from between my teeth. "It's late."

"It is."

"And you were just sleeping."

"I was."

"They'll still be good in the morning."

"They will, but they smell amazing, and I'm really hoping I can talk you into staying with me."

I gulp.

"Okay." I can't take my eyes off him as I tuck myself into a chair at his table. Luke moves in an unhurried and confident manner, gathering plates and forks. He settles into the chair next to me and slides a set my way.

He's opted for biscuits topped with butter and honey. The groan he lets out after the first bite makes my stomach flop over. I wonder what else could elicit a groan like that from him.

"Shit," he says, "these are so good. You really like to bake, don't you?"

I definitely don't notice when his leg presses against mine. "I do. I used to cook all the time."

"Used to?" He doesn't miss a beat.

"It's hard to cook for just one person now, so I stick to the basics." Ignoring the thrumming in my veins, I focus on my food. He nods in reassurance but says nothing. I like that about him; he doesn't try to dig at me for information.

Conversation flows between us, each of us grasping at any topic, eating our late-night snack at a snail's pace, trying to drag out each minute so we don't have to say good night. I'm halfway done with my biscuit when I tap out, letting my fork cling against my plate. Before I have a chance to grab the dirty dishes, he's out of his chair and already to the sink.

"I'd have gotten those."

"I know."

Unable to resist the pull between us, I stand beside him while he handwashes the dishes. He's methodical and thorough as he runs the sponge over the plates. I definitely don't notice how large and strong his hands are. I grab a nearby towel, then I dry the dishes before handing them back to him to put away.

"So . . ." he says, crossing his arms over his chest. I can't figure out what he's thinking as he stares at me, waiting for a response.

"I should let you get back to bed," I say. He nods, placing his hand on my lower back and guiding me to the patio. "Sorry for interrupting."

Luke stops short, and his hand slides up to the base of my neck. I think I might be on fire.

"Feel free to interrupt me anytime you want." He leans forward, and I wonder if he's going to kiss me.

"Okay." I swallow the lump in my throat; desire encourages me to close the distance.

But right before I think he will kiss me, Luke places a quick peck on the apple of my cheek. And for that I'm grateful. I'm in uncharted territory now, and I know crossing any boundary with Luke will be monumental. We both deserve to know I'm truly ready to take that leap.

With great effort, I pull away and walk back to my house, trying to slow my breathing. Before I disappear from sight, I take one last look at him. He's got his arm braced against the house. The light from his kitchen illuminates his figure, accentuating each dip and curve.

"Greer," he warns, making me jump.

"Yep. Okay. Well, good night, Luke."

"Good night, sweetheart."

With another awkward wave, I disappear into my house. I replay each time he's called me sweetheart when I tumble into bed and eventually fall into a dreamless sleep.

11

Luke

"**H**ey, Cap," Adam calls out, disrupting me from my daydream, "mind if we stop at Ground Up on the way to training?"

It's been a long few days of work, and the only thing on my mind is Greer. When she came over the other night, it was a sweet surprise in more ways than one. It's like every time I see her, a little bit more of her shines through the cracks in the shell encasing her. I can't wait to be blinded by her.

"Luke? Did you hear me?"

"Sure thing, Adam. But it's gotta be quick." He nods and heads to the truck. We're assisting with the live fire functionals at the academy and finally get to put our rookies through the paces.

Adam, my engineer, eases the truck along the curb of Ground Up. Typically, I avoid this place in the morning because it's always busy, but today, I could use the extra dose of caffeine. We exchange greetings with a few townsfolk before reaching the door. I hold the door open for Adam, then follow him through.

"Hey, guys!" Navy shouts from behind the counter. "Sorry, we're packed today."

"It's all good." Adam jumps in line.

Hunter is texting me some shit about going out, something I definitely don't want to do, when someone taps me on my back.

"Hey, you." My stomach dips, recognizing Greer's voice. She's right behind me, looking gorgeous as ever, hair piled atop her head, loose-fitting concert tee, and legs for days.

"Hey, G." I'll never stop smiling when she's around. "What are you doing?"

"Well, this is a coffee shop. So . . . you know, getting a coffee."

"Makes sense."

"How are you?" She rocks side to side in high-top hiking boots and purple striped socks.

"Are you going hiking?"

"Um,"—her brows furrow together—"yes, I am."

"Alone?"

"No. Why?"

"Oh, just curious." I've barely seen this woman leave her house, and now she's going hiking with someone? I can't help that the protective side roars to life, wondering who she's going with and where. Her cheeks flush as she tucks a few loose strands of hair behind her ears that have come loose of her bun.

"I'm actually going with my parents." Her smile is subtle, innocent, as if maybe she knows I'm jealous.

"Thank god," I blurt. "I mean, that'll be fun."

The line finally moves, and we shuffle forward.

"You're working a lot this week." Her gaze falls to the floor.

"Missing me already?"

I'd meant it as a joke, but she jerks, and I think maybe I'm spot on.

"Yes. I mean, well . . ." She sucks her lips between her teeth. "Shit," she mumbles before looking me square in the eyes. "Yes, I have. Not all the noise you make at the asscrack of dawn. God, you are so noisy. Did you know that? Anyway—"

"Been missing you too, G," I say.

Being a fireman is difficult in so many ways, but the time away from home is often the worst. I've lost count over the years just how many holidays, family events, and other life functions I've missed because of work.

"Shift work is hard," I tell her. She reaches forward and slides her hand in mine. I've had a few long-term girlfriends over the years, but not once have I ever felt they missed me while I was away on shift. Not like I feel it now coming from Greer. My heart stutters in my chest. It's a strange feeling, being missed by someone.

"Tell me your schedule again." She drops my hand as the line inches forward.

"Well, I work for twenty-four hours, and then I'm off for forty-eight hours." It's clear she's trying to mentally calculate my schedule. "I'll be home tomorrow and Friday and then I'm back to work on Saturday, but I've got that day off, so I'm home for a few days."

"Okay, that's what I figured. It's nice you'll have Saturday off." She gives me a shy smile and a goofy thumbs-up. She's cute when she's nervous.

Ground Up isn't a large location by any means, so we're cramped in here. Every table is occupied by patrons in various states of the daily grind. It's hard to wonder why the owner hasn't splurged for a larger location, considering they have the clientele for it.

"What'll it be, guys?" Navy asks as we approach the counter. "Oh, hey, Greer." She reaches across the counter to give her a light hug.

"My girls!" A voice that can only belong to my sister shouts from the entrance. Suddenly, I'm shoved aside as the three embrace.

"What's going on with this?" Adam says under his breath, motioning to the girl huddle.

"I have no idea, but I'm beginning to feel left out."

The girls break apart with giant smiles. "Don't feel left out, big bro," Sutton says. "You'll get your chance."

Greer's eyes dart to mine, and she toys with the hem of her T-shirt. She'll wear every article of clothing down to nothing if she keeps this up. I grasp her hand and pull it toward me. Her shoulders instantly soften.

"As much as I'm happy to see you guys," Navy says, "you're kinda holding the line up." She motions to the desperate coffee addicts behind us.

Greer pulls her hands away from mine. We place our orders and pay before moving off to the side

"You guys are going out with us tomorrow night, right?" Sutton asks. Greer's eyes grow to the size of saucers.

"They don't want to," Greer begins to say.

"To what?" I nudge her foot with my boot.

She shakes her head and glares at my sister. "Nothing really," she begins. "Sutton has decided that we're going dancing."

"Dancing? And who's this *we* you speak of?" I ask.

"Yes, big brother," Sutton says. "Dancing. All of us." Her grin tells me she's up to something.

"But you girls never go out," Adam deadpans.

Both Greer and Sutton shrug before saying, "And?"

"And now you're going dancing?" Adam says.

"Like to a bar or what?" I ask.

"God, yes, Luke. Are you guys coming with us?" Sutton says, readjusting her bag on her shoulder.

"Hell, yes." Adam grabs his coffee. "Grace has been asking me for forever to take her out."

Reaching out, I take Greer's hand again, stopping her before she can fuss with her shirt. "Do you want me to go with you?"

"Yes," she whispers, making me smile. Her eyes flicker. What I wouldn't give to know what's going through her mind at this very second.

"Great!" Sutton declares as she grabs her order. "Well, I have to jet. Busy day!"

"You let Hunter know, Sut?" Adam asks.

Sutton screeches to a halt, and without looking at us, replies, "Not yet, but I'm sure Hunter will be there." She embraces Greer again, telling her not so quietly, "Bye, babe. It can be a good thing, okay?"

Her blue eyes lock with mine over Sutton's shoulder.

"Bye, Navy!" Sutton shouts before exiting the café.

"Tomorrow night, then?" I turn my attention back to Greer.

Her tongue slips out to wet her lips before that damn bottom one disappears between her teeth. She inhales deeply.

"Tomorrow night."

"I'll come by around seven?"

"G-great," she stutters, then takes a small sip of her coffee. Her eyes don't leave mine as she backs toward the door.

"Bye, G," I say as the door closes between us. Her hand raises to give me another wave, and then she's gone.

"You are so fucked, man." Adam elbows my ribs before opening the door and motioning for me to go through.

"Tell me something I don't know."

And I'm not mad about it.

Hunter: So what's this I hear about you being in love?
Me: Adam needs to shut his mouth.
Hunter: That'll never happen and you know it. He talking about Greer?
Me: High probability.
Hunter: How's it gonna work?
Me: Meaning?
Hunter: She's a widow.
Me: Your point?
Hunter: Grief is brutal. Do you worry...
Hunter: You'll be living in her husband's shadow?

It's something I've thought about. Greer's husband died less than a year ago, and the amount of grief she suffers through on a daily basis must be incredible. Not only because of the loss of her husband but also the loss of how she used to be—uninjured, no outward physical signs of what her body endured.

Greer is quiet and hesitant, and she's definitely got walls built around her, but every moment I spend with her, she lets me see more and more of her, willingly opening a gate for me.

Yes, I missed you.

Those four words sent my heart soaring. She may not be ready to admit it yet, but I get the feeling she senses something between us too. Even though I don't know a damn thing about losing my significant other, I'm no stranger to grief, so I understood it completely when she once told me she wasn't ready for more. But the more time I spend with her and the more I get to know her, it's becoming impossible to bury down how much I like her. I want nothing more than to grab her hands and run heart first into the unknown together. But with Greer, I know I have to be patient.

Hunter: Listen, just don't do this if you're trying to fix her.
Hunter: You've done that before, and it's never worked out in your favor.
Me: I know, bro. It's different with Greer.
Hunter: Just make sure you're both on the same page, yeah? It would really suck if either of you got hurt.
Me: Look, I gotta go. See you tonight, right?
Hunter: I can't believe Sutton set all this up. She's never gone out with us. What gives?
Me: Greer and Navy. Shoulda seen the three of them at Ground Up yesterday. Had me and Adam feeling left out.

Hunter: Really? That's good. Sutton deserves to have good friends in her life.
Me: She seemed off yesterday when Adam mentioned you. You guys good?
Hunter: Who knows, man. Your sister confuses the shit out of me.
Me: What did you do this time?
Hunter: Why do you always assume it was me?

Suncrest Valley sits exactly where its name suggests, in the middle of a valley. We're surrounded by rolling prairies to the south and, in every other direction, by hills, mountains, and vast regions of forest. Our town isn't as small as a small town could be, but neither is it big. We've always been more of a summer town with outdoor enthusiasts being attracted to nearby national parks, hiking trails, mountains, and lakes. Summer season is in full swing based on the traffic today.

For being the end of June, it's actually a cool morning out. Fresh air whips through my open windows. It'd be the perfect day to get out of town. I can practically hear the forest calling my name, but I've got a pretty important date today. As I pull up to my house, a brown blur darts down the space between my and Greer's house.

"What the hell?" I park my truck, then jump out, tossing my gear into the garage, and jog toward the backyard.

A heavy bass beat thumps nearby, but I can't place its location. Our neighborhood is normally pretty quiet, but it sounds like someone is having a rave. After I round the back corner, I see Greer's wily old dog racing circles around my yard, that damn hot dog squeaking with each step. I don't see Greer anywhere. Normally, he's never outside without her, so my guess is he pulled a Houdini.

"Hey, Duke." I pat my thigh to entice him toward me.

He sits where he's at and looks right at me.

"Hey, old man. What are you doing out?" He remains calm as I approach. His tail continues wagging back and forth. I squat down and rub his ears. "Does your mama know you're out here?"

As if he understands me, he stands and walks toward their house. I follow closely behind, telling myself over and over that I'm just making sure he gets home okay. It has nothing to do with the possibility of seeing Greer.

Duke walks onto their back patio. It looks like he must have weaseled his way out the sliding glass door before making it to my house. Now, he nudges the screen door open with his nose. I still don't see Greer even though she's normally awake by now. I look down, and Duke bumps me in the leg as he steps inside. He sits and stares at me. I'm not a dog expert, but this feels like an invitation to me.

"G?" I call out. The great room is tidy and quiet but no Greer. The heavy bass beat gets even louder.

"G?" I holler louder, making my way toward the source of the early morning house party. She's added artwork to the walls, and a partially loaded bookshelf catches my eye. It's warm and welcoming. Just like her.

Suddenly, the music ratchets higher. Above it, I hear a female voice, "Eyes, knees, and nipples forward!" *What the hell?*

This first room I peek into is a softly lit bedroom—bed mussed and a nightgown thrown over the side of the reading chair. Duke's lying at the foot of the bed without a care in the world. Lucky dog.

I'm tempted to enter, but at that exact moment, the music gets even louder. Her house has a similar floor plan as mine, so I head down the hallway with guest bedrooms. The floor and walls vibrate from the heavy bass as I approach the closed door at the end.

I knock at the same time a female voice says, "Get ready to run out of the saddle. Cadence between seventy-five and eighty-five! See you on the other side! Three! Two! One!" Another massive drop of bass hits me followed by complete musical chaos. Not bothering to knock, I swing open the door.

Jesus Christ.

I'm assaulted by music blaring from a home system—and Greer. On a spin bike. In nothing but a pink sports bra and spandex shorts. Her eyes are laserfocused on the bike's display.

"That's it!" the female instructor shouts. "Don't half-ass this shit. You gotta use your whole ass! And while you're at it, give that ass a smack cuz ain't no one going to do it for you!"

Suddenly, Greer, my gorgeous, shy neighbor, who occupies my every thought, grips the handlebar, then takes her right hand and . . . Smacks. Her. Own. Ass.

"Sweet Jesus."

"Shit!" Greer yelps, and her eyes snap to mine. Her skin flames, eyes flare, and a massive smile spreads across her face.

"Five, four, three, two, one," the instructor's voice says. "Turn it down. Flat road."

"You have to stop sneaking up on me," she pants through a smile. "Everything okay?"

"I . . ." My brain has melted. Dragging my hand through my hair, I step into the room, drawn to her like a magnet. "You just smacked your ass."

A full belly laugh erupts from her, and her entire face lights up. When she finally calms down and slows her pedaling speed, she catches my eye and shrugs. "I definitely did that. I'm good at doing what I'm told." And then she winks at me. She fucking winks at me.

Sweat glistens on her shoulders, droplets running down her collarbone before disappearing between her breasts. I've never wanted to be a bead of sweat so much in my life. Her plump lips cover the opening of her water bottle. Then, taking a swig, she turns off the bike's screen. Audible clicks punctuate the awkward silence as she removes her feet from the pedals and steps away from her bike.

She stands there, silently watching me as my eyes rove over her spandex-clad body. Strong shoulders and arms compliment her muscular thighs. Her stomach is bare, and all I want to do is run my hands over every exposed inch of her. A few damp strands of hair curl at the nape of her neck. Greer may think she's broken, but this woman standing in front of me is the epitome of strength.

"Luke?" She pats her skin dry.

Somehow, I manage to mumble, "Yeah?"

"You alright over there?" She giggles. A sound I've come to love. Her eyes sparkle, a hint of *something* hidden within.

"Uh, yeah." I clear my throat. With great force, I step away from her. If I don't, I'm not liable for what I may do.

"Can I help you with something, or is walking into people's houses and watching them workout something you enjoy?" Her sarcasm pulls me from my stupor.

"Actually, I was bringing Duke home. He snuck his way out the back door while you were"—I gesture to her body and bike—"doing this."

"It's called spin class."

"And do most instructors ask you to do things like smack your own ass? If so, I might have to join you sometime."

"Oh god." She bends at the waist to take off her shoes and uses her other hand to hide her face. "Because of course that's when you'd walk in."

"What can I say?" I tease. "My timing is impeccable."

"It sure is." She brushes past me and heads to her kitchen.

Her ass sways from side to side. She's different today, more sure of herself, more confident.

"Breakfast," I blurt dumbly. Normally, she's the one nervous around me; boy how the tables have turned.

"Breakfast?" She repeats, gulping down water. Her throat bobs up and down with each swallow. My fingers twitch to caress her skin. A giggle sneaks out of her again, breaking the spell she has me under.

Clearing my throat—again—I take a seat at her island, trying like hell to hide how she's affecting me. Not necessarily the way I want to greet her after barging in on her workout.

"You like it, right?" *What the fuck, Luke? Act like you've talked to the woman before.*

"It depends." She crosses her arms. I avoid focusing on where her breasts are now firmly pressed together.

"On?" I question.

"Are you making it?"

"Of course." I fold my hands together atop the counter, the pressure grounding me. Anything to keep them from reaching for her.

"Then, yes, I like breakfast."

"Ten?"

She nods and sets her cup in the sink.

"Cool." *Cool? Good god, man.*

"I just need to get cleaned up and take a—"

"Stop," I growl, running my hands over my face. "For the love of god. Please. My brain is clearly unable to function seeing you like this." I gesture to her body. "I think it might self-destruct if you say that word."

"Shower." She extends the *sh*, her tongue swiping out to wet her lips.

"You little minx."

"Minx?" Greer says.

Great, I obviously said that out loud.

"Maybe I am," Greer says with a sly smile.

"Ten o'clock," I command with a curt nod, my voice steady despite the growing storm inside. Never before has a woman turned me into a bumbling mess just by existing.

As I push in the chair, she rounds the kitchen island and walks across the room to the back door. She holds the curtains back and gestures for me to exit. Morning air surrounds me as I step through, instantly cooling my heated skin. One would think I was the one who just worked out.

I look over my shoulder one last time and catch her watching me. She startles and quickly drops the curtains.

"Good," I say out loud. "Looks like I'm not the only one who can't stop staring."

12

Greer

"It's fine. Be cool. Everything is going to be fine." I repeat the mantra over and over as I walk the short distance to Luke's patio. Maybe if I say it enough, my body will believe it.

Duke darts ahead and runs a few laps. Matt told me he was an old-timer, but I'm beginning to think Matt lied. A droplet of water from my wet hair crawls down the center of my chest. I hadn't expected anyone, let alone Luke, to catch me working out. Not that I'm ashamed, cycling is the one exercise that's easy on my leg, and I'm proud of how strong I've become. But it's not every day your neighbor catches you mid-workout and smacking your own ass.

The me from a few weeks ago would have run and hid. The way Luke was looking at me... My body flushes thinking about it. He's been the cool and confident one, so it was a pleasure watching him struggle to form words. Every time I'm around Luke, I feel a little safer, more secure, more willing to take risks.

I knock on the back door, hollering for Duke, who comes bounding up to sit at my side. Luke's patio is pretty bare bones, just a grill and pile of camping chairs.

"Come on in," Luke calls out, his muffled voice cutting through the glass of the sliding patio door.

Cool air blasts my cheeks as I enter his home, greeted by the heavenly scent of frying bacon. At first, I'm overwhelmed. I'd been too distracted the other night to give his home a once over, but now, in the light of day, it's not the bachelor pad I anticipated. Unlike his sparse patio, every wall and surface holds the touch of a professional decorator. Warm brown and taupe tones adorn the furniture, while a stunning black wall provides a deep focal point for his TV and fireplace.

"Holy cow, this place is gorgeous."

He doesn't respond, focused instead on slicing vegetables with a towel casually slung over his shoulder. He's clearly calmed down and looks handsome in a dark T-shirt and shorts. I immediately scan his body, happy to see his feet are bare.

"I'll pass your compliments to Sutton." He gestures to a barstool and I sit.

"I thought Sutton sold houses. I didn't realize she could do *this*." Large bookshelves bracket the fireplace. It's an unexpected treasure, finding a collection large enough to rival my own—if most of my collection weren't buried in my storage unit. I can't resist the temptation and step over to check out his book collection.

"You read all these?" I run my fingers reverently over their spines, curious as to which are his favorites.

"Not all of them, but yes." Bacon sizzles as he casually flips each piece.

Perusing each shelf, I spy several books with worn spines. I'm surprised to discover a leather-bound copy of *Pride and Prejudice.* "Which is your favorite?"

"*Lord of the Rings*," he says without delay. "Yours?"

"That's like asking me who my favorite student is."

"I know you'd say all of them." He smiles. "I bet you're excited for next year."

I step around the great room, an identical copy of my house except flipped. My hands graze over the supple leather of his couch and the soft blankets folded over the back.

"I really am," I finally answer. "I've never taught the littles before, but I'm excited for something new."

"You're going to be amazing."

Large, framed nature landscapes adorn the walls as well as photos of his family and friends. A pinch in my stomach reminds me of all the frames begging to be filled in my own home.

"I hope so." I return to my barstool. "I figure a fresh start might be a blessing in disguise. I've been at my old school since I started my teaching career. Plus, it'll be nice not to deal with middle-grade hormones. Can I help?"

"Sure." Luke points to eggs as he sautés veggies.

Slipping around the kitchen island, I step into his space. I crack several eggs and whisk them together. "I'm curious, why *Lord of the Rings*?"

Luke's arm brushes mine as he reaches for tortillas, and my heart skips a beat.

"I've loved that book since I was a kid. Probably read it ten times. And I kind of relate to Samwise Gamgee."

"Ah, the trusty friend willing to risk his own life for those he loves?" I pass him the eggs.

"Something like that." He smiles. "You've read it?"

My cheeks redden. "Shockingly, no, but I'm obsessed with the movies. What are we eating?"

"Breakfast burritos. They're my favorite. That okay?"

"They're my favorite, too." I don't think I'll ever stop smiling around him.

We spend the next hour cooking and eating, the flow of conversation never dulling. I learn that his favorite food is a double-bacon cheeseburger and his favorite movie is *Up*.

"There's something about loving someone the way Carl loves Ellie," he says, and my heart melts a little more. I've only ever been loved by a good man, so I know exactly what he means.

Our laughter fills the space as he regales me with stories of growing up with Sutton. When he talks about his father, my soul warms at how close they were and the love they shared.

He asks about me too. What I was like as a kid growing up, my parents and Gemma, and random other little things. I love how his eyes crinkle with laughter when I tell him about my love for electronic dance music.

"There's just something about it," I say. "You hear all these various beats and melodies. And, if it's a good DJ, they'll make you feel like you're floating, and then, out of nowhere, the beat drops and you feel it everywhere."

"You ever been to a show?" He takes our dishes to the sink.

"I wish!" I say. "Brian never really understood my love for EDM music."

Luke looks at me, and I realize it's the first time I've mentioned Brian without hesitation. Embarrassment crawls up my spine. I'm sure the last thing Luke probably wants to hear about is my husband—the man Death ripped from my life and my heart.

"It's okay, sweetheart. You can talk about him."

I button my lips, taken back by his response. A gentle silence descends upon the room, the only sound being the steady *drip, drip, drip* coming from the faucet.

"I'm sorry," I say.

"Greer, you have nothing to be sorry for." He turns fully toward me, those amber eyes of his never straying from mine. "Brian was a huge part of your life. How can I get to know all the parts of you if I don't also get to know those parts, the ones you spent with him?"

"Luke . . ."

"Listen, sweetheart,"—my heart stutters every time he calls me that—"I don't know how to do this." He gestures between the two of us as he leans back against the counter. "I know you've been through hell and, I don't know, maybe you're still there, but I can't lie to you and say I'm not attracted to you. Because I am."

His words hang in the air between us. I pluck them out and hide them away for later.

"And," he continues, "I think, maybe, you might be attracted to me too. At least I sure as hell hope you are."

I nod, and I love the small smile he returns.

"I'm also not blind to the fact," Luke says, "that we're both in unfamiliar territory. I know you said you weren't ready for anything more, and I'm trying my damnedest to follow that request, but I really want to know you, Greer." He takes a deep breath, his shoulders rising and falling, before whispering, "I want to know everything about you."

"Okay." The word tumbles out of my mouth.

"Okay?" His eyes are bright when they meet mine.

"I want to know you too." I'd already decided the other night that I owe it to myself to at least explore these feelings I'm having for Luke.

"You do?"

"Yes . . ." I say, my heart in my throat. "But my heart . . . it's still broken, and I can't promise I won't screw this up. Grief is part of me now, and it's soul deep. The story of my life will never not be shadowed by it. It's something I can promise you'll be forced to deal with. Brian was a huge part of my life, and he always will be. I'm finally figuring out who I am without him. And, you deserve to know that I've never done this"—I motion between us—"before. I've only ever been with Brian. And . . . I'm scared." I say the last part just above a whisper.

Luke squats down in front of me, taking my hands in his. "Scared of what?"

"So much." Our eyes lock. "I don't want to hurt you or myself or Brian."

"Greer." His hands cup my face. "We'll just take it one day at a time. Okay?"

"Okay," I whisper as a tear falls down my cheek. "I'd love nothing more than to know everything about you, Luke. As long as you're okay with getting the bits and pieces of me that are left."

"I'll feel lucky to get to know any part of you that you're willing to share with me. One day at a time, right?"

I nod as he presses a gentle kiss to the top of my head.

One day at a time. I can do that.

It's just after noon when I pull into my parents' driveway. Dad's already got his head buried under the hood of his old 1960s Ford truck. He's always tinkered with projects around the house. People used to ask him about having two girls and not a son. He was quick to tell them, "I was meant to be a girl dad."

Gemma and I stuck to Dad like glue. We'd follow him around the house, eager to help with whatever project he was working on. Our favorite was this same old truck. It didn't matter that we had no idea what a radiator was or what a Phillips screwdriver was; we just liked being near him. Dad always planned to fix the truck up and take it to vintage car shows, but it's taken him a great number of years longer than we girls thought it would. Every time I see him, his *to-do list* for it grows. I'm starting to realize maybe it's just his way of keeping me and Gemma coming around.

"Hey, sweet pea," he says over the engine of his truck. "Whatcha up to?"

"Nothing, just haven't seen you and Mama much. Thought I'd stop by."

"We miss you too, Greer." He never misses a thing. "How's the new place?"

"It's really great. Mama's been a huge help, but I've had fun decorating on my own. Let's just hope she approves." I smile, thinking of her joy in beautifying a room.

"She'll love anything you do." He nods his head, fussing with a socket or wrench or something. "Mama says you've met some new friends?"

"Yes." I grin, thinking of the girls. "Navy and Sutton . . . they're . . . it's like we were meant to be friends. It's not like any friendship I've had before, ya know?"

He stops tinkering and places his elbows on the side of the truck. "That's real good to hear, Greer. They must be something special."

"They are, Daddy. I can't wait for you to meet them."

"Well, maybe it's time you had a housewarming party or something. You know, so we could meet 'em." His eyebrows rise, a hidden challenge there to my self-inflicted isolation.

"I . . . well, you know how I feel about . . . You know what,"—my eyes close as a laugh bubbles out of me—"I'll talk to Mama and the girls. A party would be fun."

Dad's jaw drops, his eyes bugging out of his head.

"What is it? What's wrong?" I look over my shoulder thinking he's seeing something I don't.

"Nothing, baby girl. I just haven't heard you laugh in a long time. I've really missed it."

My cheeks flush as I fidget with various tools.

"These friends of yours," Dad says, "must be something special if they're bringing my girl back."

It doesn't take a genius to see that my connection with Navy and Sutton is special. I never thought it possible to meet anyone, let alone two women who truly listen to me and challenge my way of thinking. They make me laugh constantly, and there's no pressure to be someone I'm not. Life has a funny way of giving you what you need when you're not even looking for it.

"I don't know about being *back*," I tell him. "But, I feel different lately."

"Good different or bad different?"

"Good different."

I'd been prepared to begin this new chapter of my life alone, but then Sutton stormed into my life. Now, she's just there, her energy and companionship swirling around me. And Navy? I don't think she had a choice. Sutton sucked her into her orbit and, like me, she's happy to stay. And then there's Luke.

My stomach whooshes as his amber eyes enter my mind. It's been too long since a man has looked at me the way he does, talked to me the way he does. After his bumbling invite to breakfast, my battered heart was soothed knowing it wasn't just me who was nervous.

The way he didn't so much as flinch or cringe at the mention of Brian's name. *How do I get to know all the parts of you if I don't get to know the part of you spent with him?* It didn't matter that he told me he was attracted to me and wanted to continue to get to know me because I'd already decided days ago that, no matter what, I had to know him. It *feels* right.

"I'm going out tonight," I say.

"No shit?" Dad nearly drops his wrench.

"Going dancing in fact."

"Well, I'll be. Who are ya going with?"

"The girls and Luke and his friends."

"Luke, huh?"

"Yeah, he's my neighbor, remember?"

"I remember. Met him a few times leaving your place."

"And? What did you think of him?"

Dad sees right through my bullshit. Never in my life could I have predicted I'd be asking my dad for dating advice again.

"Think of who?" Mom comes up behind him and hands him a glass of water.

"Greer's neighbor, Luke," he tells her before taking a gulp.

"Luke, hmm?" she says.

"Yes," I say, "a group of us are going out dancing tonight and Luke and I are going together." I say the last word quietly, not sure how they'll react knowing this could be an actual date. Like me, they only know *me* with Brian.

"Greer, sweetie, that's just wonderful," Mom says, a dreamy look appearing on her face.

"Yes, sweet pea," Dad says, "it really is."

Fidgeting with the hem of my shirt, I ask, "You don't think it's too soon?"

They share a look, communicating silently. Mom comes around the truck and wraps her arm around my waist.

"The only person who can dictate the timeline of your life is you. What does your heart tell you?"

"What about what other people will think? What they'll say? It's not even been a year."

"Now, Greer," Mom says, "your daddy and I didn't raise you to be concerned with the opinions of others. Everyone who has lost a significant other approaches the next phase of their life differently. Sure, it's been less than a year. Who cares? If we've learned anything from losing Brian, it's that life is unpredictable, and, no matter how many decades we think we'll spend on Earth, they're never guaranteed. You have to live your life fully, every day, because you never know if it could be your last." Emotion clogs her throat as she lays her head on my shoulder.

"Brian," Dad adds, "would want you to find love again."

"Do you like this Luke?" Mom nudges my arm.

"I do," I say. "Very much. He's very patient and kind. You should see him with us, Duke and me. And he's an amazing brother and friend. It's like he's the sun who keeps everyone warm." I can practically feel his warmth now even though he's nowhere nearby.

"And how do you feel when you're around him?" Mom prompts, digging in that way only moms know how.

I can't stop smiling. "I, well, it sounds lame but . . . I kind of like *me* better when I'm around him."

Mom sighs. "Well, that's just wonderful."

"It's very exciting, Greer," Dad pipes in. He's got his head buried under the hood again, so we can barely hear him.

"It is?" I ask.

"Of course." He pops up over the hood. "Opening your heart again after loss must be very difficult, but it is exciting. You fell in love with Brian and loved him completely for eight years. You'll never stop loving Brian, but now, you have the opportunity to fall in love again, move forward with your life, and find a new version of happiness."

"No one said I was falling in love," I remind him.

"You won't know unless you open your heart and mind to it," he counters.

"Have you and Luke talked about what this means?" Mom asks as she steps nearer to me.

"We did this morning," I say. "He's so . . . he's so accepting of it. He told me he wants to know all the parts of me, even the ones spent with Brian."

"Had a feeling I'd liked him," Dad says, dabbing the corner of his eye.

"Well," Mom says, "this is just wonderful."

"You keep saying that, Mama." I playfully bump her hip.

"It is, Greer," Mom says. "We are all afraid to love. Of course we are. Hearts are fragile and delicate things. You've had yours shattered, and, as your mother, I worry about you. I want your heart to be whole and happy."

"I don't think it'll ever be whole," I say.

"It won't be," Dad says. "And whoever you invite into your life will know that too. But, when you're ready, you have to be willing to allow yourself, and him, the chance to mend it."

"Now, for the most important question," Mom says, "what are you going to wear?"

My stomach drops. I've been so focused on everything going on between Luke and me, it hadn't crossed my mind to consider what to wear.

"Shit. I-I don't know. Maybe a dress."

"Greer Ashbury," Mom says, "you are not wearing one of your school dresses on a night out with Luke and your new friends. Grab your purse. We're going shopping." Mom whips around, dashing inside to grab her things.

"You walked right into that one." Dad chuckles.

"Thanks, Daddy." He's already got his arms open, waiting to envelop me in a tight hug.

"I'm proud of you, Greer. I know this is new and hard for you, but I'm so damned proud of you for being willing to try. Sounds like you've met some pretty great people."

"I really have. It's like they fell out of the sky."

"The people who are meant to find you always will."

"C'mon, Greer," Mom hollers from the garage. "Get your butt in the car!"

"Oh man, wish me luck."

Dad's laugh echoes behind me as I jog to Mom's truck.

13

Greer

THERE WAS A MOMENT this afternoon when I wasn't sure I was going to survive the shopping venture with my mom. It started out looking for one outfit and ended in a total wardrobe overhaul. Which was necessary. For the past year, I've existed in work clothes or athleisure wear. Who needed going out clothes when you never went out? Mom finally relented and let us leave when she realized I actually had to get ready for tonight.

Tonight.

With Luke.

Was it a date? Were we just arriving together because we were neighbors? These questions have been running through my mind all afternoon. Cold water runs down my back, soap suds swirling down the drain. My anxiety spirals a similar path through my body, around and around and around.

"Why am I so nervous?" I say aloud. I apply conditioner, then begin the arduous process of shaving everything. An expert at dating I am not, but even I know a woman never wants to be caught unawares with a forest between her legs. Not that I'm planning on Luke seeing or feeling my forest. *I think?*

No, definitely not. There's no way anything like that will happen tonight. I mean, maybe Luke doesn't see me in that way. Jesus, Greer, the man can barely keep his hands off you as it is. He definitely wants you that way. What if I get nervous or what if . . . what if I want . . . My chest tightens.

Inhale. Exhale.

I allow each breath to subdue the rising tide, and after only a few rounds, my thoughts clear and breathing normalizes.

I step from the shower, pat my skin dry, lather on body lotion, and begin my facial routine. A simple girl I may be, but one who's not lacking a skin care routine.

"This kind of stuff was easy with you," I tell Brian, hoping that voicing my fears will ease any lingering nervousness. "We never really had to date *date*, did we? We just were what we were, young and in love, without a care in the world." And it's true, we met in our college algebra class, and we just *were*. In fact, months later, we'd had to decide on an anniversary date because neither of us could remember when we became an *us*.

Mom helped me pick out a simple black dress to pair with my cowboy boots, so I decide to wear my hair down in loose curls.

After taking out my makeup bag, I apply the basics. I might take a little extra time on my eyes, applying mascara to make them pop. As I'm putting on the final coat, there's a knock at my door.

"Shit, who in the world could that be?" Making sure my white towel is secure, I finger comb my wet hair as I walk down the hallway.

There's another knock accompanied by a loud, but subtle, "Greer? It's me."

I freeze, hand on the doorknob. This man has yet to see me dressed in anything semi-normal, and now he catches me like this. I shake my head then unbolt the lock and open the door.

"Fuck," he mutters as his eyes rake over every exposed inch.

"Hey, is everything okay?"

"You—you're in a—"

"Oh, yeah." I look down, cheeks flushing. "You caught me getting ready."

He closes his eyes, inhaling and exhaling audibly. "Do you want to go to dinner before we meet up with everyone tonight?" When he finally opens his eyes, they don't stray from my face.

"You could have texted," I tease.

He shuffles his feet. "I could have, but then I'd have missed out on seeing you like this."

"Lord, one of these days maybe you'll catch me looking like"—I gesture to my body—"not this."

"I like you like this," he says confidently. I catch fire.

"You said something about dinner?"

"Yes, dinner. You like dinner, right? Jesus, of course you do. What I meant is, can I take you to dinner tonight before we meet everyone at Big Joe's?"

"Rest assured, Luke, I like all meals and food in general. Just in case your future self is ever curious about lunch or snacks or second breakfast." He laughs at my *Lord of the Rings* reference, and the tension between us dissipates. We've gravitated toward one another, the air around us heats from his warmth.

"Have dinner with me?" He threads his fingers between mine. Our hands are such a juxtaposition. His are large and tanned; mine are small and pale. I can't help noticing how easily they fit together, like puzzle pieces.

"Greer?" he asks again.

"Like a date?" I say. He pulls my hand, bringing our bodies nearly flush.

"Would that be okay with you if it were a date?"

"I'm okay with that. In fact, I was just having a debate with myself in the shower about what this was tonight. Is it just friends driving together, or did you see me as something *else*? It all sounds so stupid saying it out loud."

"It doesn't sound stupid at all. And, just so we're clear,"—his jaw clenches, voice husky—"I see you as something else. I meant what I said earlier. I want to know every. Single. Part. Of. You."

"Okay," I whisper, grinning, heat sizzling away any leftover anticipation under my skin.

"I know I said seven, but you about ready?"

"In a rush to take me out?" I lean into him.

"Yes." His thumb brushes along the edge of my towel.

I take a step back, straightening my spine. "Give me thirty minutes. I'm almost ready."

He nods his head and squeezes my hand before letting go. He backs down the sidewalk entry, his eyes descending so slowly it makes my toes curl. "I'm excited, G."

"Me too," I whisper, closing the door.

Turning, I lie back against the door, steadying my breathing and my body. Duke sits quietly to the side, having watched the whole exchange.

"C'mon, bud, let's go make me presentable for my date."

In the back of my mind, I see Brian watching me. I like to think he'd be smiling. When I was younger, you couldn't have convinced me that this would be my life, reentering the dating field as a widow. Maybe whatever this is with Luke should feel stranger than it does. Maybe I should feel guilty at the timing of things. But I wasn't lying when I told Luke I was excited about our date. I'm also a thousand other emotions, but excited tops my list.

"I hope you're proud of me, Brian. Trying to put myself back out into the world." Duke gives a small woof. "Okay, okay, I hear ya. I'm going."

Approximately thirty minutes later, I'm staring at myself in my full-length mirror, unable to recognize the woman looking back at me. My hair is curled and swoops over my right shoulder. The black dress Mom and I found has a subtle lace detail across the bodice and is short enough to show a little leg. I even had a few extra minutes to polish my cowboy boots.

I look effervescent, brighter, different from the me I'd become used to seeing after the accident. It's nice seeing a bit of my old self peering back at me. Well, maybe not exactly my old self. I won't ever be her again, but I like who stares back at me now.

"C'mere, buddy, let's go outside before I leave."

Duke is out the door and in the yard running in circles before I can make it to the edge of the patio. The sun has begun to set, casting the yard in a shadowy haze. As I tend to do these days, I walk to my favorite spot and absorb the view in front of me. A kaleidoscope of reds, yellows, and purples explodes at the edge of my property where the preserve begins. The sea of wildflowers, finally in full bloom, paints the otherwise green landscape a vibrant canvas that beckons to be explored. I can't wait for the day Luke takes me fishing out there.

Smoothing my hands down my dress, I feel a giant smile burst from within me. God, I forgot how good this feels. I feel topsy-turvy because I'm excited for something.

"Hey, gorgeous." This time, I don't spook at the sound of his voice.

When I swirl around, it's my turn to be struck speechless. Luke is decked out in a pair of dark-wash, blue jeans; a black T-shirt; and cowboy boots. His hair is styled back in gentle waves I long to run my fingers through. It's almost unfair how handsome he is.

"Hi," I say on an exhale.

"You look,"—he hesitates, approaching slowly, like if he moves too fast, he'll startle me away—"incredible." He reaches for me and slides his hands around my waist. My arms automatically move up his chest and my hands lock around his shoulders. He brings me into him and buries his head in the crook of my neck, inhaling deeply.

"I am beginning to think you have a thing for smelling people." I bite my lip, giggling into this shoulder.

"Nah, I just have a Greer thing." He squeezes me tighter, my heels lifting off the ground.

"Yeah, well, I have a Luke thing." At my words, he pulls back to look me in the eyes, so close our noses nearly touch. He drinks me in. Every part of me, even the hidden ones, feel exposed. But this time, it's a welcome feeling.

"You look really handsome." I slide my hands down his shoulders and grip his biceps.

A sound rumbles from him. "We better go or else . . ."

"Or else what?" I ask playfully as he leads me to the patio.

Duke runs inside, and we close the sliding glass door. As we pass through my living room, I grab my purse. Then we're back out the front door, crossing over to his driveway, where his truck waits. Luke's hand remains a constant reassuring pressure on my low back.

He drives a dark, midnight-blue 4X4 truck, and it's already running when we approach. A footboard pops out when he opens the door that I use to lift myself into the cab. As I'm buckling myself in, I glance over at Luke, his hand is utterly still on the door, eyes level with my legs.

"I might eat you up." He groans.

Goosebumps erupt across my legs and crawl up my skin. I know my face is tomato-red.

"Luke," I whisper.

A devilish smile sneaks past his careful composure as he closes my door and makes his way to the driver's side. Luke jumps in and buckles his seat belt. Before I know it, he's backing us out of the driveway and down our street. As he turns onto the highway, he slides the hand resting on the center console over my leg and rests it on my knee. I am electric.

"Is this okay?" He gestures with his chin to where his hand rests upon my thigh.

"Yes." He tilts his forehead down in understanding before focusing on the road. I, however, am unable to focus on anything except his hand on my thigh, thumb rubbing small half circles. I focus only on that and don't realize we've driven the distance to the restaurant in silence.

"Tacos!" I shout as we pull into the parking lot.

"You did say they were your favorite."

"You working for bonus points?"

"I—no. I just wanted to . . ." I like it when he loses his words and gets flustered like this. Makes me feel not so alone. He pulls into a parking spot.

"No need to work for bonus points. You've already made quite an impression on me. Just be yourself." I give him an encouraging smile.

The breath he takes causes his shirt to pull tighter around his shoulders. I don't know if the sleeves are too small or if his biceps are too big. Either way, I'm happy to reap the visual benefits.

"Sweetheart, you gotta stop looking at me like that." He groans as he squeezes my thigh.

"Y-yeah—okay, let's eat," I stutter out, shaking myself out of my Luke-induced haze.

His chuckle echoes in the truck's cab as he jumps out. Just as I unbuckle myself and reach for my door, it opens, revealing Luke with his hand held out waiting for mine. I place my hand in his and climb down.

As he starts to let go of my hand, I link our fingers, catching him off guard.

"Is this okay?" I ask. His only response is a deep swallow and a nod. "Good." I add a little pressure.

"Yeah?" he asks, opening the restaurant door.

"Mm-hmm. I find I like the feel of you, Luke."

It's a Friday night, which means most of the nice restaurants in town are busy. This is the only Mexican food place worth a damn, so we're not shocked at the wait. After checking in with the hostess, Luke guides me outside to wait for our table. His arms wrap around my waist, and he pulls me close—my back to his front.

"I like the feel of you too," he whispers, his warm breath coasting over the shell of my ear.

Tangy salt sparks against my tongue as I sip on my second peach margarita. Luke's hands wave all around as he tells a funny story about Hunter and himself from their baseball days. The tequila settles under my skin, making me feel light and airy.

Dinner with Luke has been the most fun I've had in a long time. The restaurant is busy and loud, but in a surprising turn of events, I don't mind. It is refreshing being *out.* Being in the middle of a crowded restaurant, enjoying time with a wildly interesting man. I've isolated myself away from the world for so long, telling myself it's who I am. But I know it was a lie. I didn't go out because I was afraid. Afraid to be and feel alone in a room full of people. With Luke, I don't feel afraid, nor do I feel alone.

"I gotta warn you, G," Luke says, "in our group we like to dance. You good with that?"

I give him the side-eye. "Don't you worry about me." Little does he know I love to dance. Whether I'm any good or not has yet to be determined. I'm the person you'll find having a dance party in the middle of the pharmacy simply because they put on a banger of a tune.

We make the drive to the bar and spend several minutes trying to find a parking spot.

"Has this place always been this busy?" I ask. Seems like half the town decided to come out tonight.

"Tonight's dance hall night, so it's busier than normal." With one hand, he maneuvers the steering wheel and backs his truck into the smallest parking space possible. My brain short-circuits.

"Dance hall night?" I put on a quick swipe of lip balm and stow my handbag in his glove compartment. He's watching me intently, his handsome smile stretching from ear to ear. "What's wrong?" I pat my hair and face. "Is there something on my face? In my teeth?"

"I like you in my truck."

I reach over and squeeze his forearm. A memory blasts me out of nowhere.

His forearm is warm and sticky with blood. "Just hold on Brian. It'll all be okay. They'll be here soon. Just hold on until then. Okay? Just hold on."

Tears flood my eyes as the image assaults my mind. I've had this memory so many times over the last year. I've memorized every detail. The blood dripping from the gash on his face onto the crisp white expanse of shirt. Music still pouring from the speakers even though everything around us is in pieces. My heart rate accelerates, knowing what happens next.

"G? What's wrong?" Luke's hushed voice breaks through the cacophony inside my head. "Are you okay?"

My eyes turn to his and come into focus as a few tears drip down my cheeks.

"Where did you just go?" he asks.

"That night." I'm motionless.

"Still having flashbacks?" The rough texture of his voice is gentle, soothing.

"Not in a while." I suck in a stuttering breath.

He turns to face me fully, bringing his hands toward my face. "Is this okay?"

I nod. Warm hands slide up my neck and cup my face. Using his thumbs, he strokes my cheeks and catches the tears trickling down my face.

"You're okay, sweetheart. Just breathe." I breathe in sync with him. "Good girl. Inhale. Exhale." I sigh aloud at the reminder, smiling at Brian because he must have let Luke in on our little anxiety-reducing mantra.

"I'm sorry." I close my eyes as the memory slides down my spine, leaving a cold trail in its wake.

"You have nothing to be sorry for."

"I know. I'm still sorry though. They pop up out of nowhere, but I haven't had one in a while."

"What was it this time?"

I sink into my seat and lay my head back, feeling his eyes on me. "The doctors say I blacked out after the impact and that it's possible I would never remember any of it. But I remember enough of it. I watched him die. Did you know that?"

"No, I didn't know that. But I had suspicions."

My eyes meet his. "What do you remember?"

"We'd never seen something like it before," he says. "The damage to your car was . . . we thought there was no way anyone survived. But the woman who called 9-1-1 assured us someone inside was alive. We checked Brian first." He pauses, judging my reaction. I nod for him to continue. "But he was already gone, so we focused on you. I remember you telling us *get him first*. You kept saying it over and over. By the time we got you out and into the back of the ambulance, you'd gone quiet. Even now, I can still see the desolate look on your face as we closed the ambulance doors."

"It was the smell of gasoline that woke me up," I say. "I was so confused and all I heard was screaming. I figured out later it was me. There was glass everywhere. I couldn't really see well because my right eye was swollen, but I could see Brian behind the steering wheel. I tried moving, but I-I couldn't. I was stuck. The only thing I could do, the only part of him I could reach was his forearm." Luke touches his own forearm where my hand had been just moments before I had the flashback. "I was hurt badly. Brian tried to move, to get to me, but he couldn't move either. I think he knew." I swallow the lump in my throat. "I was holding onto his forearm when he stopped breathing."

The air in the cab is heavy with memories and grief. I knew we were going to have to talk about this someday. Little did I know, someday would be right now. Luke slides his hand onto my shoulder, and cups the back of my head.

"Thank you," he says turning my face to his.

"For what?"

"For telling me all that."

"You said you wanted to know all the parts of me."

"I do." He leans forward, my face a breath's distance from his. "Do you want me to take you home?"

"You would do that?"

"I would do anything for you. Just tell me what you need."

We're quiet. Our foreheads braced together as we breathe in sync, each inhalation calming me further. When I open my eyes, Luke's worry-filled eyes stare back at me.

This man.

The old Greer would have jumped at the chance to escape, to hide in her cocoon. This version of Greer? The new one? She wants to be here with Luke, wants to spend time with her friends, wants to let others in.

"I would really like to *not* go home." I shrug. He presses his lips against my forehead.

"Okay, sweetheart. Let's go have some fun."

14

"**Y**OU GUYS MADE IT!" My sister squeals above the music as Greer and I enter the bar hand in hand; something she doesn't miss based on her grin.

"Yeah, sorry we're late," I say. "Dinner ran a little longer than expected." I cover for Greer, not sure what she feels comfortable telling our friends. I know people who have suffered traumatic events are prone to flashbacks, but I've never witnessed one firsthand.

One minute she was right there with me, and the next, she completely disappeared into her mind. There was nothing I could do but hold space for her. Greer is so much stronger than she gives herself credit for. The fact she felt safe enough to reopen that scar and let me in is proof of that. As Sutton and Navy wrap her in a hug, I'm forced to drop Greer's hand.

"You good?" Navy asks quietly.

"Yeah, I just had a bit of a flashback in the truck."

"Oh, honey, I'm sorry," Sutton says with a sad smile. Both women look at her expectantly, running soothing hands up and down her back. "Why are you here then?" Sutton asks.

"You could have texted us, G," Navy says. "We would have understood if you wanted to go home."

It's funny watching these three together. Sutton is always put together—the planner, the leader. Greer is clearly shyer and more emotional. Navy's straightforward honesty could make a grown man tremble. They are vastly dissimilar from each other, and yet the bond between them glows.

"Uh-uh, ladies," Hunter yells. "No one is going home!" He wraps his arms around Sutton's and Navy's shoulders, joining their girl huddle. He looks right at Greer. "I'm really glad you're here, Greer."

"Me too." She nods before stepping back into me. Her hand finds mine. Hunter raises an eyebrow, and I see his thoughts floating above his head.

I know he worries I'm just trying to help Greer, to fix her and help her be happy again. Maybe I am. But there's something about Greer, and this thing between us feels different from any previous relationships. She doesn't seem to need or want anything from me except my company.

"Are you two together now?" Navy asks, causing everyone in the group to stare at us. There's no beating around the bush when Navy is present.

Greer lifts her shoulders, eyes glinting in the light, and gives that sweet smile I've come to love. "We're taking it one day at a time," she says, her voice smooth as she leans into me.

"Hell yeah!" Adam hoots as he passes out beers. And just like that, our friends accept whatever this is between Greer and me.

"Alright, alright, alright!" The MC's voice powers through the speakers. "Who's ready to dance?" The crowd erupts into cheers and hollers.

The band strikes up a popular country song, and people converge on the dance floor. Dinner ran a lot longer than we anticipated, and the night is well underway. As expected, the dance hall is filled wall to wall with people. The band is finishing its last set before the DJ takes over.

"C'mon, babe, let's dance." Hunter grabs Sutton around the waist and pulls her into a spin. She shakes her head but follows him to the center of the crowd.

"Alright, handsome," Grace says to Adam, "you promised me dancing."

"You bet your sweet ass I did," Adam says. "Let's go, baby." He buries his face in his wife's neck as she leads them out to the dance floor. A longing for what they have zips through my heart.

"I'm gonna go grab some drinks," Navy says. "What can I grab you to drink?"

"Anything with tequila," Greer shouts above the music.

"You got it." Navy drags Vinnie with her to the bar.

"You ready for this?" she asks, bumping my hip with hers.

I wish I could tell her how ready I have been. In the weeks I've known Greer, she's starting to emerge from her cocoon of grief. I'm not sure how I got so fucking lucky that she moved in next door and to have her presence in my life.

"Woman," I tell her, "I was born ready."

"Let's see those moves then, mister."

I slide my arm around her waist and lead us to the dance floor. A spot opens and I claim it as ours. With a rock step, she swings out, and then I twist her in and under my arm, her back now flush to my chest. "You asked for it," I say against the smooth skin of her neck.

Her chest heaves, the low-cut neckline of her dress slipping to reveal the swells of her breasts, and I can't tear my eyes away.

"Hey, you?" She nuzzles her nose into my cheek, breaking me from my staring contest with her chest. "I thought we were dancing. If you'd rather do something else . . ." The husky whisper tumbles straight to my core, and I know she's got that goddamn lip between her teeth again.

"We are," I say. "And I'd love to *rather*, but first, we're going to have this kind of fun." I spin her around again before taking up a traditional frame. "You're good at this. How long have you been country swing dancing?"

"Since I was a kid. It's something Dad and Mom did, so I learned. We'd go out dancing a lot with Brian's friends and see a lot of country shows."

There's no hesitation this time when she mentions him. I love that she's willing to let me get to know her and be herself, even the parts buried in the dark. Greer had talked about her life with Brian at dinner. It allowed me to see how big her heart is and how strong she truly is.

Her face glistens with perspiration, and she smiles as I twirl her. Brian was a lucky man to have had this amazing woman as his wife for as long as he did. A pang hits me low in the gut imagining how he must have felt knowing he was leaving her. Any guy might question if he measured up to Brian and what he and Greer had together, or wonder if she has room in her heart for someone new, *something* new. I don't, though. She wouldn't be here with me if she didn't. I'm thankful he loved her like she is meant to be loved.

"Okay, bitches!" Navy shouts behind us. "It's shot time!"

"We're going to regret this, aren't we?" Greer says against my neck, tugging me off the dance floor.

"With Navy and Vinnie as bartenders? I'd say the chances of that happening are one hundred percent."

"I've never really done shots," she says as she takes a shot glass from the tray.

"First time for everything." I smile. "Just have fun."

Sutton hands out limes, and Vinnie passes the salt.

"Mind if I . . . ?" She gestures to the salt and lime.

"Uh, sure thing." I offer her my hand.

"I was actually thinking . . ." I see the flirtatious gleam in her eyes. God, she's fucking gorgeous like this. Gorgeous all the time, really.

Her soft fingers trail over the skin below my jaw. A flurry of fuck-knows-what dances over my skin, and I'm an immediate addict. This woman can touch me any time she wants.

Her voice is low and sultry when she murmurs out, "That I could maybe do it here." When her finger draws a lazy circle over the same spot to get her point across, I nearly combust. I'm not sure I'm going to make it through an entire night with this woman without crossing a boundary I'm not sure she's prepared to cross.

"You sure?" With a quick glance at the group, it's clear no one is paying us an ounce of attention.

"Yes." Confidence punctuates the word as she pushes me back, the bar stool wobbling as my ass lands on it. Her hand cups the side of my face, and she tilts my head to the side. I focus on not forgetting to breathe. I catch sight of Hunter in a similar position—struggling to hold back as my sister licks the salt from his neck and takes her shot before removing the lime from between his lips.

Time stands still, and I wonder if Greer's lost her nerve. But then, her cheek brushes mine, her warm breath whispers over the skin below my jaw. I stop breathing, chest constricting, when her tongue caresses the skin along my pulse point.

Buzzing fills my ears. My lungs, having been deprived of oxygen, finally heave an inhale. That little minx giggles. I'm powerless, unable to hide her effect on me. She shakes salt on the wet spot before placing the lime between my lips. Our eyes meet, creating an unspoken promise of something more.

"Ready?" she asks.

I nod.

She leans in, licks the salt on my neck, tosses back the shot, and leans over to capture the lime from my lips. Her lips briefly meet mine before pulling away, her cobalt eyes a storm of desire.

Gripping her waist, I pull her between my thighs, her breasts level with my face. There's no mistaking her pebbled nipples.

"You're trouble," I growl. Shivers course through her body, tempting me to scoop her up, throw her over my shoulder, and discover how her body truly reacts when we're alone.

Her giggle morphs into uncontrollable laughter, and she buries her face in my neck. Flames spark throughout me as she loops her arms around my shoulders.

"God, I'm . . ." She hesitates before whispering, "I don't know what you're doing to me."

"Well, I could be doing—"

"Oh my god, Greer?" A high-pitched voice interrupts. "Is that you?" Greer pulls away from me as if she's been burned.

"Annie?" she says, eyes wide. I can't help but wonder if maybe Greer is embarrassed at being caught. A swirl of shame sinks low in my gut at the possibility.

"Hi, how are you?" Greer asks Annie.

"I'm good," Annie replies. "Gosh, it feels like forever since we saw you last."

Greer visibly tenses when she notices two men behind Annie. I don't know who they are, but she's obviously not their biggest fan. My protective switch flips on.

"Since the funeral," the taller guy behind Annie says. Greer's eyes flare with shame as she starts to retreat.

"That's right," Annie says quietly, shooting daggers at the tall guy. "How are you doing?"

"Um, I'm pretty good," Greer answers.

"Who's this?" Guy two asks.

"Luke Bradley," I answer, reaching out to shake his hand. Greer's visceral reaction to these people, or, I hate to think it, her embarrassment at her boldness with me, still has me wrapped in knots. I'm normally cool and collected, but right now I have the urge to punch him in the jaw. I bury it down and make an attempt to remain civil.

"Nice to meet you, Luke," Annie says.

UNTIL THEN

"Are you two, like, together?" the shorter guy blurts out.

I push out of the stool, step into Greer, and wrap my arm around her waist. Our friends step near, readying for anything, but keeping quiet. I don't know these people, and I've never heard Greer mention them. How dare this guy come in asking questions he has no right to ask?

"Um . . . Luke and I are taking it one day at a time." Greer pushes back into me.

"It's so weird"—guy two pushes closer, spilling some of his beer—"seeing you with someone else." My jaw clenches. It's clear these guys have zero social training and have had way too much to drink.

"Jesus, shut up, Alan!" Annie chastises him.

"It is, though." Guy one shrugs nonchalantly. He reeks of whiskey. "It's been less than a year, so, yeah, it's weird as hell seeing you with someone new."

My hands splay over Greer's hip, pulling her tense body into mine. I know she's preparing to escape. I don't know these people, but I'll be damned if they make her feel shameful for being with me.

"It was good to see you guys," Greer says. "I just need to run to the restroom." She squeezes my arm, and I release her. She flees across the bar with Sutton following close behind. Hunter stands nearby, laser focused on what's happening between me and these idiots.

"What is your problem?" I step toward them.

"What do you mean, bro?" guy two, Alan, asks.

"First of all," I say, "I am not your bro. Second of all, why the hell do you think you have any right to comment on Greer being with me?"

"We're her friends," Alan says.

"Her friends, huh? If you're her friends, why haven't you seen her since the funeral?"

Idiot one bristles, puffing out his chest. "She didn't want us around."

"Are you sure about that? Did you ask her? Or was it you guys who couldn't handle being around her?"

"Jesus, man, it's not like that." Alan's shoulders slump.

Annie remains silent.

"What was it like then?" Raising my eyebrow, I dare one of them to tell the truth.

"It was just too hard," Annie relents.

"Too hard?" Hunter butts in.

"Greer was so sad. All the time," Annie says. "We didn't know what to do anymore."

I shake my head and grab my beer from the table.

"You stay by her side," I say. "She'd just lost her husband and been through something none of us would wish upon our worst enemies. If you were truly her friends, you don't *have* to do anything except be there. You couldn't do that, though, could you? So, don't you dare stand here and make shit-ass comments about her or how she's living her life now. You don't know Greer anymore. You lost that privilege when you bailed on her. A loss that has quickly become our"—I gesture to my friends—"blessing."

"You guys have a good night now." Hunter's arm brushes mine as he steps up next to me. "And the next time you see our girl, maybe start with hello instead."

Alan and the other guy nod before walking away. Annie's face is cherry-red.

"I'm sorry for what he said," Annie says. "I'm really glad Greer's doing better now. Please tell her goodbye for me."

I reply with a curt nod.

"You okay?" Hunter asks as the others step up to the table.

"God, man, I don't know. That was—"

"You like her though, right?" Hunter interrupts.

"You know I do."

"Well, you better get used to it. Greer is a widow. There's no changing the stupid and judgmental shit people might say *to* her and *about* her. Grief is part of her story."

"I know."

"I'm glad you know. Are you prepared to deal with all that? Because the last thing she needs is for more people to bail on her. So, before you let all of us fall in love with her too, you gotta ask yourself if you're willing to put in the work. Is she worth it?"

"She's worth everything." I feel it in my bones.

"Good." Adam clinks his beer to mine.

"We think so too," Grace says, tucking herself into Adam.

"Now," Vinnie adds with his signature smile, "go get your girl and let's salvage the rest of this night."

I'm halfway to the restroom when I stumble upon Greer and Sutton. Sutton's gaze meets mine and a silent understanding passes between us. She places Greer's hand in mine and heads back to our friends.

"Are you okay?" I ask.

"Um, I think so. That was very unexpected."

"Those guys were idiots," I say.

Greer laughs. "They really are. Annie was always pretty okay, but I've never liked Alan or Troy."

"I'm sorry for embarrassing you and for what they said." I wrap my arm around her shoulder and lead her back to the table, our friends already heading back to the dance floor.

"Luke, you didn't embarrass me"—she wraps her arms around my shoulders—"Honestly, I knew things like this was going to happen, but I was just caught off guard. You make it easy to forget . . ." Her voice trails off as she turns, the floral scent of her shampoo breaks through the bar's stale air.

"Sweetheart, you and I both know you'll never forget. No one will ever understand what you're going through. You don't have to carry the weight every second of every day." My heart thrums against my ribs as she relaxes into me.

"It's getting easier," she admits. Soft blue eyes study my face. I want so badly to lean in and kiss her, but I know tonight's been a lot for her. Resting my hands at the base of her spine, I ignore how thin the material of her dress is.

"Should we go home?" I ask.

She contemplates this for a moment. "Nope, I'll be good."

"If you're positive, but if . . ."

"I'll let you know," she says with a knowing glare. "I want to be here with you."

"Me too."

"Can we get drunk now?" she asks with a playful smile.

I laugh. "Let's go."

And drunk she gets.

It's well after one a.m. when I carry Greer through the front door of her house and into her bedroom. Her covers are already pulled down, making it easy to lay her down. Her boots don't want to come off, but after wiggling them back and forth, I finally wrestle them off. I toss them in the corner before tucking her feet beneath the covers.

"I wanna my bra off," she slurs.

"Okay, sweetheart." She rolls over and I reach under her dress, trying like hell to ignore the softness of her body, the rough lace of her panties, and unsnap her bra. As I slide my hands out, she pushes her ass toward me, and it brushes against my palm. I groan on instinct. There are many things I would love to do to Greer. So many. But not until she's conscious and sober.

"Behave," I tell her, shaking off the lust.

"You no fun." She snort-giggles. She wiggles her bra straps through the sleeves and tosses it to the floor. I definitely don't notice it's black lace.

"I'm tons of fun. You have no idea the things I want to do with you, to you, but I don't want you to regret them."

A soft, dreamy look transforms her face.

"I won't. Not with you."

"Get some sleep, sweetheart." I bend down and place a kiss on her forehead. Her arms wrap around my neck, and she squeezes. After tucking the sheets around her body, I grab the trashcan from her bathroom and place it by her bedside table.

Tequila and Greer made good friends tonight, but I doubt they'll be friends tomorrow.

15

Greer

The room spins as early morning sunshine blinds me, my stomach pitches and rolls. Snuggling deeper under the covers, I scoot over to grab my cellphone off the bedside table. It's nine a.m. and gloriously quiet, save for the drum line currently beating the inside of my skull. With more effort than necessary, I roll over, greeted by Duke's big doe eyes staring back from where he's snuggled under the covers.

"You're not supposed to be up here, mister." He scoots closer and lays his head on my shoulder. "It's a good thing you're cute." I kiss his wet nose.

"I think so too." Luke's voice rumbles from my doorway.

"Go away," I mumble, pulling my duvet cover over my head. The bed dips as he leans over me. Luke's scent sneaks under the covers, and I readily welcome it.

"How are you feeling?"

"Like Don Julio and I might need to break up."

His low chuckle makes my toes curl. "Are you gonna come out of your cave today?"

I lower the covers and peek out. "Do I have to?" Luke takes the duvet cover from my grasp and folds it down. I'm sure I look terrible, so I give him a goofy smile.

Even though I'd never taken shots before, my unexpected run-in with Brian's old friends left me wanting to let loose. Loose being a relative term apparently as I went full send.

I've not spent much time anywhere except work, my house, therapy, and Ground Up this past year, so it shouldn't have surprised me to see people I know at a place we all used to go to. I'd been completely wrapped up in Luke that I hadn't seen Annie and the guys approaching. I wasn't ashamed to be there with Luke, not by a long shot, but I hadn't prepared myself for drunken, insensitive questions. Hence, my running away like my hair was on fire.

"How much did I embarrass myself last night?" I ask. Luke's hand rests near my hip. The warmth coming from his body is incredibly hard to resist. He's dressed in navy joggers and a gray T-shirt. Because, of course, he looks super handsome when I probably look a mess.

"You didn't embarrass yourself at all. In fact, I think everyone likes you more than they do me."

"Yeah?"

"Might have been your dabble in '90s rap."

"My what now?"

"Oh, yes." He chuckles, smoothing his hand across my stomach and over my hip. "You made sure to let everyone know it was 'Friday night and you feel just fine.' Pretty sure Vinnie might be in love with you now."

"Did I at least do the song justice?" I'd be mortified if I butchered a classic.

"Oh yeah, sweetheart. Big Joe requested your presence again next month. Said something about karaoke night too."

I groan, then make an escape to the bathroom. In the mirror, I take stock of the mess that is me while quickly brushing my teeth. Luke's waiting patiently by the side of the bed as I skip into the room and throw myself back under the covers. He nudges me over, urging me to scoot over. Before I know it, he's lying down beside me, his arm draped casually across my hip.

"Whatcha doing?" I ask. He's so close, his bodywash swirls around us, something reminiscent of bergamot. I sniff his neck, trying to put my finger on the other note of fragrance. His stubble tickles as I run my nose along the skin of his neck.

"Greer."

"Yeah?" I close my eyes.

"You're making this really difficult." His jaw clenches, the muscles flexing beneath me.

"Making what difficult?"

"Being a gentleman."

I trail my finger along the edge of his jaw and up his cheek bone. His eyelashes flutter shut. He sighs, surrendering to my touch. I love how weathered his skin is from spending endless hours in the sun. I love the little wrinkles around his eyes. I touch each one before tracing around his eye and down the tip of his nose. I note how perfect his lips are, smoothing my fingers over each one. He kisses my fingers, my eyes locking with his molten amber stare.

"What if I don't want you to be a gentleman?" I whisper. He squeezes my hip even harder and pulls me into him. My head rests naturally in the dip between his pecs. A warm and refreshing silence settles around us. I love that about Luke; he doesn't feel the need to fill each moment with unnecessary noise.

"I don't want to do anything you're not ready for." His breaths rustle the hairs on top of my head.

"Mmmm," I say, considering. I understand where he's coming from. It's something I worry about too—not being ready. With Brian, we'd come together in such a natural way. Even though he'd been my first, being ready was never a worry. We were young and wildly in love. Our love life had been passionate, something that made me feel powerful and sexy, loved and protected. I haven't felt like that since the morning of the accident.

It was early September, and we were headed out of town for a concert. We'd come together that morning in a slow, easy way. I can still recall his soft kisses, his hands on my body and in my hair, his whispered *I love yous*. It's almost as if he knew it would be our last time together. By that night, he was gone.

I look at Luke. "What if . . ." I hesitate, and his hand pauses its path up and down my arm. "I won't know I'm ready unless I try?"

"Is that what you want? To try?" His voice is low, threaded with a rich texture.

I run my fingers across his trim waist, his soft shirt sliding beneath my hand, and hug him tighter against me. Each of my curves and divots fit perfectly with his.

"Only with you." My eyes flutter shut. The cadence of his heartbeat, warmth of his body, and rhythm of his breathing lull me back to sleep.

I'm extremely warm and cozy when I come to an hour or so later. Luke is completely wrapped around me, our legs intertwined like vines. I like it here, tucked into the safety of his embrace. He breathes steadily even as I run my fingertips over his chest and down his muscled stomach. His shirt has ridden up, revealing a patch of tan skin. I trail my fingers along the soft expanse, the sparse hairs tickling my fingertips.

Continuing to absorb the feel of his skin, memories from last night churn through my mind. When I lost Brian, I wasn't sure when or if I was ever going to be ready to be with someone else. Alan's remarks echo in the back of my mind.

I saw Luke's worry on his face when I disappeared to the bathroom. I wasn't ashamed to be there with him, but Alan's words stung. How dare he pass judgment when he—they—don't know me anymore. It didn't take much for those three to exit my life after the funeral. Sutton let me rage about it in the bathroom, and it felt good. I know people will have their own opinions, but I refuse to let them define me. My life is my own, and no one will dictate how I live it.

"Greer?" I could get used to his sleep-heavy voice.

"I'm up." I prop my hands on his chest and study his handsome face. He leans up and kisses my forehead. My heart pitter-patters at how easily he shows me affection.

"Can I take you somewhere today?" Pulling me against his body, his rough palm drags along the bare skin on my thigh, renewing my inner strength.

"Yes."

"How long do you need?"

"Not long, and I'll need to take Duke out."

"Perfect. I'll take care of Duke and make breakfast while you shower." He winks, a playful smile on his lips. A grumble rolls out of me as he wiggles out from underneath me. "Get going, sweetheart. It'll make you feel like a whole new person." He smacks my ass and calls for Duke before heading out to the kitchen. My phone pings multiple times from the bedside table.

Sutton: I'm breaking up with Don Julio.

Me: Are you in my mind? I just said the same thing to Luke.

Sutton: Why's he got to do us dirty like this?

Sutton: Grabbing breakfast with Hunter.

You two want to join?

Me: Would love to, but Luke's got plans for us.

Sutton: I'm sure he does.

I toss my phone down, then strip down and trudge to the shower, not bothering to close the door all the way.

I use the counter to hold me up, and several minutes pass as steam fills the room. Warm water pelts the skin on my back when I step in the shower, a heavenly feeling on the sore muscles of my body. I think my body is past its pop, lock, and dropping stage. I lather my hair, massaging my fingertips into my scalp. Duke's claws clack on the tile as he saunters into the bathroom, curling up on the bath mat. I'm a little disappointed it's not Luke. I'd left the door cracked on purpose, hoping maybe he might make a move. I want him to know I meant what I said—I'm ready to try, and the door is open whenever he's ready to step through.

Bubbles cascade down my stomach and trace the contours of my muscled thighs, a sense of relief filling me.

"Greer?" Luke's voice echoes outside the bathroom door.

"You can come in." I close my eyes, saying a silent thank you that we're on the same page.

The atmosphere thickens the moment Luke enters on bare feet. He leans against the sink, arms crossed over his chest; his intense gaze burns. He's like a caged animal.

"You're so goddamn beautiful." The words hang in the steam-filled air.

With a shy smile, I turn, offering myself to his hungry gaze. Luke's eyes move achingly slowly, leaving a sizzling trail in their wake. My hands trace the heat, up and over my hips, lingering on my breasts, where my nipples are already tight. Desire pools low in my belly as he approaches the shower, placing his hands on the glass.

"Do that again." He growls. My hands obediently retrace the path. The air sparks with anticipation, and I'm on fire; his proximity alone is enough to ignite my senses.

"Is this okay with you?" he asks, his voice low. His eyes burn with an intensity I haven't experienced in so long.

A quick nod escapes me, but he smirks, demanding more. "I need to hear you say it, G." His words send shivers through my trembling body.

"It's more than okay." I breathe out.

"Thank god," he responds, his voice low, desperate. My thighs squeeze together, the heat of desire rising—its been so long since I've felt this way.

"Touch yourself," Luke commands, straining through the fabric of his pants. The request feels wanton and dirty, and I love it. He makes me feel powerful, sexy.

Ever so slowly, my hands traverse my stomach. One teasingly squeezes my nipple as the other slips down to my pussy. With one finger, I trace my clit. My body jolts from the contact. I'm panting as I slide my finger between my lips and back to my clit. Luke's eyes never look away. My entire body vibrates, surrendering to the desire pumping through my veins.

"You need this, don't you?" His eyes lock onto mine.

"Yes." My hand presses against the glass, mirroring his.

"Fuck, sweetheart, this is . . . You are incredible."

"You too," I gasp, my breathing erratic.

"Can I . . . ?" he gestures to the bulge in his joggers.

"Yes. Luke, it's okay. We said we would try. Please," I beg.

He pushes his pants over his hips with one hand.

"Oh my god," I moan, my fingers picking up their pace. Luke is long and thick, the tip glistening. He wraps his fist around his length, tugging roughly from stem to tip. "You're huge."

He chuckles, silently continuing his rough movements up and down his shaft. I'm so wet my fingers slip easily inside me.

"That's it, baby. Fuck yourself."

Not one to be told twice, I dip my finger back inside me, sliding in and out, my palm rubbing against my clit. I need more pressure, more fullness, so I add another finger. I thrust them in and out, faster and harder each time. Fire licks up the base of my spine, quickly spreading like wildfire as I chase my orgasm.

"I-I-I n-need to . . ." I stutter, breathless, my eyes fixed on him as he continues to pleasure himself.

"Me too," he says. "Let go. Let me see you fall apart."

Together, we climb, each chasing that mountaintop before crashing down the other side. My orgasm barrels through my body, my stomach clenching with the force of its intensity.

"Fuck," Luke moans as his orgasm overtakes him, ropes of come shooting onto the shower glass. With a few final pulls, he removes his hand from his cock, still thick and hard, and places it back on the glass. I mirror his actions, both of us leaning into the other, separated by glass.

"We're doing things a bit out of order, aren't we?" I tell him, a giant smile on my face. Luke's face flushes a deeper red, beads of sweat glisten on his temples.

"Yeah," he sighs. "Greer, that was . . . You are a goddess."

"Would you like to—" I gesture to the shower, welcoming him to join me.

"I would like to so goddamn much, but I also think maybe we should slow down."

"Always the gentleman." I push off the glass and back under the spray of the shower. It's lukewarm now, but the fire coursing through my body at my brazenness welcomes it. This is a new feeling, something Luke brings out of me. I bite my lip and give him a devilish grin.

"You little minx." He laughs out loud, pulling up his pants. A sad whimper escapes me when he tucks himself away. He's laughing and shaking his head as he grabs a towel to wipe away the remnants of his release. "Get dressed, sweetheart. Breakfast will be done soon, and then you're mine for the day."

"Promise?" I call after him when he steps into the hall.

"I am so fucked," I hear him say to himself.

I think we both are.

Turns out, being his for the day includes doing very mundane and Saturday-like chores. I kind of hoped he'd take me fishing today, but Luke said he needed to get some things done for work. First, we stop by his station, where I wait in the car, my newest romance novel calling my name, while he runs in to grab some materials. Luke's assisting with a junior firefighter program this week, so we spend a while at the high school setting up tables and various learning materials in the cafeteria. We chatter throughout the setup process, and I love hearing the passion for his profession in his voice.

He's a first-generation firefighter, and a program similar to this made him see he could easily make a career out of something he loved—helping people. Afterward, we grab a quick bite at a local sandwich shop before heading to Ms. Carol's house. She used to substitute at our school years ago and is one of our town's most beloved citizens.

"What are we doing at Ms. Carol's house?"

"Nothing much, just some odds and ends." He taps on the steering wheel.

"Why do you seem embarrassed?" I poke him in the ribs.

"It's no big deal. I'm used to Hunter giving me shit about doing this stuff all the time."

"Do you make it a habit helping the women of this town with *odds and ends*?" I can't help the giggle that escapes.

"Well,"—he laughs—"when you put it like that, it sounds sexual. Really, I just help out. If anyone needs something done, they typically call me."

"And Hunter doesn't like that?"

"Not exactly. He more or less thinks I'm sacrificing my time and energy in the service of others and forgetting about my time and energy."

Our conversation continues as he navigates the busy Saturday traffic. Fourth of July preparation is in full swing, so the streets are busy with volunteers adorning the town with Americana decor, excited for the upcoming festivities.

My thoughts stray as I faintly hear the ticking clock of time in the back of my heart, reminding me of another big date approaching—the anniversary of the accident.

Before summer began, I kept track of every single day I had to live without Brian—a silent form of torture I knew would one day add up to 365. But somewhere along the way this summer, I stopped counting. Relief and guilt surge through me. Relief that each day no longer feels like being dragged under by the undertow; guilt that maybe I'm starting to forget about Brian.

Luke smooths his hand over my thigh. Somehow, he must inherently know I need him to pull me back to the present. I give him a reassuring smile.

"And do you?" I continue. "Sacrifice your time for others?"

"I don't think so."

"But..."

He sighs. "I hate to disappoint anyone by saying no." He rubs the back of his neck, eyes frozen on the stoplight ahead.

"Disappoint people? Why would you think that?"

He rolls down his window, resting his arm casually on the windowsill. A welcoming breeze rustles my hair.

"I guess it's the people pleaser in me."

I reach across and caress his shoulder. "People will still like you even if you can't always be their helpful neighborhood fireman."

"You might be right. At least, in regard to you." I love the boyish smile he gives me as he presses the accelerator.

"I definitely like you for you and not for what you can do for me. Although, I really liked what you did for me earlier."

My stomach whooshes thinking back on our morning. First, sleeping in bed together, if only for an hour. It's been too long since I'd felt the warmth of someone beside me, months spent lost in the endlessness of the middle of the bed.

Then, the shower. *God.*

The images of Luke pleasuring himself, taking command of my body without even touching it, have been flashing through my mind at regular intervals. If I still cared what guilt was telling me, I'd be wallowing in shame and embarrassment, knowing we've mutually masturbated together before sharing a kiss. But to me, kissing is intense and incredibly intimate. Brian was my last kiss, and I know Luke's will be different. I'm more than okay with our order of things.

Luke eases up to Ms. Carol's house, puts the truck in park and turns to face me fully. "I wasn't sure if you meant it, you know?" he says. "But then I saw you left the bathroom door open, and I took that as a sign to *try*. Are you alright with what we did?" He captures my hands in his, dwarfing them.

"Most definitely." And I am. It felt thrilling and sexy and wonderful. There was no wave of shame afterward, only a subtle thrum of energy wondering what would be next. I know he would have stopped if I asked him; he's an incredibly patient man, almost painfully so.

"Because if it was too fast or not something you liked—"

"Luke, I know this is all new—for both of us. You, being with someone who's widowed and me, being with another man who isn't Brian for the first time. At first, I didn't think I could ever feel anything for anyone again. And yes, I still feel that soul-deep loss, those pangs of guilt that linger. I don't think they'll ever go away, to be honest. But I'd be lying to myself if I said I don't *feel* something for you—even if I'm not sure what that something is quite yet."

"I feel something for you too, G."

"I know you do, and that makes me feel so many things." I stare out the windshield.

"I sense a *but*."

I smile. "But I don't need you to treat me like something fragile. If I'm ever going to know you completely, and vice versa, we have to promise to be ourselves. We said we were going to try this, right? Take it one day at a time?"

"Greer, I don't want to hurt you or push into anything you're not ready for."

"Luke, there have been a lot of things this last year I wasn't ready for. A lot of firsts I had to go through, even if I raged against them. I promise, with these firsts, I'll tell you if I'm not ready. But how will I know unless I—*we*—try? I need you to stop holding back and making decisions for me about what you think I am or am not ready for."

"I suppose my sister was right," he deadpans.

I snort. "You get the communication talk as well?"

"Something like that." He laughs and turns off the engine. As he rounds the truck to open my door, his steps are lighter, like the weight of worry he inflicts on himself has been lifted.

"Ready to do this?" There's a playful glint in his eyes as he links our hands.

"Absolutely."

"Because the sooner we get this done, the sooner I get you back in my arms."

16

Luke

Greer: Good morning. Hope you have a great day <3
Me: Thx, sweetheart. How did you sleep?
Greer: Slept pretty okay.
Me: Just okay?
Greer: Better now that I'm talking to you.
Me: Good. Sorry work has been crazy.
Greer: Yeah, you have been gone a lot.
Me: I know. Between the teen academy and shift, it's a lot.

Greer: I miss you. Did you know that?
Me: Trust me, I miss you too. You're mine for the Fourth.
Greer: Just for the Fourth?
Me: I'd tell you that you'll be mine for always, but I'm not trying to jump the gun here.
Greer: **blushing emoji** Normally, I just go to my parents for the Fourth, but I'm sure it'll be fine.
Me: Perfect. We've all got the day off, so we're going to the lake.
Greer: Are you inviting me on an infamous lake outing?
Me: Not inviting. More like telling.
Greer: Bossy.
Me: Only for what I want.
Greer: Do you want to come over for dinner after work?
Me: Count me in. Just getting to the auditorium.
Me: I'll text you later.

It's been a great week working with local teens. We've done a lot of work educating them on the pros and cons of both professions as well as allowing them to practice many of the skills. Typically, I like busy weeks like this, but knowing Greer is waiting for me has been almost unbearable.

Grabbing my coffee and backpack, I push thoughts of Greer to the side and head across the parking lot. Adam is focused on his phone, most likely texting his wife. We've known each other since high school, but it wasn't until he and Vinnie joined the department that they became some of my best friends. When Adam married Grace, his high school sweetheart, it was the first time in my life I experienced true jealousy. Adam and Grace have what I've always wanted and searched for. Something I'm starting to picture with Greer.

"Hey, Cap," Adam says. "Ready for our last day?" He's already wiping sweat from his brow, so I know this is going to be a tough day.

"Yeah, let's go. I'm ready to be home for a few days."

"It gets easier."

"What does?" I question, holding the door open for him.

"Being away from the woman you love."

"I don't—"

"Sure you don't," he says, patting me on the shoulder. He passes through the door and disappears into the auditorium, leaving me staring blankly at the door.

By the time I pull into my driveway later that day, the setting sun is casting long shadows over the neighborhood. Greer's house is lit up from the inside. My chest tightens as excitement flows through my body. I love our text threads, but I'm ready to see those eyes, her smile, and that body in person. Throwing my truck in park, I head inside for a quick shower. I know she's waiting for me, but after the heat of today, a shower is in order.

Me: Just got home. Going to shower and be over.

Greer: See you soon. :)

The house is dark except for a subtle glow from my kitchen. As I take off my clothes, my eyes wander across the yard and through her bedroom window, wishing she'd be there. I shuck off my clothes and toss them into the hamper. Then I hop into the shower, the temperate water battling to cool my rising body temperature.

I let the water cascade over my body, allowing my muscles and mind to slowly unwind. My hand slides over my chest and down my stomach, the temptation to relieve tension overwhelming.

UNTIL THEN

I'm not expecting anything, seeing her tonight, but I wonder if I should prepare so I don't embarrass the hell out of myself.

We haven't seen each other since our date, but the sight of her body, wet and covered in soap, plays on a constant loop. She was completely at ease and so beautiful touching herself, never taking her eyes off me. Her hungry expression made me feel powerful and wanted. I had to resist taking her then.

She's mentioned before that she's only ever been with Brian, so it's not lost on me what an incredible gift that experience was—for her and me. Knowing she felt safe and trusted me enough to lose herself to the inferno between us. To allow me the opportunity to have these new firsts with her. I don't know how I got so lucky. I've spent my whole life searching for this feeling, searching for Greer. I'm never letting go.

She told me she sensed I was holding back, and my denial was ready and waiting, but I know she's right. I have been holding back. The last thing I want to do is rush her or hurt her. No more holding back though. I'm no longer capable. *Only with you.* Those three little words sealed my fate. Greer wants this *with me.* How am I to deny her—deny myself—the opportunity to try? She's confident in speaking what she wants and needs. I know we'll figure it out together.

In a few heartbeats, I'm standing at her door, nerves and anticipation storm inside me. The aroma of rich Italian spices assaults my senses, making my mouth water even before I slide open the back door. My stomach growls in response. Usually, on weeks like this, I forgo home-cooked meals and settle for something quick on the way home.

I tap on the glass, and Greer's face turns to me, motioning to come in. Duke's there as I open the door, nudging me with his cold nose before trudging back to his bed in the living room. The familiar warmth of her home surrounds me. I step into the kitchen and am pleasantly surprised by the new additions to her home—some pictures now fill once empty frames, soft music plays from her TV, and a worn copy of *Lord of the Rings* sits on the counter. My stomach tightens at the sight. Knowing she's reading a book simply because I said it was my favorite sets my soul on fire.

"Hey, you." She turns from where she's standing at the stove and offers me that sweet smile of hers. She steals my breath away with her hair knotted in a messy bun, a few tendrils framing her face, her bare feet sadly covered by fuzzy socks, and an oversized sweater stopping mid-thigh. I'm tempted to skip dinner and explore what she has on underneath.

"God, I'm so glad to see you." My steps eagerly cover the distance between us. I slide my hands around her waist as she turns into me, wrapping her arms around my shoulders.

"Me too." She softly kisses my neck.

"God," I groan, running my nose up the side of hers. "You always smell so damn good." Placing a kiss just below the corner of her jaw, she stutters an exhale. "Hmm, that's interesting."

"What is?" she asks.

"This spot"—I kiss her again—"right here." She tightens her arms around me, pressing her hips into mine. "You like that?"

"Mm-hmm." She moans, nodding into my shoulder.

My lips continue their exploration, placing gentle pecks along her jaw. She leans her head back, allowing me better access, never once letting go of me. My tongue sneaks out, licking at the skin beneath her chin before my lips close and suck.

"Oh god," she whispers. "My face . . ."

"What about your face?" I ask between kisses.

"I-I can't feel it."

"Do"—*kiss*—"you"—*kiss*—"want me"—*kiss*—"to stop?" She shakes her head back and forth. "Use your words, Greer," I whisper against the shell of her ear.

"Don't stop," she replies with a breathlessness to her words. I pull back to fully take her in. She's a flushed rose, chest heaving. Sliding my hands up, I cup her face and rest my thumbs near the corner of her mouth.

"Can I kiss you?"

Her blue eyes darken, like the ocean before a storm. They shimmer with desire, pulling me in. Her tongue peeks out and wets her lips. My eyes track the delicate movement. But she remains silent.

"Greer?" My voice is low as I bring my face closer to hers, leaving mere centimeters between us. The atmosphere crackles with anticipation for our unspoken desires lingering in the air.

Suddenly, she leans in and crashes her lips into mine.

My world tilts on its axis.

We remain like that, locked lip-to-lip, as our hearts beat wildly in sync and our bodies melt into each other.

A quiet moan escapes her, and my patience snaps. I press into her, capturing her lips fully between mine. They're soft and supple, with a subtle sugary taste. Lightning shoots down my spine. My hands are rough as they move down her body, gripping her hips and pulling her into me. There's no hiding how my body responds to this gorgeous woman.

Greer angles her head and traces my lips with her tongue. I meet it with my own. Soon, we're nothing but hands and quick breaths and moans as we lose ourselves to this kiss. To each other. She thrusts her hips into me again, my rigid cock pressing into her low stomach. I'd love nothing more than to lay her out over the counter behind me and feast on her for supper.

Slowing our kiss, I move my hands up her waist and coast them over the sides of her breasts before gripping around her neck. Her exhaling sigh is music to my ears. My thumbs trace her rosy cheeks. The room fills with the heady scent of desire. Time stands still.

"Wow." Her eyes remain closed as she leans her forehead against my lips.

"Wow is right." I place another kiss on her forehead. "Dinner smells great."

"The sauce!" she yells. She spins out of my arms and quickly steps over to stir a pot on the stove.

Leaning my head over her shoulder, I peek at what she has going on the stove. One pot holds a simmering spaghetti sauce, and another is filled with noodles. When I kiss the soft curvature of her neck, her whole body shivers.

"Interesting," I say.

"Yeah, yeah, mister. I'm sure you could kiss my entire body, and it would react that way."

"You think so?" I lean back against the kitchen island.

She looks over her shoulder, continuing to stir, that damn lip of hers sinking between her teeth. "Yes." She's calm and confident in her response, and the beast inside of me wants to be set free. To take her as mine.

"How was your day?" I pour a small amount of whiskey into two tumblers and hand her a glass.

"Oh, it was fine. Just worked on some stuff for my classroom, and I cooked"—she pans her arm around the kitchen—"a lot."

Now I notice what a mess her kitchen is. Every surface has a dirty bowl or utensil or various types of food waiting to be stored. I'm pretty sure I spy a pasta maker.

"Did you do all this for me?" Smiling is effortless when I'm around her.

She grins before taking a sip. "Would that be weird?"

"No, G, that wouldn't be weird at all." With measured steps, I approach, wanting to capture that luscious mouth of hers. One kiss wasn't enough. I want all of them.

"Uh-uh, you. Sit." She points from me to her dining table. "Dinner's almost ready, and I know you're hungry."

"Starved, actually," I say, but follow her stern orders and sit at the table.

"Well, I know that, but you can have me as dessert." There's a catch in her voice at her brazen admission. Silence descends upon the room. I push away from the table, crossing one leg over the other.

"Greer?"

"Yeah?" Her voice is soft as she plates our meal.

It dawns on me that maybe she's a bit more than embarrassed by what she blurted out. "No timeline, remember?"

Her shoulders visibly relax as she brings our plates to the table and takes a seat. The food looks and smells delicious. She mentioned loving to cook and bake, but I had no idea she could do all this. There's a slight tremble to her hands as she hands me a napkin that I place over my knee, and her breaths quicken. Before she can escape, I take her hand in mine.

"Breathe, Greer." It's getting easier to read her body and know when her anxiety is starting to take over. She follows my direction, taking a slow inhale and an even slower exhale. Greer told me she's always had trouble with anxiety, but it's been exacerbated since the accident, something I know she's worked with her therapist to navigate.

"No timeline," she repeats.

I nod my head, then dig into the food, contemplating everything that's happened in the last few moments. Her demeanor has shifted noticeably since her comment. I know I said I wouldn't hold back anymore, but I'm also determined to allow Greer to move at her own pace. Just because I might be ready for more doesn't mean she is.

"Want to tell me what happened?" I ask.

She looks at me from the corner of her eye, but says nothing, just continues to eat. Mom and Sutton are more forthcoming with their emotions and thoughts. Almost too much. Normally, Greer is the same way, rambling away and letting me know every thought. Dread snakes its way into my mind at her sudden silence.

"Do you regret it?" I ask.

"What? No!" she says. "No, it's not that at all."

"Then, what is it? Talk to me."

"That was our first kiss."

"It was. I'm sorry if it was too soon."

"Luke, it wasn't too soon. I-I wanted it. It was . . ."

I reach across the table and rest my hand on her forearm, giving her a steadying presence as she processes whatever thoughts are running through her mind. She covers my hand with hers. "It was perfect."

My heart soars. As first kisses go, this one was pure magic.

"But," I prompt, knowing that's not all.

"It's just . . . about what I said after. Everything with you feels so right and natural that I almost forget." As she looks down at her plate, I'm unsure if shame or shyness is pouring from her.

"Forget Brian?"

"Yes. What I said to you? About a-about . . ." Her chest rises with a deep breath as her eyes meet mine with unshed tears.

"Having you for dessert? Yes, I recall." I smirk, trying to lighten the mood.

"Yes, about me for dessert. As soon as it flew out of my mouth, I remembered the time I said the same thing to Brian."

"I see." My heart constricts. I knew this was something we might have to tackle—her experiencing moments that feel similar to ones she experienced with him—but I secretly hoped we never would.

"I'm sorry," she says.

"Why?" I push my chair closer to hers and place my arm along the back of her chair. "You have a long history with Brian. A happy one."

"I know," she whispers.

"Unlike many of us with past relationships who'd rather forget every moment we spent with them, you'll probably never want to forget all the special moments you had with Brian."

"God, when you say it like that, I feel horrible."

"Why feel horrible? It's the truth. And I never want you to forget your life with Brian. But I do wonder . . ."

"Wonder what?" She buries her face in her hands.

I raise her eyes to mine. "Do you have room in your head and heart for new experiences with me? Maybe some that feel similar to ones you've already had but are now with someone new? Because I can't promise I won't say or do something that

Brian did, or that you might not say or do something you did with him. It just is what it is."

Her forehead smooths as she contemplates what I've said. The warmth of her home cocoons us. With steady hands, I frame her face, confusion swimming in her beautiful eyes.

"I know I have room," she says at last, her voice resolute.

"Yeah?"

"I guess it's just something I didn't consider, you know? Sure, moving forward with my life is one thing, but the memories of Brian will never leave. And as much as I think I can control when those decide to pop into my mind, I can't. It makes me feel so guilty."

"Guilty?" I lean back. "Why do you feel guilty?"

"Because I don't want you worrying that every time I'm with you I'm thinking of him."

Greer once told me she hated small talk and that she'd rather get to the heart of things instead of sitting in it and stewing. She's so unlike any woman I've ever been with; none of them could have an open and honest conversation to save their life.

"Sweetheart, I don't expect you to bury down everything you experienced with Brian. Right now, yeah, sometimes I do think about whether you think of him or me. He was your last, and I'm your next. We're in uncharted waters."

"I wasn't thinking of him." Her hands cover mine.

"No?" The memory of her closing the distance, sealing her lips with mine flashes in my mind.

She shakes her head from side to side. "It was just us, and, god, when our lips met, it felt like I was floating among the stars. It felt almost like my lips already knew yours. Which is crazy because it was our first—"

I lean forward and seal my mouth over hers. Little did I know, those were the exact words my heart needed to hear. Her hands slip from atop mine and settle alongside my jaw. Angling my head, I coax her mouth open, her tongue gently brushing mine before I capture it wholly.

I pull her bottom lip between my teeth, and her moan fills the quietness of the room. Greer pushes her body toward me, leaning out of her chair completely. I grasp her hips and pull her to me. Sliding the chair back, she straddles me and lowers onto my lap.

"Oh." She groans. Every time she grinds against me, the line between control and surrender blurs.

I pull her closer, my hands slipping under her sweater to caress the warm, silken skin of her lower back. Goosebumps rise beneath my touch, and she deliberately rocks her hips, drawing a ragged breath from me. Our mouths stay locked, tasting, devouring—lost in the intoxicating pull of each other.

"Greer?" I breathe into her neck, kissing along her jaw, biting at the skin at the curve of her neck.

She huffs a breath. "Yes?" Her hands slide into my hair and tug the strands.

She lowers her mouth to mine once again, plunging her tongue into my eager mouth. When she rocks her hips over me, I groan, straining against my joggers and struggling like hell to keep my composure.

"Fuck, you feel so good."

"So do you." She's breathless.

I pull her to me, grip her thighs, stand, and carry her to the couch. I settle into it as Greer adjusts her legs, resting them on either side of my hips.

"Is this okay?" I ask.

She nods with flushed cheeks and molten eyes. The bun atop her head wobbles as I run my hands up the back of her head. I reach up and pull the band out. Gorgeous locks of sandy-blonde hair tumble down her back.

"Words, G. I need your words."

"I'm better than okay."

I cover her mouth with my own. She sucks my lower lip between her teeth, and my hips rise up from the couch. Our bodies meld to one another. I'm greedy with my movements as I knead and grab her thick thighs before sliding under her sweatshirt. Her warm skin begs for my touch. I pull her into me.

"Oh, god." She moans against my neck, continuing to rock her hips over me. She licks my skin and kisses me. I surrender control as she covers my neck with closed-mouth kisses before capturing my earlobe between her teeth.

"Shit," I hiss as my hands crawl up the soft expanse of her back. Desire buzzes within me.

"Can you . . ." She rocks into me, capturing my mouth again.

"Can I, what?" I groan.

"Take it off."

My core ignites as I process what she's said. Sitting back, I pull her face to mine, forcing her to focus on me.

"What's on your mind?"

"You."

My fingers trace along her skin, trembling slightly as I grasp the hem of her sweater. Desire overwhelms me as I lift it. Inch by glorious inch, her skin is revealed. Greer's arms rise, unhurried, her trust in me evident. When the sweater finally falls away, and her bare breasts are revealed, the primal animal inside me roars, as though every part of me recognizes her as mine.

"Fuck me. You are extraordinary."

Greer doesn't rush to cover herself. She sits there, weight fully pressed into me, and allows me to take her in. Her breasts are heavy with gorgeous blush-colored nipples, peaked with need. Her waist nips in at the sides, but it's her soft lower tummy that has me going feral. Without thought, my hand traces the scars on the left side of her abdomen. Our eyes connect. She covers my hand with hers. I'd give anything to go back in time and take away the pain she endured, but I know it's that pain that formed the resilient and powerful woman currently bringing me to my knees. I've never seen someone as extraordinary as her.

"I need you," I say. "Can I?" I lean closer to her chest, already imagining how soft and luscious her breasts will feel.

She nods her head, the subtle motion drawing my eyes to the gentle rise and fall of her chest, each breath a silent invitation that sets my blood on fire.

"Sweetheart, you know what I need."

"I need you too." She kisses my mouth.

Slowly, I slide my hands over her skin and up her ribs, grazing the lower curve of her breasts. Covering them with a firm grip, my fingers brush over her nipples. She groans at the contact and rocks into me. I repeat the motion before leaning forward to capture one in my mouth. I flick my tongue against her hardened bud, tugging gently.

"Oh, god." She breathes out.

"Does that feel good?" I switch to capture her other nipple.

She moans in response. Another sound I love to hear from this woman. Her skin warms as I kiss between her breasts. I cover her luscious mouth with mine. She presses her pussy farther down onto my cock and whimpers. My briefs are already damp from pre-come. This woman is making it extremely hard not to take exactly what I want. I can't help but wonder if maybe it's what she needs?

Greer continues grinding against me as my hands move around to caress the expanse of her back. She presses her breasts against my chest, and I feel her stomach tremble, her motions becoming more erratic.

"That's it, sweetheart," I encourage between kisses. "Ride me. Take what you need."

"I-I..."

"You what?"

"Numb. Everything is numb."

"Is your pussy numb?"

"N-no." Every inch of her flushes.

"Good, then let go. Let me see you come."

Her hips slow down, but I grip them firmly and press myself into her center.

"Feel that?"

She nods.

"This is what you do to me. Don't think, G, just feel. Just be here. With me."

She answers with a body roll that makes my blood boil. It's easy to feel the heat from her center through our few thin layers of clothes. I'm not sure what I want more, to touch her there or watch her ride me and take what she needs from me.

She rolls into me, pushing her breasts toward my face. I smile and take them in my hands again—squeezing, licking, biting, and sucking each nipple. Greer's rhythm increases as does her pressure. Every time she brushes against me, I feel my control completely disappearing.

"Fuck, baby. You're going to make me come." I groan against her chest. I'm losing it.

"Please." She sighs. "Come with me."

We're nothing but hands, moans, kisses, licks, and bites as she rides me. My mind is blissfully clear. The only thing I see, hear, or think of is Greer, this beautiful woman finding contentment and pleasure in me.

No longer in control of my own body, my orgasm roars down my spine, my limbs tingling as I try to hold on. My woman always comes before me, but I'm barely hanging on.

Greer places one hand on my shoulder as she takes the other to caress her body from thigh to stomach to breasts. She pinches her nipple, moaning at her own rough touch. That's what does me in. What little control I have evaporates, and my orgasm tumbles through me. My cock jerks as I blow my load in my pants like a teenage boy.

Greer's eyes lock with mine and she smiles. *Little minx.*

"Nipples," she pants. "Please."

I lean forward and capture one in my mouth. I suck hard, pulling each peak, giving her the suction and pressure she needs as she rides me. She starts to lift her hips off me, but I grip them and pull her down onto me.

"Come for me."

A few seconds more, Greer detonates, grinding against me. Her thighs tighten around my hips, her stomach trembling as she gasps for breath.

"Oh god," she moans, her hips slowing their rhythmic rolling before coming to a stop.

"Watching you"—I kiss her softly, savoring this moment I know I'll never forget—"was like witnessing a supernova."

"Did you . . . ?" She looks away.

She dry humps me to orgasm and *now* she's fucking shy? "Did I what?" I raise my eyebrows. "Words, G." I'm daring her to step into her sexuality.

"Did you come?"

"Sweetheart,"—I laugh—"I never come before a woman, let alone in my pants. But with you? I couldn't hold back."

She looks down at the mess I've made, and a sly grin takes over her face. "That's so sexy."

"Yeah?" Most women don't like a man who can't last, and she thinks it's sexy? What will she think when I have her laid out every which way for hours?

"Yes." She kisses the side of my mouth. "To know you were just as turned on as I was. That we were experiencing the same thing."

"I was lost to you." She relaxes, her body heavy, and cuddles into my chest. I trail my fingers up and down her back until her breathing evens out. "Granted, I don't plan on making coming in my pants or before you a regular thing."

Several minutes pass before she stands in front of me, her sweatshirt discarded on the floor. With a dreamy look on her face, she runs her hands up her waist and squeezes her breasts. Her nipples are still hard, and I do my best to quell the hunger for more roiling inside me.

"Well,"—she begins, reaching for her discarded sweatshirt—"should we clean up dinner now?" She pulls it over her head, mussing her hair even more than my hands did.

"I'd love to, but"—I gesture to my ruined joggers—"I should probably go clean up and change."

Greer presses her palms to her cheeks, a weak attempt at soothing the permanent blush. "Probably," she says, biting that damn lip.

"Little minx." I stand before her and adjust my half-hard cock. Desire is thick in the air as she walks me to the back door.

"Thank you," I say as she slides the door open.

"For what?"

"For giving me these firsts."

I kiss the corner of her mouth.

A brief moment passes before she says, "Good night, Luke."

Her lazy, satiated smile is the last thing I see before she lets the curtains drop into place.

17

Greer

I ROLL OVER IN bed, tossing the covers aside, trying to cool my body. It's been a few days since Luke kissed me—or, more accurately, since I kissed him—and I still haven't returned to earth. Every time I close my eyes, I'm right back in the moment—his lips claiming mine, his hands exploring my body, leaving me breathless.

The memory of us together flits in and out of my mind on a near-constant basis. Even now, as my hands lazily caress my body, the urge to touch myself to thoughts of him, to us together is almost unbearable. Just thinking about his hands and his mouth on my body makes me jittery. Duke nudges my elbow, a clear indication he doesn't care what my body needs.

"Okay, old man, let's go."

When Luke asked to kiss me, I froze, my mind spinning through every possible scenario. But when my lips met his, it was like breathing for the first time after being underwater. There was no hesitation, no guilt—just want. Just need.

Then, my stupid brain had to go and ruin it.

Or so I thought.

Looking back, I know that memory surfaced exactly when it was meant to—not to allow shame or guilt a chance to get its claws into me, but to bring awareness to everything stirring in my mind. I've been so focused on forging ahead, and things with Luke have felt so wonderful. Maybe I didn't want grief to poke holes in that happiness. But now, I know I need to allow my head and heart catch up to each other.

I step onto my patio, and Duke takes off in the yard, ears flapping and tail wagging as he completes a few laps. I'm too tired to wait for him, so I head back inside to get coffee brewing. I look around, reliving it all again: our kiss, his hands, that dirty mouth of his.

"G'morning," a rough voice pulls me from my reverie. Luke steps into my kitchen, a boyish smile playing across his face when I don't startle at all. I've gotten used to him showing up out of nowhere or just walking right in and making himself at home. He eats up the space between us, wraps his arms around my waist, and pulls me into him. I relax into his embrace, happy to be in his arms again.

"Hey, you." I bury my face in the crook of his shoulder.

He's freshly showered after coming off shift—his skin smelling like his body wash. The way I've missed and longed for this man over the last several days is incredible. I don't know if I'll ever get used to his shift work.

"I missed you." His breaths whisper through my hair.

"Me too. So much." I pull away, my eyes immediately going to his mouth, and I consider kissing him but place a gentle peck on his cheek instead.

"None of that."

"Of what?"

"No playing shy now. The other night was fucking amazing."

"Yeah?" I sigh in relief, pulling him closer so I can wrap my arms around his neck.

"Absolutely. Do you regret it?"

"No,"—I bring his eyes to mine—"I don't regret a single moment. It was everything I could have hoped it'd be."

It breaks my heart a little that he worries I might regret what happened between us. I've never been an impulsive person and tend to overthink every single situation, but that night, with him, I'd do it exactly the same way every time.

"Luke, you've been incredibly patient with me, and I'm not sure how you're processing all of this, but just so you know, I haven't stopped thinking about the other night. And you're right, it was fucking amazing."

Unable to resist, I lean up and capture his lips with my own. His breath is minty, and I try to pull away to save him from my morning breath. Luke isn't having any of that, though, and pulls me flush against his hard body.

"Thank you," he says, placing kisses down my neck. "I didn't know I needed to hear that until just now. I just want to make sure you're not doing anything because of me." His lips are soft against mine. Patient. Needy. "Is that coffee I smell?"

Nodding my head, I pull away and make us each a cup. Duke has come back inside and is currently following me around the kitchen.

"Have you decided your plans for the Fourth?" Luke asks.

"Actually, I talked to my parents, and they were pretty excited that I want to go to the lake. They said they're available this weekend though. Are you on shift?"

"Nope."

"Would you like to come with me?" I hesitate before bringing my gaze to him. Who knows, maybe it's too fast. I've gone back and forth, but now I know introducing Luke to my parents is the next step forward I want to take.

He's busy filling Duke's bowl with food, but finally says, "You'd want that?"

"I do." I hand him the steaming mug. "Is that weird? I don't know, maybe it's too soon?"

"Sweetheart, nothing is weird if it's what we want. Let me remind you again—we are on no timeline."

"Is that a yes?"

"Hell yes, it is. You know, I've already met your parents a few times when they've been leaving your place."

"Not officially."

"Officially?" he questions with a grin and a raise of his dark eyebrows.

"Yeah, as my . . ." My stomach jumps into my throat. I suppose it is a little presumptuous of me to assume we're something *more*. Maybe he doesn't feel the same?

"Greer Ashbury, are you asking if we're official?" He sets his coffee cup down before gripping my hips.

"Oh, geez." I bury my face in his chest. "This is so stupid."

"It's not stupid. Nothing with you will ever be stupid."

"I'm trying to let my head and heart catch up to each other, but, Luke, this feels natural. It's starting to feel like maybe I was meant to find you."

"I know, Greer." He tilts my chin, forcing me to look at him. "It does for me too."

"Yeah?" Hope blossoms in my chest.

"Yes. I'm not sure how I got so damn lucky to have you move in next door, but, Greer, you are all I see. All I want. I don't want or need anyone but you."

I lean up on my tiptoes and kiss him. With each minute I spend with him, I'm realizing just how important Luke is to me. I never anticipated finding someone I'd want to pursue a relationship with, and maybe I should worry more about the timing of things, but all I can think about or see is Luke.

"I've officially been replaced," I say as I look out the front window blinds.

Over the last several days and even more on the drive over, I tried envisioning what my parents' reaction to Luke and me being official would be. Would they grill him like he was interviewing for a job with the FBI? Would they make it awkward by comparing everything Luke did to Brian? Would they cry and change their minds and tell me it was too soon and they couldn't imagine me with anyone else except Brian?

None of that happened. In fact, they welcomed him with open arms and hammed it up like they had known him their whole lives. Mom fawned over his being a fireman ("Oh, I just love a man in uniform") and swooned when she realized he was Sutton's big brother ("Well, ain't that something"). Dad, on the other hand, practically leaped for joy when Luke asked about the Ford he saw parked in the garage. They've been out there ever since, tinkering away and yammering on. I can't help but peek at them through the slats in the blinds.

"Greer, sweetie, your daddy would never replace you."

"Mama, look at these two." I point out the window. They're now on sliders under the damn truck. "Daddy never lets me or Gemma go under the truck with him."

She looks out the window, and presses her hand to the center of her chest. "My goodness, Luke sure has made quite an impression with your daddy."

I grumble to myself before plopping onto their soft leather couch. Tucking my knees under me, I grab the closest novel. A book about a serial killer should help me get over whatever *this* feeling is, right? I should be happy my parents adore Luke.

"You okay over there, Grumpy Gus?" Mom's haphazardly folding a large pile laundry.

"I'm not grumpy."

"Want to tell me why you've got that look on your face?"

"You and Daddy have nothing to say? Nothing at all?"

She stacks some towels. Luke's and Dad's voices trickle in through the open windows and my heart cracks just a little.

"Is there something in particular you want us to say?"

"Well, no." I toss the book on the table. "I don't know."

"Greer," she says, sitting beside me and placing her hand on my knee. "Your daddy and I always knew you would one day meet someone new."

"You did?"

She smiles, nodding her head yes. "Of course we knew. You have the biggest heart. We know losing Brian was horrific for you, but we've always known you'd eventually allow your heart to mend and let someone into your life again."

"But what is up with Daddy? He and Brian were never chummy like this?" I cringe at the petulance in my voice.

"Don't," she says firmly. "That is not fair to Brian or Luke or anyone else. You cannot compare what is now to what was then. Your daddy and Brian always respected one another. We adored him tremendously. Don't go turning this into a game of comparisons."

Comparison? Is that what I'm doing? Shame slithers down my spine, and I sink into the couch knowing she's spot on. So, this is what jealousy feels like.

"God, what is wrong with me?" I bury my face in the arm of the couch.

"Nothing at all. You're just learning to navigate this new life is all. Give yourself some grace."

I flop my head back before confessing. "I kissed him."

"And how did that go?" she asks, eyes as bright as megawatt lightbulbs.

I peek at her from hooded lids, trying to contain my smile. "It went . . . better than expected," I say, letting the words hang in the air, teasing her curiosity.

"Oh, don't you hold out on me, Greer Ashbury!"

"It was magic."

She releases a sigh that makes my heart pitter-patter as I recall *everything* we did.

"Did you make love?"

"No, we didn't. Luke is so patient and gentle with my heart and my body." It might be strange to some people, but my mom and I have always been close and have always talked about sex openly. Not that we relay the nitty-gritty details to one another on a constant basis.

"What's that look for?" I ask. Mom's cheeks are tomato-red.

"No look." She curls her mouth to the side, giggling a tad.

"Uh-huh, sure, Mama. You've always been a shit liar."

"Just happy and excited for you is all. Finding love is hard, and not everyone gets to experience it. You found it with Brian, and it was a great love. Now, you have the opportunity to discover it again with Luke."

"No one's talking about love, Mama." Shaking my head, I stand to gather my things. Only she could jump about ten guns ahead of the gate.

"Just remember what I told you; stop the comparisons. What happens between you and Luke needs to be for and about the two of you. Okay?"

"I know. I know. I've got enough room in my head and heart, even if I don't always say the right things." I give her a quick kiss on the cheek, then I gather our things and head out front to retrieve Luke.

I pause a moment before heading outside, trying to steady the rush of thoughts swirling in my mind. There's something different about how Luke makes me feel—like I'm no longer just holding onto memories, but starting to build something new. Sure, the uncertainty is still there, but it feels lighter now, like the weight of grief is lifting just enough for me to glimpse a new future. It's as if the light is slowly finding its way into the darkness I've been living in since the accident.

As we pull out of my parents' neighborhood, the streets buzzing with cars and people rushing this way and that for the holiday. Luke's hand rests on my bare thigh, grounding me in the moment. I never imagined myself moving on, but the way he's looking at me now, with that soft smile? I know stepping into this new chapter with him is exactly what I want.

18

"**G**REER?" HUNTER HOLLERS FROM behind the wheel of his red and white boat.

I jolt, having been too focused on people watching. I've never been to the lake on a holiday before, so the amount of people is insane. I'm pretty sure most of the town is here. There are groups set up on the shore, boats tied together, and all sorts of shenanigans happening.

"Hunter," Sutton says from where she's laid out across the bench seats, "there's no need to yell at the woman." Hunter shrugs and raises his bottle of water while maneuvering us near a shady cove.

"Yes, Hunter?" I tuck my beach bag underneath before wrangling my hair into my ball cap.

"You gonna try the wakeboard today?"

Sutton shoots up from her sun tanning position, eyes darting straight to me. "Oh my gosh, Greer, it's so much fun."

"Um, I've never actually done it before."

"It's pretty easy to learn," Grace says, reapplying sunscreen to Adam's shoulders. "Sutton is really good. Just copy Sutton."

"Navy, you gonna try too?" Vinnie inquires, bumping her leg with his.

"Sure," she mumbles around a mouthful of chips. Her face is barely visible beneath her giant sun hat, and it's clear she cares more about the snacks than anything else.

"We can walk you through it," Luke says from his spot near the back of the boat. He drags a coiled rope out of a storage bench and removes the board from its holder. A giant inner tube sits nearby waiting to be inflated. Sunlight glistens off his broad shoulders, his muscles stretching and flexing with each movement. His board shorts sit low on his hips, showcasing a slightly tapered *v*, hair covering his chest and stomach. I always thought I didn't like chest hair, but on Luke?

"Focus, babe." He winks.

"Yeah, G. Save the ogling until later." Hunter laughs. Sutton elbows him in the ribs as she joins them. "Ow, babe, you forget how sharp your damn elbows are."

"I'm not your babe," she says.

"Not yet," he replies.

"You—oh, never mind," Sutton says. "We all set, Luke?"

"Yep," Luke says, handing me a yellow life jacket.

The boat bobs up and down, putting me off-balance as I rise from the bench seat and take the life jacket. My sundress catches in the buckles making me pause. Buzzing fills my ear as I take in everyone's confidence in their swimsuits. I've never been ashamed of my body. No matter how it's changed over the course of my life, I've found beauty in it. Even my scars don't bother me as much anymore, but I'm also careful of who sees them. When people see them, it opens the door for questions, and questions lead to memories. I've tried my best to keep that door closed.

Luke wraps his arm around my hip, and I look up to his face. "It's just us," he says quietly.

He places a soft kiss on my temple before tossing the rope into the water. I straighten my spine. He's right. It's just us. A cool breeze ruffles the hem as I pull it over my head, revealing my Americana-themed swimsuit, red bottoms and a blue top with white stars.

"Hot damn," Navy catcalls. "Who knew you had all *that* under *there.*"

"Oh, shut up, Navy," I say.

"I mean it, G, you're a smokeshow." She shoves another handful of chips into her mouth.

"Agreed," everyone says in unison. I'm sure my cheeks now match my bottoms.

I don't miss the way everyone's eyes dart to my scars. My hands move to cover the ones on my stomach. Luke's warmth surrounds me from behind as his hands slide around my waist, pulling me close. His presence is a quiet comfort, and the reassurance of his touch settles the tension in my body.

"Nah, none of that, G," Hunter says, shaking his head. "We're family here. Invisible or not, your scars are part of the reason why we love you." He pulls me from Luke's arms and into a giant bear hug.

Over Hunter's shoulder, Sutton's face softens as she reaches for Navy's hand. Their matching smiles send a wave of strength through me. Never in my life could I have predicted Life would shatter my world by taking someone I loved with all my heart, only to rebuild it with six people who might love me just as fiercely.

"Are we ready to ride?" Sutton blurts. She pulls me from Hunter, her fingers dancing over his arm, as she leads me to the back of the boat. She side-eyes me, daring me to ask what's going on between her and Hunter. I don't get the chance before she and Luke launch into their mini lesson on wakeboarding.

"Engage your core, keep your legs beneath you, eyes up," Sutton instructs.

Seems easy enough.

"Hunter will go slowly at first," Luke says, "so you can get your legs under you, but it's easier if you go faster. Okay?" Luke's eyes meet mine expectantly as he removes my ball cap and sunglasses.

"What if my leg can't handle it?" I whisper. It took months of rehab to heal my leg and months more to gain back its strength. A spin bike is one thing; wakeboarding is a whole other level.

"Then, you say something, silly," Sutton answers. "Just keep a bend in your legs and use those delicious thighs you have there. I promise you'll be fine."

Sitting on my butt, I slide to the edge of the swim platform. Luke snaps the bindings on my boots, and I wade into the lake.

The cool water surrounds me as I float out behind the boat, the rope's rough texture anchoring me while the extra rests atop of the water.

"You ready, G?" Hunter calls.

I inhale deeply before shouting back, "As I'll ever be."

The rope goes taut, and the board plunges beneath water. My heart slams against my ribs. I'm not looking to die out here.

"Don't worry!" Sutton shouts. "You'll get on top soon enough. Brace your core, and as the boat goes faster, you'll feel the board come to the top."

A few seconds later, the board starts to surface, and I attempt to stand up but plop right back into the water. Cool water splashes over me, dousing me completely. When I shake the water from my face, those nervous tingles still, transforming into determination.

Hunter slows the boat, and I grab the rope. It pulls forward. I can barely hear Luke's voice above the boat's engine reminding me to brace my core and squat down. It takes more effort, but soon enough, I've got myself up on the board and on top of the glittering water.

"Yes!" Navy shouts, flinging the bag of chips at Vinnie.

"Way to go, G!" Sutton yells. "Ready to go faster?"

I nod, too afraid talking will cause me to lose focus. The boat pulls ahead quicker now. At first, it's bumpy as hell gliding over the wake, but I remind myself to engage my core and thighs.

"Can we go faster?" I call out. Luke smiles.

The board moves from side to side over the waves. Wind whips through my hair, and water sprays my legs and my face as the speed increases. We might be going at a snail's pace, but to me, I was flying. My heart soars out of my chest as every thought or worry evaporates from my mind. I'm free. I should have known that nature would knock me down a peg or two.

When the boat eases to the left, I don't see how big the wake is and suddenly, I'm bouncing uncontrollably. My whole body shakes, and I think I hear Luke shouting to drop the handle. I let go, and the rope jerks forward, splashing into the water. I immediately start to sink, my body tilting backward until my butt hits the water. It envelops me, and all I can picture is sinking toward the bottom of the lake.

Thankfully, because my feet are still connected to the board and my life jacket, I don't sink like a rock. My lungs heave for oxygen as I lie back, spreading my arms out like an angel. The sun's rays beam onto my face, blinding me. Covering my eyes with my arm, the boat's engine roars in the distance. Straining my neck, I lift up to see Hunter has pulled around to retrieve me. The minuscule amount of fear I had diffuses into the lake, every cell in my body invigorated. I did something new and scary, and I'm alright.

Luke dives into the water before the boat even stops and charges toward me. When his head pops above the water, there's fear in his eyes.

"Shit, are you okay?" He's doggy paddling toward me.

"Oh my god, that was awesome!" I say. Laughter and joy burst from every pore.

Luke finally reaches me and places his hand around my ankles to pop the bindings. With one hand on the board, he wraps his other around my waist, my legs naturally encircling his waist.

"You scared the hell out of me," he says.

"Did you see me? God, that was awesome! I was flying!"

"Yeah, sweetheart, you were. But are you okay?"

"Of course I am. Why wouldn't I be?"

"Most people get pretty wrecked the first time they bail on a board."

"I'm not most people, now am I?" My cheeks hurt from smiling so hard. He pulls me in and crashes his lips into mine. They're cold and wet from the water, but within seconds I'm warm all over.

"No, you're not most people," he says against the side of my neck. "Let's get you back to the boat."

We paddle back, and Vinnie helps me onto the platform. Everyone congratulates me and checks for injuries.

"Y'all can stop mothering me now!" Irritation washes through me. "I told you I was fine. Now, who's up next?"

The rest of the afternoon rushes by as we take turns on the board and inner tube, even Navy. She might have hollered at Hunter half the time for going "too goddamn fast," but her goofy-ass smile told a different story.

"See you at Luke's!" Sutton says. "We'll talk about the listing, okay?" She gives me a quick hug. She smells like coconuts and sunshine.

"Yes, of course," I say.

"Good. Love you, G!"

Stunned, I shout back, "Love you!" but she's already closed the door. I've never said that to a friend before, but in that moment, it felt *right.*

We're sun-kissed and exhausted as we drive home. Luke's hand rests over mine, and I can feel every part of me relax. I can't remember the last time my body felt this quiet. For months, I've been telling everyone I'm fine, but this is the first time I actually feel it.

Sutton has been a godsend, helping me list the house. What once felt like an impossible task is now something I look forward to. It's time for my old house, one full of fond memories, to become part of another family's story.

Luke's thumb moves back and forth over my skin, and I sink into the comfort of his touch. I once thought it would be impossible to fall for someone new, but then this man came into my life. And now? It feels inevitable.

The accident and Brian's death took so much from me, but reclaiming the fragments of myself I thought I'd lost feels good. It feels right.

"I wakeboarded today, Brian. Can you believe that? Me." I run the loofa over my body, washing off loads of sunscreen and lake water. Excitement swirls through my body. "You'd love my new friends. Did I tell you I questioned Sutton when she first invited me for coffee? I bet that doesn't surprise you. I've always struggled with friends. Well, not anymore." I grab a towel and pat my body dry. "Navy and Sutton are the best, and I think they really do love me. I mean, I'm not sure Navy is the type to say I love you, but maybe we can change that."

"Who ya talking to, sweetheart?" Luke says, tapping on the bathroom door.

"You can come in," I call out, wrapping a towel around my body.

"Well, damn. I'm too late." I love his grin as he tugs me by my towel and plants a loud kiss on my cheek. "So, who were you talking to?"

"Oh . . ." I say, busying myself with brushing my hair. "Just Brian." My cheeks flush. I've never been caught by anyone but my parents talking to Brian.

Luke steps back and leans against the wall, his arms now crossed over his chest. At first, he doesn't say anything. Embarrassment flares in my chest. I know I'm not doing anything bad, but I'm not sure how Luke will feel learning I *talk* to Brian. It's too quiet. I wish he'd say something.

He catches my eyes in the mirror. "You still talk to him?"

"Yes, sometimes," I confess.

"Why?"

"At first it was because I was sad and lonely. I didn't know how nor did I even want to do life without Brian. Talking to him made it easier in a way. Made me feel less alone."

Luke nods his head up and down. "And now?"

"Brian was always the person I told everything to. Now, I'm not sure. I guess it's just second nature. Are you mad?"

Luke erases the distance between us, pushing me against the counter. He brackets his arms on either side of me before kissing my forehead.

"Would it sound crazy if I said I was jealous?" Luke's gaze is thoughtful, intense.

"Jealous? Why?"

"Because I want to be the one you tell everything to." He raises one shoulder. "I know, it's crazy to be jealous of a dead guy, but here we are."

"It's not crazy." Smiling, I lean forward and place a tender kiss on his lips. "And you will be. Someday."

"God." He groans and buries his face in the crook of my shoulder. Warm hands press against my back, holding me tight. "I keep telling you we're not on any timeline, and, here I am, giving you one."

"It was an honest question and an honest reaction. You're not giving me a timeline."

"Maybe not, but sometimes I forget you might not be as ready for change as I am. That you need time."

"And that's why we communicate." I grin, escaping his arms, and walk to my closet. I drop my towel, slipping on a bra and haphazardly pulling a sundress over my head. Luke is still near the sink, his eyes boring into mine.

"Do you know how goddamn beautiful you are?"

He stalks over and captures my mouth. Where his kisses were once sweet and gentle, this one is fueled with desire. Firm lips trail kisses along my jaw and down my neck, nipping lightly at the sensitive skin there.

A moan escapes as I press my body into his. He grips my hips and pulls them flush to his body. Ever so slowly, his hands caress down my body, palms rough against the smooth skin of my thighs. He kneads my thighs and lifts me to him. My legs instinctively wrap around his waist. With careful steps, he backs out of the closet, turns, and places my ass on the bathroom counter. Goosebumps erupt up and down my body from the cool surface.

My hands ghost over his chest and into the hair at the nape of his neck. My thighs relax, and he settles in the space between. Suddenly, I remember I'm bare under my dress. Butterflies take flight in my belly at the thought of Luke's hands exploring every part of me. For now, he seems intent on leaving his hands where they are. My frantic impatience permeates each of his kisses.

"Luke," I murmur. Whether he hears me or not, I'm not sure, because he's completely focused on my mouth.

"Please, Luke," I say.

"Please what, sweetheart?" He lifts my wet hair and dots kisses along my neck and collarbone.

"You know what." I sigh. He laughs and sucks my skin. "You know what I want," I say. A flush descends from my cheeks and settles in my chest. Vocalizing my needs and desires is not something I'm accustomed to.

"Mmm . . ." Luke moans, kissing the flushed swell of each of my breasts. His lips close over my nipple through the thin fabric of my dress. "I love this color."

I'm antsy and try to pull him closer. I need all of him against all of me. My cheeks lose feeling when his hands smooth down my arms and up the sides of my body. His thumbs brush the sides of my breasts before descending to my waist and hips. Tingles follow the path his hands take. He brushes down my calves before sliding up and up until he's lifting the hem of my dress. I open my legs wider, and cool air brushes against my heated core. A soft whimper escapes me.

"Jesus, baby," Luke says. "You're on fire." His breaths come in ragged gasps as he takes in my flushed complexion. "Tell me what you need, Greer."

"Touch me. Please, Luke. Just touch me."

My heart soars when he smiles. His hands inch their way up my thighs, squeezing and kneading my flesh. Luke presses his my mouth to mine, rough and insistent. Our tongues dance together as his fingers brush over the sensitive skin between my thighs.

"Fuck me." He moans into my mouth. "You're bare?"

I nod. He's tentative at first, brushing his fingers over my smooth center before putting slight pressure on my swollen bud. My hips jolt in reflex. Body buzzing, I lean back against the mirror, gasping for breath.

"Can I?" Luke asks through hooded eyes.

"Yes," I answer, knowing he likes to hear me.

Without breaking eye contact, his finger places pressure at my entrance before pressing inside. I groan, both in pleasure and pain, at the intrusion of his large finger. He pulls me to the edge of the counter.

"You're so wet."

I nod.

He shoves my dress to my hips, allowing him to see me fully. Looking down, I'm mesmerized watching his finger slide in and out of me, his thumb tracing gentle circles over my clitoris. Quick pants escape me as fire crawls its way up my spine. I clench around his finger. I know I'm not going to last much longer.

"I feel you, baby." He adds another digit and coaxes my G-spot. I thrust my hips forward. Wanting more.

As if I said it out loud, Luke's ministrations become rougher, more demanding. His palm presses against my clit as he fucks me with his fingers. All at once, the damn breaks. My body clenches down on his fingers, but he doesn't stop. He draws out my climax like a maestro.

"You are breathtaking," he says.

Slumping against the mirror, I attempt to slow my breathing. Luke doesn't remove his fingers. I look from between my legs to his handsome face. I should feel shy, but I don't. The way he looks at me sends a surge of desire through my body. Placing my hand over his, I slowly thrust his fingers into me.

"Shit," he says, allowing me to use his hand how I need. He's just as desperate. Lavishing me with encouragement, kisses, and lust-filled caresses between each inhale.

Just as my climax begins to crest again, someone yells from the living, "Hey, lovebirds, party is next door. You planning to join us or what?"

We burst out laughing at the fact that no one in our life seems capable of knocking. Luke nods at me to continue, so I do, another orgasm already building.

"We'll be right over, Grace," Luke yells over his shoulder.

"Uh-huh, well, hurry it up already," she shouts back.

"You heard her," Luke whispers. He's laser-focused on the space between my legs, on my hand using his fingers to pleasure myself. "Come for me, baby."

It takes a few minutes more, but eventually I fall from the ledge. Convulsions wrack my body, my core clenching, hips lifting from the counter as uneven breaths escape my lungs. Luke takes over in firm, but slowing thrusts, helping me come back to earth.

When he slips his fingers from me, he locks eyes with me, then places them in his mouth and sucks off my release.

"Holy shit." I breathe. Snatching his wrist, I yank his mouth to mine, tasting the tangy, sweet essence of myself. He pulls away. A blaze of lust stares back at me.

"Do we have to go to this party?" he asks, helping me off the counter and adjusting my dress.

"Yeah, we do," I answer.

"Ugh, fine. Guess we better go." He readjusts himself and tucks his hard length into the waistband of his jeans.

"Yep!" I say, sauntering into my bedroom, slipping into my sandals, and heading to the living room.

"Aren't you forgetting something?" he calls after me.

"Not that I can think of." I grin, knowing I haven't forgotten anything. I'm fully aware I don't have panties on and that my legs are sticky with my release.

"Fuck me." He groans. My heart surges at the thought.

19

Greer

Our little fun delayed us a bit, so we leave Luke's house later than intended. In our small town, Fourth of July is a massive production. The celebrations last all week, building up to the highlight of the holiday—fireworks. Almost everyone gathers at the high school football field in order to watch the spectacular display.

The road leading up to the school is packed and cars are parked every which way, but thankfully, Luke finds a parking space. He pulls forward, then shifts the truck into reverse, using one hand to expertly back into the spot with ease.

"Of course you back in." I roll my eyes.

"Such a guy thing to do," Navy teases from the backseat, sitting next to Sutton.

Luke laughs. "What is that supposed to mean?"

"Guys who back into every parking spot are just trying to show off their big dick energy. Oh, this small little parking space? Watch me back my giant-ass truck into the spot that you couldn't fit your Prius in."

"I mean, I do have a big dick," Luke throws out as he jumps out of the truck.

"Ew!" Sutton makes a barfing noise. "That is not what I needed to know about my brother."

"How big?" Navy whisper-yells, jabbing her elbow into my side. Much to my dismay, my body immediately flushes beet red. Sex banter with friends is another first for me.

Through a tight smile, I say under my breath, "Big enough."

"Oh my god, did you guys have sex?" Navy probes.

Shaking my head, I wait for the rest of the group to get ahead of us before I reply. It's one thing talking about this with the girls and a whole other talking about it with everyone. Sutton and Grace fall back to walk with us. The little girl inside me loves that we're all dressed similarly in jean shorts, tanks, and boots.

"No, we haven't," I say.

"Haven't what?" Sutton asks.

Grace busts out laughing. "Uh, Sutton, are you sure you wanna be a part of this convo?"

"Of course I do. Why? What are we talking about?"

"Me and Luke."

"Oh." Sutton's tone makes me think she's contemplating whether or not she wants to run for the hills. "No details. Got it?" Sutton says. We all nod our heads in acquiescence.

"We haven't had sex yet," I say.

"Then how do you know Luke is *big enough*?" Navy blurts, causing Sutton to choke on her water while Grace dissolves into uncontrollable giggles.

"Because"—my eyes widen, warning everyone to calm down—"we've done other things."

Each intimate moment with Luke floats through my mind. Six months ago, if someone had asked me about this, I would have laughed in their face and joked that I'd already resigned myself to life as an old maid, single-handedly keeping the adult toy companies in business. But as time passed, I honestly couldn't ignore the growing ache of loneliness that crept in a little more each day. Even before meeting Luke, I'd started to realize it wasn't a matter of *if*—it was a matter of *when* I'd finally open my heart, body, and mind to someone again.

"And? How did it go?" Navy asks, resting her arm in the crook of my elbow. Grace and Sutton follow suit and we walk, linked arm in arm, casually discussing my sex life.

"Well, shit." Grace fans her face. "I don't know whether to be proud of you or insanely jealous."

"Both." Navy giggles. "And how is your shroud of guilt?"

"Surprisingly well," I say. "I mean, so far, everything we've done has made me feel like I'm getting back to my old self. Maybe not even a version of my old self. It's almost like, I don't know, I'm coming into my potential."

"That's what she said." Navy snorts. We all burst into a fit of giggles, stopping us in our tracks.

"What the hell are y'all talking about?" Hunter says over his shoulder. The rest of the guys pause, casting expectant eyes toward us. When Luke bites that damn lip of his, I know he knows exactly what we're talking about. And I'm certain my body is the exact color he loves so much.

"C'mon, boys," Luke says. "Let's grab drinks while the ladies get a spot." Desire rushes through me at his parting wink.

It takes some effort, but we finally find an open patch of grass. It's not much, but we manage to lay out a few blankets and settle in. This is the first time I've been to the fireworks show in years. Brian always preferred smaller gathering with friends, so we usually skipped the big town events and spent the evening at someone's house instead.

"What about the communication?" Navy asks. My ears buzz just thinking about how much Luke loves to communicate.

"What is that smile for?" Sutton cringes. "If you're about to tell me my brother is a dirty talker, please don't. There are some details I cannot and do not need to know."

"Luke really likes communication," I manage to say through laughter. Navy and Grace fall back on the ground, clutching their chests, overcome with giggles.

As the evening progresses, our group grows and shrinks as people from around town stop by to chat with the guys. They're like celebrities, and Navy and Sutton are just as popular.

It's weird, being on the fray, watching how in tune they all are with people. I make an excellent introvert. I will people, but only when I must. Even though Brian was an extrovert among his friends, he never judged me when I kept myself on the outskirts. Luke, on the other hand, doesn't miss a single opportunity to introduce me to someone or pull me into conversations. By the time we settle in for fireworks, I'm exhausted.

"Is it always like this?" I ask, referring to the never-ending stream of people.

"Pretty much," everyone answers simultaneously.

Luke scoots closer and leans back on his hands, pressing the sides of our thighs together. An excited buzz whispers through the air as everyone quiets down and prepares for the show. Luke crosses his feet at the ankles. I tilt away to wipe the corner of my mouth. It should be illegal to make Wranglers and a navy T-shirt look this good. Add the boots? I'm a goner.

A hush falls over the crowd as the stadium lights wink out one by one. Suddenly, color and sound erupt in the sky above. Red, white, and blue sparkles glitter down overhead. Laughter and excited *wows* from nearby children make me smile.

My hand brushes Luke's as I lie back on the blanket, crossing my feet at the ankles, to marvel at the energy of light and sound above. Each boom jars me, evoking a childlike giggle. I am levitating—my body, heart, and mind free. If it weren't for my friends around me, I'd float away into the sky and dance among the glittering display. Luke remains motionless, his gaze burning into my cheek.

"The fireworks are up there, mister."

"I know," he says.

Tilting my head toward him, our gazes lock. The wrinkles around his eyes are smooth and his breathing is slow and steady, but his eyes are clouded with something else entirely.

My stomach tumbles over the edge into infinity as Luke leans down on his elbow. Warmth seeps into my skin when his free hand traces the side of my neck before pulling my lips to his.

Something changes inside me then.

A crack in my heart, one I believed was irreparably shattered, begins to mend. His lips tenderly brush mine, healing another fissure. Under the canopy of light, Luke seeps into every cell, coaxing life back into me. With each kiss, each gentle caress, my heart slowly stitches itself together until only a small, fragile fracture remains.

There.

In the very back.

Buried deep.

Luke settles next to me, shoulder to shoulder, and gathers my hand in his. No words are needed. In that shared silence, a world of understanding unfolds between us.

"I can't tell you how badly I want what they have," I hear Navy whisper to Sutton.

"Me too, babe," Sutton says. "Me too."

The fireworks show continues overhead, but I'm no longer paying attention. My head tilts to the side, and our eyes meet. In that moment, my soul expands, and a quiet sigh of relief escapes me. A wave of happiness washes over me when I catch the glisten of tears in his eyes. It's as if, in this moment, everything stretches out before us, infinite and full of possibility.

We stay like that—hand in hand, our souls entwined in the quiet space between us—while the finale unfolds somewhere beyond, just a faint echo in the background.

Even as the crowd erupts into cheers and people prepare to leave, we don't move. Our friends call their goodbyes, but we remain lost in our moment.

The crowd fades, night fully descends, and still . . .

We stay like that.

20

Greer

Lounging on my vibrant green lawn, the sun kisses my skin, casting playful shadows over my body. Peering over the rim of my sunglasses, I spot Luke sitting on that big ole stump. He's focused on oiling his axe, his forearms flexing with each deliberate movement. A bead of sweat glistens on his cheek, and he dips his chin, wiping it on his shirt.

My phone buzzes. His eyes lock on mine, catching me as I dab the corner of my mouth. The wink he gives me kickstarts my inner vixen. I unlock my phone, trying not to go up in flames.

Sutton: Meet me at Ground Up, okay?
Me: What if I'm busy?

Sutton: We all know you're still in your pjs and buried in a book.
Sutton: My guess is you're in lizard mode outside.
Me: You think you know me so well.
Sutton: I do. So, are you coming? Navy's about to murder someone so . . .
Me: Yikes! Be there soon.

I toss my phone aside, then I lie flat on my giant beach towel, collecting a few more minutes of the mid-July heat. Sutton was wrong about one thing; I'd opted for my swimsuit instead of pj's because this body of mine needs a tan.

I stretch my arms above my head and roll to my stomach, resting my head on my hands. Doing nothing has never felt so good. I'd dreaded summer, afraid of being alone with nothing to do as my thoughts barrel toward the day Death changed everything. But something changed; I changed. The loneliness I usually feel during summer has faded. For once, I have friends who seek me out, challenge me, encourage me. It's easier to sit with my emotions and talk about what's on my mind. For once, I'm not so scared to come out and play.

"It should be illegal," Luke says, "for you to be looking this sexy so early in the day." He abandons his axe and prowls toward me. His large hands span the width of my lower back before tracing up my spine. He rests a knee on either side of my body, settling his weight atop my ass. He runs the backs of his fingers along my heated skin before settling them into my hair. I think I stop breathing.

Luke slightly grips my hair and turns my face, pressing his mouth to the corner of mine. His tongue seeks and claims mine. Unable to take it any longer, I break our kiss and push him back so I can roll over. Shivers dust my heated skin as his hands traverse the outside of my thighs. My knees naturally part, and he leans forward, pressing his weight into me. Yep, I definitely stop breathing.

"Fuck." He moans against the curvature of my neck as he brings my thighs to wrap around his waist. When the hard length of him presses against my center, I somehow manage a stuttering inhale.

"What are you doing to me?" he whispers as I lift up and kiss the slope of his neck. His hips press into me, sending a wave of desire from the tips of my toes to the top of my head.

"Nothing yet."

He pulls away, resting on his left forearm, and palms the side of my face. Amber eyes bore into mine, suddenly serious.

"Luke . . . ?"

"Yeah?"

"I want you," I whisper.

"Fuck, sweetheart, I want you too. I've been trying not to bother you, but watching you over here is sweet torture. And this"—he tugs the ties of my yellow bikini—"is my new favorite thing, but it's driving me absolutely insane."

"Take it off."

His hand disappears behind my neck and pulls the ties. Cool air trickles over my skin as he pulls my top down. Warm hands glide over my ribs, teasing and kneading my bare breasts. His cock is heavy and hard where it rests against my pubic bone. I push my hips against his, seeking friction.

"What do you need?"

"You."

"You have me. Always."

Smiling, I bring his face to mine as my hands glide over his shoulders and down his chest. Bare skin greets me, and his eyes close when I push his shirt up. With one hand, he reaches behind his neck and pulls his shirt off in one fell swoop. With my legs still wrapped around his waist, Luke sits back on his knees, allowing me to see all of him. My heart beats erratically as I take my fill of his bare torso. For the first time, I reach for him, but my simmering nerves make me hesitate.

"Is this okay?" I'm unsure which part to touch first.

He takes my hands and places them on his stomach. I take that as permission and slowly trace the expanse of his abdomen. Luke's body is firm, strong, and corded with muscle—muscles forged through everyday hard work.

When I trail my fingers through his chest hair, his nipples contract with desire. My touch remains featherlight as I drag a finger over the sensitive peak. He closes his eyes.

The sun's warmth seeps into our skin as my hands move down his body. My fingers move along the waistband of his shorts. When I peek back at his face, Luke's eyes are full of fire. My fingers dip beneath the waistband.

I palm his hard length, pulling a needy moan from him. After our shower adventure, I knew he was big, but now that I have him in the palm of my hand, I'd underestimated just how big. The skin is smooth, and a large vein runs along the top of his shaft. I close my hand, squeezing hard as I stroke him from root to tip.

"Goddamn, that feels so good."

"Yeah?" I pant.

"I need to touch you."

"So touch me." He captures my mouth and pours every ounce of desire into me. Without hesitation, Luke glides his hand down my body, squeezing my breast.

"I fucking love this," he says, his fingers grazing over the soft curve of my lower tummy. My body responds, arching into him. I squeeze him harder. He doesn't ask this time as he pushes his hand beneath my swimsuit bottoms and glides his fingers through my damp center. "You're soaked, sweetheart."

"Is this—am I doing this okay?" I gesture to his cock. He groans and pushes his pants over his hips. I cover the crown and beads of pre-come stick to my palm. He thrusts into my hand while sliding his finger into me.

"It's incredible. You are incredible." Thick fingers fill me, sparking every nerve in my body. My cheeks tingle, and I know I'm panting like I've run a marathon. "Just breathe, sweetheart," he coaxes, leaning down to take my mouth.

Inhale. Exhale.

We are a tangle of tongues and limbs and hands as we savor each other's bodies. I grip him harder as he thrusts his finger in and out of me.

"I'm gonna come," I moan. My pace quickens, and our labored breaths fill the atmosphere around us.

"Me too." He grunts against my neck. "Come for me."

I detonate on his command, euphoria spreading throughout my body as I plummet into my orgasm. His cock thickens in my hand, his thrusts growing more erratic. He's close.

"Let go, Luke." With a final thrust, Luke sucks the skin at my pulse point and releases onto my lower belly.

"Holy fuuuck." He strains, his whole body convulsing as I continue to stroke him. "Baby, you gotta s-stop."

With a final tug, I slow my hand and release him. He's slow to remove his fingers from me. I combust when he places them in his mouth and sucks off my essence. My tongue darts out to wet my lips, and he gives me a devilish smirk.

Luke tugs his shorts back into place, then uses his discarded T-shirt to wipe off my stomach. He then lays my swim top over my bare breasts before collapsing next to me. Our skin glistens with perspiration, but that doesn't stop him from snuggling into my side, his arm slung over my lower stomach.

"That's one way to say hello," I say, then chuckle.

"Mm-hmm. Definitely ranks at the top of the list."

"It's a good thing you're my neighbor or else they would have surely gotten a good show."

"Good thing because no one sees what's mine," he says.

My heart slams against my chest. *Mine.*

"What are you doing today?" I run my fingers through his chest hair, loving how it contrasts with the smoothness of his sun-kissed skin.

"Nothing much. Why? What's up?"

"I'm going to Ground Up to meet Sutton. Wanna come?"

"Just did." He cackles.

"True story," I say through a fit of giggles.

Once he's got his laughter under control, he pulls my palm to his mouth and kisses the center. Turning and twisting our hands together, he kisses the freckles on my arms, his own game of connect-the-dots.

"I'd love to go with you," he says, breaking the easy silence, "but I've got a few errands."

"Okay," I say, kissing the center of his chest. He pulls me on top of him.

"Does that mean I have to let you go?"

"No, but I should probably put some clothes on so I can go and then get back home to you."

Now that my body has floated back down to earth, I bask in his warmth and strength. Never in my life have I done something like this out in the open where anyone could see. I tense as the fire ignites again. "Oh!" I blurt, if only to soothe the desire rushing through my body. "Can I get your help later?"

Luke pops up. "You want my help?"

"I do." I smile. "I want to paint my workout room and could use you to be tall for me."

"I can do that." His goofy grin gives away his eagerness.

"Great, I'll text you later." I sit up, and my bikini top and his shirt drop to my lap. My breasts hang heavy and he leans forward to capture my nipple between his lips. He sucks deeply, dragging a sharp inhale from me.

"Yeah." Luke winks. "You text me."

"Excuse me, but have you seen my friend anywhere? Her name is Greer?" Sutton waves her hand in front of my face, pulling me from my haze. Ground Up hums with energy this morning, but I'm too distracted by thoughts of Luke to focus.

"Huh?" I say. "Sorry. What were you saying?"

"Housewarming party."

Because, of course, my mother and Sutton have become best friends now, too. I'd kind of hoped Mom would forget about the housewarming party idea but, alas, here we are.

"Do I have to?" I whine.

"No, you don't, but it'll be fun. Plus, we have even more to celebrate than just your new house."

My brain fog clears immediately. "What do you mean?"

"Oh, nothing. Just that I have a buyer for your house."

"For real life?"

"What's for real life?" Navy asks as she steps up to our table. Idle chatter and noise fill the busy shop. She's hardly had a moment to stop moving and join us.

"I found a buyer for Greer's house," Sutton answers.

"No shit? That's awesome."

We placed the house on the market at the end of June, but I didn't think it would sell this fast. My heart and mind war with conflicting emotions.

"That's awesome, right, G?" Sutton asks.

"Yeah." I nod. "I think."

"You think?" They parrot.

"I guess I knew it would sell eventually, but I didn't think it would sell this fast."

"I'm not the top realtor in the region for nothing," Sutton boasts. "You still want to sell, yes?" Her steady gaze holds a gentle intensity.

Another weight lifts from my shoulders as I answer honestly, "Yeah, I do." The matching smiles they give me tell me they're proud of me.

"Do you want to see it one last time?" Sutton questions.

I ponder it for only a moment, but I know there's no need for me to see it again. A house is just a house. The memories I had from that house will always be with me. "No, I don't need to see it again."

"So, I've been wondering something . . ." Navy's voice fades as she crosses the café to wipe down tables.

"What's that?" I ask.

"How come you don't have anything of yours and Brian's at your new house?"

"Oh, um, I'm not sure." Guilt settles into the pit of my stomach. I've been so distracted this summer that I have not thought about my storage room since I moved in. I know they would understand, but I retreat, not yet ready to dive into this particular conversation.

Navy glares at me with a scrunched forehead. We both know I'm lying, but she doesn't press me for the truth. My phone pings with a text from Luke.

Luke: I'll be home later. We still on for painting?

Me: Yep. I've got dinner covered.

Luke: Lucky me. See you soon, love.

Love. My heart fucking soars.

"Oh, shit," Navy says, interrupting my daydream.

At her exclamation, I realize she and Sutton are both staring at me with goofy grins on their faces. "What?" I ask.

"Don't give us that innocent *what,*" Navy says. "You know exactly what. You are head over heels in love with that man. "

"Ha!" I say. "No, I'm not in love with Luke."

"Yet," Sutton adds, eyes widening with excitement.

While I'm not there yet, I get closer every day.

Falling for this man is inevitable.

After spending a few hours with the girls, I return home, excited to start on my first official house project. Over an hour in, I realize just how much it sucks. In fact, I'm pretty certain DIY projects should come with the warning label: *Can Be a*

Massive Pain in the Ass. The ladder wobbles as I stretch a few extra inches to swipe the brush along the corner where the wall meets the ceiling.

"This was a spectacularly bad idea, wasn't it?" I say.

Duke whines in response.

Here I thought it would be a fun project to paint my workout room, and now I'm dangling off a ladder. Luke agreed to come over to help, but I haven't heard from him since earlier. The ladder teeters as my hips press into the top.

"C'mon arms. Just. A. Little. More." With a quick swish, I cover the last patch of bare wall.

"Well, it's not perfect, but that'll do, pig. That'll do," I say in my best Farmer Hogget voice.

After setting the paintbrush on the tray, I go to step down the ladder, but as luck would have it, my foot catches on the last wrung, and I topple backward into the handlebars of my spin bike. Pain blooms instantly, and I know I'm going to have a giant bruise on my hip. Duke can't be bothered and leaves me for the comfort of his bed.

"Some help you are." As I step away from the ladder, pride fills me as I take in my little project. Working out is essential for my mental health and now I have a perfect sunshine-yellow room to use.

I clean up my paint supplies and tackle a few more minor projects on my list. I enter my bedroom, and my eyes immediately look toward Luke's house, but his windows are still dark. I'm tempted to text him and see if he's alright. He was supposed to help me after all. But I don't want to come off as *that* kind of girlfriend. I push the nervous gremlins in my mind back into their corners.

Scanning my room, I take one last look at the picture frames filled with people I don't know. I pull out several photos from a manilla envelope and set about filling my new house with memories. There are photos of the girls and me in our comfies baking cinnamon rolls; another from when Mom, Dad, and I went hiking; and even a group photo of all of us from the lake on the Fourth.

My favorite is one Navy took of me and Luke on our first date. He's got me tucked into his body, holding my hand against his chest. He's looking at me the same way he looks at me when I catch him staring, like I'm his whole world.

I shower quickly and check my phone. Again. There's still no answer. This time, I can't quell the nervousness that seeps into my heart. I try distracting myself by whipping up dinner. I love feeding Luke, so I make him a plate and place it into the fridge for later.

I zone out completely washing dishes, but I'm unable to wash away the fear sticking to each nerve. Eventually, I snuggle into the couch, and Duke squeezes in next to me. I call Luke this time. No answer.

Inhale. Exhale.

I turn up the TV volume in a weak attempt to drown out the roaring in my mind. Minutes tick by, but still, I don't hear from Luke. *Why isn't he home yet? He said he'd be here. Why isn't he answering me?* The movie plays idly in the background as my thoughts rage, a tempest of worry.

Me: Are you okay? I'm worried.

No response. I give up on the movie and choose the safety of my bed. Before lying down, I open my curtains, hoping maybe I'll see when he gets home later. I bury my face in the pillow

Luke used, inhaling his masculine scent, hoping it'll calm my racing thoughts.

Inhale.

Exhale.

There's no stopping it now—every worst-case scenario blasts through my mind. My thoughts spiral and coil and twist until, eventually, I fall into a fitful sleep.

21

Luke

I**T'S PITCH-DARK BY THE** time I arrive home. I'm out of my truck and across the yard in seconds, praying like hell she's still awake. No lights illuminate her bedroom when I sprint by heading toward her back door. With a little luck, maybe she's left it unlocked. I'm fully aware how stalker-like this is, but I don't care. I need to see her.

It hadn't been my plan to be gone all damn day. A buddy from work needed help moving furniture, so I thought it would be quick, a few hours tops. I couldn't wait to get back home to her and help her with her project. Then, Ms. Carol asked if I could pick up some groceries for her because she hasn't been feeling well. And then I just had to answer when Sadie called—her piece-of-shit car broke down. Again.

I should have texted Greer again. I should have made sure my phone was charged. I should have had a damn charger in my truck. I should have done so many things differently. I borrowed Sadie's charger while I fixed her car, and when I got back in my truck later, there was a flood of mixed calls and texts, each one like a punch to the gut. Her last message broke my heart.

"Are you okay? I'm worried."

No, everything wasn't okay. All I wanted was to get to her, but I couldn't just leave Sadie stranded. We may not be on great terms, and I know most people would have ignored their ex's calls, but *what if* I don't answer and something terrible happens? I couldn't live with myself if it did.

The patio is dark and no interior lights are on, but I try the sliding door anyway. It doesn't budge. I spy a few paintbrushes and paint trays lying on the ground drip drying, and my stomach drops. This girl never asks for help, and when she finally does, I leave her hanging. I know she's probably sleeping, but I send a text, my heart lodged in my throat.

Me: I'm home now. I'm sorry. I can explain.

Me: Hope you're sleeping well.

I close the screen, and then I trudge to my house. She's been through hell, and here I go causing her unnecessary worry. I've got my head low, so I almost miss the plate of food sitting on the log near the door. I unfold the note perched on top and heave a great sigh of relief at Greer's loopy writing. *Hey, you, I'm really worried & hope everything's okay. XO*

Peeking under the tinfoil, I see my favorite—BBQ mac-n-cheese. Knowing Greer, it's homemade, and that makes me feel like a bigger asshole. I run my hands over her writing, then take the plate inside and reheat the food. I'm a glutton for punishment and choose to eat outside, in plain sight of her house, hoping like hell she'll wake up.

In the back of my mind, I hear Hunter's *I told you so*. I know he's right. I have to learn to cut people off who are using me or, at the very least, learn to find balance.

Giving up on her waking, I call it a night. I clean my dishes and head for the shower, but not before double-checking my kitchen light is on. She needs to know I'm home. Lying in bed, my mind and emotions eventually settle, and I drift off to sleep.

I'm completely tangled in my sheets when I hear it. *Tap, tap, tap.* Darkness hits me as I slowly open my eyes. *Tap, tap, tap.* Sitting up, I wipe sleep from my face, scanning the room, searching for the source of the sound. *Tap, tap, tap.* Tossing the sheets aside, I venture into the kitchen, following the sound. My scalp prickles seeing Greer at the back door.

"Hey, sweetheart, it's one a.m. What are you doing here?" I ask as I open the door.

She steps inside and Duke slinks by, his soft fur brushing my leg. Her hair is mussed, and she's wearing only a pale-blue nightgown. Without a word, she slides her arms around my middle and tucks her face into the crook of my neck. Sobs wrack through her body as tears drip onto my shoulder.

"Hey, hey . . ." I say. "It's okay. I'm okay." She mumbles something, but I can't understand her. I gather her in my arms, and she tucks her face against my bare chest. It takes little effort to carry her to my bedroom and sit her on the bed.

"In," I tell her.

She quickly follows my command and snuggles under the covers. Following in behind her, I pull them over us. Her head rests on the pillow, sandy-blonde hair fanned around her, and she stares at me, lost in her own thoughts. Worry lances through me. I open my arms, and she tucks herself into my side. Her breaths coast over my skin as she settles across me. After several minutes, her breathing evens out and her grip on my waist loosens.

"You're okay, sweetheart." I kiss the top of her head as her soft fingers trail through my chest hairs.

She's warm against me, and her gown a little damp from whatever nightmare woke her. It was clearly a bad one.

"I was worried," she whispers, her voice trembling.

"I'm sorry, love." My gut twists with guilt, so I add, "For so many things."

"Goddamn it, Luke." Her teeth grind together, vibrating against my sternum. "I know your friends might be used to this with you, but I'm not. You said you'd be here. Then you just fall off the face of the planet? Do you know how many versions of hell I've gone through tonight, wondering what happened to you?"

"You have every right to be pissed as hell. You have no idea how sorry I am, Greer."

"I appreciate that, but sorry doesn't take away all the horrible scenarios I pictured tonight. I've already lost one man. I can't lose another."

The weight of her words presses down on my heart. For years, my friends have given me hell for situations similar to this. I always brushed them off, hoping they'd leave it alone, and made excuse after excuse to make my actions seem noble.

But the tremble in her voice and tears on my chest rip me open. The truth is that I wanted nothing more than to spend time with Greer today. It's what *I* wanted, and yet, every single choice I made today was in direct opposition.

Holding her to me, I smooth my hand up and down her arm. I'd continue to apologize over and over, but I know words mean nothing without action. I hope like hell she's still willing to give me her time and maybe someday she can forgive me.

"I know it doesn't make it better," I say, "but I'm sorry all the same. You didn't deserve the fear I caused you." I press my lips against the crown of her head.

Endless minutes of silence tick by before she finally asks, "Where were you?"

"I was helping John move some furniture, and then Ms. Carol needed some groceries. On my way home, Sadie called. Her car broke down again and she was stranded on the byway exit. I couldn't leave her stranded."

"Who's Sadie?"

"My ex-girlfriend."

"Oh." She doesn't pull away. "Is she okay?"

Only this woman would want to make sure my ex-girlfriend was okay instead of continuing to be furious at me for my disappearing act.

"She is. I'm sorry I didn't text you. I meant to, but I got caught up and, fuck, this sounds like a lame excuse, but my phone died, and my charger wasn't in my truck."

A tearful giggle escapes and she squeezes me tighter. "Guess you're not immune to word vomit either."

"Guess not." I smooth my hands over her hip. "I really am sorry, more than I can say."

"Is this what Hunter and everyone are always talking about? That you don't always think things through and drop what you're doing for others?"

Talk about a kick to the gut. "Yes. I don't mean to, I just—"

"I forgive you," she says, and my heart sighs in relief. She smooths her hand up my chest and holds the side of my neck. "I mean, I almost died painting the room. I was actually doing fine at first, but then . . . I was so fucking worried about you."

"I know."

"I'll worry about you a lot though, won't I? You do have a dangerous job."

"Sometimes it can be dangerous, but we prepare for the unknown and don't take unnecessary risks. Does it scare you, being with someone who does what I do?"

She considers briefly. "I've learned the hard way there are a lot of scary things in this world. Does your job worry me? Yes, but it won't stop me from being with you. Nothing could make me give you up."

She has no idea how incredible and brave and strong she is. I don't deserve this woman. "I know it's just empty words right now," I say. "But I promise I'll be better."

She nods.

"Thank you for dinner," I say.

"You're welcome."

I relax when I hear the smile in her voice. "Did you have a bad dream, too?" I ask her.

"Yes, I did. I-It was different." I trail my fingers over the smooth skin of her arm, giving her a chance to gather her thoughts. "The details are usually so clear," she says, "but tonight they were fuzzy. Brian wasn't even there. And then, I don't know, everything went dark, and all I could see was you, and that's when I woke up."

"Have you had many nightmares lately?"

"No, not since the beginning of summer. Brian said something weird to me then."

"Yeah?"

"He told me it was time for me to go. I still can't figure out what he meant, but n-now he wasn't there in my dream tonight, and I don't know what to think."

"Yes, you do," I tell her. She inhales a quick breath before rolling out of my arms to lie out wide.

"You're right." She turns her head toward me. "Did you know I listed my old house finally?"

I shake my head no.

"I asked Sutton to help me a few weeks ago," she says. "She told me earlier today she found a buyer for it."

I'm not shocked to learn that she's been in possession of her old house this whole time. I've noticed that, aside from a photo album, she doesn't have much of anything that was hers and Brian's around her house. I know grief is different for everyone. Some people want to be surrounded by their loved one's memories, but for others it's too painful. My mom struggled to let go, and it was years before she let Sutton help her remodel the house and pack away Dad's things. I think I know which type Greer is.

"Are you having second thoughts?" I ask.

"No," she affirms. "It's been empty this whole time, and I know I won't go back. It's time."

She threads her fingers through mine and brings my hand to her mouth. She kisses each knuckle before letting it settle on the bed between us.

"I worry I'm going to forget Brian."

"Why do you think that?"

"I know it sounds crazy," she says, then pauses. "Some dreams are terrible—I relive every moment of the accident. But, sometimes, they're good dreams, and it feels like Brian's really there. The last dream I had of him, I think he was saying goodbye."

"Why do you think he was saying goodbye?"

"Because I think . . . I think he knew I was stuck."

"Were you?"

"Luke, I didn't know life without Brian. I was sad and lonely. It didn't matter if the dreams were bad as long as I got to see him or talk to him. Of course I was stuck, but I didn't know how to get myself unstuck."

"And now?" I hold my breath.

"Now . . ." she rolls over to face me, tucking our hands beneath her chin. Clear blue eyes gaze back at me, free of tears. "I don't feel stuck anymore."

"Is that a good thing?"

"Yes."

My heart soars.

Leaning forward, I press my lips to hers. She snuggles into my body and lays her head on my pillow. Eventually, her breathing evens out and her limbs get heavy.

"I won't let you forget him. You know that, right?"

"I know." Her contented sigh lets me know she's finally drifted off to sleep.

I should sleep on the floor or on the couch, but I can't bring myself to be away from her. I need her next to me tonight. Bringing the covers over her shoulders, I pull her tight to my body. I dream about her when I finally fall asleep.

"How many people are coming over tonight?" I call out.

"Not that many," Sutton shouts back.

Greer's house has been a flurry of activity for days now preparing for her housewarming party. Sutton and Greer's mom are busy setting out snacks and drinks on the kitchen island. Mr. Abrams, Greer's dad, and I realized we were safer staying out of the way, lest we risk life or limb, and have relegated ourselves to the patio.

I lean to the side and catch sight of Greer flitting around her house finishing last-minute details. I'm almost positive she's straightened the items on her sofa table ten times now. I love her house. It's full of life now. Where picture frames once remained empty or full of stock photos, they now contain snapshots of our summer.

I helped her touch up her workout room and painted her bathroom and bedroom. Of course, we got sidetracked by that shower of hers. Since the night of her last nightmare, we've spent countless nights together—cuddling, talking, exploring each other's bodies long past midnight. Being with Greer is effortless.

"I think that's everything." Greer stands in her living room with her hands on her hips. This is my opening.

"Not quite." I step inside and hand her a blush-pink gift bag. "You forgot this."

Her eyes narrow on mine as she takes the bag from me. "What's this?"

"Open it and see."

Bouncing on bare toes, she perches on the coffee table's edge, tucking her new floral dress under her butt. She moves to twist her hair into a bun, but I still her hands. I love it when she lets her hair free. With a tiny smile, she sweeps the blond locks behind her shoulders, and they tumble down her back. Her parents and Sutton watch closely as Greer removes several pieces of tissue paper. She freezes when she sees what's inside.

"Luke, what is this?" She pulls out a wood frame with a picture of Brian in it. "How did you get this photo?"

"Your mom helped me."

Mrs. Abrams wipes at the corner of her eye.

"But, Luke, why?"

"I told you I wouldn't let you forget him."

Greer freezes. The room stills. I'm sure I hear a pin drop. It's right about now I'm wondering if I messed up.

"I'm sorry. I just thought—"

"It's perfect," she says, jumping up to wrap her arms around my neck. When she doesn't immediately let go, the others make themselves scarce. She finally lets go and turns to place the frame on one of her bookshelves. It's a candid photo of Brian in front of their Christmas tree in a hideous sweater. She runs her fingers over the photo, whispering something I can't quite hear, then comes back to me.

"You are everything, Luke Bradley." She squeezes my hand and presses a kiss to my lips.

"So are you, sweetheart. So are you."

A few hours later, the fire crackles, and the cool night air settles around us. Music drifts from inside along, mingling with the hum of conversation. As parties go, this one seems to be a great success. All our friends showed up, along with several of Greer's former coworkers. She'd hemmed and hawed for days about inviting them, worried that she missed her opportunity at friendship. But with some encouragement, she reached out. She's been anxious for days thinking they wouldn't show up. I'll never forget the look on her face when Lucy and the rest of her former team walked through the door. Greer doesn't realize how magnetic she is—just how much people long to be in her atmosphere.

My phone buzzes in my pocket, and I pull it out to see a text from Mom: *In the driveway.* She's known about Greer from the moment I met her, but with all her traveling this summer, tonight will be their first time meeting face-to-face. I'm halfway to the back door when Greer opens the front door, revealing my mom on the other side. I can't make out their words, but next thing I know, Greer steps forward and pulls Mom into a tight hug. By the time I reach them, they're still embracing, and my chest tightens.

"Hey, Mom," I say. They pull apart but remain close. "I see you've met Greer."

"I sure have." She smiles. "How you doing, Son?"

"I'm good. Glad you could make it."

"No way was I going to miss the chance to meet the woman who's captured your heart."

Greer reaches for my hand and interlaces our fingers. "I'm so glad to meet you, Mrs. Bradley."

"Oh, none of that, sweet girl. Just call me Carissa."

"Carissa." Greer smiles. "Well, come on in. There's plenty of food and drinks. And people. There are so many people here. I didn't know I knew this many. I'd love for you to meet my parents. Do you want to meet them?" Greer's cheeks flush and she swallows past her nerves.

"By all means," Mom says, "lead the way." When Greer walks toward the kitchen, Mom says to me, "Hold on to her. I can tell she's a good one."

"She is."

Everyone gravitates toward Greer throughout the evening, laughing at her wild stories from the classroom and begging for house tours. Every now and then, she'll walk by and graze her hand across my shoulders, or I'll go looking for her to give her a kiss. We're like electrons in an atom, in and out, constantly finding little ways to let the other know we're here.

Our parents, who spent most of the evening together, most likely telling embarrassing stories about our childhoods, left a while ago. Greer is busy saying goodbye to her last few guests, so I take her glass with me outside.

Our crew is already seated around the fire pit we've moved to the middle of our yards. Sutton curses under her breath as she struggles to open several packages of graham crackers. Navy muffles her laughter and hands out marshmallows.

"Hey," Hunter says, passing me a roasting stick. "This was a pretty great party."

"Turned out alright, didn't it?"

"Sure did." He takes a sip of whiskey. "She's pretty amazing."

Glancing inside the house, I immediately catch Greer's gaze. She smiles and blows me a kiss before grabbing her blanket.

"She is."

"You love her?" Everyone stills as not to miss my answer.

"Sure do."

"She loves you too," Hunter says. "You know that, right?"

"I hope so, man."

To some, it might seem too soon, too fast for me to feel this way about Greer. But when you find your person, falling in love feels less like a choice and more like an inevitability. I've been infinitely falling for Greer since the moment I met her. And if it takes her a day, a week, a month, or even a year to be ready to love me back, that's okay. I'll wait.

"Hey, Cap. You got a visitor."

"Thanks, John."

My office is tucked in the back of the station in a little dark room, so it's a relief to be interrupted. Walking across the station, I notice John and Adam doing station duties. Good thing because I'm starving, and we still have to figure out what the hell to make for dinner.

I open the back door, and summer heat blasts my face. I'm pleasantly surprised to find Greer standing idly in the empty bay. She's wearing my favorite black cutoff shorts, a green tank that makes her eyes pop, and a cream-colored cardigan. I'm only slightly disappointed to see she's got her white sneakers on.

"Sorry, mister," Greer says with a smile as she lifts a foot. "Station rules. No shirt, no shoes, no boyfriend."

I bury my face in her neck and wrap her in my arms. "I'm the captain. I can change the rules."

"You and my feet." She giggles. Don't ask me to explain it, there's just something about a barefoot Greer that I love.

"You and your everything," I say against her neck. She pushes away, and I reluctantly let her go.

"Whatcha doing here, sweetheart?"

"Well,"—she turns to grab the bag at her feet—"Navy and I were hanging out and decided to bake, and well, you know how that goes."

"Let me guess, you made enough to feed a small army?"

"Pretty much." She shoves the bag into my hands.

I'm unsurprised to see it's filled with bags of cookies, a loaf of what looks to be banana bread, and . . .

"Are those cinnamon rolls?"

"Of course," Greer says. "We're working on a new recipe. They're pumpkin spice flavored."

I raise an eyebrow. "That's a crime."

She crosses her arms over her chest. "Something wrong with pumpkin spice?"

This is surely an argument I'll lose, so I settle with "Nope."

"Good! Navy's been asked to develop some new menu items for Ground Up, so you boys are now our official taste testers."

"Gee, we are so bummed," Adam laments as he leans out the door to snatch the bag of goodies. "Thanks, G!"

"New recipes for Ground Up, huh?" I ask.

She beams. "I'm not sure if you heard, but Mr. Jones is going to retire, and he's looking for someone to buy Ground Up."

"And Navy wants to buy it?"

"She'd really like to, but she needs to find an investor to help financially. She's also not sure if she can run it on her own and is thinking of finding a business partner."

"Why not you?" Greer spends just as much time at Ground Up or in the kitchen with Navy; she's practically an employee.

She scoffs. "Yeah, right. I couldn't do that. Plus, I've got a job, one that I actually really like. Most of the time."

"You do, but what if you changed careers? Could be fun and you know you'd be great at it."

"They've got me under contract for the next school year already, so it's probably not an option. Anyway, when do I get to see you?"

July has flown by in a blink. It feels like yesterday we were celebrating the Fourth, and I was falling head over heels in love with Greer. We've been pretty busy on shift lately with the wildfire season. John is here covering for Vinnie who's out on assignment a few towns over.

"I work today and tomorrow, but then you're mine."

"Okay, well, I better let you go. Be safe. I lo—" Her cheeks flush. "Um, okay, bye!" She gives me one of her classic awkward waves. *Yeah, I love you too.*

22

"**O**H GOD." I GROAN, muffling the sound against the pillow. "That feels so good."

"Harder?" he asks, his voice low, almost teasing.

I peek out from beneath the pillow. "Please."

Lord of the Rings plays idly on the TV in the background, though it's barely a distraction. We've spent almost every day he's not working together—doing everything and nothing at all. Projects here and there, decorating, time with family and friends, and helping Navy have filled the gaps, but otherwise, I've done a whole lot of nothing.

Luke's thumbs dig into the arch of my foot, pressing on a tender spot. My stomach quivers in pleasure-pain. I've spent the last few days on my feet setting up my classroom, so every muscle in my body screams from his skilled hands. Normally, I'm ready to go back to work, but this year it feels bittersweet. I've actually enjoyed having an empty agenda.

"Just like that," I say. Groaning, I drop the pillow and turn my hungry gaze to Luke. His large frame takes up most of the couch, where he's reclined in the corner. With one leg propped on the cushion and the other on the coffee table, he tugs at my foot, pulling me closer to him. His hands slide up my calf, fingers dancing over my constellation of scars. On instinct, I pull my foot back.

"None of that," he warns and pulls my leg back into his lap.

"But they're so—"

"Beautiful?" he says. There's a glint in his eyes, daring me to challenge him. Luke sits up and pulls my foot to rest on the center of his chest.

"I guess," I reply. It's just one of the physical reminders I'll have forever from the accident.

"You guess?" He purses his lips.

"I've gotten used to them, but I know they probably gross people out."

"You've never told me about them," he says as his fingers drift over the skin of my legs.

"Do you want to know?"

He nods.

"Somehow during the accident, I broke my tibia, so that one is from the repair surgery."

Luke's thumb rubs over the area.

"And these"—lifting my shirt, I expose my stomach and the scars scattered there—"are because my spleen ruptured."

"Trust me, Greer, they're beautiful."

"Yeah? Let's see some of yours then." I nudge my toes into his leg. I always love hearing his stories, so I'm sure he's got some good ones behind some of his scars.

"This one right here?" He flips his arm over and gestures to a faint white line marking his forearm. "Got that one when I was ten. Hunter dared me to climb this giant tree, and of course, I wasn't about to let him know I hate heights. And this one"—he runs a finger along the skin near his hairline—"is from Sutton and a hockey stick."

I burst out laughing, wondering what could have possibly happened that would cause Sutton to choose violence.

"Scars are beautiful, G. They tell us the journey we've taken in life." Leaning forward, he cradles my calf in his hands and presses a kiss to the bottom of my scar. "They're reminders of challenges we've overcome,"—his lips ghost farther up—"the battles we've fought,"—his tongue traces my scars length. I sink deeper into the couch—"and the lessons we've learned." Warm hands slip under my thigh, kneading the flesh as he kisses just below my knee.

Loud symphonic drumming fills the room, each beat echoes the pounding of my heart. It races as Luke's lips trail over my knee. I tilt my head to the side, my thoughts drifting away as shadows dance behind my eyelids. His teeth graze my thigh, his hands disappearing beneath my oversized T-shirt. Amid the drumming and shouting from the television speakers, a tsunami of heat rushes beneath my skin as his fingers find purchase on my hips, spanning their width.

"You shall not pass!" we suddenly shout our favorite line in unison, our grins mirroring each other's.

"The best part," I murmur, my breath catching in my throat as my hips respond instinctively, rising to meet his touch.

"Take these off." He groans against my flesh. His fingers tug the waistband of my underwear. Subtly lifting my T-shirt, I wiggle my fingers beneath the band, and together, we shimmy my underwear down my body. Luke kneels between my legs, his eyes dark with want, their heat trailing over every exposed inch of my core, setting my body ablaze.

As my legs loosen, I willingly offer more of myself to Luke. He moistens his lips, sliding his hands down my thighs with purpose, gripping my waist firmly. He settles between my parted thighs, intent written on his face, his touch sending shivers down my spine. His tongue traces a tantalizing path along the delicate skin of my upper thigh, his lips grazing and teasing, inching closer to where I burn for him.

My fingers twist in his tousled locks, locking his amber eyes on mine. A suppressed whimper escapes my lips as I bite down, begging for more. With a knowing smirk, Luke maintains eye contact, his tongue tracing the length of my core, sending sparks of pleasure through me.

"Oh god." I moan, surrendering to the sensation of his mouth against my heated flesh. He worships me, each lick and tug fuels the desire coursing through my body. Luke's hand slips between my legs, teasing my entrance, all while licking and tugging at my clitoris.

"You respond so well to me," Luke murmurs, his voice a low rasp against my flesh. My control slips, my inner muscles clenching around his finger, as my orgasm roars to life, begging to be released.

"Please, Luke," I say, desperate for more.

"You never have to beg," he says, pressing deeper into me, his mouth continuing to lavish my sensitive bud with the attention it needs. With deft fingers, he grazes my G-spot, sending waves of pleasure rushing through me. My stomach convulses as my orgasm crashes through my body.

"I love the way you taste," he whispers, his tongue licking the remnants of my release.

My hands find purchase on his shoulders, urgently tugging him up my body to capture his mouth with mine. Our tongues meet in a passionate dance. Pulling at his shirt, my nails scrape at his exposed skin.

"Take this off," I say. The need for him consumes me. In one swift motion, he reaches over his head and rips his shirt off, tossing it on the coffee table, the credits of our forgotten movie scrolling across the screen.

"These too," I say, my fingers gently pushing at the waistband of his shorts.

"Are you sure?" he asks.

"Yes." I sigh. Luke's gaze intensifies as he obliges, pushing them down his hips. Impatient to see him, I use my toes to help him, sliding them under the fabric and shoving them down his legs. They get stuck on his foot, and we laugh as he kicks at them until they lie discarded behind him on the couch.

"Now you," he says, desire filling each word, as he lifts my shirt over my breasts and peels it from my body.

Greer. A voice echoes in my head.

"Holy..." Luke's breath catches as he exhales, his eyes fixated on my body. My cheeks flush with a numbness that spreads across my skin. Ignoring the voice, I reach out and wrap my hand around his length. Luke reacts immediately, his shoulders tensing and his stomach muscles contracting with need. With each stroke, desire and longing ignite in my heart.

I want him. I need him.

I sink back and draw him nearer, the head of his cock brushing against my inner thigh. He drops his mouth to mine in a demanding kiss, our lips battling for dominance. Each lick, bite, and suck fueling the fire between us.

But then, lights flash behind my eyes.

Brakes skid. Glass shatters.

I flinch involuntarily, and Luke starts to pull away. I push the vision aside, desperate for him, and wrap my hands under his arms and grab at his shoulders. His lips trail along my jaw, sucking at the tender skin beneath my ear.

The scent of gasoline lingers in the air, and Brian's face floats across my vision.

Not now. Not now. I chant silently, forcing the memory back as I link my feet behind Luke's back, pulling him closer. A groan rumbles deep within me when he presses against my entrance.

"Sweetheart, are you sure?" Luke questions again.

Why does he keep asking me that?

Determination drives me as I lift my hips to meet his, seeking connection. Our groans fill the room as the inferno within my chest rages, and the bare head of his cock swipes through my slickness.

"I'm sure," I say. "I'm on the pill." I'm so ready to cross over this boundary with him. Only him.

"Okay," Luke whispers, the anticipation palpable in the air. I hear the crinkle of a wrapper, and then he sheaths himself. His grip tightens behind my neck as he leans down to kiss me. His lips move along my cheek before finding my lips once more. He places himself at my entrance.

I always thought we'd have more time.

The memory comes rushing in—rubber burning, sirens wailing, and screams echoing in my ear.

I recoil from Luke and scramble up onto my elbows. Luke pulls away, shock and shame etched across his face. I gasp for breath, tears cascading down my cheeks.

"Shit," he says, pulling me upright with him. His hands are gentle as he wraps a soft blanket around my shoulders.

"Just breathe, Greer," Luke says against my hair, the soothing timbre of his voice calling me back to him. His firm hands rub up and down my arms. "I'm right here."

"I'm sorry," I say in a barely-there whisper.

"Why are you sorry?" he says softly, tilting my chin until our eyes meet. There's no judgement in his gaze, only quiet understanding swirling within it.

"Because I want you," I say.

"I know you do."

Luke closes the distance between us, pulling me into a tight embrace. We sit there naked on the couch, holding one another, as silent minutes tick by.

"Want to tell me what happened?" Luke's voice is gentle, coaxing me to open up.

"I'm not sure," I say, squeezing him tighter. "I was here, wanting you, wanting everything, and then suddenly I was back there. I'm sorry. I'm so sorry, Luke."

"Stop being sorry. You didn't do anything wrong," he says, his voice firm but tender.

"But I wanted . . . I want you . . . I don't understand. My body wants you." Tears stream down my cheeks, my breathing erratic and ragged.

"Breathe, sweetheart," Luke demands softly. "Inhale. Good. Now, exhale."

I follow his instructions, allowing his presence to anchor me until every ounce of energy drains from my body. He cradles me in his arms, lifting me carefully as he stands and carries me to his bed. Laying me down, he pulls the covers up to my chin.

"Are you leaving?" I ask as he sits on the edge of his bed.

"Do you want me to?" His gaze searches for reassurance.

"No."

"Then, I'll stay." He disposes of the condom as he walks into the other room.

He turns off the lights in the living room, and darkness descends throughout the house. As he joins me beneath the covers, pulling up his briefs, his warmth wraps around me. His arm wraps protectively around my hips, drawing me into the safety of his embrace.

"We just need a bit more time," he says, his warm breath trails over my shoulder before his lips press gently to the dimple there.

"Why are you so patient with me?" I whisper into the darkness, barely more than a breath.

"Because I knew from the beginning we might try something you weren't quite ready for. And I also know one day you will be, and I told you I'd wait until then." He kisses the side of my neck. "No timeline. Remember?"

"No timeline," I say.

As his breathing evens out and his arm becomes heavy, I turn to face him, my fingers tracing patterns over his face and through his hair. *How did you find me?*

A sparkle catches my eye, and my heart sinks when I spot my wedding ring, still adorning my left hand. In that moment, a deep understanding washes over me. There are some things I have to take care of first before I can fully embrace the future, before I can move forward with Luke.

Luke: I want to take you somewhere. An overnight trip.

I stare at the text. My stomach flutters at the thought of going away with Luke overnight. Two long days have passed since we almost made love. That night has replayed over and over and over. He stayed the night but left early the next morning for a double shift. Forty-eight hours has never felt so long.

"Whatcha doing?"

I startle momentarily at Sutton's voice.

I whip around, spotting Sutton and Navy halfway across my yard. I should be surprised they're here, but I'm not. They've been texting me nonstop, but I haven't felt up to talking to anyone. Instead, I reverted to my natural instinct of isolating and overthinking.

"Nothing," I say. I've been sitting in this spot for nearly an hour, staring at Luke's message, not knowing what to say to him. Scorching August sun beats down on my bare shoulders, but I don't care.

"When someone says nothing," Navy says, "they really mean everything." She and Sutton plop down next to me.

"G, what's going on with you?" Sutton nudges my arm, pulling me from my spiral.

"We almost had sex," I say.

"Almost?" Navy asks gently.

Sighing, I lie back on the grass, my arms and legs splayed out. "Yep, but then I messed it up."

"What makes you think that?" Navy asks.

"Because just as he was about to—" I look sideways at Sutton to gauge her reaction. She nods for me to continue. "We were about to cross that line, but then my mind decided it didn't like that plan and I—oh god, I'm so embarrassed."

"There's no need to be embarrassed," Navy says, her tone gentle but blunt. "You knew this could be a possibility. Why are you so shocked it actually happened?"

"Because we've done *other* things and I was fine. It was just him and me, and I wanted him."

"Well, of course you do," Navy says. "You're a horny woman with a hot-as-hell man in your life. Of course you want to fuck his brains out."

My cheeks flame at Navy's summation. "He must hate me."

"My brother does not hate you one bit," Sutton says. "He's just worried about you. We all are."

"You are?"

"Of course we are, knucklehead," Sutton says. "You've been MIA the last two days. You should have texted us."

I groan outwardly. They lie back on the grass and turn their bodies to face me, each grabbing one of my hands. They know exactly how to root me into the present.

"You are not a burden to us," Navy says. "We are your best friends, and we want to be here for you."

"Exactly," Sutton says. "No more isolating."

"You're right," I tell them, squeezing their hands.

"How long has it been since you've had a flashback or nightmare?" Navy asks.

Looking at Navy, I answer honestly. "Not since our night out dancing at Big Joe's."

Navy nods before continuing. "What do you think caused this one?"

"Did you know I still have all of our stuff?" The confession flies out, a truth I can no longer contain.

"All of it?" They say leaning up on elbows.

"Yup. All of it. It's in a storage room near my parents' house."

"That's why you don't have anything in your house, isn't it?" Navy asks. I nod.

I'm suddenly in a vacuum, unable to hear any sound except the thumping of my own heart. Guilt presses down all around me, forcing me further into the earth. I grab the center of my chest, feeling those few cracks still in the back of my heart widen—the ones that haven't fully healed, the ones that won't allow me to fully give my heart to someone new until I face what I've forcefully hidden away.

"Why?" Navy's question isn't meant to be hurtful, but I feel hurt all the same.

"I couldn't be around any of it," I say. "The memories were too much. After I moved in with my parents, they put all our belongings in a storage unit. It's not that I haven't thought about going there, because I have, but I couldn't bring myself to take the leap. And then, I met you girls and Luke and our friends, and everything was amazing. I didn't want to start slashing away at our happiness. I thought I could ignore it."

"What about now?" Navy sits up and crosses her legs out in front of her.

"Now?" I ponder the question. "Now, I know I can't ignore it. Luke deserves to have my full heart, and he isn't going to get that with the amount of literal baggage I have."

They both smile at me as the tension and heaviness of the situation eases.

"Do you want our help?" Sutton asks.

I considered asking them, but after thinking—then overthinking—the situation, I decided this was something I'd like Luke's help with. "I was thinking of asking Luke."

A bittersweet smile appears on Sutton's face. "I'm sure he'd like to be there for you in this way, Greer."

"Really?"

"Duh," Navy says. "That man is head over heels in love with you and would walk through the bowels of hell if it meant making you that much happier."

"She's not wrong," Sutton says. "Have you asked him?"

"Not exactly. We haven't really talked since he left for work." Pulling out my phone, I show them the text messages. "And now he wants to take me somewhere, and I really want to go, but I know I can't until I deal with my life. My old life."

"God, you're such a dumbass sometimes," Sutton says, shocking both Navy and me. "What did we tell you when you and Luke started this thing?" She pauses for dramatic effect.

I shrug my shoulders.

"You have to communicate with him!" Just then another text pings through.

Luke: I'm on my way. Have your bag packed.

"What's it say?" Navy asks, and I show them. Sutton rips my phone out of my hands and types out a fevered response.

Me/Sutton: I would love to. I think there are some things we should talk about.

Luke: That sounds ominous.

Me/Sutton: It's not. I can't wait to see you.

Luke: Me too. <3

"See!" Sutton says, handing me my phone back. "Was that really all that hard?!"

"Guess we better go help you pack," Navy says. She holds out her hands and pulls me to stand. Together, we all head inside to pack my bag for whatever Luke has planned. I hope they pack enough confidence in there for me, too.

23

Luke

Staring down at my phone, relief floods through me seeing Greer's texts. Ever since the other night, she's been giving me one-word responses, if she even bothered to respond at all. Not necessarily the reaction I was expecting after almost making love.

Never in my life has working felt like torture. I was slated to work a forty-eight to cover for a shift-trade I need soon, so I couldn't exactly cancel it. It was an unusually slow two days, which made staring at my phone, anticipating Greer's texts, that much easier.

My relief walks through the bay doors, and without a goodbye, I all but run to my truck. I've got plans for me and my girl today. Ain't nothing going to get in my way.

"Hey, Luke." Groaning at the sound of that voice, I turn to find Sadie walking up to my truck. I can't help the eye roll when I notice the very un-Sadie-like outfit she's wearing. I bury down the laugh threatening to escape at her poor attempt to dress more like Greer—deep brunette hair piled high on her head in a messy bun and sporting an oversized T-shirt.

Early morning sun beats down on the asphalt. My shirt is damp with sweat and sticking to my skin. Shoving things into my backseat, I double-check my fishing gear is all accounted for. All I want to do is get home to Greer; maybe if I ignore her enough she'll leave.

"Hey, Luke" she says again, leaning against my truck.

"Hey, Sadie," I respond curtly, breathing deep to push down my growing annoyance.

"I was hoping maybe you could stop by my house and look at my water heater." She steps near enough to place her hand on the outside of my elbow. I jerk away from her, my body outright rejecting her physical touch. She balks at my reaction.

"Wish I could, but I've got plans already."

"Oh? What plans?"

"None that concern you."

Her face hardens at my gruff response. "It'll only take a few minutes. I promise."

And here it is, another realization that I've done this to my own goddamn self. I knew I shouldn't have helped her with her car twice, knew she would take my assistance as me opening the door between us again. I've lost count how many times Hunter warned me not to allow my time to become inconsequential to the needs of others. And yet, as I stand here, looking back at Sadie's expectant face, it all comes full circle. I have no one to blame but myself.

"Sadie," I soften my tone, "I know you're used to coming to me whenever you need help, and I've always been willing to drop whatever I was doing whenever you—or hell, anyone in this town—need me, but I can't do it anymore."

"Can't or won't?" She steps back, tucking her hands into the front pockets of her shorts.

"Can't. My time is important too. For so long, I've allowed it to become less so, always allowing someone to pull me from whatever I have planned or what *I* wanted."

"This is about her, isn't it?" Sadie's voice is soft, almost ashamed to ask.

Shaking my head back and forth, I say, "It's about me. For once in my life, I'm telling someone no when they need help. I've already made plans, so I can't come by right now. If it's an emergency, call the plumber, okay?"

"I've seen you two together a lot," she says.

I nod, having already guessed she'd done some recon based on her sudden change in style.

"You seem happy."

"Happiest I've ever been," I say, even though I know my words might hurt.

Sadie's smile falls a fraction, but she recovers quickly. "I'm happy for you, Luke." She nods her head and continues down the sidewalk.

I know it's the last time I'll hear from her, and I'm glad for it.

The engine roars to life as I look back at Greer's last text. *There are some things I think we should talk about.* No other phrase in the world could be as anxiety-inducing as this one. I know we have a lot to talk about.

But I'll face it all because I love her.

I've known it since the Fourth, laying with her while fireworks exploded above us. I know she doesn't realize it and, hell, may not even be ready to hear it, but Greer has completely captured my heart, and I have no plans on taking it back.

Call it lust, call it hormones, but we got ahead of ourselves the other night. I should've known better than to keep going. In that moment, I couldn't hear or see anything other than the woman I love begging for me. For us.

The fear in her eyes when she'd jolted away from me, breaking the spell we were under, the tears falling from her eyes? That nearly broke me. She can say what she likes, but I know Greer has a few things locked away in that heart of hers still. It's time for a little nature therapy. It's time to lay it all out on the line.

Pulling into my driveway, I notice Navy and Sutton pulling away from Greer's house.

Sutton rolls down the window. "Hey, big bro."

"Hey, sis. Hi, Navy." I walk to where they're waiting in the middle of the street.

"Luke," Navy begins, "that woman in there is a whole storm of emotions currently, so be gentle. But make her talk to you."

"Exactly." Sutton grabs Navy's shoulder. "Luke, I don't think she's realized it yet, but she loves you. She's also scared and confused. Help her make sense of the mess in her mind, okay?"

"I plan on it." I wave as they drive away.

I turn back to my house and hustle inside for a quick shower and change of clothes. Dipping into the garage, I grab my hiking pack and shove food and supplies inside. I make one last stop to grab my fishing gear from the back of my truck before going to get my girl.

As if sensing I'm home, she meets me halfway between our houses, right at our usual spot.

"Hi," she says with downcast eyes.

"None of that." I tilt her chin, so I can see her eyes and kiss those lips. "Whatever is going through that mind of yours, it'll be okay. It's just us." My shoulders relax when she smiles. "Let's grab your bag and get Duke. We've got a little bit of a hike ahead of us."

"Say what now? Did you just say hike?" Her smile wanes.

"Sure did," I say, heading toward her patio.

"And where are we hiking to?"

Stopping, I turn and point to the preserve behind our house. At this, she bites her lip, attempting to hide her excitement.

"For real life?"

"I've been saying all summer I'd take you fishing, and today seems like a perfect day for it." Her back door is open, so I grab her backpack and attach Duke's leash. She's still standing in the middle of the yard. With a quick assessment, I see she's dressed appropriately for our outing. I'll have to thank Sutton for that.

"Here, let's get this backpack on and make sure it's snug." I make a spinning gesture with my open hand, and Greer turns and puts her arms back like a child. "You good?"

She nods her head, but then follows up with, "I'm good. I thought maybe you'd still be mad at me."

I spin her to face me and grasp her hands. "No reason to be mad. I'll say it again: Whatever is running through that mind of yours, it's going to be okay."

She leans up and presses her lips to mine. They're soft, and I distinctly taste a bit of frosting.

"Did you pack any of that frosting?" I ask, even though I know she's got some baked good squirreled away from all the stress baking she's done.

Her deep belly laugh soothes my frazzled heart. "What gave me away?"

"You taste like frosting. So, did you?"

"Of course." She rolls her eyes. "Ugh, how is it that you know me so well?"

"Because you're the other half of my soul." The words fly out before I can stop them. We pause, eyes and hearts locked. I smile softly before saying, "Let's go."

Hand in hand, we walk into the preserve using the hidden trail just beyond her favorite spot. Her steps are tentative, eyes never leaving the ground in front of her. She gives little grunts of frustration every now and then as we gain elevation. It's clear she's not much of an outdoors woman. All around us the preserve is coming alive with the rustling of animals and morning twittering of birds. Wildflowers are in full bloom all around. Duke tugs on the leash, so I kneel down and unhook him. He immediately runs down the path before coming back toward us to take up the lead position.

"So," she says casually, "about the other night." She picks up a large branch, inspecting it carefully before deciding to use it as a walking stick.

"What about it?"

"Don't you think we should talk about it?"

I've thought of nothing else the last two days. Even going so far as to get advice from Hunter, which was surprisingly helpful. *If you love her, talk to her about it. Don't let this shit fester.*

"I do," I finally answer.

She slows her pace to walk by my side. Peeking from under her ball cap, she says, "I haven't been truthful with you."

My stomach plummets to my feet. "What do you mean?"

"I have a storage unit."

"Okay? Like for dead bodies or something?"

"Not real ones." She laughs.

"You've lost me, G."

She reaches out with her open hand and places it into mine. I squeeze, hoping to give her a boost of confidence. We continue forward along the path.

"After Brian died, I moved in with my parents. What most people don't know is they also moved all our stuff into a storage unit. I couldn't"—she pauses, swallowing hard—"I couldn't be around our things. And . . . well, they've been locked away in that unit ever since."

Understanding trickles in. She's done a great job looking the part of a woman who's moving forward, but it sounds like maybe she might finally be ready to face a crucial part of her journey, parting ways with the physical objects from her old life.

"What does this have to do with the other night?"

She pauses and faces me fully. Tugging my hand, she leads us over to sit on some nearby boulders.

"I think in order for me to give you my heart completely, I have to take care of the physical elements of my life with Brian. I'm almost me again, and I think this is the last piece."

My heart aches for how hard this must be for her. She reaches for me and links her fingers with mine. There's a sudden stillness in the air as sunlight filters through the branches.

"I was wondering, if maybe you could help me?"

At first, I'm stunned. She wants me to be part of this intimate moment with her? Doesn't she want to do this with her parents or even her friends? Why me?

"Because"—she starts to reply but stops herself—"aren't you supposed to be taking me fishing?"

"Yeah, let's go." I pull her up. It's important to me that she finally feels ready to discuss this with me, but I'm okay giving her a few more minutes to gather her thoughts.

Almost forty-five minutes later, we come to an opening in the trees. Glittering before us is a small lake. The sun is just nearing its pinnacle, and the water's surface has taken on a glassy sheen. Greer stops to my left and wipes sweat from her brow. Buffeted by forest, this lake is tucked far enough away into the preserve that most anglers don't venture here.

We continue in silence toward a shady spot on the western bank. It's my usual spot for when I stay overnight because it has a flat area above the shore for laying out sleeping bags, a small fire pit, and easy water access. Duke runs ahead through the water before taking refuge in the shade. Greer sets her bag against a stump and sits to pull off her shoes and socks. She wiggles and stretches her toes. I smile.

Greer isn't like the other women I've spent time with. With them, everything felt forced, each of us intent to fill every moment with meaningless chatter, saying plenty but never truly connecting. Greer is different. Even when we're surrounded by silence, we speak volumes—reading each other like our favorite books, every glance and breath filled with understanding.

As I'm setting up our fishing poles, Greer walks cautiously toward the shore. She dips her toes in, but sucks in a quick breath at the cold water. It may be summertime, but our lakes and rivers never get all that warm. She studies the water, her feet swinging back and forth, and then takes a few more steps.

"Jesus, this water is cold," she says, looking over her shoulder at me, her signature grin lighting up her face.

"High altitude tends to do that."

She rolls her eyes and steps in a little farther, the hem of her cutoff shorts dips into the water. Giggling, she dips her hands into the water and swishes them from side to side. I can't take my eyes off of her, captivated by watching her experience something for the first time. She's in her own world, and I'm the lucky bastard that gets to watch.

"You going swimming, sweetheart?" I ask, not taking my eyes off of her even as I continue preparing our fishing poles.

"Could I?"

I set down the poles, remove my boots and socks, and stand to unbutton my jeans.

"What are you doing, mister?"

"Well, I didn't bring any swim trunks, and I'd rather not wear wet jeans all day." I wink at her and shimmy out of my jeans.

A slight breeze cools my heated skin, and pinpricks move from my feet up my legs, making my skin break out in chill bumps. The water passes my knees as I ease in farther, until I'm mid-thigh. Reaching over my head, I pull my shirt off, leaving me in nothing but my briefs.

"You coming?" I toss my shirt toward the shore, then dive under the water.

At first, my lungs seize, and I think they might explode, but as I surface, the sun's heat makes the water more refreshing. Greer's got her eyebrows scrunched together, and I know she's debating diving in. She grumbles something, nods, and slips her shorts down her legs, tossing them toward our stuff. She takes off her tank next, leaving her standing in only a bra and underwear.

"Are those strawberries on your undies?"

Her cheeks blush cherry-red as she glances down at her undergarments—a matching yellow set covered in tiny, red strawberries. When she looks up, her smile sends my heart spinning.

"Yes, yes they are." She straightens her shoulders and braces herself before swan diving into the water. A few seconds later, she surfaces, sputtering water. "Holy shit, that's cold."

"You'll get used to it." I float backward farther into the lake.

"Oh yes, I am sure my nipples will thaw out in twenty to thirty years or so."

"I could help them thaw out faster if you'd like me to," I say, waggling my eyebrows.

She rolls her eyes, then dips back under the water before coming to float on her back near me.

"How did you find this place?"

"Hunter and I found it not long after I moved in. There are a few hidden lakes back here, but this one is my favorite."

"Hunter's a good guy," she says almost to herself.

Approaching slowly, I swim next to her as she continues floating on her back.

"He really is. If only my sister could see that. Our lives would be much easier."

"Mmmm," she says, turning her head toward me. Water drops glisten on her eyelashes. "I think she knows it. She's just scared to do something about it."

"Could be." My hands caress her back under the water.

"You scare me," she whispers.

"Why do I scare you?" Confusion leeches from each word. In my whole life, I've never had anyone say I scare them. Intense, yes, but I'm usually easy-going.

"Because of how much you make me feel." She rolls over in the water and swims a few feet away. I follow, drawn to her like a fish to a lure.

Greer turns swiftly, startling when she finds me so close. My hands skim her waist as I pull her to me. She wraps her legs around me and interlaces her hands over my shoulders.

"Is what you feel a bad thing?"

She shakes her head no, but then says, "No, it's not bad. I used to feel guilty for it. In the beginning. But now I think it scares me because I never thought I'd feel this way again."

"And how do you feel?" Her lips hover centimeters from mine, and I can't help but pray she closes the distance.

"Like I'm falling for you." She presses her cold lips against mine. "Now, didn't you say something about fishing?"

Pulling her to me, I kiss her on the tip of her nose and walk us to shore. I take our poles and place some power bait on each.

"Alright, ask any angler and they'll tell you fishing is all about the cast." I laugh at her befuddled face. "Don't worry, it's easy."

I am, in fact, wrong. Minutes later, I find out casting is not as easy as I thought. Especially not for Greer.

"It's all in the wrist," I say. "Keep a bit of tension, and as you come forward, release your finger. Got it?"

Greer nods and watches me model a few more times. She takes her pole, prepares to cast, and then proceeds to release the whole damn thing into the lake. "Oh, shit!" she yells, splashing through the water to retrieve her pole. "That is not what I was supposed to do, was it?"

"I mean, beating the fish over the head by tossing your pole at them is one way to do it." My body rumbles with laughter when she smacks me in the chest. I reach to take the pole from her to show her the proper technique again, but she swats my hands away.

"I got it."

I hold my hands up in mock surrender. She prepares to cast again, so I step back. This time the hook gets stuck on a nearby tree branch.

"Goddamn it," she says, stomping over to untangle her line. Her strawberry-covered ass sways back and forth. My mouth waters watching her sexy, muscular thighs jiggle.

This goes on for several more attempts. So many, in fact, that I take a seat on a nearby boulder to watch the show. After the tree, it gets stuck between rocks, on her discarded shirt, on my boot, and even me.

"Oh my god!" she says, rushing over to see where her hook embedded itself in my arm. "It looks so easy when others do it. I didn't think I would suck this bad."

"Would you like some help?" I ask as I remove the hook from where it's barely stuck in my arm.

She shakes her head no and returns to her pole. It's been a learning curve, allowing Greer to figure things out on her own, realizing all she needs from me is me. My hands feel empty with nothing to do, so I move a few steps away, take up my own reel, and cast out.

"Show off," she says.

I shrug.

Out of the corner of my eye, I watch her talk to herself, working through each point I gave her. Then, she walks to the edge of the water. Her feet are submerged in mud. She settles, brings her arm back, places the reel in perfect position, and brings the line forward smoothly. It zips through the air before making a *plop* as it breaks the surface of the water.

In true Greer form, there aren't any squeals of delight. She just gives me a cute smile and a thumbs-up. I swallow past the lump in my throat. *This woman.*

"Wow," she says hours later. "Who would have thought I'd be a better fisherman than you?"

"Beginner's luck," I mumble. Only I could take a woman who's never done anything remotely outdoorsy fishing, and she'd out fish the hell out of me. "Now, it's time for the real work to begin—time to learn to gut 'em."

"Um, no. Nope, I am not doing that." She crosses her arms over her chest, pushing her breasts together. Her skin glows pink from the afternoon sun. It's only now I realize neither of us bothered to put clothes back on.

"What are you laughing at?" she asks.

Gesturing to her body and mine, I say, "I've never actually been fishing in my skivvies before. It's no wonder they liked you more than me."

Greer looks down at her body before planting her hands on her hips, grinning ear to ear. Her gaze is hot on my back as I squat down near the water's edge. We're both quiet as I prepare the fish for dinner. I'm so focused I don't notice she's approached until her warm hands smooth over my shoulders. She squats down behind me, her legs bracket mine, and the smooth skin of her inner thighs brush against my waist.

"Be good," I say as her hands continue to caress my shoulders and arms. This wasn't why I brought her out here.

"I really like you, Luke," she whispers against my skin. She slides her hands around my chest and hugs me to her. "Thank you for today and for teaching me to fish."

"You're welcome." I bend my head enough to kiss her arm. "Now, get dressed, and I'll teach you how to start a fire."

"Great!"

Night settles quickly around us. Dinner was a success. Greer's prattled on and on most of the evening. I remember when I first met Greer, how shy she was, often getting caught up in her mind so much that her words would get stuck or they'd come tumbling out. It's hard to believe how much she's changed, hell, how much I've changed, over the course of a summer.

I pull her legs into my lap and knead her feet and calves. The ridges of her scars are soft beneath my fingers.

"How did you do it?" I ask.

"Do what?" she asks.

"Come out the other side?"

"I'm not sure exactly. In the beginning, there were times I wasn't sure I wanted to." She looks up, gauging my reaction at her confession. My eyes lock on hers, heart aching as I imagine the pain she felt. "But then," she says, "I found Muriel and that helped. To be honest, I spent most of the last year in automatic mode, doing what I needed to do to get from one minute to the next. There's no way to prepare for the grief Death leaves behind, no way to know how much it fucking sucks, no way to prepare for all things you have to do alone now. Hell, I barely made it through the holidays. Brian was a Christmas fanatic. It was brutal trying to pretend to have Christmas cheer. All I wanted to do was talk about Brian while simultaneously trying to forget him. It was hard, talking about him, but I was afraid if I didn't, I'd forget him." She pulls her feet from my lap, crosses them over the other, and scoots closer to me.

"Love, I'm too big to be sitting criss-cross applesauce."

"The fact you know that phrase." She giggles, pulling my hands into her lap. "Earlier, you asked *why me?*"

"I didn't realize I'd said that out loud."

"Never, over the course of the last year, did I ever think I would feel *this* again." She presses our hands over her heart. "You've helped me realize I'm not as lost or hopeless as I once thought. You've never shied away from my grief or made me hide it."

"Never," I say firmly. "Losing my dad shook my entire family. Watching my mom grieve was, and is, very difficult. I can't know what it was like for her, or you, to lose the man you love. There are days I wonder why my mom hasn't found someone else, but now being with you? I can't imagine losing this, losing you."

"It's not something I ever imagined being, a widow. But that's Life, beautiful and unpredictable. My life didn't end that night, and I know"—she looks into my soul—"I still have so much life left to live."

"Are you sure you really want my help with your storage unit? I don't want to overstep again."

Settling one hand over mine, she brings her other to cup the side of my face. "I know I can do this part on my own, but I don't want to. Luke, you make me feel strong. You make me incandescently happy. I'm ready to start fully living my life again. With you."

Later, we snuggle into our sleeping bags. The night sky comes to life above us, stars peeking out from behind paper-thin clouds. We lie there, hand in hand, both of us lost in thought.

"Greer?" I whisper.

"Yeah?"

"I'd be honored to help you."

24

Greer

After our trip, we go to Luke's mom's house for family dinner. Carissa is already waiting for us in the middle of the driveway and doesn't even give me a chance to get out of the truck before pulling me into a tight embrace. She leads us inside, leaving Luke standing alone in the driveway. Sutton relaxes when I give her a reassuring smile. By the time Luke makes it into the house, we're two photo albums and a thousand stories deep into his childhood.

The four of us work in tandem finishing dinner. Knowing the beautiful weather is winding down, we end up on the patio.

"Greer, honey," Carissa asks from across the table, "will you pass the sweet potatoes?"

"Mom," Sutton says, "did I tell you that the police station got approval for renovations?"

Luke shakes his head and rolls his eyes. "They get a fancy new station while we've still got one station working out of a trailer."

"I couldn't care less what the city does with their money," Sutton says. "I just hope they pick me to run the remodel."

"Pick you?" Carissa asks. "Are you finally going to get into interior designing?"

"Uh . . ." Sutton hesitates. "I'm not sure, just something I'm thinking about."

"That's really cool, Sut," I say. "When is your proposal due?"

"Sometime after Labor Day," she says nonchalantly.

My heart jumps to my throat. *Labor Day.* It seems like only yesterday school was letting out for summer, and I was moving into my new house. How is it that an entire summer has gone by in a blink? How has it almost been one year since my life irrevocably changed?

Luke's hand finds my thigh, a quiet comfort. His eyes meet mine, and a small nod says what words can't: hHe remembers, just like I do, what that date means to me.

"Shit," Sutton says. "I'm sorry, Greer. I totally forgot."

"Oh," Carissa says, "is that the day you lost your Brian?"

"It is," I say.

"November fifteenth," Carissa says. "That's the day I lost my Daniel." She smiles. Sutton and Luke don't move.

"Does it ever go away?" The room grows heavy with loss.

"No, dear. It doesn't go away, but it does get easier."

"Mom," Sutton says, "why did you never date again?"

"Well,"—Carissa gives a shy smile. Color peppers her cheeks—"I tried a few times, but there was always something not quite right. So, I stopped looking. I figure your dad found me, so if I'm meant to find someone new, we will somehow find each other. For now, I just keep loving on these two beautiful children I have and living this new life. I know it's what your dad would have wanted."

"Mom," Luke says, "I didn't know you tried dating after Dad." His voice carries surprise.

"Of course you wouldn't have known, Son. It wasn't as if I was out there advertising that this old gal was trying to get back in the saddle. I didn't need Susan gossiping about my sex life at bunco night, you know?"

Luke chokes on his food, sending the whole table into a fit of laughter. Carissa grins unapologetically—filters are clearly not her thing.

After supper, Luke takes over the dishes, and Sutton disappears to work on her proposal, leaving Carissa and me alone on the back porch. Her luscious garden is alive with color under the dreamy glow of her garden lights.

"Can I ask you a question?" Carissa takes my hand in hers.

"Of course," I say. As if anyone could deny her anything.

"Things between you and Luke, they're serious?"

"Yes." Easiest answer in the world.

"That's good. Makes this mom's heart happy to hear that. For both of you."

"Can I ask you something now?"

"Anything." She fixes the cashmere blanket over our legs.

"What did you do with all of Daniel's things? With the things from your life together?"

She sighs deeply before reaching forward to wrap my hands in hers. "Let me show you something."

Inside, we pass the kitchen, where Luke gives me a curious expression. I shrug as she leads me into her bedroom. From her closet, she tugs out a medium-sized trunk. Upon opening it, I'm met with all the mementos of a life well-loved. There are papers and photo albums, what looks to be her wedding dress and veil, and other various items all neatly folded inside.

"This is the house Daniel and I raised our children in. It's the house he died in. Over the years, Sutton and I have redecorated the majority of it, and I've slowly said goodbye to the physical pieces of our life together. The rest, well, it's all right here."

"How did you know what to keep?"

"Your heart will tell you."

"Do you think I'm asking too much of Luke, to help me with my storage unit?"

Inhale. Exhale.

Her smile is serene, calm. "No, my love, I think it's quite wonderful. Luke would do anything for you."

"I know he would, but I don't want to hurt him." Luke's love language is acts of service, that much has become clear, but I don't want him offering without thinking of his own heart first.

"That's a risk you're both going to have to take, but it's a lot less scary than going at it alone. If you and Luke really want this to work between you, your story and your grief will always be a part of your lives. A sad part, yes, but I think by seeing your old memories and helping you say goodbye, I don't know, maybe it can be something therapeutic for you both."

Carissa pulls me in close. "It's not easy, losing the one we love," she whispers. "It's not fair that you had to experience this type of loss so early in life."

"Life really does suck sometimes," I say against her shoulder as my tears soak through her blouse.

"That it does," she says. "But it's also really beautiful. After we lost Daniel, there were moments when I didn't think my heart would ever heal. Not only did I have to mourn the loss of my husband but I also had to watch my children grieve the loss of their father. We took it day by day and, eventually, it stopped hurting as much."

"I'm afraid Luke agreed to help me because that's just who he is, always willing to sacrifice himself in service of others."

"That is a personality trait my son has, but I can guarantee he doesn't feel like he *has* to do anything. He wants to do this."

We stay like this for several minutes longer, taking comfort in the arms of someone who knows the same pain you feel.

Town is less busy tonight when we finally leave Carissa's and head back home. My mind wanders as I watch trees, signs, houses, and cars flash by my window. Streetlights illuminate and cast shadows throughout the interior of Luke's truck. His hand finds mine, threading our fingers together.

"Greer?" Luke's voice is low, gaze set forward. Shadows cover the side of his face, but his eyes flick from the road to me.

"Yeah?"

"I want to be there for you. Not just because it's what I do. All I want to do is be a part of your life in any way you'll let me. I care about you."

"I care about you too," I say with a sweet, lazy smile. "Even if you eavesdrop."

I love the boyish smile he gives me. "Then, together?"
I kiss the top of his hand. "Together."

"Greer?"

"Just hold on, okay? They'll be here soon."

Brian's hands are clammy and sticky from sweat and blood. "You know I love you, right?" he says.

"Of course I know that. I love you too."

"It's time."

"I know, but I'm afraid I'll forget you."

"You won't."

"I'll always love you, Brian."

"And you know I love you. But it's time for you to live. Are you ready?"

"Yes."

"Good. Now, just breathe . . ."

Inhale.

Exhale.

Darkness stretches across my vision, broken only by faint moonlight seeping through the slats in of my window blinds. The silence lingers, but it's no longer heavy like it once was. Duke nuzzles closer to me, his warm body pressing against mine as my fingers find the soft fur at his neck.

"I'm ready." And for the first time, I know it.

Morning comes and I savor the soul-deep calm that seeps into every corner of my body. I dress quickly in a pair of shorts, a tank, and sneakers. After feeding Duke, I cozy up on my couch. It's been a week since our fishing trip, and last night, I decided that today would be the day I face the mementos of my life *before*.

My phone sits heavy in my hand. I stare at it as nervous anticipation fills my tummy. It's been a few months since I last spoke to Brian's parents. Initially, we kept in touch with one another regularly, but, like relationships sometimes do, our phone calls became further and further apart. Brian and I didn't have children, so with him gone, there haven't been many reasons to try hard to stay connected.

It's important for me to check in with them now. They deserve to know I'll be emptying the storage unit. I want them to have an opportunity to take any of Brian's items they'd like.

Steadying my hands, I dial Mrs. Ashbury. After a few rings, she picks up.

"Hello?"

"Hi, Mrs. Ashbury. It's me, Greer."

"Oh, Greer, honey. It's so good to hear from you. How are you doing?" A muffling sound comes through the receiver, and she calls for her husband. "Greer, Bob is here too."

"Hey, Bob. How are you both?"

"Oh, we're doing just fine, dear. It's been a busy summer. We'll actually be headed to Europe again next week. How are you doing?" It's easy to hear hints of Brian's voice in his.

"I'm doing really great actually. Summer has actually been surprisingly fun and relaxing. I, uh, moved to a new house and met some new friends. They're really great. You'd like them a lot. I . . . um, I wanted to tell you . . . Well, I met someone." My heart locks. I'm sure this isn't what they expected to hear.

"Oh, Greer," Mrs. Ashbury says, then inhales sharply. "That's wonderful. Tell us about him."

We spend the next several minutes talking about Luke, my friends, my new school, and even my new house. It feels strange, talking to them about Luke, but they seem genuinely happy for me and interested in how I'm doing.

"I also wanted to let you know I'm going to be emptying our storage unit, you know, in case there's anything you both thought you might want."

"That's so sweet of you to think of us, dear. We actually helped your mom and dad transfer your items to the unit, so we've already had the chance. We didn't take much, just a few of Brian's items from when he was little. Your mom said you wouldn't mind."

I should be hurt that they took things without asking me, but I find I'm actually relieved. "No, that's great. I'm glad you got those things. If I find anything else I think you might want, I'll save it for you, okay?"

"We'd appreciate that, Greer," Mr. Ashbury says.

The weight of loss lessens each minute that passes, but soon, the conversation peters out.

"It was really good to talk to you both."

"You too, Greer," says Mrs. Ashbury. "Losing Brian was hard on all of us. He'd never have wanted you to spend your life alone, and we know he's proud of you. We're proud of you. We couldn't be happier for you."

We stall for a few minutes more before saying our goodbyes. I know it's probably the last time I'll ever speak with them.

When I finish up my phone call, Luke's already waiting in his truck. It's time.

Our drive through town passes by without conversation. Even as we walk into Ground Up, we're oddly quiet. Navy eyes us both questioningly, but I reassure her with a smile.

"You two okay?" she asks when she brings us our coffee and food. We'd taken a table near the window to enjoy the sun's warmth that's already filtering through the glass. Luke's eyes move to mine, uncertain of what he should say.

"We're going to my storage unit today," I say before taking a tentative sip, unsure of how she'll react.

"You are?" There's hope in Navy's voice.

I nod and reach across the table to grasp Luke's hand in mine. His warmth steadies me, grounding me in the moment.

"*We* are," he says for me. Navy looks from him and back to me, searching for confirmation.

"And this is what you want?" Navy says. "You're ready?"

My dream from last night flashes through my mind, but for once I'm not filled with fear or guilt.

"I know it'll be hard," I say, "but I'm ready." I smile and catch her gaze before shifting to Luke's.

"Sutton and I can help too if you want," Navy offers.

"I know, but I only decided last night that now is the right time to do it. I can't expect y'all to drop everything for me. Plus, it'll be good for us"—I gesture between Luke and me—"to go alone first."

"I understand," Navy whispers as she pulls me in for a tight hug. "I'm so happy for you."

"Me too." My gaze locks on Luke's. His eyes are warm and so full of love.

Luke doesn't let go of my hand as we finish our drive. He doesn't let go as we exit the truck. He doesn't let go as we wind down long rows of doors. He doesn't let go as we locate the storage locker, number 1111.

From my pocket, I remove a silver key. The lock gives way easily and, together, we lift the door. Within moments, the automatic lights flicker on. The air is heavy and stale after being left undisturbed for so long. With a deep breath, I step into the unit and come face to face with a life I once lived.

At first, confusion fills my brain. I expected everything to be shoved every which way, no rhyme or no reason. Instead, I'm greeted with the most organized and well-thought-out storage room in the history of storage rooms. Furniture is stacked neatly on one side while boxes are stacked on the other.

"This is not what I expected," Luke says.

"You and me both," I laugh.

Together, we edge around tables and chairs to the middle of the room. From the corner of my eye, I see the label "Things you might keep." Next to it, I spy a box labeled "Things you might donate." A laugh bursts from deep within me when I notice all the boxes labeled "Why do you have so many books?" Tears prick my eyes as I see each and every box is labeled in this way.

"My mom—" My heart lodges itself in my throat. Tears threaten to overwhelm me when Luke pulls me to him.

"You don't have to do this right now," he says.

"No, it's not that. It's all of this." I gesture to the boxes. I know my parents and Brian's parents carefully packed and labeled them like this knowing someday I would be ready to face my old life.

"So, where should we start?" Luke asks.

For months, I have been too afraid to do this. Afraid I'd be overwhelmed by everything that was and will never be again. But this—what my, *our,* parents have done—banishes that fear. They've given me peace during a moment that could have shattered me completely.

Over the next few hours, Luke and I take each box, and I carefully go through their contents. From kitchen and living room boxes to office and guest room boxes, I allow whatever memories or thoughts or words pour into me. Finally, I face the boxes from our bedroom.

"Do you want me to step out?" Luke asks as we stare down at boxes labeled "Brian's clothes."

"If you want to, you can," I say as the tape breaks easily.

He shakes his head no and stands behind me, his warmth and steadfast nature calms me.

Brian's clothes are folded neatly inside. On top is his favorite plaid shirt. I pull it from the pile, bringing it to my face, my lungs expanding on a deep inhale, wondering if it still smells like him. I'm not sure if I'm relieved or saddened when it doesn't. I return the shirt, close the box, and hand it to Luke. "I think he'd like it if I donated those."

"I think so too." Luke's voice soothes my frazzled edges as he takes the box, stacking it with the others to be donated.

"Is it weird that I'm not taking much?" The cart we borrowed from the storage unit office has only a few boxes labeled "Things you might keep" for me to take home.

"Only you can answer that, sweetheart."

A manic laugh bubbles out of me. "For so many months, this goddamn storage unit has felt like a dark cloud hanging over my head. I was so scared to come here, and then I even let myself think I could forget about it. But now that I'm here? It's like I don't even remember half of this stuff. And that's what it is, isn't it? Stuff. I'll always have the memories. But the rest? It's just stuff."

Grasping the final box labeled "Things you might keep," I rip the flap open. My heart simultaneously breaks and soars as my wedding dress and veil are revealed, nestled into a neat pile—still as beautiful as I remembered, still as full of memories of that special day.

"I bet you were the most beautiful bride," Luke says next to me, his voice low and sincere next to me in the silence.

Rough beading on the satin bodice scratches the soft skin on my palms. A small black ring box is hidden within the fabric. It creaks when I open it, revealing Brian's black wedding band. My fingers rub over the one I've worn on my left hand for the last nine years, one of which I spent without the man who gave it to me. The diamond catches the light, sending prisms bouncing here and there. It slides off my finger just as easily as it went on. With a final kiss, I tuck it next to Brian's and close the lid.

"Is it okay to keep this one?" My tears fall freely now.

Without a word, Luke takes the ring box and places it back in the storage box before adding it to my pile to bring home. When he returns, he stands like a sentinel next to me, holding my hand as I succumb to the emotions bubbling out of me.

"Hey guys, I think they're down here." Hunter's voice breaks the heaviness.

"What in the world?" Luke whips around, grabs my hand, and leads me into the hallway. If I weren't already crying, I would be now as I spot our friends walking down the hallway.

"What are you guys doing here?" I ask.

Navy and Sutton try to reach me first but are beaten out by Hunter, who wraps me in a bear hug.

"You didn't think we'd let you do this by yourself, did you?" he says as he places me back onto solid ground.

"Hey, babe." Sutton smiles at me as she wipes away my tears that seem to never stop today.

"I told you earlier I didn't expect you to just drop your plans for this. For me." I pin Navy with a serious look. "How did you even get up here?"

"I have my ways." She winks. "And, Greer, you're going to have to realize that we'll do anything for those we love. And we love you, so,"—she holds her arms out wide—"here we are."

"Guys?" a voice that sounds distinctly like Vinnie's hollers from the elevator. "Wanna come give us a hand?"

Luke rushes ahead and stops dead in his tracks as Vinnie, Grace, and Adam step from the elevator with empty boxes and another cart.

"We weren't sure what we might need," Grace says, "so we brought it all." Grace pushes by Luke to hug me.

"Alright, G," Adams says, "put us to work." He drags the empty boxes down the hall.

They're all chattering as they head toward the storage unit, leaving Luke and me dumbfounded in the middle of the hall.

"You guys!" I shout.

"Yeah?" They say, turning around.

"What are you guys doing? You don't have to be here."

"Of course we had to be here," Vinnie says. "You're family and family sticks together. We wouldn't be anywhere else."

My tears run freely down my face as laughter erupts from within me.

"Is this good laughter or bad laughter?" Hunter mumbles out of the corner of his mouth.

"You guys . . ." Luke begins, but emotion clogs his throat.

"Oh, for Christ's sake," Vinnie says. "Group hug!" He corrals us all together.

Our arms overlap as everyone crowds in to surround Luke and me. For a brief moment, we're silent, content to sit in this embrace of friendship, of family.

"I don't know what to say," I tell them.

"No need to say anything." Hunter grips Luke's shoulder with quiet strength, offering unspoken reassurance.

"Alright, put us to work," Adam says, and we all break apart, moving into action.

Together, our friends help us unload the storage unit. I already decided to sell most of the furniture, a task Sutton volunteers to manage. With Hunter's help, he and Sutton load a trailer and head to the consignment shop. Everything else I choose to donate. Adam and Grace take those boxes to the donation center. Vinnie takes my boxes of books to drop them at my house.

That leaves Navy, Luke, and me with everything I am going to keep. We carefully load them into the bed of Luke's truck.

"Well," Navy says, "I think that's everything."

"Yeah," I say. A task I thought would take forever is now complete in a day. Air fills my lungs to capacity, and I audibly release it. "I don't know how you managed it but thank you."

Navy reaches forward, holding my face and places a kiss on my cheek. She takes a step back, looking at me. "You're welcome. You guys will call if you need anything else, right?"

"Yeah, we will," Luke tells her, wrapping his arms around my shoulders, pulling my back against his front. She smiles again before disappearing out the door.

"You good?" Luke's breath coasts over my head as we look inside the empty storage room. A place that once stored everything from my life with Brian is now empty.

"Yeah, I'm good."

"You need a minute alone, or are you ready to go?"

"I'm ready."

Just breathe.

I slide the door shut.

Music fills the cab of the truck as wind whips through my hair on the ride home. We're exhausted physically and emotionally. I knew today would be hard, but our friends coming to help was not something I ever expected and based on his reaction, neither did Luke. My hand rests in his firm grasp as his thumb smooths back and forth over the spot my wedding ring used to be.

"Let's pick up pizza and wings on our way home and watch a movie."

My stomach grumbles in response. "Sounds perfect."

When we get home, we make quick work unloading the back of Luke's truck by placing all the boxes in my garage. We forgo plates or silverware, choosing instead to eat straight from the box on the coffee table.

"Ugh," I moan an hour later, washing down my food with a swig of beer. "I don't think I can eat another bite."

"Are you sure? I think you might have missed a crumb or two." He snickers, kicking his foot against mine.

"Says the guy who ate a whole pizza. By. Himself." I raise an eyebrow at him.

"Hey now, I'm a growing boy." He lifts his shirt to pat his non-existent belly. I shove my feet into his thigh, but he grabs them and lays them in his lap.

We settle onto the couch and put on one of our favorite movies. Another hour ticks by before I realize I'm not even watching it. Instead, I've been watching Luke. He's lying out across the couch, his long limbs hanging off at strange angles. There are so many little things about him that I love—how he breathes, how he laughs, how he mouths the words to almost every movie we watch even if he won't admit it, how his eyes crinkle in the corners when he laughs, but, most of all, how he loves me. This man has absolutely no idea what he's done for me. After months and months of never-ending internal chaos, I finally feel at peace, and he helped me get here.

"I have something for you," Luke says, his voice pulling me gently from my thoughts and back into the present.

"You do?" Anticipation tingles at the base of my spine. After everything he's done for me today, I can't possibly imagine what he has for me.

"Yeah." Redness creeps its way up his neck and embeds itself into his cheeks. His fingers drum against my thigh as he has some kind of internal battle.

"Am I supposed to guess, or do I get to see it?"

"No, you don't need to guess." He sits up, tugs me up from the couch, and points down my hallway.

"Luke, you're making me nervous."

"Don't be. It's in there." He nods toward my guest room. With his hand on the base of my spine, he pushes me inside. I click the light on.

"Luke." My lungs constrict when I see what he's done.

"I thought maybe you'd want some place special to keep your memories, something just for you."

I drop his hand, then kneel down in front of the most beautiful chest. I easily life the lid, and the rich and familiar scent of mahogany fills my nose.

"Luke, I-I—thank you. It looks just like your mom's."

"She might have helped me. And your parents."

At that, I collapse against the trunk, my laughs turning to sobs. He takes a seat on the ground next to me and nestles me into the safety of his embrace. I burrow deeper into him, one hand wrapped around his back while the other is pressed against his taut stomach.

"Today was a lot," I say.

"It was." He nods as he traces up and down the skin of my arm and side.

"But it was a good *a lot*."

A laugh rumbles through him. "It was that too."

"Thank you. For everything." Beneath my ear, his heart beats a slow and steady rhythm. I smile, grateful for this man who came into my life and helped me find my way back to me.

"Anything for you, Greer."

25

Luke

Greer: Hey you <3
Me: Hey gorgeous, how is work going?

The next few weeks blur together. Whether we're fishing at our spot, out dancing, boating on the lake, or just relaxing at one of our houses, Greer and I are inseparable.

But, like all good things, her official summer came to an end. She's been busy with meetings, classroom setup, and lesson planning. I'd honestly underestimated how much work goes into being a teacher. Granted, I wasn't always the best in school growing up and couldn't have cared less about school. But maybe, if I had a teacher like Greer, I might have paid more attention. Still, I've embraced my role as a teacher's boyfriend pretty well. My laminating and cutting skills are top-notch.

Greer: Oh, you know, just watching another required health safety training video.

Greer: I swear, the people who make these videos have no idea just how gross kids are.

Me: That might be true. Although, I've been on calls and seen people do some nasty shit without proper personal protective equipment.

Greer: Personal protective equipment, huh? I love when you talk medic to me.

Me: I'll remember that next time I see you.

Three dots appear and disappear on my screen multiple times. I can picture Greer perfectly—sitting in her meeting, brows pinched together, debating whether or not to send the text. I chuckle. Greer may look like she's shy and hesitant when it comes to sex, but I know what a minx she is.

"What's that laugh about?" Adam asks from across the dining table. It's been a quiet morning, giving us time to cook a real breakfast and sit down to eat together as a crew.

"Let me guess," Vinnie says, leaning against the doorway with a smirk that's almost too smug for his own good. "I bet you're talking to your wifey."

I level him with a serious gaze. I've wanted to shout it from the rooftops how crazy I am about her, how much she's changed me for the better, how much she owns my heart, but I'm still trying to figure out if she's ready to hear those three words. I should get a gold medal in patience.

"She is not my wifey," I say before quietly adding, "yet."

"You tell her you're ass-over-heart in love with her yet?"

I shake my head. "Pretty sure that's not a real phrase, Vinnie. And no, I haven't. Don't want to rush her."

"You're part of the equation too, bro," Adam says from the sink. "It's okay to do things on *your* own timeline, too."

"Just tell her," Vinnie says. "We all know she loves you."

"You think so, huh?" I say.

They raise their eyebrows and shake their heads.

"It's obvious to anyone with two brain cells," Vinnie says, slapping his hands on the table, then quickly fleeing to the bay.

"What's his deal?" I ask.

"Your guess is as good as mine." Adam shrugs. "He's been a grumpy bastard since the last time we all went to the lake."

"Always something with him. So, about this weekend, you and Grace meeting at my house or what?"

With the school year about to begin and the anniversary of the accident coming up, I decided to surprise Greer with a trip to see her favorite EDM artist—something to give her a good experience and, maybe, lighten the weight of the anniversary.

Over the last two weeks, Navy, Sutton, and Grace helped wrangle the group and nail down the details of the trip. We'll be driving about six hours south to a famous outdoor amphitheater. Thankfully, Greer's been too exhausted and distracted to piece anything together.

"Grace has instructed me to tell you," Adam says, "that we'll meet at your house to surprise her. She also said we need to be leaving by eight a.m. sharp if we want to make our dinner reservations. She also said—"

"I better like glitter?" I ask.

"Exactly." His brow furrows. "What kind of show are we going to anyway?"

"It's one of Greer's favorite EDM artists. I've heard it blaring through her house enough times, and she's never seen him live. I thought it would be fun."

My phone finally buzzes in my pocket with a response from Greer. Adam heads toward the office as I pull it out. A photo of her smiling in a bathroom mirror fills my screen.

Greer: I swear, you'd think I'd be good at this
whole sexting thing.
Me: You know what they say, practice makes perfect.
Greer: It's not like we haven't seen each other
naked or anything.
Me: Speaking of, you were magnificent last night.
Greer: So were you.

I made us dinner but decided to have *her* instead. Even now, I can feel her hands ravaging my hair as I kissed, licked, and sucked every inch of her body. The way she writhed on the counter as I devoured her. The sound of her voice in my ear as she jerked me off. The serene look on her face when she orgasmed.

We've both pulled back since our first attempt at making love, but after cleaning out her storage unit, she seems lighter. I'm a man dying of thirst whenever she's near, but I know we'll both sense when it's the right time to cross that final boundary.

Me: So, this weekend?
Greer: We're going to disappear together and do
absolutely nothing?

Me: Not so much. Pack a bag and be ready by 8:00 a.m. Friday.
Greer: Yeah? Where are we going?
Me: You'll see. ;)

Hours later, I'm taking what little downtime I have to enter some paperwork, which might be the worst part of being a captain. After every call, it's my job to complete the on-scene reports and make sure our i's are dotted and our t's are crossed. I rub my forehead from the headache brewing between my eyes.

Vinnie leans into my office, seemingly in a better mood. "Hey, Cap, Ms. Carol stopped by earlier trying to find you," he says.

"Oh yeah?" I call out as I finish my last on-scene report.

"Yeah, she seemed a little out of sorts to be honest."

"What do you mean?"

"I don't know. She's normally a filthy old broad, flirting it up with everyone, but she only wanted her best friend." Vinnie shakes his head, a slick smile tugging at his lips.

"Jealous?" I tease.

"We'd all be lucky to have a friend like her." He shrugs.

I nod in agreement, then set aside my papers. "I haven't seen her since I stopped by a few weeks ago. I'll reach out to her before we leave for Colorado."

Ms. Carol has been coming around the fire station since before I was a rookie. She's been married a few times but prides herself on being a bachelorette. Over the years, she asked me to do odd jobs around her house, and we quickly became close friends. She's come to trust and rely on me, but, honestly, I think she's just lonely.

A few minutes pass, but I can't shake the feeling that something's off. Deciding to play it safe, I call Greer.

"Hey, you." I hear the smile in her voice.

"Hey, sweetheart. I hate to bug you, but do you think can you do me a favor?"

"Of course."

Greer's met Ms. Carol a few times this summer. I actually think she only asks me over now to see Greer. After filling her in on the situation, she promises to stop by Ms. Carol's house on her way home from school.

We're in the middle of cooking dinner when tones pierce the air. We drop everything, double-check the stove is off, and rush to the engine. I'm pulling up the location when my stomach immediately drops, recognizing the address.

"Shit," I say.

"What's up, Cap?" Adam asks, catching me out of the corner of his eye.

"It's Ms. Carol."

"Fuck," Vinnie says from the back seat as he slams his door. "I knew something wasn't right with her."

Adam puts the truck into gear, turns on the lights and sirens, and exits the station. As first responders, we all know the odds of running a call on someone we know are low—but never zero. In a small town, though, those odds are almost a guarantee. So far, I've only experienced it twice: Greer's accident, something I wish had never happened, and now Ms. Carol.

The tension in the cab is so thick you could cut it with a knife. They might not be as close with her as I am, but with her frequent visits to the station, everyone is fond of her.

Adam pulls along the curb and ensures a safe surrounding. As soon as we're in park, we grab our gear and rush inside the open front door to find Greer comforting Ms. Carol.

"She's here," Greer's panicked voice calls from the living room, sharp and urgent like an alarm bell.

Vinnie, my acting medic, helps me move the furniture to make room for our equipment. "Pulse is weak," he says. "We've got it from here."

There are no further pleasantries. We focus on our patient. She's breathing, but her pulse is weak. An IV line is started, and we check her other vitals. When the ambulance arrives, we load her onto the gurney and into the back of the rig.

"Ma'am, are you coming?" the EMT asks Greer. Without hesitation, she grabs her purse and jumps in the back.

"We'll meet you at the hospital," I tell Vinnie, who rides in with our patients. Greer gives me her awkward thumbs-up.

When we arrive, the hospital is busy for a Wednesday. Normally, the hospital staff take over upon arrival, and we tend to the paperwork before going back on call. This time, we go in search of Vinnie and Greer. They're waiting outside the hospital room.

I wrap Greer in my arms, whispering reassurances. Guilt slides down my spine. I should have just made us do a welfare check and not given this responsibility to Greer. Not when my gut said something wasn't right. "I should never have asked you to go," I say.

"I'm glad you did," she says against my neck.

"Ms. Carol stopped by earlier but wouldn't tell Vinnie what was up. Should have known better."

"Don't do that," Greer says. "You couldn't have known she wasn't feeling well. I got there right in time, and I'm sure the doctors are doing everything they can."

After nearly half hour, the doctor finally comes out to give us a report on her condition and permission to see her. I don't hesitate, grabbing Greer's hand and heading toward the room. She doesn't move.

"Greer?" I ask. Her eyes are glazed over, body utterly still.

"I really don't like hospitals."

Bracketing her face, I force her to look at me. Her blue eyes are filled with tears.

"I don't like them either. You don't have to go in there."

She shakes her head. "No, I want to check in on her too."

Hand in hand, we peek behind the curtains to find Ms. Carol resting in bed. "You know," I tell Ms. Carol as I take a seat in the visitor's chair, "if you wanted to see us, you could have just asked. No need for the show."

This gets a weak laugh from her. "Yeah, yeah, smart-ass."

Greer goes to Ms. Carol's other side. "Why didn't you tell us? We could have helped."

Ms. Carol takes a deep breath. "Now don't be mad at me, Luke," she says and then proceeds to tell us everything. Turns out, she was diagnosed with bladder cancer and had recently started presurgical chemotherapy. Dehydration coupled with the side effects of the chemo had done a number on her today.

"Why didn't you call 9-1-1 to begin with?" I ask.

"I'm sorry, Luke. You know me, I don't want to go making a fuss where a fuss isn't needed. I was on my way back from the store and just wasn't feeling too well, so I stopped by to see you, but you were in a meeting. I headed home to get some rest, and, well, you know the rest. I'm lucky you showed up when you did, Greer. Thank you."

"You scared the shit out of me," Greer says.

"Scared the shit out of myself."

"How long will they keep you?" I ask.

"Oh, just a day or so."

I look to Greer. "We are headed out of town for the weekend, but we can cancel and stay here."

"Absolutely not."

"Why not?" I know Ms. Carol's family isn't close by, so I don't understand why she's refusing my help.

"Luke, honey, if I've learned anything since my diagnosis it's that life is short. Something I think your Greer knows something about too." She smiles at Greer before turning her attention back to me. "You two go on your trip and enjoy the hell out of it. You'll know where to find me when you get back. I expect a full report."

"But—" I say.

"But nothing, Luke Bradley," Ms. Carol says. You know I love you, and I appreciate our friendship, so, listen to me when I say take your girl and go on an adventure. You can't live your life if you're always putting it on hold for other people." She gives me *that* look.

My arms drift out in surrender. "Fine, but I'm going to check in on you while we're gone."

"Wouldn't expect anything else from you, my boy. Now don't you have something better to do than stand around here with this old gal? Plus, *Jeopardy* is starting, so you two get going."

We say our goodbyes and meet the crew by our truck. Greer wraps her arms around my stomach, pulls me in close, and kisses the base of my neck.

"Thank you for being there for her," I say against the crown of her head.

"Of course. Are you okay?"

Part of my job is facing mortality. As firefighters, we have to process quickly and try not to think too hard about what we've seen or experienced. Standing here now with Greer, I feel the weight of time. The ever-present ticking clock.

"Yeah, I am. It's always nerve-racking running calls on people you know." I kiss her temple, and she squeezes me tighter. I can't help thinking of that dreadful call almost one year ago. "I'm glad you were there for her, and I'm glad she's going to be okay. Well, as okay as someone who's been recently diagnosed with cancer can be. I won't lie, I have the urge to cancel all our plans so I can be there for her myself. I want to do everything for her. I also know she's right. I don't need to put my life on hold to prove I'm by her side. She already knows it."

It's hard admitting to oneself that you've been stubborn. My friends have always given me shit about my inability to say no. I'd let their words roll off my shoulder, telling them it's no big deal. But now, with Greer in my arms and Ms. Carol's words in my head, I see that it is a big deal. It's okay to serve others, but it's also okay to protect your own time.

The rest of the week flies by, and thankfully, it's less eventful. Ms. Carol's daughter was able to bring her home after her labs came back normal. Greer and I went over last night to bring her dinner and keep her company. She's not a fan of being "locked up like a criminal" and refuses to take it easy.

"You ready to go?" I peek into Greer's room, where she's frantically packing.

"I wish you'd tell me where we're going. I feel like I'm bringing everything I own." She throws a few more items into her suitcase.

"What you're bringing is fine."

"And you promise your mom is okay watching Duke this weekend? Mom said they could too, but—"

"G," I say, "relax. Everything is taken care of. Okay?"

She huffs and rolls back her shoulders before turning to face me. "Fine."

"Good. Now, let's get this stuff in the truck. They'll be here soon."

Greer stands there, slack-jawed. Ignoring her, I grab her suitcase and backpack, putting distance between us as the torture of keeping this trip a secret reaches its boiling point. Her flip-flops smack against the tile floor as she runs after me toward the front door.

"What do you mean, *they*?" Her voice fades off when she slides around the corner and sees all of us standing on her front porch. She stops mid-motion, arms out, legs splayed, as if she's made of stone.

Hunter waves his hand in front of her face. "I think we broke her," he says with a smirk.

"You ready to go?" Sutton asks, shaking Greer's shoulders to pull her from her stupor.

"Go where?" Greer asks. "What are you guys doing here?" Her brow crinkles when she finds me in the crowd. "I thought *you* were taking me somewhere this weekend."

"*I* am. They just happen to be going too." I wink then turn to put her suitcase in the truck.

"Man," Adam says, "this is gonna be so fun." He reaches for Grace's hand and leads her to their vehicle, with Vinnie close behind.

"I can't believe I have to drive with you," Sutton mutters to Hunter before turning to get into his car.

"Well," Hunter says, rolling his eyes, "this should be fun."

Navy grips his shoulder. "Don't worry. I'll play referee. Or maybe I'll leave you both at a rest stop to work it out."

Greer says goodbye to Duke and locks up her house before literally jumping into the truck. She's wearing those cutoff shorts I love so much, so I can't resist squeezing her thigh.

"What did you do?" Her tank top strap slides down her arm as she buckles up.

"You'll see." I slide my fingers beneath the strap, the back of my fingers dragging up her arm, to pull it back into place. Goosebumps pepper her skin.

She narrows her eyes at me and her breathing speeds up. "I'm feeling very anxious right now, but I'm trying to be all YOLO and shit, but, like, can you please give me some information, so that I can stop freaking the hell out?"

Bringing my hand to rest at the base of her neck, I pull her toward me and capture her mouth with mine. She's tentative, but after a few delicate kisses, she opens fully. Our tongues collide, desperate for the other. Pulling away, I take in the pink speckles along her cheeks. She sighs dreamily.

"We're going on a little road trip to Colorado."

"Colorado? What's in Colorado?"

"A place you might have mentioned a time or two."

She smacks me across the chest, and I cover her hand with mine. "No way." Shock fills her face. "No fucking way."

"Yes way."

"But? Wait, what day is it?" She pulls out her phone and checks the date, as if she doesn't know what the date is, as if we both haven't been tracking each day that passes this month, bringing us closer and closer to the anniversary.

She clicks on her events tab and bounces in her seat. "Are we going where I think we are?"

"Possibly."

She throws off her seat belt and clambers over the console to me. Her hands burrow into my hair, and she yanks my mouth to hers. My fingers graze bare skin when I grip her hips, pulling her to me and forcing her full weight onto my lap. Our hands feverishly explore every inch of the other—hair, neck, face.

"Oh my god." She pulls back panting. "I can't even believe this is happening. I didn't think you even heard me mention this show." Still seated on my lap, she rolls down the window, leans halfway out, and yells, "Are we really going to Red Rocks?"

"Hell yeah, we are!" Grace yells back.

Greer pulls herself back into the truck and grips me by the sides of my face.

"How did I find you?" she asks, suddenly serious.

"Technically, Duke found me first."

Greer bursts out laughing, throwing her head back as she wiggles her way her way back into the seat, a grin still plastered on her face.

"Well?" she yells at me. "What are we waiting for? Let's go!"

26

Luke

WE MAKE IT HALFWAY into our six-hour trip before stopping for gas and provisions. Everyone scrambles out of their vehicles, stretching and loosening up, before heading inside the corner store.

"You want anything?" Greer asks over her shoulder.

"Whatever you pick will be fine." I probably should have been worried by the look she gave me. I'm not ashamed to admit I watch her ass until she's out of sight.

"You know," Hunter says, his voice cutting through the hum of both gas lanes, "it's nice seeing you like this."

"Like what?"

"Happy."

"Have I not always been happy?" I finish before going to stand next to him.

"Sure, you've been happy, but she makes you different."

"Greer is the best thing that's ever happened to me," I tell him, my voice steady with conviction. "You think you'll ever find a woman to tie you down for life?"

Hunter smiles, his gaze shifting toward my sister as she enters the store and disappears from sight. "Already have."

"So," I say, "when are you going to tell her?"

"When she's ready to hear it."

"Don't wait too long, Hunter. Life is too short. You and Sutton both deserve happiness and living in this perpetual state of . . . hell, I don't even know what to label it, isn't fair to either of you. Remember your advice you gave me about Greer?"

He nods his head.

"If you love her, don't let this shit fester." With that, I leave him to sort through his own thoughts and head inside after my girl.

Gaudy fluorescent lights greet us as we step inside, all of us laughing and goofing off while picking out drinks and snacks. I spot Greer in the middle of the girls, their heads huddled together as they whisper excitedly, her smile wide and infectious.

"You think you two will finally seal the deal?" Vinnie asks.

"Watch it, Vinnie," I say, shoving him away from me. His boisterous laugh draws everyone's attention. Greer's eyes meet mine with a wicked half smirk. I nod in warning. Little minx just bites that damn lip of hers, laughs, and disappears into the restroom.

After much delay and with our goods acquired, we finally hit the road again. Greer's scanning through my music app looking for the perfect song. That's one thing I've learned about Greer this summer—she loves to ride in the passenger seat and play DJ. It doesn't matter how many times I try to command our playlist when we go for a drive, she weasels her way into control. So far, our playlist has gone from Broadway musicals to rock and even some hardstyle EDM.

"Your musical choices are always interesting," I say playfully as I lace my fingers with hers.

"Says someone who listens to one genre of music only."

"Hey now, nothing wrong with '90s country."

She laughs. "There is absolutely nothing wrong with '90s country. You know I love it, and I'm sure they love it way down yonder on the Chattahoochee. I'm merely suggesting there's a whole world of music out there. Why limit yourself?" She traces her fingers up and down the inside of my arm, each pass inching her fingers farther under the sleeve of my shirt.

"Whatcha doing?" I ask, trying like hell to focus.

With a devilish grin, she says, "Touching you."

I slide my hand from hers and trace the smooth expanse of her thigh. I love how warm her skin is. Her hand stills as mine finds its way under the hem of her shorts, toying with the edge. She takes a steadying breath and relaxes her thighs open. My fingers trace the delicate skin of her inner thigh, and her eyes close. I want so badly to slip my hands under her panties. With great difficulty, I pull my hand back to the steering wheel.

Greer breathes heavily before leaning over and kissing my shoulder. Her free hand runs up the side of my neck and caresses my earlobe.

"Be good."

"I am, but I . . ." she hesitates.

"But you what?" I ask, dying for her to finish her thought.

"I want you."

A semi-truck slows down and suddenly changes lanes in front of us. Greer tenses, squeezing her thighs together. I reach over, then smooth my hand over hers. The atmosphere is charged with anticipation and apprehension. My phone pings with a text. I glance at Greer and nod, signaling for her to check the message. She smiles, as if this smalls gesture proves how much I trust her.

"Oh no," she says, after reading it and burying her head on her arm.

"What's it say?" I laugh.

"Navy is not a happy camper right now. She's threatening to jump out of the truck."

"I kind of figured driving with those two would not be fun," I say, replacing both hands on the wheel. I maneuver our truck out from behind the semi, pulling up behind Hunter's once again.

"Those two have a lot of history, don't they?"

"Yeah," I say. "Not that I could describe any of it to you. Ever since Dad died, Sutton keeps her private life very private, and Hunter's protective of her."

"But they like each other?" Her hand trails up and down my shoulder.

"Oh, they're totally in love with each other, but I think they're too blind to see it."

"You'd be okay with them being together?" Greer replaces my phone and changes the song.

"Hunter is a great guy, even if he seems like someone different to the general population. Granted, he's my best friend, so I might be biased. They just need to get out of their own way."

She nods and minutes tick by.

"I meant it," she says out of the blue, her voice serious. She must read the confusion on my face because she continues, "I need . . . No, that's not quite right. I want to be with you, Luke. I'm ready."

Taking our joined hands, I press my lips to the back of her hand. My chest feels tight, knowing she finally feels ready to take this step with me.

"Okay, sweetheart. I am too."

We arrive at our hotel in the late afternoon. It isn't fancy by any means. Thankfully, Grace pulled some strings and got us rooms at the last minute. Pine-green carpeting lines the hallways, and gold accents adorn the walls, giving it a definite '70s-roadside-hotel feel.

"Here are your keys." Grace passes them out one by one. After loading into the elevator, we agree to meet in the lobby in an hour.

"This place is nice." Greer tries to contain her laughter.

"Let's just hope the room is better," I say.

"As long as I'm with you," Greer smiles, "it could be a box outside Taco Bell."

"I wouldn't do that to you. It'd be a Chick-Fil-A at least."

She playfully bumps her hip into mine as I swipe the key card. Holding the door open, she enters, and I drag our bags inside. We're pleasantly surprised to find the room has been recently renovated sporting a navy, forest-green, and gold color scheme. The best part though is the view.

"Holy shit." I motion for Greer, who's busy unpacking. "C'mere and look at this."

"Oh my god." Her mouth hangs open as she takes in our view, the Front Range of the Rockies. "This is incredible."

A knock echoes at our door. Greer opens to reveal Sutton and Navy, already decked out in glitter and bright colors.

"Did we do this right?" Sutton spins, barely containing her excitement. I can't remember the last time I've seen my sister this relaxed and ready to let loose.

"Why am I wearing about eighty pounds of glitter?" Navy groans as she plops down on our bed. "I don't even allow Rowan to use glitter in the house."

"Because that's what people wear at EDM shows," Sutton says. "Right, G?"

"I mean," Greer says, "I guess a lot of people do, but I've never actually been to one before."

"You mean to tell me," I say, "for all the bass and house music I hear blaring constantly from your house, the *music of your soul* as you like to tell me, this'll be your first show?" Greer told me about the concerts she saw with Brian and their friends, so I assumed she'd already been to an EDM show before.

"Brian wasn't the biggest fan of electronic music," she says. "But he finally relented and got us tickets. That's where we were headed the day of the accident."

Fuck. We'd talk about the details of her accident many times. I'd known they were headed out of town to a show, but she never said anything more than that. I feel like an asshole now, planning this whole trip not realizing it's a bigger deal in more ways than one.

"Greer, we had no idea." Sutton keeps her eyes low.

"I wouldn't have brought you here if I knew," I say.

"You guys." She's holding her hands out in her best *calm down* teacher pose. "I promise this is more than okay. Actually, I'm so freaking happy we're doing this. The anniversary is going to be hard enough. I'm glad I get to experience something like this with people I love." Her eyes sweep over to me.

"Cool," Navy says, "so now that the awkward part of the trip is over, can someone please explain to me why the hell I need to wear this much glitter? I am not a glitter person." Navy presses her fingers over her glitter adorned cheeks.

"Because" Grace says, stepping into our room, "glitter is like shiny bits of joy and happiness."

They're soon lost in a sea of makeup and sparkles helping Greer get ready. Not one to intrude, I change quickly, give her a kiss, and head down to meet the guys in the bar.

We arrive at the venue early enough to get decent spots in line. I'm not sure what to look at—the venue or the people. Some are in jeans and T-shirts, but the ones in full rave attire garner my full attention. Bright colors, jewels, braids, platform boots, and glitter (a lot of glitter) adorn a majority of the fans.

"This place is insane," Hunter says, his gaze sweeping over the crowd and the surrounding amphitheater.

As we enter through the gates, we're awestruck. Even though we saw pictures of Red Rocks, thank to Greer, they do not do this place justice. We meander through the entrance, and within two hundred feet, the walkway opens up to reveal a massive open-air amphitheater tucked between rock structures. We make our way to the edge of the venue and look over the railing. Row upon row of massive step-like benches lead down to a large stage. The name Red Rocks fits perfectly because the rocks are a gorgeous rust-colored hue.

"What is EDM music anyway?" Vinnie asks as we make our way to the merch booth.

"EDM stands for electronic dance music," Greer says. "It's created digitally and with analog equipment. It's traditionally played for large crowds at clubs and raves. Think music you can dance to. And there are so many subgenres. The guy we are seeing tonight is melodic house." Greer spouts off her musical knowledge all while guiding us into the venue like some kind of tour guide. It's not until she realizes she's walking alone that she whips around to find us cemented to the ground.

"You're really into this, aren't you?" Hunter walks up to Greer and slings his arm over her shoulder.

"Just a little bit," she answers with a full belly laugh. She waves her hand, motioning for us to hurry up, and we clear the distance to the merch line. She's only told us a hundred times that it would be our first stop. I love seeing her in baggy concert

T-shirts back home, and now I know most of them are from shows she's attended. After she's gotten her goods, we take our time exploring the venue.

We attempt descending to the bottom of the venue, but we give up to find a bar somewhere at the mid-level. We find a spot near the middle of a row just as the opening act, a local DJ, comes on the stage to get the crowd primed and ready.

The sky is a vibrant fire of oranges, yellows, and pinks as the sun makes its final descent. One by one, the lights of the amphitheater fade, leaving us in a semi-darkness. The crowd erupts into screams and surges to their feet.

I should be watching the stage, but I'm captivated by a certain woman. Greer stands dwarfed between me and Hunter with her hands bracketing her face, eyes and mouth open in wonder. Lights flash on stage as a low drumbeat begins, and she bobs her head to the beat.

Flashes of light dance in her eyes and bounce off the glitter speckled over her cheeks. Other sounds join the drum beat, building in tempo before dropping out completely, as the stage opens to reveal the artist. The beat picks up, and Greer bounces on her toes, wide-eyed and eager, like a little kid.

"Here it comes!" she yells.

The beat drops at the same time smoke and fireworks erupt on stage. Greer and the crowd go absolutely wild. As one, they jump and wave their hands in the air. It's hard to hear anything over the roar of the crowd, their voices merging into a deafening chorus as they scream-sing every lyric.

"Holy hell," Hunter yells over the music. "This is fucking crazy! I've never experienced anything like this."

"I know!" Greer yells back. "Isn't it amazing!" She reaches for my hand and interlaces our fingers. She can't control her dancing and jumping though, so I move behind her. She wiggles back into me, and I rest my hands on her hips.

No one in our group has ever experienced a concert like this before. It's not soon after the artist begins to play that we're lost.

Lost to the lights.

Lost to the music.

Lost to the beat.

Each song seamlessly blends into the next. Some are fast; some are slow and moody. I'm surprised by the number of songs with little to no lyrics. However, it's the ones with lyrics that are fan favorites; everyone around us belts every word. Each beat drop causes the crowd to surge, collectively pulling in, deep down, before exploding in a burst of energy.

I can't help but laugh at my friends varying states. Greer is completely immersed—singing, jumping, even headbanging. Sutton and Navy are on the Greer party train, copying everything she does. Hunter can't take his eyes off my sister. Vinnie stands there, mouth open, staring at the stage, possibly having an out-of-body experience. Adam and Grace are snuggled up together, faces bright, soaking in the energy of the crowd. But as the show progresses, Greer gets more and more subdued.

"Are you good?" I say into her ear.

"Yes." Her chin wobbles.

"Hey," I turn her to me. "What's wrong?" She buries her face in my chest and wraps her arms around my middle as tears soak through my shirt.

She looks up at me. "This is . . . this is . . . " she pauses and attempts to get control of herself. "I'm so overwhelmed right now. In the best way possible. Thank you for this." She stands on tiptoes and presses her lips to mine. Before I can deepen our kiss, the DJ transitions into a new song, and Greer reels away from me, eyes wide as can be with a smile to match.

"Oh my god!" she says. "It's my favorite song!"

Lasers illuminate the dark sky around us, cutting through the night with their vivid colors. Greer must intuitively know it's the last song. I've never seen someone experience music like her—hands raised high, voice loud and full of life, tears streaming down her face. She keeps reaching back to make sure I'm still there, so I pull her close, wrapping my arms around her.

As the seconds tick by, I pull her closer into the warmth of my body. Bending down, I place my mouth near her ear, the words I've longed to say for weeks finally slipping out:

"I love you."

Her body sinks into me as she pulls my arms tightly around her chest. More tears fall, and her heartbeat thrums erratically beneath my touch. Her chest rises and falls with quick breaths.

Suddenly, she wheels around and throws her arms over my shoulders. Just before the beat drops one final time, she says loud enough for everyone to hear, "I love you too."

27

Greer

As we make our way back to our vehicles, everyone is bursting with energy, all talking over each other to share their favorite part or favorite song.

Normally, I'd abandon my introverted ways and chime in, but, after a live show, I prefer to disappear into my thoughts and replay every song. I savor the way my body tingles, that sensation when my soul feels like it's overflowing with happiness. For some, music is just music, but for me, it's transformative. I feel that shit deep in my soul.

"Shit, G," Hunter says, leaning over Sutton, whose hand is clasped tightly in mine. "I'd have never pegged you as a headbanger type."

I bite my lip. "You haven't seen nothing yet, Hunter."

Luke and Sutton hold my hands, like they know I need to be tethered to earth or else I'll float away on a cloud of pure euphoria. There's no chance for my heart. It's already floating in the stratosphere. Those three little words, said by this man I love, fly free among the stars.

Crisp Colorado air cuts through my thin layers, so Luke wraps his arm around my shoulder and pulls me closer to him. Sutton squeezes my hand. I look at her, and she smiles before mouthing, "We love you too." Of course I tear up. I feel ripped open, my heart beating right out in the open for all my friends to see. It's overwhelming realizing I've never before had friends like this—friends who love me for me, who make me feel safe, who see me at my worst and stay.

Darkness settles inside the SUV like a blanket from the world. When the doors shut and lock, it releases the pin on everyone's energy, and there's a collective exhalation as we float back down to earth.

Luke and I squeeze into the third row of Adam's SUV. I'm pressed tightly against him with my hand resting on the center of his chest. I never thought I would fall in love again. I didn't think it was possible. But now, here with Luke, my emotions threaten to bubble over.

He loves me.

And I love him.

Sliding my hand up his chest, I wrap mine around the side of his neck. He pulls me in closer. If I were under his skin, we still wouldn't be close enough.

A year ago, if someone told me I was lucky to have Brian for as long as I did, I'd have raged and told them Life sucks. I'd have yelled that Life hates me because it took Brian from me. But I realize now, you can't predict how Life will present your story to you.

If someone asked me right now if I felt lucky, I'd have no choice but to say yes. Where once I was lonely and lost, now I am surrounded by supportive family and friends. Not only did I get to love Brian and be loved by him but now I also get to love Luke and be loved by him.

I don't even realize I've started crying until he whispers, "It's okay, sweetheart. I'm right there with you."

Traffic leaving the venue crawls at a snail's pace, a constant flow of brake lights illuminating the interior of the vehicle. Eventually, we make it back to our hotel and pile into the lobby.

"There was a bar down the street. Anyone want to go?" Vinnie asks, pointing over his shoulder.

Adam and Grace are oblivious to the world and head straight toward the elevator.

Sutton yawns. "I'm down."

To which Hunter says, "Nah, babe, you need sleep."

"Don't be a fun ruiner, Hunter," Sutton says.

"Not trying to be," Hunter says. "But I don't want to have to carry your ass all the way back here after you fall asleep at the bar. Like you do every time we go out this late."

"You act like you know me or something."

"I do know you," Hunter replies, wrapping his arm around her shoulder. Sutton nods in agreement and allows him to lead her to the elevator.

"Navy, you in?" Vinnie asks.

She only contemplates it for a minute. "Why not. Let's go." With his hand at the small of her back, they exit the lobby.

"You want to go?" Luke turns to face me.

He's leaving the choice up to me, but there is no choice.

I just want him. I want us.

"No," I say as he threads our hands together and guides me toward the elevator.

The doors open and close on a whisper. Interior lights bathe us in a warm glow. Luke pulls me into him and wraps his arms around my back. I slide my hands around his firm stomach, reaching up and up, gripping his back. He pulls back slightly. Our eyes lock before he drops his forehead to mine.

His lips kiss my temple—sweet and tentative.

The apple of my cheek—my eyes fall shut.

Just to the edge of my jaw—goosebumps pepper my skin.

The corner of my mouth—my breath stutters.

When we arrive at our floor, Luke pulls me behind him and guides me to our room. The key card lights up, and he opens the door, leading me inside. The door closes with a quiet *snick* at the same time he turns on the ambient room lights.

He's quiet and unhurried as he toes off his sneakers before kneeling down to unlace mine. A warm hand slides around my ankle, lifts my foot, and slides my shoe off. He places it next to his. I thread my left hand through his hair as he leans forward, placing an open-mouth kiss on my thigh. Hands slide up the length of my other leg, cupping the back of my thigh. I can't help my stuttering sigh. Luke's eyes find mine as his hands coast down my leg and remove my other shoe.

He remains there, on his knees before me. Lowering myself down, we sit knee to knee. Neither of us moves or talks. We sit in this moment, knowing what comes next changes everything.

Leaning forward, I grasp his face, and his stubble tickles my palms. I wiggle forward and climb onto his lap. My knees rest on each side of his legs, my thighs on top of his.

I kiss him—he inhales sharply.

The corner of his mouth—a moan rumbles out of him.

Just to the edge of his jaw—his hands slide up my shirt, gripping bare skin.

The apple of his cheek—his hands drag down to brace me under my thighs.

My lips at his temple, sweet and tentative—he's lifting me, crashing his mouth to mine.

Luke carries me into the bathroom and sits me on the counter. His hands skim my arms before bracing behind my neck. His mouth is hot, insistent as he coaxes mine open. Warmth invades every part of my body. My skin flushes from anticipation. With a tug of my lower lip, he pulls away, reaching over to turn the shower on.

As the water heats, he turns his attention back to me. His hands move up my thighs. My shirt bunches, caressing my skin as Luke continues pulling my shirt up my body. My nipples pebble as I lift my arms above my head, and he slips my shirt off. I grasp the hem of his T-shirt, and ever so slowly, peel it from his body.

Without breaking eye contact, I slide my hands down to the buttons of his jeans, popping the button in time with him unhooking my bra. The straps fall to my elbows as I slip my fingers beneath his waistband and push down. Luke steps back, dragging me off the counter. He nudges my bra off, exposing my breasts to the cool air.

"You're so beautiful," he whispers, running the back of his fingers down my chest and over each sensitive peak.

My body is tight, expectant, both wanting him to go faster and slower. Farther down his hands go, his eyes searing my skin as they follow the path of his hands. My shorts unbutton easily, and he pushes them off my hips. I wiggle them down until I can kick them behind me. With an open-mouth kiss to the top of my chest, he steps back and slides his jeans off, kicking them to the side.

"Luke . . ." My breath stutters as I catch sight of his hard length beneath his briefs.

He smirks before stepping back into my space. Chest hairs tickle my bare skin when he bends to capture my mouth once again. This time he doesn't hesitate.

With a few side steps, he brings us closer to the shower, and, with our mouths still fused, he slides my undies down. I shiver as they slip down my legs, stepping out of them. I grasp his waistband and wiggle them over his thick thighs. I can't look anywhere else but his rigid cock, long and heavy between us.

"In," he says, motioning to the shower.

I smile. The man who constantly demands my words is one of few right now.

Steam creates a foggy haze in the small bathroom. He holds my hand as I step into the shower and under the spray. The water feels heavenly on my sore back muscles. Luke follows, his gaze tracking every bead of water as it slides down my body.

"Are you gonna come closer?" I ask, then bite my bottom lip and tilt my head back under the spray. At first, I think he'll answer with that filthy mouth of his, but he doesn't say a word.

"You okay?" I slide my hand over his pecs and up through the back of his hair. Again, he says nothing. I plant a kiss above his heart. Another at the base of his throat. A tiny bite to the edge of his jaw. My lips seal over his. His hands grip my waist and hold me to him. His hard length presses against my stomach, and I tremble with anticipation.

"Luke? Is everything okay?" I ask between kisses. "We can stop if you want."

But still, he says nothing. Simply melds his mouth to mine, my body to his. He tugs at my lower lip with his teeth. My hips roll into his, eliciting a groan.

"I'm just trying to go slow." He sucks the skin at the curve of my neck. "I want you so goddamn bad." He's focused on my mouth now, his tongue pushing in, meeting mine, demanding more.

"You have me." Our tongues dance as his hands trace over my bare skin, setting every nerve alight.

"And you have me." His eyes are serious. "Can I?" he asks, gesturing to the bath products hanging on the wall. I can't contain my smile at this sweet gesture.

We take our time shampooing each other's hair, getting distracted often with fevered kisses. Our hands caress bare skin as we lather and clean each other's bodies. Luke turns and grabs a washcloth from the towel rack close by. Wetting it, he begins to carefully wipe the remnants of glitter and makeup from my face.

He's on his tenth pass or so when he says, "What the fuck is up with this glitter?"

"Well," I say, "it's meant to last throughout a full-day festival, so maybe I should try."

"Yeah, that might be good," he says.

I turn and grab my face wash before placing my face under the spray. Luke brings his hands around my body and pulls me to him. We groan as his cock skims up my body.

"I love this," he says, gripping the flesh of my ass with both hands. "I love you," he whispers as he kisses my shoulder.

"Luke." I press my hips back, bringing my backside more firmly against him. He pulls my hips and thrusts into me.

"Sweetheart, you gotta hurry up."

Figuring the skin care gods will forgive me just this once, I abandon my routine, scrubbing and rinsing my face before turning my body back to him

"Fucking finally." He shuts the water off, grips me behind my thighs, and lifts me to him. I wrap my thighs around his waist, which proves difficult when I'm dripping wet. I immediately lose traction and slip-slide down his body.

"Towel," I pant as he licks and sucks the skin along my collar bone.

"Good idea." He sets me back on my feet and reaches for two towels. He drapes one over my shoulders and quickly pats himself dry. Just as I'm about to wrap the towel around myself, he lifts me back to him, my legs now able to grip his dry skin. The towel is forgotten somewhere between us.

As I wrap my arms around his neck, he fuses his mouth to mine and walks us into the bedroom before dropping me onto the bed. The towel pools around me. He stands there, hands hanging limp at his sides, once again not saying anything.

"You're so quiet tonight." I lie there, letting him devour me with his searing gaze, the silence thick between us.

"I've searched my whole life for you," he says. "I'd begun to think maybe there wasn't someone out there for me. But there was—you. How did I get so lucky?" He kneels on the bed and pushes my thighs apart. They fall to each side, my body relaxing completely when he settles between them. I pull him to me, desperate to feel his body weight on mine. Our kisses are frantic now, more insistent. Hands grip flesh, hips rise and press into the other.

Luke pulls away from my mouth, kisses along my jaw, over my collarbone, and down my chest. He covers my nipple with his mouth and sucks gently. My hips rise off the bed, and the head of his cock brushes against my thigh.

"I need you," I say.

"I need you," he answers back as his mouth closes around my other nipple. His hands knead my breasts, pushing them together, so he can easily move back and forth more between my nipples. His teeth graze a turgid peak, and my hips thrust to meet his.

"Luke." I'm desperate to have him.

"I know, love." His kisses descend down my sternum and over my ribs, biting the skin there. I don't know what else to do—I'm lost and numb. Closing my eyes, I allow myself to just *feel*. He caresses my scar and places another kiss there. Trembles wrack my body when he kisses my lower stomach. He bites the soft skin there, placing open-mouth kisses from one hip bone to the other. Luke's hands skim down and bring my thighs over his shoulders. I shiver as he licks my inner thigh.

"Damn, baby, you're so wet for me."

With a firm tongue, Luke licks my pussy from its entrance up to my clit. My hands fall to the side as I suck in a deep breath. Nerves tingle up my legs, settling low in my stomach.

"Oh god. It's—it's so good." Reaching out, I grip the sheets.

"Fuck, you taste good." Luke takes another slow pass and gently sucks at the sensitive bud. My body is an inferno.

"Eyes open," Luke says.

I force them open, and look down to find his locked on me. Light from the bathroom silhouettes his body. I stifle a giggle when I notice the mess I've made of his hair. With one hand pressed against my lower stomach, he takes his other and slips a finger inside me. My body responds immediately, my hips lifting to meet him. He presses down on my hips to keep me still.

"More. I need more." More pressure, more force. Just more. Inhale. Exhale.

"Not yet." He lowers his mouth over my clit, licking it in time with his thrusting finger. "I need to get you ready," he says as he adds a second finger. They coax a spot deep within me, and there's a gush of fluid. "That's it, sweetheart." Luke continues his ministrations with his hand and mouth, my body twisting higher and higher.

"Luke," I moan on an exhale. "I n-need . . ."

"I feel you, sweetheart. Just let go. Let me feel you come on my tongue." He releases the pressure on my lower stomach, allowing me to push up and against his waiting mouth. His fingers slide in and out of me as he lashes and sucks at my clit.

My thighs tremble and press against Luke's head as my orgasm flares, rushing down my spine before flooding my body.

"Gorgeous." He places a last gentle kiss on my pussy.

Luke crawls up my body until he's kneeling between my legs. Threading our fingers together, he pulls me to sit. He lets my hands go and grips my ass and pulls me to him.

"Luke," I say, but am interrupted with his mouth on mine. I moan when I taste myself on his lips. His hands grip me tight, and his cock slides along my inner thigh. So close to where I need him. Where I want him.

With a firm kiss, I cup his handsome face and hold him away from me. His chest heaves with quick, forced breaths. He's looking at me. I'm looking at him.

"Just breathe," I whisper. His eyes melt as he inhales and exhales. His hands slide up my back as I kiss each eyelid.

"I'm trying to go slow, baby. But I don't know how to slow down anymore."

"I don't want you to slow down."

Our gaze locks as he lays me back on the bed. The sheets are cool against my overheated body. Luke settles his weight over me, kisses me deeply, and pulls my legs around his waist. I reach between us to grab his hard cock. The skin is soft in my hand as I stroke him from root to tip. I drag the tip of him through my slit and back down. As I notch him at my entrance, he suddenly leans back, eyes molten, control slipping. He moves to grab a condom from the bedside table, but I stop him. We've already had this discussion.

"I just want you." I reach for him.

"Are you sure?"

"I'm sure if you are."

He leans forward, pressing his lips to mine. "I'm sure."

He settles at my entrance. "Eyes on me," he says.

As if I could look anywhere else.

He presses into me. "You feel like heaven."

He stills, allowing me to adjust. I've never felt so full or stretched before. Pressure builds, but he doesn't move.

"Luke?"

"Yeah, sweetheart?"

"Make love to me."

And he does.

Those four words unleash whatever tether he had on himself. He pulls out before thrusting back in, each longer and deeper than the last. My hands drift over his shoulders now glistening with sweat. Without losing rhythm, he bends down and claims my mouth. His arms sneak under my body and wrap around my shoulders. With each thrust, he pulls me closer to him.

"You were made for me."

Electricity races across my body, tempting my eyes to close. Instead, I kiss along his neck, sucking at his skin. My hands move under his arms to grip his lats. My hips meet his, thrust for thrust. I tuck my face against his biceps and place a kiss there. Then, I bite him. He groans in response.

"You like that?"

"I think you'll find out I like a lot of things." His thrusts become quicker, more forceful.

Another orgasm builds low in my stomach and spreads out. Each time my nipples rub against his chest, they become more and more sensitive. Leaning on his left elbow, Luke brings his other hand to my face—kissing me, licking into my mouth, pulling at my bottom lip. With each thrust, each kiss, I summit the mountain, the pressure building and building.

"Luke, I'm going to come." His pelvis rubs my clit. I know I won't last much longer.

"I'm right there with you." He pulls back, not stopping his maddening pace even as his hand disappears between us to rub my overly sensitive clit.

"I love you, Luke. So much." Soft amber eyes stare deeply into mine.

"I love you too." His words echo into the deepest parts of my heart, mending more cracks that still linger.

"Are you close?" he asks as my pussy spasms, clenching around his cock. "Damn, you're already there." Luke pushes his entire length into me. Each time, his cock stretches and fills me, each rigid vein caresses my inner walls. I ride the wave of my orgasm, not sure if it'll ever stop.

"Sweetheart, I'm close. Where do—"

"Inside me," I pant. "I want to feel you come inside me."

I barely get the words out before he buries his face in my neck, and I feel the first spurts of his orgasm. He continues to push in and out of me, pouring everything into me. As our breathing comes back to normal, Luke's pace slows before stopping all together, leaving both of us breathless.

We remain connected, not moving for several minutes. He brings his head up and presses a kiss to the slope of my neck, the corner of my mouth, and finally seals his mouth over mine one final time.

He slips from me, and I whimper at the loss. Luke rolls over and lays his head on a pillow. He snakes his hand over my stomach, wraps it around my hip, and drags me to him.

Splayed across his body, I feel his heart beat steadily beneath my ear. Our legs twine together, and he never once lets go of me even as he wiggles around to pull the blankets over us. Before I completely succumb to the exhaustion spreading through my body, he kisses me on my temple.

"I will spend every day of forever loving you," he says, "no matter what Life has in store for us."

28

S UNLIGHT FILTERS THROUGH OUR hotel window, casting a warm, golden light. The peaks of the Rockies rise in the distance. Greer remains nestled against my side, her leg draped over mine, toes tucked under my calf. Her hand cradles the side of my face, anchoring us.

Golden strands of her blonde hair lie tousled across the pillow framing her peaceful face. I tenderly explore the exposed patches of skin, partially hidden by the crumbled sheets. Sunlight dances along her cheekbones, leftover glitter shimmering slightly. Her lips, now a gentle shade of red, carry the memories of our night together. She stirs slightly, and, for a moment, I think how mornings like this could be enough.

From the moment I met Greer, she felt different to me. Dancing with her, wrapped in each other's arms, I knew we were different. Underneath the fireworks, I understood my life would never be the same now that she was in it. But last night rearranged my soul, pieced together my heart, and showed me what true love really is.

Greer breathes deeply beside me, constantly drawing closer. A soft laugh escapes me at how much she resembles a koala right now. She'd crawl all the way inside me if she could. My hand traces along her arm, down her ribs, and over the curve of her hips. Even in sleep, her body responds to my touch, and goosebumps cover her golden skin. The desire to roll her over washes over me. After making love, we'd fallen into a deep and restful sleep.

"What are you thinking about?" she asks, her sleepy voice cutting through the quiet morning air.

"I was thinking of rolling you over and having you again."

"Oh, I like that idea."

She moves her hand from around my neck, tracing a path down my chest until she grips my hip. I turn toward her, gently guiding her onto her back, eager to see her face. A red mark blooms over her cheekbone where she slept against my chest the majority of the night.

"Last night was—"

"Beautiful," she finishes for me.

The word escapes her lips, floating in the air around us. We kiss in a soft and unhurried way for several minutes as we greet the day. My hands slip around her shoulders, drawing her closer to me. Her legs ease apart, inviting me to lie between them. There's no mistaking the desire pulsating through our bodies.

Unable to resist, I brand every inch of her face with my lips. Each touch elicits a gasp, a moan, or a subtle shift of her hips. My dick presses along her inner thigh and against her center.

"Damn," I say. It would be so easy to slide right into her.

"Yeah." Her hands slide down my back, gripping my bare ass and kneading the flesh.

"Be good."

"It would be good," she sighs, her hips meeting mine in a tempting thrust.

"Fuck, but do I know it would." My mouth descends on hers, tongues colliding in a heated dance. "I don't want you to hurt."

"You won't hurt me." Her teeth graze my lower lip, sending a shiver down my spine. "Luke. Please."

"Please what?"

"Fuck me."

At her words, I reel back, taking her in. Every time this woman fully owns her sexuality and allows her shyness to fade, it shocks me to my core. The denial dies on my lips when she looks at me like this.

"Oh, I'll do more than that, but we should probably get downstairs. They're probably all waiting for us."

Sitting back on my heels, my erection stands at full attention between us. She launches up to a semi-seated position with her arms braced behind her.

She huffs out a breath. "They can wait."

"Greer," I bend over her body, gripping her face, trying to calm whatever emotion is swirling in that beautiful mind of hers. "I'm also a selfish bastard, and if I take you now, we might not ever leave this room."

That goddamn lip of hers disappears between her teeth, her gaze downcast. Her breathing accelerates. Her legs wrap around my hips, rubbing along the bare skin.

"Then be selfish with me, Luke."

By the time we finally make it to the lobby, it's crawling with people in various forms of outdoor gear—some heading out for a hike, others just returning.

"Well, well, well," Hunter says, rising to greet us. "It's about time you graced us with your presence."

"Shut up, bro." I grip his hand and he pulls me into a one-armed hug.

"I'm happy for you, man," he says pulling back, keeping a firm grip on my shoulders. "Jealous as hell, but happy." Judging by the girls surrounding Greer—huddled in anticipation, letting out bated sighs and *oh my gods*—it seems everyone knows what happened between us last night.

"Jesus," Vinnie says. "Can we go to breakfast now? I'm starving, and this happy couple's bullshit is too much on an empty stomach." He shoves his hands in his pockets.

"Yes," Navy says, pulling out of the girl huddle. "Let's go eat. We've got shit to do today."

"Oh yeah?" Greer reaches for my hand. "What kind of shit? You going to be our tour guide?"

"Not sure yet," Navy shouts over shoulder. "We'll figure it out." She leads our raucous bunch to breakfast. Spilling onto the sidewalk, we head to a boutique breakfast joint nearby. My stomach grumbles in annoyance and anticipation.

"Gee,"—Greer bumps her hip with mine—"someone sounds mighty hungry."

"Someone might have worn me out." I bump her back. "In the best possible way."

"Oh god," Vinnie says, rolling his eyes, "today's going to be a long day."

"Vinnie," Navy says, "just because you were turned down by a gorgeous woman last night doesn't mean you get to ruin the day for everyone."

"Gorgeous woman? Do tell," Sutton chimes in.

"You guys,"—Vinnie gets a faraway look in his eyes—"she was everything." He goes on to tell us the whole sordid tale.

After breakfast, we decide to hit a popular hiking trail nearby, supposedly an easy trail with spots for picnics and water access. We pile into two vehicles and grab lunch from a sandwich shop. Soon, backpacks are loaded with food, water, and other snacks, courtesy of Navy.

"The trail says it's intermediate level," Navy says. "About two miles round-trip."

"Sounds fun," Grace says.

We head out, but it's not long before our group separates. Hunter and Sutton take the lead, like always. Navy and Vinnie stick with us while Grace and Adam bring up the rear. Most of us have grown up together, but this is the first time we've ever left our hometown to do something together. Vinnie, Adam, and I knew how lucky we were when I got assigned to their shift and truck, but it's still a pain to match schedules to do anything outside our usual routine.

"Hey," I say as we pause on the trail, "what if we do something out of our norm?" We're surrounded by spruce trees, sweeping views of the valley below, and an endless azure sky. It's astounding that we get to live on a planet where places this incredible exist.

"What do you mean?" Sutton asks.

"I was thinking," I say, "after this, why not try something different? I saw a sign for zip-lining on the way here."

"Zip-lining?" Vinnie raises an eyebrow. "Sounds fun."

"Sounds like a hell of a lot of fun," Hunter chimes in.

Navy looks intrigued. "Ugh, why not? Together?"

"Together," we chorus.

We hike for a bit longer, before turning back toward the truck. It's midday when we find a swimming hole tucked off the trail and surrounded by massive boulders to have lunch.

"We should do this more often," I say as I unzip my backpack and pass out food.

"What?" Vinnie says. "Go on vacation where everyone has sex except me?"

"I haven't either," Navy says. Greer giggles, trying to hide it by gulping down water. Hunter and Sutton are oddly silent. I'm curious what drama is going on now.

"C'mon." I gesture to the beauty around us. "You guys know what I mean. When have we ever made time to do anything like this?"

"You getting sentimental on us, Cap?" Adam calls.

"And what if I am?"

"Nah, I agree," Adam says. "We should do this more often. It would be fun to see more of the world than just our backyard."

"Agreed," Greer says softly. "Life is short." A somber look passes through the group. I appreciate how everyone seems to be treading lightly—I'm not sure where Greer's at mentally.

"How are you feeling, G?" Scratch that, everyone but Navy. "It's almost the anniversary."

"I actually feel pretty good." Greer gifts them a smile as she toes off her sneakers and steps into the water. "If you'd asked me three months ago, I'd have said something different. But now? I feel more settled than I have all year."

"What changed?" Sutton asks, struggling to unknot her laces. Hunter swats away her hands so he can unlace them.

"Isn't it obvious?" Greer raises her arms out to her sides, dragging them through the water. "It's you guys. Over the last year, I isolated myself so far away from the world that I kind of forgot it was out there, but somehow, you guys found me, and I haven't been the same since."

"Me either," Navy and Sutton say as they step next to Greer, followed closely by Grace. The four girls wrap their arms around one another's waists.

"So, uh, should we hug too?" Vinnie opens his arms wide.

"Why the fuck not." Hunter rushes into Vinnie, pushing him up against the girls, who open to include them.

"God, what's happened to us?" Adam asks, motioning me to join the group hug. "It's like all we do is talk about feelings and hug and shit."

"Greer happened to us," I say, placing my arms over their shoulders. We've always been an affectionate group, but it's at a whole new level now.

"Sometimes," Navy says, her voice thick with emotion, "the people we need most in our lives find us." She shakes her head, blinking back the tears threatening to emerge. "Okay, enough of that." She wiggles out of the group, and Sutton and Greer burst into laughter.

"What the hell are you laughing at?" Navy narrows her eyes at them.

"Your grumpy ass, that's what. Someday, someone's gonna find you, and your heart is going to grow three times its size." Greer winks as she turns back to the stream.

The silence of our secluded swimming spot is broken by the shrill sound of my phone going off. I gather it from my bag, only to notice it's the fire chief calling.

"Hey, Chief." I walk out of earshot of the group.

"Bradley, where are you at?" His tone is urgent.

"Went out of town for the weekend, sir."

He grunts, and I can tell he's debating whether to ruin our weekend. "Thing is, there's a pretty serious wildfire burning east of town. We're gathering our resources and mobilizing our engine boss units to respond."

Dammit. "Copy that, sir."

"How far out are you?"

"Over six hours, sir." Hunter catches sight of me and walks over to where I'm standing. Concern fills his face. Chief is silent on the other end of the line. "What do you need from me?"

"Well, I need you to be here and ready to run this crew."

Hunter's face turns angry, and he shakes his head back and forth as he eavesdrops on the conversation. A clear indication where he stands on this issue.

"I understand that, sir. What about Tyler or Brandon?" Hunter nods his head in encouragement. Normally, I'd never question or say no to my chief. Normally, I'd drop everything and do exactly what's asked of me.

"You're the best one we have, Luke. If you leave now, you could make it here by this evening and report to command immediately." Hunter rolls his eyes, mouthing *for fucks sake*.

Turning back toward the water, I catch sight of Greer. She's removed her tank and is stretched out on the rocks, bathed in golden sunlight. Her eyes light up when she sees me, and her lazy smile sets my heart to pounding. But it's her words from earlier that echo in my mind, making this decision feel effortless.

Life is short.

"Sir, as much as I would love to help out, I won't be available until after I get back." I can't take my eyes off Greer. This, right here, right now, with her and my friends, is what's important.

"Okay, Bradley," Chief says. "I understand. Good for you, getting out of town. I'll talk to you when you get back."

I end the call, dropping my hands to my sides. That was easier than I thought it'd be.

Hunter grips and squeezes my shoulder. "Proud of you, bro."

"Life is short, right? It means nothing if I miss out on actually living it, right?"

29

Greer

As Luke stows his phone in his backpack, a sudden tug of worry and anxiety needles my stomach. It's like I hear the ticking of time, the real world waiting for us just beyond the bubble we've created.

"Everything good?" I ask when he joins me, sitting on the bank of the stream.

"Yeah. Chief called. Sounds like there's a pretty good fire getting started back home."

"No shit?" Vinnie says. "Where?"

"I didn't ask," Luke says.

"Does that mean we need to head home?" I can't mask the disappointment in my voice.

He reaches forward and pulls me next to him. "Nope. I told him I'm not available until I get back."

"Damn," Sutton says. "I never thought I'd ever hear you say something like that."

"Things are different now."

"How so?" I ask.

"Work will always be there, but my friends and family might not be. I want my memories to be filled with moments like this." He gestures to our group and leans over, kissing me.

We do just that. After our hike, we go zip-lining and fill our weekend making every moment count, creating new memories. But time flies when you're having fun. Isn't that how the saying goes? And before any of us are ready, it's time to head home.

Back to our lives. Back to the real world.

Looking around my classroom, anticipation crackles in the air. Rows of desks wait patiently for my new little friends, our walls are covered with brightly colored posters, and this teacher is ready for her new adventure. My phone pings with a message.

Sutton: I have to ask, what is your plan for tomorrow?

Earlier today, I finished my back-to-school meetings, so I've been given the remaining days before school starts next week to work in my classroom. I've learned my lesson throughout the years—if the school gives you time to work, you work, because once the school year begins it'll be a chaotic whirlwind until May. I stare at Sutton's messages, taking a deep breath.

Tomorrow.

One year since the accident.

One year from almost losing my life.

One year from losing my husband.

One year since my life was shattered.

When we returned home from our weekend trip, Luke had to report for duty. His chief called him about the fire, although slowly being contained, it's still a risk to some nearby areas. Luke took another crew to relieve the first. He's had spotty signal, so we haven't gotten to talk very much, which has been hard.

Me: I'll go see Brian.

I know that much is true. Truth be told, I haven't been back to visit his grave since the funeral. It was too much, too hard. I haven't *spoken* to Brian for a few weeks. I haven't needed to, not with Luke and my new friends in my life. It's important for me to go there now. To tell him I'm okay.

Sutton: Do you want us to come with you?

Me: Nah, you guys don't want to hang around a graveyard.

Navy: We will for you.

And don't I know it. If I've learned anything this summer, it's that your people will never back away from the hard stuff. They'll stand by you through thick and thin.

Me: I'm not even sure if Luke will be home.

Sutton: He will be. And if he's not, we are.

Me: I'll be at the cemetery around ten, but you don't have to come.

Navy: We got you, G.

The school is blessedly silent for the rest of the day. Most teachers finish up early to get a jump-start on their final long weekend of summer. I keep busy writing lesson plans all the way into the evening. As the sun begins its descent beneath the horizon and my room darkens to a burnt orange, I know it's time to head home. Another message pings through as I pull into my driveway.

Luke: Missing you.

Me: Missing you too.

Luke: I'm sorry I'm not there with you. Sometimes, I really hate my job.

Me: No you don't. I also know you'd be here if you could be.

Me: It's hard, missing out on so much, huh?

Luke: Yeah. About tomorrow?

Me: I'm going to go see Brian.

Luke: That's what I figured. Will you be okay?

Will I be okay? I've asked myself that same question a million times over the past year. But now I'm not lying when I answer.

Me: Yeah, I will be.

Luke: I love you, sweetheart.

Me: I love you too.

Duke greets me with plenty of jumps and kisses as I open the door. I place my bags down on a stool at the island. My house is quiet, almost too quiet. Melancholy surrounds me as I head to my bedroom to wash off the day and put on my jammies.

Just as I'm slipping my feet into a pair of fuzzy socks, a knock echoes at my door. In a daze, I shuffle toward it, feeling outside my own body, as if I'm watching myself from afar. Duke jumps and barks at my heels, but I barely register it. Without a second thought, I open the door—and my heart drops.

"Hey, baby girl," my mom says. She and my dad stand just beyond my welcome mat. "Want some company tonight?"

"Y-Yes, I do." I'm already crying as Dad approaches, pulling me into a warm embrace. Mom wraps her hands around us both, providing a steady comfort I've always been thankful for.

"We've got you, sweetie," Mom whispers into my hair.

"Oh, you beat us!"

Brushing tears out of my eyes, I look up to find Navy and Sutton waiting at the end of my walkway, laden down with pizza boxes and grocery bags, reminiscent of the first time they came to my house.

"What are you two doing here?" I'm confused but elated to see them. I thought I wanted to be alone, but I'm glad they know me better than I know myself.

"As if we'd let you be alone," Navy says, shooting me a look of incredulity as she squeezes past my parents.

"We're here for you, G," Sutton says, shrugging her shoulders before heading past us into my house.

"C'mon, Greer," Dad says, taking my hand. "Let's go inside." He leads me through the door and shuts it behind us. Instantly, the heavy cloud of grief that weighed on my house fractures and dissipates, replaced by the comforting noise of family and love. For the first time, I feel truly grateful—and at peace—knowing I no longer have to grieve alone.

We spend most of the evening spread out on the couch eating pizza, laughing, and telling stories. We talk about the concert, Sutton's interest in interior design, and Navy's possible business venture with Ground Up. We even talk about Brian. The girls help me unpack all the boxes from the storage unit. Most of the mementos are placed into the storage chest Luke bought me. Sutton even brought a special garment bag to protect my wedding gown. We all wipe tears away as I tuck the ring box on top and close the lid.

Eventually, Mom and Dad head home. Hugs and *I love yous* and *we'll see you tomorrows* rustle the atmosphere on their way out.

"Thank you for coming over," I tell the girls.

"You know we're here for you," Sutton says, tucking her feet under her body.

"Do you need to get back to Rowan?" I ask Navy.

"Nope. He's with his dad." Navy pulls a fluffy blanket from my wicker basket, before burrowing into the corner of the other couch like a mole.

"It's getting late, though," I say. "Don't you both want to head home?"

"Nope," they say in unison. My brows knit together.

"We told you, Greer,"—Sutton reaches over to squeeze my foot—"we got you."

The dam holding back my tears breaks loose again. You'd think I'd have no tears left tonight. Navy and Sutton squish in around me on the couch. Navy tucks me against her shoulder and pats my back like I'm a small child.

"Let's head to bed," Sutton whispers.

They guide me to my bedroom and start turning down the sheets while I brush my teeth. Duke's claws click against the floor as he circles his bed before settling in. I turn off the light and head back to my bedroom. A laugh escapes when I see Navy and Sutton tucked under my covers, leaving just enough space for me between them. But this time, as I lie in the middle, I won't be alone.

Wiping more tears, I crawl over Navy's legs and wiggle my way into the bed. Sutton tucks the blankets around us, and they turn on their sides, wrapping an arm around my stomach.

"This is another first," I say.

"First?" Sutton asks at the same time Navy says, "First time sleeping with two women?"

We can't contain our giggles as we burrow deeper under the covers. Darkness settles in my room, the only light being a faint glow from a streetlight that peeks through my blinds. Little do I know this will only be the first of many sleepovers to come.

"What's up with you and Hunter?" Navy asks Sutton.

"I'll answer," she says, "if you plan on telling us about you and Vinnie."

"Easy," Navy says, "he likes me, or at least he thinks he does. He said as much at the bar that night on our trip. Problem is, he's not really my type. He took it pretty well though, and I got to play wingwoman for him."

"What is your type?" I ask.

"Not too sure any guy can handle me," Navy says. "Rowan's father didn't want to."

"Your guy is out there," Sutton says with a soft smile. "When you least expect him, there he'll be."

"So . . ." I say, elbowing Sutton lightly in the ribs. "What's up with you and Hunter?"

"Hunter and I"—she takes a deep breath—"have a lot of history, so it's complicated."

"You ever going to tell us the story there?" Navy asks.

Sutton contemplates this as she fingers the fringe on the comforter. Several minutes pass, and I'm certain she's not going to answer, but then she says, "I'm just not sure the timing will ever work. Maybe we're not meant to be."

"Why do you think that is?" Navy asks on a yawn.

Sutton looks at me then. I see the confession right there at the tip of her tongue. "Not sure," she says, covering her face with one hand. "I guess there are some things I'll never know."

I give her a sad smile, knowing she must have more to say.

"You talk to Luke tonight?" Navy asks.

"He texted me earlier when he was about to have dinner. I really wish he were able to be here. As weird as it sounds, I'd like Brian to meet him."

"That doesn't sound weird at all," Sutton says. "I know my brother. He'll be there."

My eyes fall shut as exhaustion overtakes my body and mind. No matter what you do, you can't pause time or speed it up. It passes regardless of your opinion. I knew I couldn't stop the anniversary of the accident and Brian's death from coming. Honestly, I feared I would have to face this last first alone. Like I did so many others.

"I'm really glad you're both here." Reaching beneath the covers, I take their hands in mine. "Thank you for tonight."

Navy rolls over and sleepily says, "No *thank yous* needed."

"No matter what, Greer," Sutton says, "we've got you."

30

Greer

M Y ROOM IS BATHED in a hazy, golden light. Sutton is squished into my side, legs entwined with mine. Navy is turned away from me with her butt tucked against my thigh. The fan spins above me like the hand on a clock.

1 year.

365 days.

52 weeks.

8,760 hours.

Death irrevocably changed my life in a matter of seconds and now 35,536,000 have since ticked by. Many of those, I spent in denial. How could he be gone? Others I spent in shock. What happened to me? Countless more I spent frozen, unable to move beyond. Then, there are the ones I spent pretending everything was okay even though I was dying inside.

I couldn't tell you when things changed. Maybe it's not even important, except for the simple fact that they did. I changed. And now . . .

Here I am.

"Jesus," Navy says, kicking off the covers. "You're like an inferno. I'm burning up."

I giggle and manage to whisper, "Well, be thankful you don't have Sutton using you as a real-life body pillow." Navy looks over her shoulder, eyes going wide, and bursts out in a fit of giggles.

"Why are you two so loud?" Sutton mumbles. "It's early."

"What time is it anyway?" Navy asks.

Sliding out from Sutton's grasp, I wiggle my way out of the covers, sitting at the foot of the bed. "My guess would be six a.m."

Behind me, Navy shuffles to the edge of the bed to grab her phone. "How do you do that?"

I laugh. "Natural gift. I'm going to make coffee."

"Hey, wait." Sutton sits up, grabbing my shoulder. "How are you?"

How am I? A question I dreaded any time it was asked over the last twelve months. But now?

"I'm good," I say.

Duke meets me by our bedroom door, and we walk to the back door. The sky is filled with fluffy gray clouds, bright-blue sky peeking through every now and then. All the flowers I've planted enjoy their last blooms before fall.

Duke doesn't hesitate as he dashes into the yard, making quick circles that get bigger with each lap. I stifle a laugh when he slips on the dew-covered grass and goes sliding. He instantly recovers and sprints back to me. *Old dog, my ass.*

Gliding across the lawn to my favorite spot, my feet sink deep into the soft grass. The once-vibrant sea of wildflowers are beginning to fade as fall makes its quiet approach. A small giggle escapes as I realize it's almost time to mow again. Before me lies the lush green preserve, a gentle breeze whistling through the branches and rustling my nightgown.

"Beautiful."

I take flight—*Luke.* "Hey, you."

He steps behind me, his warmth seeping through my thin gown and settling deep in my bones. His hands slip around my hips, linking together over my lower stomach, and his chin rests in the dip of my shoulder.

"I'll never get sick of this view." He kisses me on the side of my neck. Any tension I may have had disappears instantly.

"Oh yeah?"

"I still remember that first morning I saw you out here. Just like this." He slides his hand down and jostles my pale purple nightgown. "I think I loved you then."

Leaning over, I kiss his stubble-covered cheek. Having not had a decent shower in a week, he reeks like smoke.

"I thought you were working?"

"I was, but I told them I had somewhere to be today." The weight of him, holding me close and pressing into my body, soothes me.

"Thank you." I bury my face in the slope of his neck.

"No *thank yous* needed. I got you."

I know. "The girls are inside," I say. "You want breakfast?"

"You bet your ass I do if you and Navy are making it. Let me go shower first, yeah?"

"Of course." I seal my lips over his.

"God, I love you so fucking much. Do you know that?"

"I do." Tears cloud my vision. "I don't know why or how I've gotten to love two incredible men, but I'll never stop being grateful. Thank you, Luke, for loving me like you do. I hope you know how much I love you."

He pulls away, creating space between our bodies, and cradles my face in his large, calloused hands. "I do know. And I'm the luckiest man in the world to be loved by you."

Navy and Sutton are already up and rummaging around my kitchen. I sidle up to the counter and seat myself on a barstool. I'll happily let them take care of me today.

"Okay, G," Sutton says, "coffee is brewing. I'm going to take a shower." She makes for the guest bathroom.

"Hey," Navy says, "get your cute butt in here and help me whip up some food."

UNTIL THEN

Not one to deny Navy's commands, I do just that. We work side by side in perfect synchronization. She makes a batch of cinnamon rolls while I throw together a quiche.

"It smells so good in here." Luke enters in the back door and immediately heads toward the coffee. He's fresh from his shower in a T-shirt, jeans, and his boots. His beard is trimmed up, and I internally groan in delight. It's not every day I get lumberjack Luke.

"Hey, big bro." Sutton exits my guest bath, looking immaculate as always in jean shorts and a flowy top. "What is that smell? I want to eat the air; it smells so good."

"Just a little breakfast we whipped up." Navy pokes my side as she exits the kitchen to get ready.

"Just a little something" Sutton mimics. "Yeah, right." I can feel Sutton's eye roll from here.

"I don't know, Greer," Luke says. "Maybe you missed your calling and should go into the restaurant business with Navy, instead of educating the youth of America."

"I used to want to be a chef when I was younger," I say.

"And?" Sutton asks. "What happened?"

"I don't know, actually. I guess maybe I thought that was a pipe dream and I needed to get an actual job."

"You ever think about giving it a go?" Luke says, seating himself in his chair at my table. In my mind, I see flashes of our moments in this kitchen. The smirk on his face tells me he knows exactly where my mind went.

I sip on my coffee and pull out a chair. "If the right opportunity came along, yeah, I think I would. Any news on Ground Up, Navy?"

She mumbles to herself before finally saying, "I still need a financial partner. But Mr. Jones said he'd let me take over and stay on as a silent partner until I can buy him out."

"Navy," I say, "that's amazing. Even if it's not exactly what you wanted. It'll work out eventually."

"You're not wrong," she says. "And if you ever think about getting into the restaurant business . . ."

"You'll be the first to know." I smile at her, trying to picture myself leaving the classroom. I've had a lot of change over the past year, I think I'll give it a while longer before possibly adding career shift to the list.

We spend the morning together. A plethora of coffee is consumed, even though Navy is annoyed that I don't have an espresso machine. Food is served and devoured. And soon, I've taken leave to get myself ready.

At first, I think Luke will come in to join me, but my door remains firmly closed. It's like he knows I need this time to myself. I shower and dress quickly before applying a minimal amount of makeup.

They're all three waiting for me as I open my bedroom door. I chose to wear the dress Brian always loved, a light teal floral number. I grab my sneakers and, with a final pat on the head, leave Duke curled up in his bed.

Sutton and Navy lead us out the door with me following closely behind. Luke never removes his hand from the small of my back. I'm shocked when we pile into Sutton's SUV and not Luke's truck. Luke doesn't say anything, though, just squeezes his large body into the small backseat, my hand held firmly between both of his.

Everyone's lost in their own thoughts as we drive across town. The tourist traffic has started to ease now that summer is winding down and fall is just around the corner. Witnessing the leaves transform into vibrant hues, signaling another season of change, sends a zing of anticipation through me.

Sutton makes each turn effortlessly, familiar with the route to the cemetery. The funeral, a blur in my shock and denial, had been orchestrated by Brian's parents and mine. Now, as we approach, I see how beautiful the cemetery is—filled with large trees and various gardens.

It's a fitting resting place for Brian.

The car eases up to the curb before coming to a stop. Luke turns to me, bringing my face close to his. "Good?"

"I am." He leans in, and our lips meet in a reassuring kiss. When I step out of the car, the sight before me takes my breath away, and my eyes well with tears.

"What are you guys doing here?" I ask, my voice filled with surprise as I'm greeted by all the people I love— Luke, Sutton, Navy, Mom, Dad, Hunter, Vinnie, Adam, and Grace. Mom and Dad approach, enveloping me in a tight hug, then guide me toward my friends.

"As if we'd let you do this on your own." Vinnie rolls his eyes before dragging me into a hug. Hunter steps forward, stealing me from Vinnie to hug me even tighter. I notice Sutton's face soften when she sees him.

"We told you before," Hunter says, "we're family. And family doesn't let family go through hard shit alone."

"You're stuck with us now," Grace says as she and Adam push through Hunter's grasp. When Adams hugs me, he lifts me off the ground.

"Well, baby girl," Mom says, sniffling, "do you want us to come with you?"

"No," my dad promptly responds, winking at me. "She's got this." I give him a nod and a soft smile. I turn back to Luke, who wraps his arms around my waist.

"I'll be right here." His lips brush my temple.

Stepping away from my family, I move slowly toward Brian's grave, nestled beneath a large tree that provides a comforting shade in the afternoon. My gaze lingers on the headstone, and I trace the engraved letters with my fingertips, a silent apology for my absence. Beautiful fresh flowers surrounding his headstone catch my attention. Glancing back at my parents, Mom wipes her tears. She's been caring for Brian, just like she's been caring for me this last year.

I sit on the ground, crossing my legs underneath me, the grass cool against my skin. I remove my sneakers and place them to the side. It's as if I hear Brian's laughter in my head. He knows I never liked wearing shoes.

For a moment, I enjoy the fresh air and listen to the birds twittering in the trees. A glance over my shoulder reveals my friends and family sitting or lying on the grass, not speaking, just existing in this moment for me.

"Hi, Brian."

Inhale.

Exhale.

"I can't believe it's been one year since I lost you. It seems hard to believe sometimes that I can't just call you or text you or see you. I'm sorry I haven't been to visit. Things were really hard for me back then. I didn't know how to exist in this life, in this world, without you. So . . . I did what I could. Even if I couldn't see you, I talked to you almost every day. It helped. So much." Emotion clogs my throat. "But I think even you knew I needed to be strong. I needed to move forward. Maybe it was you, or maybe it was me, but the dreams eventually faded, and so did the constant visions of you. I've changed a lot this summer. Little by little, I've emerged from my cocoon. Instead of being frozen and forcing myself to move on, I met people, wonderful people. God, Brian, you would love them. They helped me see that I don't have to move on. I just have to choose to continue moving forward every day."

Threading my fingers through the blades of grass around me, I feel a peaceful silence settle around me.

"I met someone." I let the words scatter into the wind. "That feels strange to say to you. I thought you were my forever, but our story ended sooner than either of us thought it would." I take a settling breath. "His name is Luke. I know you'd like him. He's kind, incredibly patient, understanding, and challenges me when I need it." I smile. "After I lost you, I never thought I could ever open my heart to someone new, but he found me and, Brian . . . he loves me fully and deeply. Just like you did. I'm so lucky to have been loved by you. Thank you for the love you gave me and for our beautiful life. I miss you every day, and I'll love you forever. I just . . . I want you to know I'm okay now."

Just breathe.

I press a soft kiss onto my fingertips and with a final caress of the engraved letters bearing his name, I whisper goodbye.

Inhale. Exhale.

After a few more minutes in silence, I make my way back to Luke, my parents, and my family. Sutton and Navy reach me first and pull me into a tight embrace. The others stand around, their presence providing me with undeniable strength.

Next, Luke pulls me into his chest, and his fingers thread through my hair. I center myself with the scent of him.

"You good, G?" Hunter asks.

I pull back and look into Luke's eyes. "Yeah, I'm good."

"I love you," Luke says with a huge smile.

I feel it then . . .

That final fracture . . .

Deep in the back of my heart . . .

Healing closed.

Looking back, I thought Death had stolen everything from me, and I never imagined I'd get here. But with the embrace of my family, the support of my friends, and the love of Luke, I know I've finally made it to the other side.

Life has taught me so much over the last year through its painful, beautiful, and unpredictable nature. I'm not sure what the rest of my story holds or when my final page will turn, but until then . . .

I will live it fully and out loud.

The End

"This woman is a pain in my ass," I say. I huff out a breath, then press down on the bike pedals more aggressively. I refuse to be bested by a cycling class, especially not today. After last night, I've got too much residual energy, and it's called for an exorcism.

I've watched Greer ride the hell out of this bike to quiet her demons, so I figured I'd give it a shot.

"Resistance up to forty-five now," the instructor says. "Keep that cadence at around eighty." It's hard to believe how calm her voice is even though the music—and me—are definitely not.

"Shit," I say. "I really need to get in better shape." I focus on the screen, but in my mind, I can't stop thinking about last night. It was one for the books.

Now that it's the middle of November, most of the out-of-towners have vacated the city, but the few stragglers and handful of newcomers sure are causing a shitstorm for our small town.

Hunter's been dealing with an uptick in crime for several months now but hasn't been able to nail down any perps. I got a call from him last night just after dinner. He gave me a heads-up about a tip he received from an anonymous source that there might be trouble at the old mill. Even with a lack of details, he had no choice but to go check it out with his partner. We're not ones to mother each other, but I appreciated that he checked in with me.

I didn't bother going to my bunk room to sleep, not with Hunter walking into the unknown. Instead, I sat in my office listening to the scanner. I eventually nodded off and fell asleep on my desk but was abruptly awoken just after midnight when the tones rang through. When the dispatcher relayed the location, my heart lodged itself in my chest, fearing the worst.

Sweat flies from my forehead and lands on the mat under the bike. I've created quite the sweat angel as Greer likes to call them. I swipe a towel across my forehead, my heart rate pulsing wildly, then toss it to the side. Normally, I do well with the pressures and the unpredictable nature of the job, but never before have I been that overwhelmed with panic that something had happened to my best friend.

I try to shake away the thoughts of what could have been and focus only on the music and the instructor's voice, but still, the images flash in my mind.

By the time we arrived, the old mill was billowing smoke as black as night. It wasn't until I spotted Hunter waiting for us at the gate that the adrenaline in my body calmed. Flames poured from broken windows, flaring and sparking close enough to the surrounding forest to cause alarm. Almost immediately, I knew we had to abandon an interior attack and commanded the crew to set up a defensive attack until other units arrived. With so much debris and fuel inside the mill, it was slow going, but after two hours, we finally got the fire out. There wasn't much left to salvage of the building, and I suspect it will end up being condemned.

We won't know for a while what caused the fire, but Hunter and the fire investigator suspect arson. By the time we got back to the station, the crew and I had nothing left in the tank. Thankfully, A-shift was already there and offered to clean the rig so we could go home. Not one to look a gift horse in the mouth, I barely muttered goodbye before grabbing my gear and getting the hell out of there.

My thoughts won't stop spiraling, so with one hand, I reach over and turn the volume up even more. The heavy bass and drumbeats pulse through the speakers, rattling the pictures.

"Get ready to run out of the saddle!" the instructor yells through the screen. When the beat drops, I lift up, hovering just above my seat—and do my best impression of a badass cyclist. My vision blurs as I push my body to the limit, my quads ready to burst from exertion.

"Fuck me!" I say.

"I'd love to."

My focus slips momentarily at her voice, but my smile is immediate as I lay eyes on her. "Hey, sweetheart." I laugh. "You get off early or what?"

She plops down on a yoga bolster stacked in the corner. "Yeah, it was a half-day, and we had meetings, but something told me to come home." Her eyes rove over my bare chest, and her lip folds beneath her teeth as she looks where my shorts ride low on my hips. "*Something* is definitely better than meetings."

The instructor calls for us to return to the saddle, but I'm only half listening now. I can't take my eyes off Greer. She's a vision in black leggings and a long, off-the-shoulder, cream sweater, hair down and curled in soft ringlets. She slips her feet from knee-high, brown boots and stretches them out in front of her, showcasing a new pair of socks.

"I dig your socks," I say as I grab my water and take a much-needed drink.

"Figured you would." She grins and wiggles her feet clad in *Lord of the Rings* socks proclaiming *my precious* on the bottom.

"They're actually very fitting . . ." My voice fades off as I suck in more oxygen, doing a piss-poor job following the instructors commands. "This woman is brutal. I don't know how you do this."

"It's because you're out of shape, old man."

I roll my eyes and laugh. The last two minutes of class feel even more difficult, especially under Greer's watchful gaze. Nothing says pressure like your girlfriend—an indoor cycling addict—watching you get your ass handed to you by a bubbly instructor decked out in a sequined jumpsuit and space buns.

"Who you calling old man?" I say as I finally unclip, then grab my towel. "I'm only a few years older than you."

Greer pops up from the yoga bolster and leans into my chest. She wraps her arms around my waist and goes to pull me in for a hug, but I push against her shoulders.

"I'm disgusting right now, sweetheart. You don't want all this"— I nod down to the sweat pouring off my body—"all over you."

"Mmm, I beg to differ." Her eyes narrow as she steps back. She studies me, and I suspect her internal senses are blaring some kind of alarm. That's something Greer's good at, knowing when someone's got too much on their mind.

"You need a shower," she finally says.

Duke, Greer's dog, who'd been waiting outside the door, leads us into her room, then proceeds to jump onto the bed and make himself right at home.

"Don't get too comfortable, old man," I say. "My back can't take anymore trying to sleep while you're in the bed."

The side-eye he gives me looks almost human. He yawns and stretches out, putting his head right on my pillow.

"Maybe I should get a bigger bed," Greer says. She wiggles out of her sweater and leggings leaving her in a matching bra and underwear set.

I grin. "Love the undies. The pumpkins and leaves are very seasonally appropriate."

She places her hands on her hips. "I thought so too. Don't worry, I got you a pair."

"Sweetheart," I say standing on one leg peeling off a sock, "I doubt they'll fit."

"Har har, smartass." She disappears into her bathroom only to return with a pair of matching boxer briefs. She tosses them at me.

"Don't say I never gave you anything," she says.

I pause what I'm doing as she lowers her panties, unsnaps her bra, and saunters into the bathroom. Snapping out of my Greer-induced haze, I toss the briefs onto her reading chair, peel off my sweaty shorts, and chase after her. She's leaning against the glass waiting for me as I stumble into the bathroom.

I stop dead in my tracks. "I'm so happy to see you," I say.

I breathe deeply, then smile for the first time today. She opens her arms and welcomes me into her warm embrace. All the stress and anxiety bubbling beneath the surface instantly settles as she caresses the back of my neck and shoulders. She runs her fingers into the back of my hair and down the back of my ears before framing my face. She leans forward and presses her lips against mine. They taste like her strawberry lip balm.

I'm never one to *need* anything. But right now, I need her.

Greer's arms loosen, then she opens the shower door, steps in, walks to the tub sitting against one of the shower walls, and starts the bath water.

I raise my eyebrows. "I'm not so sure we're both going to fit in there." I gesture to the tub.

"We will," she says, "but right now, it's just for you."

I step into the huge shower, then sit on the small bench along the back wall. I'm not sure who decided it was a good idea to put a tub *in* the shower, but they deserve some kind of award. Greer ensures the temperature is perfect, places the stopper, and then begins filling it with flower petals, bath oils, and who knows what else, as though she were some kind of woodland healer.

"You making a potion over there or what?" I ask.

She smiles. "No, silly. But it'll help you relax."

When the tub is almost half full, she motions for me to get in. I step over the lip of the tub and ease into the water. Its warmth immediately seeps into my pores, and my tense muscles start to release. I can't contain the groan that escapes. I close my eyes, then surrender to whatever she's got planned.

"Scoot down a bit so I can get your hair wet," she says.

"Sweetheart, you don't—"

"I know I don't," she says, "but I want to take care of you. Now, scoot. Your hair needs washing."

I do as commanded, the distant clicking of shampoo bottles punctuating the stillness. She trickles water over the top of my head, repeating the process several times. Next, she applies shampoo, expertly massaging my scalp. I groan again and she kisses my forehead.

"So," she says, "want to tell me about it?"

I smile. "How'd you know something was wrong?"

"Because someone would only pick a cycling class like that if their brain were too loud. You've ridden my bike a grand total of six times, and it was always because you had a tough shift."

Her hand slips down the back of my neck, squeezing and kneading my tense muscles, while the other combs through my hair and rubs around my ear.

"It was." Several quiet moments pass. "But I'm not sure why it's in my head so much."

Greer washes, rinses, and conditions my hair while I tell her about the anonymous tip, the fire, and my worry for Hunter. Before she finishes, I tug her arm. She comes around the side of the tub, and I pull her into the water with me. She straddles my lap, and I run my hands up the smooth skin of her thigh before wrapping them around her back and holding her to me. She lays her head on my shoulder and allows me to hold her.

"I know Hunter can take care of himself, but . . ." I hesitate, trying to gather my thoughts. "When we got the call, I was worried about him."

"I'm sorry, Luke." She kisses my shoulder and wraps her arms around me. I appreciate that she doesn't try to say anything to make me feel better; she simply holds space for me to feel what I need to.

The truth is, it doesn't matter how much you bury it down, fear is always a part of the job. You never know what to expect on calls, and realize early on that anything can happen in an instant.

"Are you still okay with everyone coming over tonight?" she asks, slipping from my arms and settling on the other side of the tub. She places her feet on top of my thigh.

I take in her body, covered in water and suds, her breasts sitting just under the water's surface.

She giggles. "Luke?"

"Uh, yeah?" I finally bring my eyes to hers. She raises her eyebrows and I shrug.

"Tonight," she says, "are you still okay with everyone coming over for movie night?" She runs the toes of her right foot along my thigh. I grab hold of it and press my fingers into the soles. She groans in delight, slipping farther under the water.

"I'm more than okay with it," I finally say. "In fact, I think it's just what I need."

We talk and enjoy our bath for a while longer until we're both on the verge of turning into raisins. I step from the tub, grab a towel, then motion for her to stand. She puts her arms out like a child, and I wrap the towel around her. I pull the plug in the tub, then grab my own towel.

"C'mere," she says, pulling me into her body.

I raise an eyebrow. "Aren't the girls going to be here soon to help you set up?"

"We've got time." She winks, tugging me by the hand and leading me into her room.

It glows with a soft white light from the bedside lamps, bed still mussed from the previous night. Greer drops her towel, then pulls mine free. We crawl into bed and, like it always does when we're together, the weight of the world disappears.

"I love you," I say an hour later as we lie snuggled under the covers. "And thank you."

I feel her smile against my chest. "No *thank yous* necessary. Now—"

Suddenly, a loud banging ruptures the silence of our cocoon, making us both startle.

"Greer? Luke?" A voice that can only be Navy's shouts from the front door. "Are you guys home?" Navy bangs harder.

"We see your vehicles in the driveway," Sutton shouts, "so we know you're home. Get your cute butts dressed and come open this door, or I'm going to use my key. And lord knows we don't need to be seeing what y'all got going on."

Greer groans and tucks her face into the side of my neck. "She'll totally use her key."

"Yup," I say. "Better get a move on." I yank off the covers and smack her butt cheek.

"I'm going, I'm going." She gives me one last kiss before pulling on her clothes again.

"Sutton," she shouts walking out of the bedroom, "don't you dare use that key. It's for emergencies only!"

"This is . . . something," Adam says as he steps up next to me at the kitchen island.

"With our girls," I say, "everything turns into *something*." We both laugh, taking in the organized chaos around us.

The girls decided another kick-off event like our lake day was needed and thus Holiday Cheermeister night was born. I have no idea what that even means, but if it makes Greer happy, I'll do anything for her. The day after Halloween, she and the girls took down the plethora of Halloween decor, then transformed her entire house into a holiday smorgasbord.

Looking around, I can't help but smile at everyone's holiday gear. The girls and Vinnie are making gingerbread houses while Adam and I eat our weight in holiday treats. Navy shouts something at Vinnie, and tosses a candy at him. They're having some kind of heated battle over candy walking paths. A fourth holiday movie creates the perfect soundtrack.

I snort when Greer elbows Vinnie for trying to steal her licorice. He feigns innocence and her face lights up with a smile that takes my breath away. I know how blessed I am to have this woman in my life. Her eyes catch mine and she winks, mouthing *I love you*.

"Luke," Grace calls from her spot at the end of the kitchen table, "your phone's ringing."

I step around the island, then grab my phone off the sideboard. I don't recognize the number and almost silence the call, but something tells me to answer. I press accept.

"Hello," I say.

"Hi, yes, is this Luke Bradley?" a woman asks.

"This is he. Who's speaking?"

There's a rustling sound through the receiver, then some muffled voices. "Hi, Mr. Bradley, this is Ashley Bloom. I'm a nurse over here at Suncrest Valley Memorial Hospital."

My stomach bottoms out. "How can I help you, Ashley?"

There's more rustling and a deep voice in the background. After several moments, a new voice comes on the line.

"Luke, it's me."

My heart lodges in my throat, and I brace my hand on the back of the couch. "Hunter?"

Every eye in the room is on me, but I keep mine locked with Sutton, communicating a silent message. We aren't twins or anything, but our sibling bond gives us a strong ability to talk without talking.

"Yeah, bro," he says. "Look, something happened . . . " There's a beat of silence before he continues. "I'm okay, but I need you."

"We're on our way. What room are you?" Without thought, I wheel around and grab my keys from the basket on the counter.

"Don't freak out," he says.

"Already am." I pause at the edge of the kitchen island and look back to Sutton. Aside from the movie in the background, the room is completely silent.

"I'm in the burn unit."

My eyes snap shut. "What happened?"

"I'll fill you in when you get here," he says.

"We're on the way." I watch as everyone jumps immediately into action—chairs being pushed out, whispered calls for shoes, keys and purses.

"Luke . . ." he hesitates, emotion clogging his throat. "Please tell Sutton I'm okay."

"You can tell her yourself when we get there."

The line is silent and I wonder if he's hung up, but before I end the call he says, "Thanks, Luke. See you soon."

The call cuts off, and I tuck my phone into my back pocket.

Greer steps forward. "What's going on?" she asks.

"It's Hunter," I say. "I'm not sure what's happened, but he's in the burn unit at Suncrest Memorial."

Sutton's eyes go wide and she falters. Navy wraps her arm around Sutton's waist at the same time Greer takes her hand. Vinnie and Adam make quick work of turning off the TV.

"Luke," Sutton says, "is he okay?" Tears pool at the corners of her eyes.

"He says he's okay, but he needs us."

———————-

Will Sutton and Hunter finally find their way to each other?
Find out what happens in book two of
The Blue Collar Boys Series.

Acknowledgements

To the girl in her teens writing stories and reading every book she could get her hands on, to the young woman in her twenties who wrote a book that went nowhere and then proceeded to shove it in drawer, to the mom in her thirties who was trying to discover her true self, to the woman in her forties who found the courage to pursue the dream she thought disappeared because she hadn't gotten to it yet . . .

We did it.

To my husband, Blake: You've loved me since I was fifteen. Through every version of me—teenager, teacher, roller derby player, mother, wife—you've been there to support and love me. Thank you for having faith that I could write this story even when I had my doubts. Also, the flowers and copious amounts of coffee and snacks were greatly appreciated.

To my daughter, Henley: You've been cheering mama on from day one. Thank you for all your smiles, drawings, and being my writing buddy. It's not easy having a mama who isn't always available because she was busy writing and talking to voices in her head. Thank you for your patience.

To Mom: You read every draft of this story, and you never once told me I was anything shy of great. I hope you love this final draft, even though I know you'll find a comma I missed. Thank you for your endless love and support.

To Dad: Thank you for believing in me. You told me once you're living vicariously through me as I work to publish a book. Well . . . look at us.

To Mom Miller: Thank you for stealing that early draft from the kitchen counter and reading it in one night. I never told you, but it meant a lot to me.

To my friends and family: Sorry I've been a hermit this last year. Thanks for pulling me from the writing cave and providing me with great writing material. (Joking. Or am I?)

To Jayme Rosales-Speck and Elizabeth Martin: You read this book in its infancy. Your thoughtful suggestions and notes helped me transform this story into something magical and meaningful, something more than just a love story.

To Allyn Hamrick, Camille Durant, Amanda Wright, and Saundra Watts: Thank you for being the absolute best beta readers an author could ask for.

To Sara Tallary: Your beta-read-turned-developmental edit helped me find the heart of the story. I am so lucky to have had your assistance and support as I navigated the world of writing and publishing.

To Jenni Misener: You've been on team Luke and Greer from the get-go when I first told you I was finally going to write the book. You've been there to listen to me cry and bitch, you've been there to celebrate the little moments, and you read and fell in love with this story in its early stages. I will forever be grateful for your friendship.

To Kristen Weber, Breanna Call, and Amy Guan: Thank you for your eagle eyes and editing expertise.

To Jess King: Thank you for being the best spin instructor to ever exist and for teaching me that you've got to use your whole heart and whole ass to make shit happen.

To Spotify: Thank you for providing the musical therapy I needed to write this book and for not judging me when I listened to the same songs over and over. I was going through some things, okay?

To Starbucks and Dutch Bros: You kept me caffeinated. Keep that shit up.

To my readers: Thank you for taking a chance on a debut author and being the best damn hype team a woman could ask for. You fell in love with this story and characters just as much as I did. I'm sorry (not sorry) if I made you cry. I can't wait to meet all of you someday and give you a giant hug!

To the dreamers: your dream hasn't disappeared just because you haven't gotten to it yet. I know it's hard. I know it's scary. But I promise you, it's worth it.

Love Ya, Mean It!
Sara

Sneak Peek

I know, I know, how dare I write a cliffhanger epilogue!

You'll have Sutton and Hunter's story before you know it.

Until then . . . here is a sneak peek.

Now and Then

Sutton

"It's just you and me tonight, Don," I say. Sparkling lights bounce along the dark mahogany bar top as I twirl my shot glass around and around, the golden liquid spiraling like my thoughts. I tap my phone screen. It's late, later than I ever choose to go out in public alone. But after the day I've had, the last thing I plan on doing is begging my friends to join me while I drown my sorrows in as much Don Julio as I can stand.

After entering my password, the screen sparks to life and glows brightly. The three words I've come to loathe glare back at me from the offending email. I inhale deeply, toss back the honey-toned liquid, and slide the glass across the counter.

"Pour me another, Joe." He doesn't say anything as he refills my glass, but I don't miss the way his eyes narrow in that dad way. The *I love you, but . . .* look, the one with the judgy eyes.

"What's that look for?" I beckon him to pass the shot.

"No look, Sutton. No look at all." He sweeps a dingy white cloth over the counter, cleaning up non-existent spills. "Haven't seen you in a while, that's all."

I toss back the shot, then slam the glass down on the counter this time. "Yeah. Don over here requested the pleasure of my company."

He braces his hands on the bar and leans in close to me. A low buzzing starts in my stomach, but I'm not sure if it's the tequila or the look he's giving me. Joe's run this bar for as long as I can remember. He and Dad were best friends, at least they were until Dad died. I grew up watching Joe give the look to Luke and Hunter, but not me, never me. I was the perfect kid.

"You okay?" Joe nudges me to open up. He can nudge all he wants, but he should know by now I don't easily offer up my pain, my secrets.

"Nothing at all," I lie. "Just celebrating."

"What are we celebrating?" I don't like his use of *we*. I'm not in the mood to be a *we* tonight. This pity party only has room for one.

Mentally fortifying my defensive walls, I put on my best Sutton-like smile. "Oh you know, just the fact that I closed on another house and have two others under contract."

"That's amazing, girl. You were born to be a realtor." He heads down to the other end of the bar to serve a few bikers.

"Was I though?" I say aloud to no one.

Growing up, I was always the girl who was naturally good at everything I tried. I had excellent grades, all my teachers loved me, and I was a go-getter, involved with more clubs than necessary. I was Sutton Bradley, perfect girl with the great smile and all the energy, and I played the role well.

It's easy to pretend you have it all together when you have everything going for yourself. But most people had no clue I was also a girl without a clue in the world about what I wanted to do with my life. I dreaded being asked, *What do you want to be when you grow up?* because it always felt like someone parked a bus on my chest. Truth be told, I liked a lot of things but couldn't picture myself doing any of them every day for forever.

I became an expert at answering that question, ready and waiting with an arsenal of prepared answers because most people didn't like it when you said you didn't know. Princess, teacher, garbage truck driver, president, and pediatrician were some of my favorites. At first, it was fun to spin tales of the life I'd have someday. They were always a lie, but it was fun, trying one on for size to see if it fit. They never did.

But apparently the older you get, the more people expect a legitimate answer. Being a princess wasn't as readily accepted when you're fifteen. It felt like as soon as I started high school, teachers and guidance counselors demanded to know where I planned to go to college (nowhere) and what I wanted to do professionally. (Their guess was as good as mine.) All my friends had their whole lives mapped out in front of them; my brother and his best friend included. All I knew was I wanted to do *something*.

"Man," I say to myself, "it's hot in here." I slip my arms from my black suit jacket and roll up my white shirt cuffs.

"It could also be the tequila." The man next to me snorts and mumble-laughs.

"Could be." I fold my perfectly manicured hands in front of me.

"You're a realtor?" mystery man asks. He's wearing a green baseball hat low on his head paired with some kind of adult neighborhood baseball league jersey and jeans.

"Something like that." Turning my focus to my glittering bracelets, my mind opens fully, allowing past memories to slip through the cracks.

It was summer of my junior year, and Dad was busy in his office preparing an offering. I snuck in like I always did and sat nearby sketching. I'd started rattling off questions about what he did for work, and before I knew what was happening, he was offering to let me tag along. At first, it was fun helping Dad find great features in a home that would help a family imagine living in the space. The more I went, the more excited he got, and the more he encouraged me, and, like all things, the more I excelled.

I'm not sure exactly when it happened, just that it did. But soon, he was talking about me following in his footsteps; that we'd run his real estate firm together. Within a year after graduation, I'd nailed my real estate exam and officially joined forces with my dad.

We were the Bradley Team, a father-daughter power duo who could sell a tree to a forest. We were unstoppable. I even started to think maybe it was my calling, but then he died, and everything changed.

My phone buzzes next to me. It never stops ringing or buzzing with phone calls, texts, and emails. I have this urge sometimes to chuck the damn thing into a river, but that's definitely not something the Sutton everyone knows would do.

I press in my passcode but get an error code. I try again. And again. On the fourth attempt, I finally get my screen unlocked. With a rapid swipe, that damn email disappears, and I pull up my text threads. Seeing our group name, Wildflowers, my heart grows heavy. I'm not in the mood to play the role of sunny-side-up Sutton tonight.

Navy: I'm bored. Want to hang out?

Greer: Yep. Luke's on shift, so I'm in.

For a second, I consider not responding, but I know better. We may only have known each other for a few months, but I know how they work. They'll text non-stop, or worse, they'll come looking for me. I love them like sisters, but tonight, I'm not sure I want to be found. Closing one eye to focus on the letters starting to swim in front of me, I relent and respond.

Me: Sorry, I've got a date with Don.

Greer: A date? You didn't tell us you had a date!

Navy: Sutton's like a vault. She doesn't tell us shit.

Me: Do to.

Greer: Wait, Don as in *Don* Don?? Are you drunk?

"Not yet," I mumble aloud. The guy one barstool over side-eyes me, so I give him a thumbs up. He shakes his head and manages a laugh but returns to the hole he's currently staring through the counter.

Navy: She's definitely not drunk, G. Sutton

wouldn't do that.

Me: Why do you say it like that?

Navy: We all know you're not the type to do anything risky without provocation.

I toss the phone onto the counter, startling the guy next to me. His eyes meet mine. I smile sheepishly and am glad when he smiles back.

Navy's right, this isn't the Sutton everyone knows. One by one, I tug all the little threads of *me*, frayed and fluttering around me, and wind them back up onto their neat little spool.

Suddenly, the bar door opens, the incoming draft fluttering a few red strands that have fallen from my perfectly coiffed bun. A gold light illuminates the doorway, casting a man and woman in a hazy silhouette. Hairs prickle on the back of my neck, and my hand instinctively rubs soothing circles over the center of my chest, begging my heart to stop its thrashing. I don't need to see their faces to know it's *him*. My body always knows when *he's* around.

About the Author

Sara Miller writes emotional stories full of love and light. She calls Arizona home. When she's not in the classroom, you can find her buried under a pile of books, enjoying the outdoors, spending time with her family, attending concerts and festivals, and consuming more than the daily recommended limit of iced coffee. She always has a book within reach, ready to escape to a fantastical world or a small town full of love and friendships.

Visit saramillerbooks.com to sign up for the newsletter and get updates on future projects and new releases.

If you enjoyed *Until Then*, I'd be grateful for a quick review.

Follow on most socials: @saramillerbooks

Made in the USA
Coppell, TX
21 February 2026

71948213R10260